Joanne Kormylo's debut novel, *The Resistance Daughter*, is a work of historical fiction inspired by true stories. She is the daughter of a WWII bomber pilot and prisoner of war. As part of her research for this novel, she studied her late father's Wartime Log, interviewed veterans, served on the board of an Air Force Museum, and traveled to the UK, Poland, and Germany. Joanne holds both an MA and a JD, leading to a career as a lawyer and business owner. She has one daughter, Andrea, and resides in Western Canada.

The
Resistance
Daughter

JOANNE KORMYLO

HODDER &
STOUGHTON

First published in Great Britain in 2025 by Hodder & Stoughton Limited
An Hachette UK company

The authorised representative in the EEA is Hachette Ireland,
8 Castlecourt Centre, Dublin 15, D15 XTP3, Ireland (email: info@hbgi.ie)

1

A CIP catalogue record for this title is available from the British Library

Paperback ISBN 978 1 399 74488 1
ebook ISBN 978 1 399 74489 8

Typeset in ITC Garamond Std by Manipal Technologies Limited

Printed and bound in Great Britain by Clays Ltd, Elcograf S.p.A.

Hodder & Stoughton policy is to use papers that are natural, renewable
and recyclable products and made from wood grown in sustainable forests.
The logging and manufacturing processes are expected to conform
to the environmental regulations of the country of origin.

Hodder & Stoughton Limited
Carmelite House
50 Victoria Embankment
London EC4Y 0DZ

www.hodder.co.uk

To my daughter, Andrea

1942

CHAPTER ONE

Midnight

SEPTEMBER 1, 1942

Poland

Five glowing lanterns formed a cross, illuminating the drop zone in the dew-soaked clearing. Hidden in a pine forest near Warsaw, Anna Kowalski waited with her back to the trees, gripping her light.

When the thundering roar of engines broke the eerie silence of the night, her brother, Michal, flashed Morse code signals to guide the pilot in. The plane, a Wellington bomber, was coming in too low. Anna bolted into the clearing, thrusting her lantern into the air, swinging it back and forth as high as her trembling arm could reach so the pilot could see the trees.

Air vibrated. Hot exhaust swept over her as the pilot pulled up at the last second. Overhead, propellers sliced through the pines, tossing heavy branches to the ground.

She stood transfixed, watching the plane climb hard to gain altitude and circle back over the drop zone. The bomb bay creaked open, sending clusters of containers tumbling out. Parachutes deployed and the cargo floated to the ground.

The plane returned one last time to tip its wings. It looked to Anna as if the pilot were saying goodbye. She raised her arm high and again swung her lantern in the air as the plane disappeared into the darkness, the sound of its engines fading.

Papa drove his battered Fiat truck out of the woods. He jumped out, door left open, engine running.

Wet grass brushed against Anna's ankles as she ran to meet him. Papa looked more worn than his Fiat. Michal, so much like their father, with his square chin and fair hair—minus the wisps of gray—had fought with the Underground Resistance every day since the German occupation had begun.

They dragged tubular metal containers through the grass to the pickup.

"I can help," Anna offered.

"It's too heavy," Papa said.

"I'm not a child. I'm seventeen."

"You've done enough."

With no time to argue, Anna climbed onto the tailgate, crawled into the open truck bed, and huddled against the rear of the cab. She reached for the wool blanket heaped in the corner and spread it over her lap. Kicking off her wet shoes, she tucked her feet underneath her to warm them.

Papa and Michal opened the containers and loaded burlap bags of tightly wrapped cargo into the back of the truck. Anna didn't need to see beneath the burlap to know what they contained: Sten guns and explosives.

"Your mother would be very proud of how brave you were tonight," Papa said as he threw bales of hay on top of the weapons.

Inside her trouser pocket, she touched the beads on the rosary she carried everywhere. Her most treasured possession had once belonged to her mother.

Life as she'd known it had shattered during the Siege of Warsaw. September 25, 1939, to be exact. Black Monday. The day the Germans razed her neighborhood in the bombings.

Tonight, she had fought back. Instead of waiting at home alone, she'd been hustled out to the forest at the last minute to fill in for the Weiss family members who had disappeared. Maybe it wasn't much, standing in a field and swinging a lantern, but she'd helped the pilot avoid the trees and find the drop zone. And it felt good. Exhilarating even.

Papa stepped up into the truck, followed by Michal. Doors slammed and tires spun as they pulled out of the meadow and onto the dirt road. They sped along the Vistula River valley in east-central Poland, past the willow and poplar trees that graced her sandy bank, evading checkpoints on their way back to Warsaw.

Leaning against the back of the cab, Anna studied the constellations overhead. She imagined the Wellington darting in and out between the stars and wondered what it was like inside the airplane.

CHAPTER TWO

0400 hours

SEPTEMBER 2, 1942

Johnnie Nowak peered down from the cockpit of his Wellington bomber into darkness blanketing the Netherlands. Although no lights were visible, he knew there were buildings below. Enforced blackouts were intended to disorient the pilots flying overhead. Without visual bearings, he had to rely on his navigator, Tubby Edwards. Crammed into his tiny workstation in the belly of the plane, he was plotting their flight path using charts, a compass, and the stars. Any minute now, they would cross the Dutch coast and soar out over the Zuider Zee to the North Sea. Nine hours into their mission, and Nowak almost had his crew of three Brits and a Yank back to base safe and sound.

Almost.

Not many crews could have achieved what they had four hours earlier, deep inside enemy lines. Nowak's first assignment with the Special Operations Executive—the British agency formed to aid the Underground Resistance. They'd taken off in the twin-engine bomber on a moonlit night from a secret airfield camouflaged to look like an old farm at RAF Tempsford, England. Round trip, 2,000 miles. The exact coordinates of the drop zone so secret that only Nowak and his navigator had been briefed in case they were shot down and captured.

It felt damn good delivering crates full of arms and ammunition for the Home Army, the military arm of the Polish Underground Resistance. They called themselves the *Armia Krajowa* or AK for short. Men, women, and children desperate to defend themselves against the Nazi bastards destroying the country he was born in twenty years ago. After his father's death, he had left Poland as a child with his mother and sister to start a new life in Canada. But his grandparents had stayed behind in Warsaw.

He felt a sense of kinship with the people who had risked their lives to guide him into the drop zone. A swinging lantern had warned him of the pine trees. He'd pulled up just in time, skimming the treetops.

His four crew members, at first jubilant after the successful drop, had been quiet in the hours since. Nowak knew that they, like him, were counting the minutes until they passed through the Kammhuber Line—a coastal chain of enemy stations with radar units, searchlights, and anti-aircraft fire from 88mm flak guns—and saw the Thames Estuary on the English coast, welcoming them back. He rotated his broad shoulders and stretched his neck to release the tension while he waited for his navigator to let him know when they reached the coast.

"Pilot to crew." Nowak spoke into the bomber's intercom, the only way to communicate over the thundering roar of the engines. "Who's buying when we land?"

"Bomb aimer here," said Freddie Yates, whose job now was aiming supply containers out of the bomb bay. "You are, Skipper. Forgotten last night's poker game already?"

"I was hoping you'd forget," Nowak replied. "We've got a lot of celebrating to do. It's your last night as a free man." Once back at base, Nowak planned to eat breakfast—a post-operation tradition of bacon and eggs—catch a couple of hours' sleep, and then head down to the local pub. He'd been planning Freddie's surprise bachelor party for a month.

"Navigator to Pilot," Tubby said, cutting in. "Passing over enemy coast."

"Roger Wilco." Nowak checked his instrument panel. He still had enough fuel to make it across the sea thanks to the installation of additional tankage. Then he patted his vest pocket that held the lucky rabbit's foot his sister had slipped into his kitbag the day he crossed the pond for active duty overseas.

Brilliant beams of light shot straight up from the ground in front of him, sweeping across the night sky, blinding him as an intense cone of searchlights swallowed the bomber.

"Damn it!" Nowak took evasive action in a corkscrew to starboard by slamming the yoke on the control column forward and pushing the nose of the bomber into a steep dive as arcs of white tracers and exploding munitions surrounded them.

Red, yellow, and orange anti-aircraft fire spewed from the guns below, forming a curtain of flak that burst into thousands of metal fragments. He pulled back on the yoke with all his strength and began a steep climb to port.

He thought about the words Freddie had painted in red over the door of their Wellington—*Nil Bano Panico*. Above All Don't Panic. The only thing that mattered now was getting his crew back to base. He had to get higher, try to get out of the range of the deadly guns. The torque of the ascent threw him back into his seat as he watched his altimeter, his fingers gripping the throttle. Twelve thousand feet. Twelve fifty. Thirteen thousand. Thirteen fifty.

Bam.

An exploding shell ripped through the airframe, and the bomber reared as pain shot through Nowak's shoulder and chest. A rush of frigid air filled the cockpit. Fire burst from the port wing, igniting the plasticized lacquer on the fabric-covered exterior. Flames streamed rearward.

"Petrol cocks!" Nowak shouted into his microphone, ordering his crew to shut off the flow of fuel to the burning engine. "Port engine on fire."

"Bomb aimer here," Freddie shouted back. "Hold her steady, Skipper. I've got it."

Nowak yanked the lever activating the fire extinguisher, pulled back on the throttle of the burning port engine, and gave the starboard engine full throttle. They swung with a severe starboard yaw. Applying full rudder, he fought with the yoke to stay level.

Freddie edged his way into the cockpit from his position in the nose. Another explosion rocked the bomber and he slumped to the floor.

"Freddie? Freddie?"

No response.

"Petrol cocks. Petrol cocks!" Nowak repeated. Adrenaline surged through his body. "Somebody divert the fuel. Bloody hurry."

"Rear gunner here. I can do it, Skipper," Edwin Branch said. Nicknamed Twig, only eighteen years old and just two weeks out of training, he had to rotate his turret and crawl in the dark along the narrow catwalk leading into the fuselage to shut off the petrol lines.

"Pilot to Navigator: How far are we from land?"

Silence.

Nowak called out a second time. "Tubby, you there?"

No answer.

"Wireless Operator, what's happening back there? Check on Tubby. See if he's plugged in."

"Tubby's hit," Raymond Cooper said in his East Texas drawl. He'd moved his family across the border into Canada to join the RCAF a good two years before the US joined the war effort. The navigator's table was immediately aft to his station. At twenty-three, he was the old man in the crew. "We're on fire."

Through his earpiece, Nowak heard Ray tapping out an SOS in Morse code on his wireless radio set. *Dit Dit Dit Dah Dah Dah Dit Dit Dit*.

"Strap Tubby in," Nowak said.

At six-foot-five and lean but muscular, Ray would have no trouble moving Tubby's hefty frame from the navigator's table to the fold-down cot. After fastening the straps and securing him, Ray would activate the inflation bottle on Tubby's life-jacket and top it up by blowing into the mouthpiece. Nowak trusted he could do it.

Smoke and the acrid smell of explosives filled the air. Intense heat rose through the floor. Out of the corner of his eye, he saw movement. Freddie clambered to his feet, blood oozing from his forehead.

"Tear out the wires. Break the circuit. Douse the flames," Nowak shouted.

Freddie grabbed the fire extinguisher from behind the pilot seat and unscrewed the cross handle. Pumping it fast, he splashed retardant on his way out of the cockpit.

The flak stopped somewhere over the North Sea. Without his navigator, Nowak wasn't sure where he was, but he knew it would take at least another hour to reach the closest point on the English coast. They'd never make it. His men couldn't parachute into the cold water this far from shore. That would be suicide. They'd all die from exposure.

As pilot and captain of the aircraft, Nowak was responsible for the safety of his crew. They called him *Skipper*, a title he was proud of, and they trusted him. He wasn't about to let them down. Not now. Not ever. He had only one way to save them: make an emergency landing on the water and hope like hell the rubber dinghy inflated on impact.

"Prepare to ditch, fellows. We're going in," Nowak said, as calmly as he could.

His crewmembers all knew the ditching drill. Remove the astro-hatch in preparation for escape. Secure the pilot's shoulder harness. Jettison loose equipment. Destroy secret papers. Pack emergency supplies. Radio location back to base. Assume ditching position crouched in the belly, backs against the wing spar, hands clasped behind their heads.

The altimeter spun counterclockwise, leaving Nowak without an accurate reading of his altitude as he piloted the plane toward the choppy sea. He had to land on the crest of the swells, parallel to the troughs. He flipped the switch for the landing lights to judge his height. They didn't work. If the nose smashed into the surging waves, the Wellington would disintegrate on impact.

He tore off his leather flying gloves to wipe his sweaty palms on his trousers, then dumped his fuel, lowered the flaps, and pulled back on the throttle. He wrestled with the yoke to keep the nose of the shuddering bomber up and the wings level, with only the reflection of the moon on the water to guide him.

If a wing tip hit the water first, it would cartwheel like a leaf dancing in the wind.

"For Christ's sake, boys, hold on," Nowak hollered over the deafening roar. The bomber plunged downward. In his mind, he made the sign of the cross and thought about his mother and sister back in Canada, Freddie's wedding set for Saturday, and Ray's kids.

The tail hit the sea first. Then the belly. A second later, the nose smashed violently into the waves. Saltwater rushed into the cockpit and the plane lurched to a stop.

They had one minute, two max, before the damaged plane sank. Nowak pulled the pin to release his harness and jumped out of his seat, ripping off his goggles and leather helmet. Freddie and Twig rushed into the cockpit and clambered out of the escape hatch over the pilot seat. Ray was right behind them with Tubby slung over his shoulder. He boosted Tubby up through the hatch to Freddie and Twig, who pulled him out. Ray squeezed through next.

Nowak crawled out behind Ray, pulling the cord to inflate his lifejacket as soon as he emerged. He was relieved to see Freddie and Twig already crouched on the partially submerged wing, trying to keep their balance as the waves pounded them. Ray inched his way down with Tubby in his arms.

Scrambling along the top of the bomber, Nowak slipped on the wet surface and recovered by kicking his foot hard through the fabric. By using the basket weave construction of the geodetic airframe to grip his boots, he worked his way rearward, counting the seconds in his head. It had already been about half a minute.

He slid down onto the wing. The two hot engines crackled as sea water washed over them, forming a cloud of hissing steam.

The rubber dinghy had inflated on impact, but it floated upside down, attached by a rope to the starboard side. Somehow, they had to right the dinghy, board it, and cut the rope that tethered them to the plane and certain death.

Nowak took a deep breath and plunged down into the saltwater. Gasping from the cold, he swallowed mouthfuls. Freddie followed, crawling onto the capsized dinghy to pull the handling strap as Nowak pushed up on the underside. It slammed back down, forcing him under water. He bobbed up again, sputtering. Eyes burning, he could see the dinghy straining against the rope that tethered it to the plane as the smashed nose of the bomber slipped underwater. Within seconds, the plane would drag their only means of survival to the bottom of the sea.

The two of them tried again, this time succeeding in flipping it right side up. They held the bouncing dinghy steady while Ray and Twig hauled Tubby in off the wing.

"Where's the bloody knife?" Freddie yelled. "It's not in the sheath."

"Who's got a knife?" Nowak shouted.

Ray whipped a switchblade out of his pocket, flipped it open, leaned over the side and sliced the tether.

Relief and regret flooded over Nowak as he watched his Wellington sink nose first into the dark water. He clung to the side of the dinghy, fighting against the buffeting waves as he strained to lift himself in, but his strength was draining away. His hands slipped on the slick rubber just as Ray grasped hold of the grab handles on his life jacket and heaved him aboard.

His crew huddled together. Tubby lay sprawled between them with his head in Edwin's lap.

"Tubby's in bad shape." Ray used his silk scarf to wipe blood from the navigator's face. "His nose is damn near shot off."

"Bloody hell," Freddie said.

"Apply pressure. Try to stop the bleeding," Nowak said. "Freddie, find the kit."

Freddie rummaged through the contents of the metal first aid kit stowed in the dinghy. Pulling out a syringe and an ampoule of morphia, he pushed up Tubby's sleeve, jabbed him with the needle, and pushed down the plunger. Nowak turned his attention to the rest of his crew.

"Ray, you hurt?"

"Nuthin' serious."

"Twig?"

"My arm's shot up a bit."

"Freddie?"

"Just this gash." Freddie touched his forehead. "How about you, Skipper?"

"I'm okay," Nowak said, then asked Ray, "Did you send our coordinates back to base?"

"Only a guess. Best I could do without Tubby."

Nowak needed the flare gun and cartridges to shoot a distress signal and mark their position. "Where's the Very pistol?"

Ray hesitated, then said, "Had it in my bag. Got washed away in a surge of water. Had to make a choice, Skipper. Save Tubby or save the Very."

"Don't worry. Air-Sea Rescue will pick us up," Nowak reassured his men, not wanting to tell them how worried he was. He shivered as he pulled his wet flight jacket up under his chin. Blood from his wounds felt warm as it seeped down his chest.

The dinghy bobbed up and down in the howling wind as raging waves splashed water inside. Freddie bailed it out as fast as it came in. Twig hung over the side, seasick, while Ray held him by the scruff of the neck so he wouldn't fall overboard. Nowak kept his eyes glued to the western horizon, his fingers clamped around his lucky rabbit's foot, hoping for rescue. Tubby remained unconscious.

At daybreak, a vessel appeared, and while Twig blew his whistle and waved his arm, the rest of the crew cheered.

Until the black swastika on a red-and-white Nazi flag loomed into focus.

CHAPTER THREE

Kowalski Residence
Old Town Warsaw, Poland

A stone gargoyle rested on the roof of the blue house on Piwna Street. Anna always glanced up at it on her way out and said a silent prayer for the gargoyle to ward off evil spirits, but today, in her excitement, she had forgotten.

Her favorite poet, Krzysztof Kamil Baczyński, a student of Polish literature at the Underground University, was coming to do a reading at her school, so she'd woken early to finish sewing the silk blouse she'd made from a parachute in the air drop. Then she'd polished her only pair of shoes and rushed out of the house to go pick up Ewa Jeska.

It was only a few blocks along the cobblestone streets, just past the Gothic St. John's Cathedral and the Jesuit Church to the house on Market Square where the Jeska family lived. At five years older than twelve-year-old Ewa, Anna had offered to walk the girl to school after several children in the neighborhood with blond hair and blue eyes had gone missing.

Most days, she took the long way to Ewa's house to avoid seeing a block of houses destroyed during weeks of relentless bombings, but today she took the shortcut, past the wooden crosses scattered amidst the rubble, fighting the memories they evoked of Black Monday. Wandering for hours among the scorched ruins, panic-stricken and lost until she recognized a bedpost from her parents' bedroom, sticking out of the rubble. Digging through the debris with her bare hands, calling out her mother's name, and scraping her fingers until they were bloody by lugging bricks, pipes, beams, and shards of glass to find her mother's body.

She wiped her eyes before entering the front door of the burnished yellow burgher house on Market Square. As usual, she found Ewa sitting behind the wooden desk in her father's upstairs office, with a stethoscope hung around her neck.

"Here's your prescription, slow poke." Ewa scribbled something on a prescription pad and handed it over with a flourish.

Anna laughed when she read it: *Two sugar lumps and a piece of chocolate.*

Ewa stepped out from behind the desk, wearing a floral dress with forget-me-not flowers, and fancy new shoes. Both girls wore their wheat-blonde hair in a single braid, but Ewa always threaded hers with a purple ribbon. They looked so much alike that people often mistook them for sisters.

Since the Nazis had banned education above Grade 4, Anna and Ewa had attended secret classes set up by the Underground at a private residence in New Town about two kilometers away. They walked side by side through the pointed archway of the red brick fortification wall that surrounded the Old Town, then down a quiet back street the Nazis usually didn't patrol. Linden trees flanked the street, branches so low they formed a tunnel, the heart-shaped leaves almost brushing against Anna's face as they walked underneath. They turned left at the end of the street where a massive oak tree stood.

Ewa talked nonstop as they walked. "Purple is my favorite color," she said. "What's your favorite?"

"Blue. Like the sky," Anna said, looking up.

Ewa stopped beside a cluster of white baby's breath wild-flowers. She lowered her voice to a whisper. "I heard my sister talking to our parents. Zophia said Samuel and his family disappeared. She's afraid someone told the Germans they're Jews."

Anna rubbed the goosebumps on her arms, thinking back to the night at the airdrop. She was worried about her childhood friend Samuel Weiss. Soft spoken and shy, he used to meet her almost every day after school to practice for dance competitions at his mother's studio before the Germans shut it down. Their mothers had been close friends since meeting at a ballet class when they were children.

"It could be true. The Gestapo are handing out rewards for information on Jews in hiding," she said.

"Why do the Germans hate the Jews so much?" Ewa asked.

"Hitler thinks everyone should have blond hair and blue eyes."

"That doesn't make any sense. Hitler doesn't even have blond hair." Ewa tugged her braid and fiddled with her blue ribbon. "But we do and he hates us too."

"Hitler hates all Poles. He calls Christian Poles like us, *Untermenschen*." Subhumans.

"They're the *Untermenschen*."

Anna checked her watch. "We better be quick. We don't want to be late." She took Ewa's hand as they crossed a busy street, checking both ways for German soldiers. "Hurry," she said to Ewa, quickening her pace.

They turned onto a gravel road that led downhill. A woman wearing a heavy-looking black coat stood at the bottom, and though she looked harmless enough, something felt off. As they approached, Anna noticed a gray dress with a white apron poking out the front of the woman's unbuttoned coat. It looked like the uniform of the Brown Sisters—the Nazi nurses. She tightened her grip on Ewa's hand.

"Keep walking," she whispered, "and keep your head down." For a moment Anna thought they would pass by safely, but then the woman stepped in front of them.

"*Guten Morgen*," she said.

"*Guten Morgen*," Anna replied in her best German, while glancing up and down the road.

"Where are you going?" the nurse asked.

"Out for a walk. Such a nice day," Anna said.

The nurse directed her next question at Ewa. "How old are you?"

Ewa didn't answer.

"Don't be afraid, my dear. I won't hurt you," the woman spoke in a gentle voice. Digging into her coat pocket, she brought out a wrapped candy bar. "Do you like chocolate?"

Ewa nodded.

"Would you like to have it?"

Anna took a step backwards and pulled Ewa with her. Ewa yanked herself free from Anna's grip and stepped forward, holding out her hand.

Anna spun around when she heard a rustling sound in the trees, her heart hammering when she saw a man in a black uniform holding a scary-looking German shepherd with a torn ear on a tight leash. The double sig rune and the *Totenkopf,* the death's head insignia of a skull above crossed bones, identified him as a member of the Schutzstaffel. The dreaded German SS.

His jaw tightened and she caught the glint of a gold tooth as his hand moved to the MP-40 submachine gun slung over his shoulder. She knew her guns as well as her Polish authors.

"Don't take it, Ewa. There's an SS officer watching us and he's got a dog. Run!" Anna yelled.

The two girls sped off down the road. Anna thought about heading to the school for help, but that would expose the secret location and put everyone there in danger.

She could hear the officer and the panting dog behind them. They cut through a vacant yard and wriggled under a fence. Just ahead a steep incline led up to the main road. Cars and trucks whizzed by. If they could reach the busy street, they might be able to find help or dodge through the traffic to lose him.

The girls clambered up the sandy slope, using scattered grass and rocks for grip. Anna reached the top and climbed over the guard rail with Ewa just a few steps behind. She put out her arm to help her young friend over the metal rail but Ewa lost her footing and slid back down to the bottom.

Anna watched in horror as the officer unleashed the dog. It jumped on Ewa, front paws on her chest and black nose inches from her face, teeth bared in a growl.

"Anna. Help me. Please help me," she screamed.

Anna slid down the incline to where Ewa lay motionless, eyes closed, fists clenched. Swinging her bag at the growling dog, she screamed at it to get off. The officer swung his submachine gun and knocked her to the ground.

"Don't hurt her. She's just a little girl," Anna pleaded.

He pointed the gun directly at Anna, finger on the trigger. "Leave or I'll shoot you," he said, narrowing his hazel eyes.

Scrambling to her feet, she raised her arms. She was no match for the officer, his gun, and his dog. She had to find Papa. Fast.

She crawled back up the embankment. Climbing over the railing, she ran all the way to the arched entrance of the crumbling fortification wall back into Old Town, through Market Place, and down the cobblestone street past the bombed-out apartment complex. Everything felt threatening now, even the familiar multi-colored row houses on Piwna Street.

Bursting through the front door of the house with the weathered gargoyle, she found Papa and Michal sitting at the kitchen table.

"Anna, my dear. What's wrong?" Papa got to his feet.

She could barely speak. "They . . . they have Ewa!"

"Who has Ewa?"

"The SS . . . the SS has her," Anna tugged her father's arm to pull him toward the door. "There's no time to talk. We have to go back and help her."

"Slow down. Tell me everything." He brushed the strands of hair that had fallen loose from her braid away from her eyes.

Still trying to catch her breath, she recounted what had happened.

"*Lebensborn*." The Fountain of Life. Michal smashed his fist on the table and stood, grabbing his Sten gun and a box of ammo.

"Sounds like they've got the Brown Sisters helping them do their dirty work." Papa nudged Anna toward her brother and said to him, "You stay here with Anna, Michal. I'll go alone."

"This is all my fault. I was supposed to protect her. I felt so helpless." Anna squeezed her eyes shut to hold back tears. "Please can I come with you?"

"No."

"But—"

"Anastasia. I said *no*."

The sharpness of his voice told her not to argue. Papa slipped his Vis 35 pistol out of his holster and released the magazine to make sure it was fully loaded. He slid the mag back into position with a firm tap and grabbed his felt hat—the one with the partridge feather that Mama had tucked into the headband on the day that she'd died.

"Michal, keep an eye on your sister. Lock the door behind me." He stormed out of the house.

Michal bolted the door and wedged the blade of a butcher knife between the wall and the wooden door frame. "Did anyone follow you?" he asked as he opened a box of ammo and dropped 9mm rounds into the magazine of his gun.

She shook her head. "What's *Lebensborn*?"

"We have few details. Only what our cryptographers have pieced together from deciphered Nazi communications. It's some kind of secret program."

"What will they do to her?"

"Assess her for racial purity. Compare her to their ideal. They're trying to create a Master Race with blond-haired, blue-eyed children."

"She's Polish!"

"Her birth records will be changed."

"But the Nazis call us *Untermenschen*." If the Nazis believed Poles were subhuman, why would they kidnap their children and pretend they were German? "What if she doesn't measure up to their ideal?"

Michal hesitated. "Let's just pray that she does."

"Tell me."

"She'll be sent to a concentration camp for extermination."

Did she hear Michal correctly? Ewa would live or die depending on the measurement of her features. Anna kicked the wall in disgust at the reign of terror the Nazis held over her people.

She headed upstairs to her bedroom. Nothing made sense anymore. No sense at all. She examined her tear-stained image in the mirror—wheat-blonde hair, almond-shaped blue eyes—and promised herself she'd do everything she could to aid the Resistance.

CHAPTER FOUR

Ziekenhuis
Amsterdam, Netherlands

Nowak woke, feeling groggy. A glass bottle hung from a metal pole, feeding saline into his vein. Tubes protruded from his chest.

A doctor in a white lab coat with the SS insignia peered down at him. In his mid-thirties and freshly shaven, he smelled of antiseptic that brought back fragments of the last few days: the squeaky wheels of a gurney; a powerful light shining in his face; forceps digging pieces of shrapnel out of his chest without anesthetic.

Placing the ends of a stethoscope in his ears, the doctor pressed the apparatus to Nowak's chest. "Take a deep breath," he said in a thick German accent.

Nowak sucked air in through his mouth and coughed up a small amount of blood.

The doctor wrapped the stethoscope around his neck. "You're ready to travel," he declared and moved on to someone moaning in the next bed before Nowak could respond.

A nurse dressed in a dark blue uniform with a white apron removed the IV from Nowak's arm and the tubes from his chest. She dabbed his wounds with a cotton swab and sprinkled yellow sulfa powder on them, then she wrapped paper bandages around his chest and left shoulder.

He struggled to sit up and fell back, his head spinning into darkness. Sometime later, he awoke to the nurse offering him a cup of coffee and a piece of dark bread.

"Where's my crew?" He scanned the white iron beds in the crowded recovery room and, at the same time, checked the doors and windows for a way out. *Wehrmacht* guards in field-gray uniforms and shiny black jackboots stood at each exit with Mauser K98 rifles slung over their shoulders.

She held the cup to his mouth without responding.

Nowak sipped but could barely swallow the awful-tasting coffee. Dizzy and nauseated, he pushed the cup away.

"My crew. Where's my crew?" he insisted.

"No English. Dutch," she said.

She returned with his clothes. His blue cotton shirt and battle jacket were laundered but torn from the shrapnel. The pilot's wings and patches had been cut off his jacket. He made sure no one was watching before he checked for the brass button with a reverse thread that doubled as a compass when unscrewed. Gone. He looked for the silk map issued by MI9, the British intelligence agency tasked with escape and evasion, sewn into the lining of his jacket. Gone.

But the bastards had missed the compass hidden in the button that fastened the fly on his trousers. Good. He was going to need that button. When suspended from a thread, it would oscillate until coming to a rest with the single dot on the underside facing magnetic north.

The nurse returned to help him dress.

"Where am I going?" he asked as he ran his fingers through his dark hair. He might be in intense pain, but they hadn't killed him yet.

The nurse didn't respond.

He pointed to his wrist and tried to lift his left arm. "I need my watch. My rabbit's foot. And my money."

She walked away.

A guard stomped over, swung his rifle, and gestured for Nowak to follow. He stumbled along the polished floors and glaring lights between rows of beds lining the ward. Searing pain tore through his chest and he stopped.

That's when he spotted Tubby, though he was almost unrecognizable, with bandages wrapped around his head, nose, and part of his mouth, but Nowak couldn't miss the tattoo of a red heart and the name of his girlfriend, Betty, on his left forearm.

Nowak headed to his bedside, thankful to see his navigator alive. "How're you feeling, Tub?" he asked as he rested his hand on Tubby's shoulder.

"Okay," Tubby said, his voice muffled.

The guard waved his rifle toward the exit.

Nowak ignored him. "They're shipping me out."

"Nurse said. I have to. Stay. Here." Tubby took frequent breaths.

"You still have your watch. The bastards kept mine."

"Nurse. Hid it. Brought back. I think. She likes. Me."

"I'm sure."

"She. Even kissed. Me. On the cheek." The edge of Tubby's mouth twitched slightly.

"You always had a way with the ladies."

This time, the guard poked Nowak in the stomach with the rifle to get him to move.

"Hold your horses." Nowak glared at the guard. He turned back to his navigator, wishing there was something more he could do than say goodbye. "I've got to go, Tub. See you in England after the war."

The guard pushed Nowak out of the exit into the gray misty morning. Outside the building, two armed guards and an officer stood beside a camouflaged army truck. Nowak winced in pain as he climbed into the back of the vehicle.

"I was beginnin' to think you'd never wake up." Ray sat forward, his elbows on his knees, too tall to sit up straight under the truck's canvas canopy. Both of his hands were dressed in mesh gauze, with pressure bandages up to his wrists. Twig sat across from Ray with his arm in a sling. The skinny rear gunner fit easily inside the cramped space.

Relieved to see his two crew members inside, Nowak sat beside Twig and asked, "How long have we been here?"

"'Bout a week. You lost a lot of blood," Ray said.

"What happened to your hands?" Nowak asked Ray.

"Got second-degree burns when I was movin' Tubby." Ray held up his hands. "Nuthin' serious."

"Where's Freddie?"

"Haven't seen him since we got here," Ray said.

Nowak noticed Twig squinting. "Where're your glasses?" he asked.

"Lost 'em when we ditched." Twig rubbed his green eyes, then whispered, "Where are we going?"

"The train station. They're shippin' us to Germany. We're prisoners of war now, and they're gonna lock us up behind barbed wire." Ray's expression hardened. "Stalag IVB."

"Jesus. That's one of the worst. Are you sure?" Nowak asked. The living conditions for Allied Air Force personnel were much better in the POW camps run by the *Luftwaffe*, than they were in the Army camps. "Why not a Stalag *Luft*? We should be headed to an Air Force camp. Not an Army camp."

"Most are full. The Germans are establishing Air Force compounds inside the Army camps," Ray said.

The guard climbed into the back of the truck and sat beside Nowak, who edged closer to Twig.

"*Für euch ist der Krieg zu Ende*," the guard said as he tightened his grip on his rifle.

Nowak looked at Ray. "What'd he say?"

Ray shrugged.

The German officer hopped into the front cab. The coal-fired engine growled, sputtered, and stalled, then started again and rumbled forward on the washboard road.

Nowak wondered if the Germans had found the silk map Ray kept hidden in the hollow heel of his size thirteen flying boot. The map detailed rail lines, waterways, and roads providing escape routes out of Germany.

"Ray, is that boot of yours giving you any trouble?"

Ray tapped his foot. "No trouble at all."

"Glad to hear it." They were going to need that map where they were headed.

CHAPTER FIVE

Kowalski Residence
Old Town Warsaw, Poland

Anna had to get rid of the evidence, fast. Her kitchen table was strewn with half-drunk bottles of homemade potato vodka. Shot glasses. A suitcase radio. Morse key. Truck battery. And most dangerous of all, a decoded message.

She tossed the piece of paper with the message into the fireplace and the burning logs collapsed inward, as if the weight of the words were too much to bear. A member of the Home Army in Kalisz, a city in an area taken over by the Nazis called Warthegau, had received information that Ewa was being held in a monastery seized by the SS and surrounded by an electric fence. Anna had been so worried; it was all she could think about. The guilt was unbearable.

When Papa called a Home Army meeting, the main floor of her house on Piwna Street became Command Central. Men shrouded in tobacco smoke engaged in heated conversation crowded around the kitchen table. As usual, they had slipped out the back door into the alley, leaving her behind. She was determined to do something more important for the Home Army than clean up.

This house was nothing like the house they lived in before the German invasion in the days when Papa had been a language professor at the university and Mama had cooked traditional Polish meals of duck blood soup, pierogi stuffed with potato and cheese, cabbage rolls in creamy tomato sauce, and smoked kielbasa. Michal had played Chopin hunched over their grand piano while friends and family danced the mazurka. As a child, Anna had loved standing on Papa's feet while he whirled her around the room.

Mama's murder had devastated Papa. He'd vowed to avenge her death and fight to liberate their country. That was when he joined the *Armia Krajowa*, the Home Army, and they'd moved to Old Town Warsaw. She had vowed to avenge her mother's death too, but she was only fourteen then, and Papa wouldn't let her join.

Now she was home alone and waiting for word on Ewa. She turned down the burner on the stove to bring the wild mushroom soup she'd made to a simmer. Not that long ago, Ewa had stood right here in this very spot cleaning the mushrooms they had gathered and cutting them into thin slices.

Anna lit a candle and ran a sewing needle through the flame to sterilize it, then used the needle to thread the slices onto strings. After that, she climbed onto a chair and hung the strings from the curtain rod above the kitchen window for the mushrooms to dry in the sun. She remembered how Ewa had grabbed one and holding it up to her neck like a necklace, had done a little dance. They had a good laugh over that.

Anna couldn't remember laughing since.

She looked at the box filled with components for a prototype submachine gun, based on the Sten guns the British had delivered, that she was supposed to hide in the cellar, beneath the floorboards concealing the trapdoor. Twenty different workshops had been set up in the city by the Home Army, each one making a different component and mined with explosives in case of a raid by the Gestapo. That way, if the Germans discovered one workshop, it wouldn't jeopardize the entire operation.

She pulled out a metal butt-plate fashioned from an oven handle made by a manufacturer of electric stoves. Her fingers traced over the three lightning bolts carved into the aluminum that gave the guns their name: the *Błyskawica*. Lightning. She placed it on the table and picked up a magazine that could be loaded with stolen German 9mm ammo. Next, she lined up a couple of small springs and an end cap for an upper receiver, then a barrel.

The sound of a truck pulling up in front of the house startled her. She rushed to the window and opened the burlap curtains she'd sewn out of the bags wrapped around the cargo in the airdrop, to see Papa and Michal climbing out of the dusty Fiat.

"Did you find Ewa?" she asked as soon as they opened the front door.

"I'm sorry," Papa said. "We were too late."

"What do you mean?" Anna gasped, fearing the worst.

"We made contact with the caretaker at the monastery. He's a Pole that worked for the nuns before the Germans occupied it." Papa took off his felt hat. "He's the one who passed the information about Ewa on to the Home Army. But she's not there anymore."

"Where is she?"

"Probably Germany or Austria. They're kidnapping our children and showing them off as their own. There's nothing more we can do until the war is over."

"It's my fault. All my fault."

"Don't talk like that." Papa reached out to comfort her, but she moved into the kitchen so he wouldn't see her wipe away a tear.

"You must be hungry. I made soup."

Michal took off his fringed, brown suede jacket and threw it on the green sofa with horsehair batting that doubled as his bed. Papa noticed the submachine gun components lined up on the table.

"This work is nothing a young girl needs to concern herself with. Practice your dancing for me," Papa said as he moved the coffee table out of the way to give her room.

"But Papa, we don't have any music. I don't want to dance. I want to help assemble the guns."

Her father sighed and stuffed tobacco into the bowl of his carved cherrywood pipe. "My own daughter." He paused to light the tobacco. "I'd still rather you were interested in music instead."

The Nazis had declared the possession of a radio punishable by death. They forbade the playing of musical works by Polish composers, and Papa could no longer afford a piano because the Nazis had closed all the universities, followed by *Intelligenz-aktion*: the mass shootings of the Polish intelligentsia.

"Close your eyes and hear the music of Fryderyk Chopin." Papa settled back on the sofa and crossed one leg over the other as he began to hum the first few bars. The sweet fruity scent of his pipe tobacco filled the room. "You must carry the music of our Polish composers in your heart."

As her father instructed, Anna stood and held her head high, torso straight. Closing her eyes, she imagined Michal seated at the keys of their old piano, instead of on the ramshackle chair. When the music started, a triple meter Mazurka, she lifted her hands into position and, raising her bare foot, she danced.

In her mind's eye, she danced to Chopin's Opus 50 while wearing a fancy folk costume sewn by her mother: a lace-up embroidered vest, white blouse, flowing striped skirt, and a flowered wreath with colored ribbons. Samuel danced beside her in his tailored waistcoat and striped trousers, like he used to do when their families got together for special occasions.

It felt good to see her father smile. He even clapped and tapped his foot. Afterwards, she placed the pot of steaming wild mushroom soup on the kitchen table, set with their blue-and-white ceramic bowls hand-painted by a younger Michal who dreamed of attending the Academy of the Arts. Once they were all seated, they bowed their heads and folded their hands.

"Father in heaven," Papa said. "We thank you for the food we are about to eat. Please help us understand the circumstances in which we find ourselves and grant us the strength to carry on. We pray for our beloved wife and mother, Basia. For the safety of our family, the safe return of Ewa, the liberation of our country, and peace for all. Amen."

Anna picked up the ladle to fill Papa's bowl.

"We have other news," Michal said and he glanced at Papa as if waiting for permission to continue. "Tell her, Father."

Papa looked lost in thought.

"The Home Army and the Jewish Fighting Organization are joining forces to form a council to aid the Jews. Codenamed *Żegota*. I've accepted the position of director of the children's division." He spoke slowly. "It's top secret. We can't let the *szmalcowniki*, the blackmailers, get wind of this. When we don't have the money to pay them, they'll report us to the Gestapo."

"Yes, of course," Anna whispered.

"We estimate that around three hundred thousand Jews have been deported from the Warsaw ghetto to death camps at Treblinka and Auschwitz-Birkenau since the liquidation started in June. There are only about fifty thousand people left inside,"

Papa continued. "Now that the deportations have stalled, we plan to smuggle as many Jewish children out of the ghetto as possible. We need to act fast before the liquidation resumes.

"Once the children arrive on the Aryan side of Warsaw, they'll need Christian documentation. Michal will work with the Underground press to form the legalization cell. Each child will receive forged identity documents and a biography about a fictional family. Those who are old enough will be taught certain beliefs of the Catholic religion. If they only speak Yiddish, we'll teach them Polish. Dr. Jeska will address any medical concerns."

"What can I do?" This was her chance to do something important. She poured soup into her brother's bowl.

"You're too young to get involved in this," Papa said.

"There are couriers much younger than me."

"You're safer here at home," he insisted.

"Michal is a soldier. He's only a year older than me."

"A year and a half older." Michal raised a spoon of steaming soup to his mouth and blew on it.

"That's different."

"Why?" Anna asked.

"Anastasia—" Papa heaved a tired sigh. He leaned back in his chair and rolled the sleeves of his blue-and-black plaid shirt up to his elbows.

"Mother would never approve," Michal said between mouthfuls.

"Mama is dead." Anna slammed her spoon on the table. She reached into her pocket to touch her rosary. "What do you expect me to do? Just sit here? The bloody Germans murdered my mother. They kidnapped Ewa. And now Samuel is missing."

"Anna! Where did you learn to talk like that? You sound like a British soldier," Papa reprimanded her.

"I want to help rescue the Jewish children."

"Your German has to be perfect."

"My German *is* perfect."

Papa stirred his soup, moving his spoon around and around. He looked up at her. "You can work with the children after they arrive. Many will have a hard time separating from their families and adjusting to new identities."

Visions of the three-meter-high red brick wall that surrounded the ghetto, barbed wire strung along the top, flashed through her mind. It sealed the Jews inside; there was no way out for them.

"There are armed guards everywhere. They shoot anyone seen leaving. How will we get the children over the wall?"

Papa paused. He pushed his soup away.

"Not over. Under."

CHAPTER SIX

Centraal Stationsplein
Amsterdam, Netherlands

Nowak stood with Twig and Ray on the wooden platform of the Amsterdam train station, surrounded by Army and Air Force prisoners of war from Allied countries, his spirits boosted by an enthusiastic crowd of Dutch citizens. Some risked cheering in support, others shot the V for victory sign. An elderly man in a dark suit and plaid bow tie tossed Nowak a package of cigarettes. He waved and bent to pick them up, but a German officer shoved him out of the way and pocketed the cigarettes for himself. Nowak turned away, seething, and looked at the waiting boxcar with the words: *HOMMES 40: CHEVAUX (en long) 8* painted on its side.

Standing beside him, Ray pointed at it. "What the hell does that mean?"

"Forty men or eight horses in length," Nowak said. "It's French. The Germans use the boxcars for transport."

"They're going to cram forty of us in there?" Twig asked.

"Looks like it," Nowak replied.

A burly guard stomped up to Nowak and poked him in the ribs with the barrel of his Mauser. "Boots, Boots."

Nowak saw that the other POWs were taking off their boots, marking them with chalk, and throwing them into a crate.

"Why do we have to take off our boots?" Twig asked.

"To make it harder to escape." Nowak picked a piece of chalk up off the platform and wrote his initials on his. He passed the chalk to Ray. "Make sure you mark those boots of yours really good," he whispered, thinking about the map hidden in the heel.

A guard pushed Nowak into the boxcar at gunpoint. It was sweltering hot with straw on the floor, vertical slats for ventilation, a narrow window covered by crisscrossed barbed wire high up the wall, and dozens more than forty servicemen already jostling for a place to sit. He found a spot just inside the door. Ray squished in beside him, and Twig slipped his willowy frame into the corner.

A guard appeared and handed out black bread. Three pieces per man. Moments later, the door slammed shut, silencing the crowd. The whistle blew, the steam engine hissed, and the train rolled out of the station.

Nowak noted that there was just one pail of drinking water for the entire car. It didn't take long for the men to drink it all. Once emptied, it became the communal toilet.

Twig had the runs. He fidgeted and talked nonstop between trips to the pail.

"Let's take off as soon as the train stops." Twig fumbled with the button on his fly, with one arm in a sling.

"They'll shoot us if we do," Ray said.

"Twig, try to settle down," Nowak said as the train rumbled eastward toward Germany. He felt responsible for his rear gunner but there wasn't much he could do. He was fighting the urge to throw up from the suffocating heat laced with the smell of sweat and the stench from the pail slopping onto the floor. He took off his jacket and unbuttoned his shirt. His eyes felt heavy. He leaned back against the rough wooden interior.

Ray used his unbandaged wrist to touch Nowak's forehead. "You better get some rest, Skipper. You're burnin' up."

Nowak closed his eyes, picturing the Dutch countryside with windmills, steep-roofed houses, and canals. When thoughts of the war-torn villages entered his mind, he tried to envision springtime with miles and miles of red, white, and yellow tulip fields.

He had planted bulbs for his mother along their concrete sidewalk back at home. Tulips and purple crocuses were always the first to bloom after a long Canadian winter, sprouting bursts of color up through patches of snow.

Just as Nowak was about to drift off to sleep, Twig let out a yell. Opening his eyes, Nowak stiffened as he heard the faint drone of an aircraft engine. They were sitting ducks. The roar of the aircraft grew closer, machine gun fire blasted, and an explosion rocked the compartment. Twig wrapped his arm over his head. Ray stared straight ahead.

Nowak peered through the slats and saw nothing but darkness. At any other time, he'd be cheering the pilot on, but getting killed by Allied fire locked inside this wooden coffin packed full of men like sardines in a can, would be one hell of a way to go. He pressed his ear against the wall and listened as the gun fire receded into the distance.

The train remained stationary. Twig tried to force open the door. He yanked at the barbed wire covering the window, cutting his fingers. Hours later, the door finally opened, and the prisoners poured out into the early morning air. There wasn't a tree in sight, just vast potato fields in every direction.

Standing beside the train track, Nowak ripped off his shirt, taking deep breaths after so long in the stale and close confines of the cattle car. The cool breeze dried the sweat on his back. Ray stood on one side of him. Twig on the other.

Nowak surveyed the number of guards surrounding them. Most looked young and fresh out of the Hitler Youth. Five to the left. Three to the right. All armed. Voices of more behind them.

"Let's make a run for it," Twig whispered.

"I don't like this any better than you, but we've got to use our heads."

Twig shifted his weight from one foot to the other.

"Twig, we don't stand a chance." Surely the kid had more sense than to try something here. No trees or bushes nearby to hide in. No boots. No weapons.

"They're going to lock us up." A look of panic spread over Twig's face.

"Listen to me, Twig. Not now." Nowak reached over to grab his arm.

Too late.

Twig bolted into the potato field, and the guards didn't hesitate. They levelled their rifles.

"Halt," a guard yelled.

Twig kept running.

A shot rang out. Nowak watched in horror as Twig's body jerked, then he fell head first into the field.

Nowak took a step forward. One guard turned his rifle toward him. He lifted his hands in the air. Step by tentative step, he started across the field, his heart pounding and back tensed, expecting a bullet at any second. He reached Twig and knelt beside him, using his sweat-stained shirt to staunch the wound in Twig's back. Feeling for the large artery on the side of Twig's neck, he felt a faint pulse. The kid was still alive.

"Hang on, Twig. I'll get you some help," Nowak said.

A second later, a guard kicked Nowak hard in the shoulder with the toe of his hobnailed jackboot. Pain shot through him as he tumbled backward.

The guard cocked his rifle and aimed it at Twig.

"No! Don't shoot. He's just a kid," Nowak shouted.

The guard glanced back at Nowak, then held the barrel to the back of Twig's head and pulled the trigger.

Blood spattered Nowak. He reached for his shirt to wipe his face and held it there for a moment to stop the tears that fought to flow. He moved his shirt from his eyes and saw the barrel of the rifle inches from his face. *Jesus, don't let the fucker pull the trigger.*

The guard yelled, "*Los. Los,*" and motioned toward the supply car, jerking the rifle sideways.

Nowak hobbled over to the train where a guard handed him a rusty shovel.

"I need my boots," Nowak said.

The guard shook his head.

Nowak thrust the metal tip into the ground and lifted out some dirt; his stitches tore from the strain and blood ran down his chest. Ray strode up and ripped the shovel out of his hand.

"Let me do it, Skipper."

Ray went to work. When he reached the depth of a shallow grave, they lowered Twig's body into its final resting place. His once soft green eyes stared up at them. Nowak swallowed hard, knelt, and lowered the boy's eyelids. Ray lifted a shovelful of dirt and sprinkled it on top of the corpse. Once the grave was full, he scooped gravel from beside the tracks to scatter on top. Nowak arranged a series of larger rocks in the shape of a cross.

Scrambling back onboard, he took one last look at the mound of gravel before the door slammed shut and the train continued its journey, leaving Twig alone, in an empty field, with nothing more than a few scattered rocks to commemorate his life.

The shock of Twig's murder left Nowak numb. He sat in silence. Only a week or so into captivity and Twig was dead. Tubby was missing his nose. And where the hell was Freddie?

Now, it was just him and Ray. Some skipper he turned out to be.

CHAPTER SEVEN

Jacobsthal, Zeithain
Germany

The heavy wood door slid open with a crash. Sunshine burst into the boxcar. Nowak rubbed his eyes and grimaced as he crawled out into the light with Ray right behind him.

Armed guards and German shepherd dogs waited on a wooden platform at a brick building. "*Totschläger!*" Murderer, yelled a harsh voice. No cheering crowds here.

Nowak scanned his surroundings. A sign read *Jacobsthal*. A train station right in the middle of nowhere, with all trees cut down to keep the line of fire clear. No chance of escape.

"What now?" Ray asked.

"Figure we gotta march the rest of the way," Nowak said, breathing in fresh air.

Two sallow-skinned men climbed aboard the boxcar and unloaded the body of a soldier who had died during the last day of the journey. The crimson collar patches on their worn uniforms told Nowak they were Russian prisoners from the stalag. They threw the corpse into the back of a cart.

Nowak dug around to retrieve his boots from the large pile dumped on the ground. After making sure Ray found both of his, he joined the column of prisoners and began a march along a dirt road, surrounded by goose-stepping guards and barking German shepherds. Once strong, determined soldiers of the Red Army now harnessed to a corpse cart followed behind.

Nowak's shoulder throbbed and his chest ached, but he was determined to march. He wasn't about to become another body in the back of a cart pulled by skeletal Russians. He didn't know if they'd be marching for days or hours.

Head held high, arms swinging shoulder height, marching faster and faster as his legs limbered. Ray stood taller than most of the men, and his one step matched their two strides. Let those bastards work to keep up.

They must have been marching for some four kilometers when an appalling odor almost stopped Nowak in his tracks: the smell of open-pit latrines and rotten food. As the road veered off to the right, the prisoner-of-war camp came into sight. Double barbed wire fences and snarling dogs secured the perimeter. Guard towers manned with machine guns and searchlights hovered above.

A swastika flew high over the main gate flanked by wooden pillars and the words *M. Stammlager IVB*. Nowak marched through the gate past uniformed guards holding Mauser rifles with fixed bayonets. To the west, the sunset draped them with a curtain of darkness.

Anger consumed him: anger for his plane getting shot down, anger over Twig's murder, and just plain damn anger at the horror of it all.

He was directed to a grimy delousing center housed in a red brick building where they were all ordered to strip.

"We might not get our boots back this time," Nowak whispered to Ray.

They both maneuvered their way through the throng of men to the back of the room. Nowak deliberately stood in front of

Ray so he could remove the silk map without being noticed. There were five guards. One remained at the front, while the other four circled the room, two on each side, scrutinizing the prisoners. With rifles in hand, they were getting close. One watched Nowak, tightening his finger on the trigger.

Nowak glanced at Ray who was squatting down still fiddling with his boot. It seemed like he was having trouble replacing the heel.

"Hurry," Nowak whispered. Taking a few steps back, he undid the buttons on his shirt, exposing the blood-soaked bandages on his chest, and stretched out his good arm to shield Ray from the view of the guard.

"*Was ist los?*" the guard hollered, using his rifle to ram his way in between Nowak and Ray.

Nowak clutched his chest and moaned in pain.

The guard raised his rifle.

Ray jumped up. "Let me help you with that, Skipper." He pulled at the sleeve of Nowak's battle jacket with one hand while slipping his silk map into a pocket with the other.

The guard looked puzzled, eying them up and down. Seemingly satisfied, he continued on.

Nowak bunched his clothes inside his battle jacket and tied the sleeves around the bundle. He entered a room that was bare save for nozzles in the ceiling and a drain in the floor. After a spray of ice-cold water and no soap, a scruffy-looking Russian prisoner with a tin pail of insecticide brushed him with liquid under his arms and around his balls, burning his skin. He cringed when a medic jabbed him in his pectoral muscle with the same needle used on all the prisoners, hoping it was a vaccine to ward off typhus. He'd heard the disease raged rampant through the lice-infested camps.

He rummaged through heaps of steaming clothes fumigated in delousing ovens to find his bundle. While he dressed, he held his breath against the chemical vapors that had seeped into the fabric. His boots had disappeared, replaced by wooden clogs. After that, he was fingerprinted, photographed, and registered as *Kriegsgefangener*, Prisoner of War, 12679. Kriegie for short.

An old guard with yellowed teeth and a bit of a belly motioned for Nowak and Ray to follow him, and Nowak stepped out of the building into darkness. Searchlights stationed on guard towers tracked his movement as he shuffled in clogs down a dirt road past rows and rows of drab wooden barracks to a gate with a padlock and a heavy chain wrapped around a post.

The guard's keys jangled as he unlocked the gate to the RAF compound, an area separated from the main camp by extra rounds of barbed wire. Inside, Nowak counted four barracks and a hut with a Red Cross emblem. The guard led them up to a door and motioned them inside a dimly lit building. The door slammed behind them and they heard the sound of a key turning in the lock.

An airman with an unlit cigarette dangling from his mouth and tufts of chest hair poking out of his unbuttoned shirt said, "I'm your hut commander. Name's Snowshoe. RCAF. I've been expecting you. Lights are already out. I'll show you to your bunk assignment." He maneuvered his way through rows of three-tiered wooden bunks, using the light of a burning wick inside a tin can, and pointed to empty beds. "I bet you could use some sleep. We can deal with everything else in the morning. There's no rush. You're not going anywhere."

Exhausted, Nowak climbed up onto a filthy straw-filled mattress with a threadbare army blanket on a middle bunk.

With every breath, his chest burned. He needed to sleep and rolled on his side. Just as he closed his eyes, something crawled across his face. He brushed his cheek. The straw crackled. Sitting bolt upright, he smashed his fist against the mattress.

"Jesus! What the hell?"

"Bed bugs," said a gruff voice from below.

Nowak lay back down. "Fuck this place and fuck the Germans."

"Amen."

The sounds and smells of the barrack that was to be his new home surrounded him. A cough. Stale smoke. Sweaty bodies. Snoring.

CHAPTER EIGHT

A large roll of blueprints held down by a bottle of homemade potato vodka lay open on the kitchen table. Papa stood, his arms crossed in front of him, talking to Mr. Baranek, a short, pudgy man with a handlebar mustache from the Department of Sanitation.

"Can we trust the sewer workers to help us? The Germans have issued the death penalty for anyone aiding the Jews," Papa said. "The plan will not work unless we have their full cooperation."

"Most have agreed to help. A few are demanding bribes, but we've made the necessary arrangements." Baranek twisted the waxed tip of his mustache with his fleshy fingers. "We're ready to start. I've called a meeting for tomorrow."

Papa poured two shots of vodka. He handed one to Baranek and picked up the other. They clinked their glasses and drank the alcohol, then slammed their glasses down. Baranek gathered his coat, smiled at Anna, and left.

Anna approached the table. "Show me."

"This is too risky for you to concern yourself with." Papa poured himself another shot of vodka and set the bottle aside to roll up the blueprints.

"Just a minute." Anna held the papers down with her hand.

Papa sighed. "These sewer lines run under the ghetto wall to the Aryan side of the city. This is how we plan to bring the children out." He ran his hand along his stubbled chin. "The question is . . . which route is safest?"

Anna pulled up a chair and leaned forward over the drawings. With her index finger, she traced her way through the maze of white lines drawn on a blue background, picturing one route, then another, and back again.

After a few minutes, she planted her finger against the blueprint and said, "I think this is the best place to start." Her tone was serious, confident.

"What makes you say that?"

"Ewa and I used to walk this way to school. This back street is quiet and lined with linden trees. I can get close to the manhole cover without anyone seeing. And look here," she pointed. "If I turn in the other direction, the sewer line leads all the way to the outskirts of the city."

"You can't do this."

"Yes, I can. The ghetto is only about a kilometer away. First you turn right, then you pass through four junctions and turn left and then—"

Papa wrapped his arms around her. "Anna, my dear child."

"I want you to be proud of me, Papa."

"I am proud. There is nothing you could do that would ever change that. I would never forgive myself if something happened to you."

"You said you have to get the children out. And I want to do it with you."

"The sewers are very dangerous."

"Everything we do is dangerous."

CHAPTER NINE

A blast of a bugle jolted Nowak awake on his first morning behind barbed wire. Rags and cardboard covered the glass on the windows. Three-tier wooden bunk beds stood in groups of four on a red brick floor with laundry draped over ropes strung between them. The foul odor of urine emanated from a bucket used after curfew.

A couple of hundred aircrew milled about starting their daily routines. Many from Allied countries, who either flew with, or had their own squadrons within, the RAF. Nowak swung his feet over the edge of his middle bunk and eased his way down, careful not to burst anymore of his stitches. Heading over to a wash area that separated the two sides of the barrack into Hut A and Hut B, he waited in line to cup his hands underneath a pipe dripping freezing water into a concrete trough, collecting enough to refresh his face. With no towels, he used his sleeve.

Snowshoe appeared and handed him a yellow and brown tin can with *KLIM* printed in white and a small handle soldered on the side. "Here's your klim. Have a brew," he said.

Nowak cocked his head and gave Snowshoe a puzzled look.

"The Krauts only give us a spoon. We have to make everything else for ourselves." Snowshoe tossed him a rusty nail. "They're in short supply. Put your initials on it."

After scratching *JN* on the bottom of the tin can, Nowak joined Snowshoe in another long line at a brick cook stove with a sheet metal plate top. When he reached the front, an Aussie dipped a ladle, made from a jam tin attached to a piece of wood with wire, into a massive copper cauldron to fill his klim. Nowak thought about how good a cup of brew was going to taste. He sipped the lukewarm liquid and wanted to spit it out. The same horrible tasting coffee they served him in the hospital in Amsterdam.

"What the hell is this?" Nowak asked.

"Ersatz coffee made of roasted barley beans and crushed acorns," Snowshoe said.

"Where's the latrine?" Nowak set his klim on a table.

"Around here we call it the *shizen haus*. Go out, turn right, and follow the smell."

Nowak found the brick shit house at the western end of the compound. It took a few minutes for his eyes to adjust after he entered the dreary building. There were four rows of raised wooden platforms with open pit holes and no privacy.

He headed to the last hole in the back and unbuttoned his trousers. Just as his rear hit the wood, an airman moved toward him.

"Don't sit down, Skipper."

Nowak looked up.

Freddie stood right in front of him. He was bald and had a nasty scar on his forehead, but it was him.

Nowak jumped up, fumbled with his trousers, and fastened the button. Relieved to see his bomb aimer alive, he threw his arm around his friend and patted him on the shoulder.

"Jesus, Freddie. You had me worried. I was afraid you were dead."

Freddie stomped his feet a few times and kicked the wall of the latrine. "There, it's good now. You can go."

Nowak sat back down. "What the hell was that all about?"

"Rats," Freddie said. "They bite your balls."

Nowak jumped up again. His trousers fell around his ankles. "Are you kidding?"

"Just remember to kick the wall before you sit and be quick. I'll wait out front." Freddie grinned and walked away.

Nowak gave the wall another kick. And then two more, just to be sure.

*

Nowak found Freddie outside, leaning against the shit house with his hands thrust deep in his pockets. They walked together past a gaunt Russian prisoner cranking a lever up and down to suck the contents of the open pit latrine into a wheeled portable tank.

"Gotta watch out for those *shizen karts* as they drip their way out of camp. They make a real stinkin' mess," Freddie said. "After the Russians dump the shit on the fields, they smuggle vegetables back into camp on hooks installed inside the tanks. They receive fewer rations and no Red Cross parcels because the Soviets refused to sign the Geneva Convention.

"There was an uprising by the Russians before I got here. The Krauts refused to enter their barracks. Rumor has it the guards sent their dogs in and the Russians ate the dogs," Freddie told him.

"The bastards ate the dogs?" A gagging sensation lodged in the back of Nowak's throat. He felt sorry for the dogs. Not for the Russians. After all, they had collaborated with Hitler and invaded Poland from the east back in '39, sixteen days after Germany invaded from the west. Poland got hammered from both sides.

"Where the hell have you been?" Nowak asked.

"I didn't need to be hospitalized so they shipped me out right away." Freddie stood at attention with his right arm outstretched in a Nazi salute and clicked his heels together, mimicking a German officer. "Velcome to *Dulag Luft*. You are now *zee* guest of *zee* Third Reich. For you, *zee var ist* over."

Nowak was used to Freddie's antics. His friend used humor to ease his anxiety. The more nervous he was, the more of a comedian he became.

"How bad was it?" Nowak had heard stories about the infamous Interrogation Center known as *Dulag Luft* where a special unit of the *Luftwaffe* interrogated captured airmen.

"They locked me in an overheated cell. Grilled me every day. A German officer impersonated the Red Cross to try to get me to talk. The bastard even knew my mother was a widow," Freddie said. "When they didn't get any information out of me, they shipped me here."

Nowak thought of his own widowed mother. She had probably received a letter by now informing her he was missing in action. It would be months before she learned he was a POW.

"They didn't put any effort into interrogating me at the hospital. By the time I woke up, any intelligence information I had was too old to be of any use to them." Nowak brought Freddie up to speed on Tubby and Ray.

"What about Twig?"

Nowak kicked the toe of his clog into the dirt a couple of times and adjusted his battle jacket to hide the blood stains on his shirt. He didn't want to talk about it. The air drop had been Twig's first mission: replacing Cunningham, the usual fifth member of his crew, who had remained back at base on sick leave.

"The kid got killed on the way here." Nowak's voice wavered. The memory of Twig's death was still so raw. "Panicked. Took off running and the bastards shot him in the back. I should've realized how scared he was. It all happened so fast."

"Maybe he knew he'd never survive this place."

Nowak and Freddie stood together in silence, peering through the barbed wire fence at the rows and rows of wooden barracks in the main Army compound.

"This is a damn big camp," Nowak said. "How many prisoners are there?"

"Snowshoe says twenty-some thousand. We get to enter the Army camp a few times a week for soccer games in the exercise compound. Army against Air Force. Snowshoe's negotiating with the commandant to get us more freedoms. He's the acting *Vertrauensmann*, our man of confidence, until we hold an election. It's for officers only. That would be a good job for you, Skipper."

"How'd he get a name like Snowshoe, anyhow?"

"British humor. A Canadian with big feet."

The blare of a whistle interrupted them. A booming voice shouted, "*Raus. Raus.*" Out. Out.

"That's just Ukraine Joe." Freddie checked his watch. "It's time for morning roll call. Rows of five on Parade Square. They call it *Appell*."

Parade Square turned out to be the dirt yard in front of their barrack. At the far end stood a tall man with deep-set eyes, pockmarked skin, and a small cap perched on a big head— Ukraine Joe, Nowak supposed.

Freddie and Nowak stepped into position. Ray stood a couple of rows up ahead.

"Try to pay attention, Skipper," Freddie whispered. "Keep the lines straight. And remember, the Krauts can only count in fives."

As soon as Ukraine Joe turned his back, Freddie whistled the tune from the *Wizard of Oz*. It had been Freddie's favorite ever since he took his fiancée, Izzie, to see the film release in London. Nowak sang along in his head.

Ukraine Joe whipped around. His hand went for the Luger pistol in his brown leather holster. The whistling stopped. Moving down the rows of airmen, he went back to his count, muttering to himself, "*Fünf, zehn, fünfzehn . . .*" while blowing his whistle in short bursts when the lines weren't straight enough. When he finished the count, morning roll call was over.

"We like harassing him," Freddie said. "But you can only push old Ukraine Joe so far. He's got a real temper. Word is he used to be a prisoner in the penal block until he made a deal with the Krauts and joined the *Wehrmacht*. Now the bastard is one of the guards."

Freddie shoved his hands in his pockets. "I need to talk to you about something. Let's sit here by the tree. The only one they planted in the whole damn camp."

Nowak kicked a cone out of the way and sat cross-legged on the ground.

"I don't know what to do about Izzie." Freddie put his hands to his face and rubbed his temples with his fingers.

"Nothing you can do. She'll have to wait, that's all. She'll be okay."

"She's pregnant."

"Shit, Freddie. That's all you need!"

"I'm happy about it," Freddie said.

"You are?" That was hard to believe, given the mess they were in. Nowak thanked his lucky stars it wasn't him. He'd kept things casual with a girl who worked at the local pub he called Red. The name suited her and the relationship. Fun. Uncomplicated. And far from serious. They were more friends than anything else.

"Why didn't you say something?" Nowak asked.

"She asked me not to. We were supposed to get married. I thought everything would be okay," Freddie said. "I should've made arrangements before we left. This is going to be hard for her. Her parents are very religious."

Nowak thought about his mother and how she'd struggled after his father's death, as a widow emigrating to a new country with two young children to bring up and only a grade three education of her own. When they'd reached Canada, she'd worked at a Chinese laundry during the day and brought clothes home to press at night. As a child he'd been the man of the family, selling newspapers on the street corner in his white shirt and striped tie, and later working in the coalmines when he was older.

"I always wanted a family. I grew up an only child, remember?" Freddie reached into his pocket and pulled out what appeared to be a crumpled church bulletin. "Anyways, not like there's much I can do about it in here. Still, I want her to know I'm thinking about her. I'm going to send her this. Copies have been circulating around camp."

Freddie held the paper up and read the poem "High Flight" by RCAF fighter pilot Magee, written a few months before he was killed.

When Freddie was finished, Nowak said, "I've never been much of a poet, but that's pretty good. It ought to butter Izzie up some, huh? Don't forget to tell her you can't wait to get home."

Four airmen passed by lugging a copper cauldron, with poles slid through the handles, resting on their shoulders. Two men on each side, front and back.

"There goes our lunch." Freddie shoved the paper back in his pocket. "Don't get excited. I've been hungry since I got here."

Back at his hut, Nowak grabbed his klim and stepped into line. The Aussie poured watery looking soup into it using the jam tin ladle. A Czech airman handed him half a piece of black bread.

Nowak and Freddie headed over to the battered wooden table where Ray was seated.

"Well, I'll be damned," Ray said, standing. He was a good eight inches taller than Freddie. "How'd ya get here, ya ole cuss?"

"Been here all along. About time you showed up." Freddie pulled up a chair.

Nowak raised his mug and took a sip of the lukewarm broth. "What *is* this?" he asked, screwing up his mouth.

"Swede a.k.a. turnips," Freddie said. "Wait till you taste the bread. They make it out of tree flour."

Nowak broke off a piece of black bread and stuffed it in his mouth. After a few chews, he asked, "Tree flour?"

"Sawdust."

Nowak stopped chewing.

"They put it in the soup too." Freddie reached into his bag and brought out a can of sardines. "Been saving this for a special occasion. Got it in a Red Cross parcel. We'd all be dead if it wasn't for our parcels." He opened the can and cut each sardine into portions using an odd-looking knife.

"Where'd you get that knife?" Nowak asked.

"Sharpened a piece of metal from a ring on the rain barrel."

"How secure is this place?" Nowak asked.

"As you can see, we're locked in the center of the camp." Freddie stabbed a slice of sardine with his knife and offered it to Nowak.

Nowak ate it slowly to savor the taste.

Freddie served Ray and kept talking. "The outside perimeter of the camp is surrounded by two ten-foot-tall, barbed wire fences separated by coils of wire attached to tin cans."

"To alert the guards if we make it over the first fence?" Nowak asked.

Freddie nodded. "Problem is, we'll never make it over the first fence. A low warning wire runs along it on the inside. Guards are under orders to shoot if we step over it." He stopped talking long enough to take a bite. "They lock us in our huts at twenty-one hundred hours and shut off our lights. Searchlights fan the grounds outside. That's why the windows are covered. Guards patrol the compound all night with dogs and orders to shoot us on sight."

"Ever try to escape?" Nowak asked.

"Not yet," Freddie smirked. "Been waiting for you."

CHAPTER TEN

Warsaw, Poland

Papa offered his arm to Anna as they walked out of Old Town on their way to the meeting with Baranek. They crossed Piłsudski Square, renamed Adolf Hitler Platz, and strode past Saxon Garden. The sign at the entrance of the park read: *Nur für Deutsche*. For Germans only.

She treasured one of the rare moments she got to spend alone with her father. In her mind, she strolled through the avenues of chestnut trees and Baroque statues inside the park, just like her family used to do every Sunday after church. Anna loved the crisp autumn air, and the way the leaves turned endless shades of red, yellow, orange, and brown. When she was younger, she used to collect as many varieties as she could find, dash home, and press each leaf carefully between the pages of the family Bible.

"There's still time to change your mind. Are you sure you're ready to work for Żegota?" Papa asked. "Once you take the oath of loyalty and secrecy to the Home Army, there's no turning back. As a soldier, you must carry out the orders you're given."

"I'm sure."

"Your codename will be Hope. You must never use your real name."

"Yes, Papa."

"We're living in a time in history when saving lives is a crime and murder is legal. Do you understand?"

"I understand."

Her father looked at her tenderly. "You've grown so much, Anna. But you'll always be my little girl."

They crossed a busy intersection and turned onto Żurawia Street.

"See the building marked twenty-four?" Papa asked as they neared a six-story, whitewashed building with rows of rectangular windows, tiny balconies, and a large arched doorway at the entrance. Clematis vines crawled up one side.

A man sweeping the sidewalk gave Papa a slight nod as they passed by. They turned left at the corner and walked halfway down the block to enter the alley. Papa tipped his hat at another man before he rang the bell at the back entrance to Apartment 4.

A dark-haired woman welcomed them inside. Michal stood in front of a narrow window looking out onto the street. Baranek, the overalled man with the mustache from the day before, sat at a dining room table littered with *Błyskawica* submachine gun components and a stack of papers. He stood when they entered.

"We'll start the meeting soon." Baranek looked Anna up and down as if he was assessing her.

She glanced around the room. Three young women, who looked to be a few years older than her, sat on wooden chairs. Ewa's older sister, Zophia, sat on a brown upholstered sofa. It was the first time they'd seen each other since Ewa's kidnapping.

Zophia was the same age as Michal. She worked with her father as a nursing assistant and still wore her white uniform. An older version of Ewa, she had the same blonde hair and striking blue eyes.

If Anna wanted to work for *Żegota*, she'd have to face Zophia sooner or later. She headed over and sat down beside her, expecting to hear harsh words.

"I'm glad you're all right." Zophia gently squeezed Anna's hand.

Zophia's kindness eased Anna's anxiety. She wanted to say how sorry she was, but the tears welling in her eyes spoke for her. She shifted in her chair and straightened her skirt.

The room was so quiet, she could hear her father and Baranek whispering.

"She's too young." Baranek tinkered with the submachine gun parts on the table.

Papa looked across the room at Anna. "I wouldn't allow it if I didn't think she was ready."

"Girls her age are too emotional. I have daughters of my own." He fumbled with two small springs and an end cap, trying to put an upper receiver for a firing assembly together.

"It is very important to her. And to me," Papa said.

Unable to assemble the component with his fat fingers, Baranek put the parts down on his desk. Anna walked over and effortlessly slid the inner bumper spring into the end cap, fit the outer driving spring around it, inserted the cap and the springs into the rear part of the receiver, and screwed it tight. Then she placed the assembled component down on the desk and headed back to the sofa, feeling a twinge of satisfaction at the look of amazement on his face.

Papa smiled. "Shall we proceed?"

Baranek twisted the tip of his mustache and walked to the front of the room. "Welcome, ladies. Thank you for coming this evening."

Anna and the girls sat at attention. Papa remained standing.

"Each of you will receive a map showing your route under the wall into the ghetto." Baranek gestured to the stack of papers on the table. "In some places, the sewer system is narrow and dark. The fumes may disorient you. And rats run rampant."

Anna squirmed in her chair at the word *rat*.

Baranek stopped talking.

She sensed all eyes in the room on her. Her cheeks burned with embarrassment. She told herself soldiers didn't worry about such things and tried to hide her fear of rats by forcing a smile.

Baranek broke the awkward silence. "For your safety, we've installed a series of ropes hanging from the ceilings at the tunnel junctions. Knotted ropes of various lengths will serve as signposts showing you which direction to go. Even though you know the route by heart, check the knots at each junction. Two knots mean to turn right. One knot, turn left."

The girls nodded.

"You'll know when you've reached your destination when you find two ropes hanging instead of just one. Do not go past this point. There will be someone waiting there to bring the children to you. Lead the children out the same way you came in, by feeling for the ropes." He picked up a roll of cable and showed it to the girls. "We'll give you a cable to carry with you. If there are several children to rescue, they must hold on to it so they don't get lost in the tunnels. Be very quiet. Any noise will alert the Germans and jeopardize our operation."

Baranek hooked his thumbs under the straps of his overalls. "Questions?"

Zophia raised her hand. "Where do we take the children when we get them out?"

"Several orders of nuns have agreed to house them in their orphanages until we find foster families. The Sisters of Immaculate Conception, Sisters of Charity, Franciscans, and Grey Ursulines, among them," Baranek replied. "We've chosen escape routes that end near the convents. Someone will be waiting for you on your return. Once you turn the children over, your job will be done."

"When can we start?" Anna asked.

"Right away. Members of Żegota have entered the ghetto with Department of Sanitation passes to speak to families. As you can imagine, many are reluctant to give up their children," he said. "The time and place of your first mission is written on your map."

"What if we run into a sewer worker?" the girl in a navy polka dot blouse asked.

"My men have been briefed. If you run into one along the way, they'll help you." He studied the room and rested his hand on the stack of papers on the table. "Take a copy of the map on your way out. Memorize it, then destroy it. Show it to no one."

Anna stood.

"Anna, before you leave you must take your Oath of Allegiance to the Home Army." Baranek took a silver crucifix out of his pocket and handed it to her. "And remember, the Underground judiciary issues the death sentence to our members for any acts of treason or collaboration with the Germans."

Anna gripped the crucifix in her palm and recited the words:

> I swear loyalty to my Fatherland, the Republic of
> Poland. I pledge to steadfastly guard her honor,
> and to fight for her liberation with all my strength,
> even to the extent of sacrificing my own life.

CHAPTER ELEVEN

Roman Catholic Cathedral
Warsaw, Poland

Anna clutched a cloth bag to her chest and peered up at the spires of the Gothic red brick cathedral. After checking to make sure no one followed her, she climbed the steps, adjusted her kerchief, and pulled open the heavy front door. Incense from a funeral lingered in the air, and images of her mother lying under the ruins of their home, still gripping her Holy Rosary, again came back to her. The very same, black-beaded rosary now wrapped around her hand.

Sunlight filtered through the arched stained-glass windows and etched colored images on the floor. A gilded crucifix hung on the wall. Angels on the painted ceiling watched as she dipped her trembling fingers into the basin of holy water. It felt cool on her sweaty hand. Making the sign of the cross, she mouthed the words: *In the name of the Father, and the Son, and the Holy Ghost. Amen*. She headed down the aisle, genuflected to the main altar, and slid into a pew.

She had attended this church every Sunday when her mother was alive. It was a special day for them all. Papa and Michal wore suits. Anna and her mother wore their best dresses. The church had always given her a sense of calm when she entered.

But not anymore. Now the church housed a concrete-lined tunnel underground used by the Home Army to test-fire guns and practice shooting at targets. She had talked Michal into taking her there for target practice. It had only been a few weeks and she could tell he was impressed, although he didn't want to admit it.

Today, she was here not for target practice or absolution, but to receive her first assignment for the Home Army. To give herself courage, she recited the Lord's Prayer. Then she recited it again. Then a third time for good measure.

Footsteps shuffled up the aisle. Had someone followed her? She'd made a mistake choosing a pew with her back to the entrance. The side altar at the back of the cathedral where a Baroque statue of the Blessed Virgin Mary beckoned, and votive candles burned, would have been better. Standing, she turned, ready to run, but it was just an old woman with missing teeth and ragged clothing, looking for a warm place to sleep.

Anna walked along the red carpet as nonchalantly as she could and entered the door to an empty confessional. Kneeling in the darkness, she held the rosary tight and scared herself when she accidentally knocked it against the wall. The partition covering the small window slid open. Behind the wooden screen, a priest in a white-collared cassock and a purple stole around his neck sat with his head bent in such a way that she couldn't see his face.

"Bless me, Father, for I have sinned," she said, in a soft voice. "It has been a month since my last confession. I didn't listen to my brother. I talked back to Papa twice." She paused. "The SS kidnapped a young girl I was supposed to look after. I ran away. I shouldn't have left her."

The priest raised his head.

"I am Hope," she blurted, remembering to use her codename.

The screen between them slid open a crack, and the priest slipped her an envelope. She knew it contained the birth and baptismal certificates of deceased child parishioners needed by the legalization cell to forge Christian identity documents for the Jewish children. She grabbed the envelope and shoved it inside her bag, then changed her mind, took the papers back out, hid them inside her blouse, and buttoned her coat.

"For your penance, say three Hail Marys and the Lord's Prayer two times." The priest raised his hand and blessed her in the form of a cross. "*In nomine Patris et Filii et Spiritus Sancti. Amen.*" In a low voice, he added, "Go in peace, my child. If you had stayed with your friend, the SS would have taken both of you. You are here today to help others. God is with you."

Anna moved to the side altar and knelt to say her penance, breathing so loudly that she feared someone might hear her. She held her hand against the envelope inside her blouse, an envelope that held the future of the children she planned to rescue. Each certificate a life.

A wave of self-doubt swept over her. The last time she was in charge of a child, she'd failed. Could she do this?

She studied the angels on the painted ceiling and told herself that her mother was safe in heaven. Stroking the beads, she asked her mother for guidance and strength. She stared at the statue of the Blessed Virgin Mary, Our Lady of the Home Army, and asked for protection.

Her first trip through the underground sewer system was scheduled for tomorrow. She needed all the help she could get.

CHAPTER TWELVE

Nowak paced back and forth in front of the camp commandant. Colonel Gustav Müller sat behind an oak desk with a bronze statue of the sovereign symbol of the Reich: an open-winged eagle holding a swastika framed by a wreath of oak leaves in its talons. An oil painting of Adolf Hitler and a swastika flag hung on the wall behind him.

The aroma of cooked bacon and fresh bread from a private kitchen lingered in the air, tormenting Nowak. Since he was one of the few officers in the RAF compound, he had volunteered to stand in for Snowshoe, who had his hands full dealing with an incoming shipment of airmen.

The well-groomed commandant had just delivered devastating news. Nowak slammed his fist on the desk. "I forbid you to shackle my men."

"There's nothing I can do. These are my official orders from Berlin." The commandant spoke as he smugly waved a document at him.

"Whose orders?" Nowak adjusted the borrowed RAF officer's cap.

"*Der Führer*. Our supreme commander. Adolf Hitler." The commandant laid the papers down. He shifted in his leather chair and placed his hand over the holstered P-38 pistol on his desk. "You don't have a choice. Your men are lucky to be alive."

Nowak wanted to grab the pistol and blow the bastard's head off. "I'll file an official complaint with the International Red Cross."

"It won't do you any good."

"We'll see about that."

The commandant waved his hand in dismissal. "That will be all."

Military protocol dictated that the two officers salute each other as a matter of respect but Nowak just glared at him, then spun around, and marched out of the room. He'd rather spend a week in the cooler than salute the arrogant son of a bitch.

Nowak wasn't running in the upcoming election for an official man of confidence. As a POW of officer rank, he considered it his duty to escape, and he had a plan. Step one: Make friends with Polish prisoners. Step two: Establish contact with their Underground. Step three: Head to Warsaw.

Today's development was a major setback. Wrist restraints would make escape virtually impossible. He strode back to his barracks. It was drizzling rain, which fitted his mood. Guards stationed at the perimeter of the camp stood with rifles cocked, ready to shoot. A machine gun in the sentry tower followed his movement.

He entered his compound where hundreds of airmen were anxiously waiting on Parade Square to hear his report. Ray stood near the front with his arms crossed. Freddie paced off to the side.

Nowak hated having to break the terrible news, but there was no way around it. He cleared his throat and announced, "Hitler has issued an order. Starting today, the RAF compound will be in lockdown. Our wrists will be bound for twelve hours a day. From zero eight hundred until twenty hundred hours."

"What do you mean, *bound*? With what?" Ray demanded, breaking the quiet.

"Binder twine from the Red Cross parcels."

"Well, I'll be damned," Ray mumbled.

Someone in the crowd let out a shout. "No way."

"For how long?" Freddie asked as he paced.

"Until further notice," Nowak was forced to tell them.

"Why?" yelled a voice.

"In retaliation for Dieppe," Nowak said, referring to the August '42 raid by more than five thousand Canadian and British troops under the protection of RAF fighters on the German-occupied French port. "Hitler claims German soldiers were found after the raid with their hands bound behind their backs."

Words of protest flew through the air, and he didn't disagree with any of them. "Bullshit," "Liars," "Bastards."

"We're under orders to return to our huts. Immediately," Nowak told the airmen. "Look, I don't like this anymore than you do, but there's not much we can do about it."

Nowak stormed back to his hut as the grumbling crowd dispersed. Snowshoe caught up to him inside. "What the hell is going on? What's all the yelling about?"

Nowak brought him up to speed on the news.

"I'll talk to the commandant. See if there's a way around this. But we've got to settle our men down," Snowshoe said, clearly stunned by the news.

Ray joined them. "They can't get away with this."

"They're doing it," Nowak said, grim-faced.

Within minutes, the door burst open and Ukraine Joe stomped in, blowing his whistle and shouting. Two guards marched in behind him with reams of binder twine strung over the leather ammunition pouches on their belts. Their silver buckles were inscribed with the imperial eagle and the words *Gott mit uns*, God with us.

"Form two lines," Joe shouted, but not one airman moved off his bunk.

"Go to hell!"

"Shove it up your arse."

"Fuck off."

Someone chucked a wooden clog at Joe. He ducked. Cherished cans of food from Red Cross parcels were flung. Powdered eggs. Spam. Minced collops.

"Silence!" Joe drew his Luger and shot at the ceiling, while the guards behind him raised and cocked their rifles.

"Bloody hell. As if the roof didn't leak enough already," Freddie muttered.

It was a no-win situation. A full-blown riot was about to erupt. Nowak glanced over at Snowshoe, afraid that someone might get killed in the chaos. Snowshoe gave him a nod of resignation. They both walked to the front, stretched out their arms and crossed their wrists. If they didn't do it, they couldn't expect anyone else to. A guard slipped a piece of twine from his pouch, wrapped it around Nowak's wrists, and tied a secure knot. The men, all of them complaining, shuffled off their beds, collected the cans of food they'd thrown, and formed two ragged lines.

As the day wore on, Nowak's arms began to ache from being in the same position and, with the circulation reduced, his hands and wrists swelled and itched. He was bone cold and damp, but with his hands bound he couldn't put on the great-coat issued to him by the Red Cross.

It was that damn Kammhuber Line that got him here. The coastal chain of stations he had to cross to get out of enemy territory. RAF Bomber Command had incurred heavy losses by sending night bombers through that danger zone on solo flights. Over the summer, they had come up with a new strategy, sending thousands of planes across in successive waves to overwhelm the enemy below.

It worked. Losses were way down. Nowak and his crew had flown in all three of the thousand-bomber raids targeting Cologne, Essen, and Bremen. But that night they'd been sent out on orders from the Special Operations Executive, which meant they were flying solo and were vulnerable to concentrated flak.

Images of his plane being hit haunted him. The voice inside his head questioned every move, every dive, every decision he'd made. If only he had climbed higher, dove lower. He'd let down his crew and ended up in this hole.

He could very well die here. There was a rumor circulating that the Germans planned to shoot every fifth POW. He didn't know whether it was true or if they were trying to wear the prisoners down with psychological torture.

With muscles tense and palms sweaty, he tried to use his teeth to loosen the twine around his wrists, to no avail, and slammed his fists onto the table.

"*Nil Bastardo Carborundum*, Skipper," Freddie shouted from his bunk. Don't let the bastards grind you down. Freddie's favorite mock Latin expression.

Nowak thought about the day Freddie wrote those words over the door of their Wellington and, underneath, his next favorite line in the made-up language, *Nil Bano Panico*. Above All Don't Panic. He repeated the words to himself a few times and felt better.

"Did you hear about Radaski from the Army compound?" Freddie asked.

"No. What about him?"

"He escaped from a work party. He's on the run."

Nowak felt a ray of hope. Hundreds of Army personnel marched out of camp every day under armed guard for forced labor on farms, at factories, or in mines for work that didn't directly further the German war effort. The problem was that members of the Air Force, with a rank of sergeant or higher, weren't allowed to work. And that included him.

Goddamnit, he needed to find a way into one of those work parties. But how?

CHAPTER THIRTEEN

Twelve Meters Underground
Warsaw, Poland

Anna stood under the linden trees and stared down at the manhole cover. Even though it was early morning on the quiet backstreet, she felt exposed. The trees would have offered some protection, if only she'd been here a week earlier, but now the branches were bare and golden colored leaves littered the cracked sidewalk.

Edging closer, she pulled out the miniature crowbar she had hidden in her sleeve. She scanned the street to make sure no one was watching, then bent to pry open the metal manhole cover, and scrape it across the cobblestones. The smell from the sewers hit her like a wall.

Legs shaking, she climbed into the entrance shaft, taking a few steps down the iron rungs embedded in the bricks, before stopping to drag the heavy cover back into place, sealing the manhole with a clank and plunging her into darkness. She tightened her grip on the iron rungs and began her twelve-meter descent, fighting waves of nausea from the suffocating odor. So much of her wanted to turn back and climb the ladder up to the sunlight, away from the stench and the danger. But she knew that her contact was waiting for her in the ghetto with children who counted on her for escape, and she couldn't let them down. Steeling herself, she carried on, counting the rungs and feeling for the bottom with her feet.

Stepping off the last rung, she flicked on her flashlight. The beam shone on a large pair of black rubber boots, perched on a small platform just where Baranek had said they would be. She slid them over her shoes and set the crowbar down on the ledge to pick up on her return, buttoned up her jacket and took a step into the ankle-deep sewage.

She sloshed forward, trying to reassure herself. Then she slipped. The flashlight jiggled in her hand, casting a beam of light against the ceiling. She reached out, her fingers desperately scrabbling for something to hang on to and saved herself from a fall by clinging to the brick wall.

At last, she came to the first junction where she had been told to expect a hanging rope to orient herself. She shone her flashlight to the left side, but its beam revealed nothing but darkness. She swiveled her flashlight to the right, and there it was, hanging against the wall. To preserve her battery, she switched off her light and reached up to catch the end of the rope, inching her fingers upward until she touched a knot. Standing on her tiptoes, she reached further and felt a second. Two knots. A clear sign to turn right.

She continued, running her hand along the wall, turning right, or left according to the hanging ropes. Raw sewage poured out of pipes. The tunnels narrowed and the ceilings lowered.

Struggling over to a faint light filtering down through a grate high above, she heard the distinctive sound of hobnails on cobblestones. Terrified, she froze as jackboots stomped onto the grate and stopped.

A stream of urine sprayed past her. She stumbled back into the darkness, collapsing against the wall. To stop herself from gagging, she pressed her hand against her mouth and waited for his footsteps to retreat. Then she threw up.

It took a few minutes to convince herself to continue, leaning against the wall, desperate to take deep breaths, and unable to do so with the overwhelming smell. She'd come this far. The meeting place had to be close by.

As she waved her flashlight up and down the sewer canal, the beam shone on an unexpected, raised passageway. Two suspended ropes dangled at the entrance, marking the meeting point with her contact, codenamed Józef.

She climbed up into the passage and crawled on her hands and knees through dusty cobwebs to an underground bunker. In candlelight, a silhouette of a man flickered.

"Hope?" he said as he rose from a chair and moved toward her.

"Samuel, is that you?" Anna brushed the sticky webs from her face, hardly believing who stood before her. He had grown a beard and wore a white armband with a blue Star of David on his left arm.

"What are *you* doing here?" he whispered, hugging her.

"Hope is my codename," Anna whispered back. "I've been so worried. You just disappeared." As she looked around the bunker, all she saw was a candle, a chair, and a blanket. "What do you need? I can bring it on my next trip."

"We need weapons. Father is mobilizing the Jewish fighters. We plan to fight back."

"I'll speak to Papa," she said. "How many children are you sending out with me?"

"One."

"Just one? I can take more."

"Many families oppose our plan. They're suspicious. They think converting to Christianity is spiritual destruction."

"It's the only way to protect the children once we get them out."

"I know. But to the very religious, it violates one of our commandments."

"And you, my friend, what do you believe?"

"I'm not that religious. We don't have a lot of time. I'll get the boy."

Anna sat on the chair as Samuel retreated into the darkness. It felt good to rest, until a rat scurried across the room in front of her. She wanted to bang on the wall to scare it away, but she knew that any sound would echo through the tunnels, so she lifted her legs and lowered them, one after the other, as fast as she could. That didn't seem to do much. Another rat ran out.

She reached into her pocket to stroke the rosary and silently counted the beads. *One, two, three, four, five, six.* Footsteps drew near. Samuel entered the bunker, dragging a frightened little boy.

"Let go of me," the boy pleaded, trying to break free of Samuel's grip.

"Shhh," Samuel whispered. "You have to go with this girl."

"No."

"Your parents talked to you about this."

Anna knelt beside the boy and spoke softly, "My name is Hope. I'll lead you out of here."

The boy crossed his arms and refused to budge.

"What's your name?" she asked.

"Aaron," he whispered.

"How old are you?"

"Six."

"I know you're scared. I'm scared too."

He wiped his nose with his little hand. "Where are you taking me?"

"Somewhere safe."

His shoulders slumped and he looked at the ground. "Why are my mama and papa sending me away? Don't they love me anymore?"

Anna rested one hand on each of his shoulders. "Aaron. Your parents love you very much. You'll see them when the war is over."

"Promise?"

"I promise," she said. The words felt heavy in her throat.

How could she explain the insanity of war to this six-year-old child? That the world stood so divided by race, religion, and nationality—that Polish Jewish children were sent to the Aryan side of the city to pretend they were Christian, and Polish Christian children were kidnapped and taken to Germany to pretend they were German. She couldn't understand it herself.

The boy shivered. She took off her jacket to wrap around him. "We have to leave now. You must be very quiet."

Aaron nodded.

Samuel handed Anna a cigarette paper listing the child's name and family members, which she hid under the face of her watch in case she was caught and searched.

"You shouldn't come here again," he said. "This is no place for you."

"I'll be back." She kissed him goodbye on the cheek with a pang of regret for leaving him behind.

Anna and Aaron crawled through the narrow passageway out of the underground bunker into the sewers. Soon, they reached an area where the sewage was too deep for the small child to wade through. "Climb onto my back and hold on tight," she said, bending down. She labored forward, carrying him piggyback the rest of the way.

They arrived at the designated manhole on the Aryan side of the city. Aaron was sobbing. She held her hand over his mouth, fearful a German above would hear him.

The cover lifted, and a man dressed like a sewer worker stood looking at them. Sunlight glared down, masking his features.

"You're late. Hurry," he whispered.

Aaron scrambled up the ladder while Anna kicked off the rubber boots and grabbed her crowbar. Once they were both on the street, the man lugged the cover back into place.

"This nice man will take you to the orphanage," Anna said, indicating a horse-drawn lorry parked under the linden trees.

"I'm not an orphan. I have parents," Aaron said, tears streaming down his flushed face.

Anna leaned forward. "Aaron, please."

He threw his little arms around her neck. "Don't leave me," he pleaded.

"There's no time for this." The man lifted Aaron off the ground, tearing his grip away from her. He carried the child over to the wagon, hiding him in one of the wooden barrels stacked in the back and latching it shut, then jumped into the lorry and gripped the reins.

Anna bit away her own tears as the wheels spun and the horse's hooves clopped down the cobblestones, disappearing around the corner.

Thirty minutes later, she burst through the front door to find Michal sitting at the kitchen table, forging signatures on identity documents. Without saying a word, she hurried past him and fled upstairs to her bedroom. Inside her small room, she slid the cigarette paper out from under the face of her watch and set it on top of her dresser. Her instructions were to write Aaron's assigned Polish name on the paper, then insert it into a glass jar buried under the massive linden tree in the churchyard. After the war, the jar could be dug up so the child could be reunited with any surviving family members. According to Polish folklore, linden trees were a symbol of love and family and believed to have protective powers. She hoped they would protect Aaron now.

She stripped off her clothes. Dipping a washcloth into a basin of water on top of her dresser, she lathered it with soap and rubbed the cloth all over her body. After putting on a nightgown, she clenched her rosary and crawled into bed to warm up.

She couldn't get the sweet, innocent face of Aaron and the way he pleaded with her to stay with him out of her head. Despite her assurance, the chances of him seeing his parents after the war grew fainter by the day. She had lied to the child and it haunted her. The Home Army had sent their intelligence information regarding the extermination of the Jews to the Allies by radio transmissions and couriered microfilm. The world was as aware as she was of what was happening. Britain had suspended all supply drops to Poland. Why had they abandoned her country?

She found solace in the pages of her dog-eared *Airplane Recognition Handbook*. Ever since that night in the forest, flying had fascinated her. Flipping through the pages, she looked at photographs, imagining what it was like inside an airplane and longing to escape her life through the freedom of flight.

Her thoughts were interrupted by two loud knocks on her door, followed by two soft. Michal's secret knock.

"Don't come in," she said.

"Why not?"

"I stink. That's why." Anna hastily splashed herself with rose-water she'd made from wild rose petals, as Michal opened the door.

"I can tell you've been crying," he said. "Was it that bad?"

She nodded.

"Then don't do it again."

"Someone has to," she said. "I saw Samuel. He's in the ghetto. His family's there too."

"Thank God they're alive."

"Things just keep getting worse," she sighed. "I want our lives back. The way it used to be."

"Those days are over. Things will never be the same." Michal hesitated. "You need to make friends with members of the Home Army. We're planning to get together for a poetry reading. Do you think Zophia would come with me if I asked her?"

"That's a really good idea," Anna said with a smile, remembering a conversation she had with Ewa on the way to school earlier in the day she was kidnapped.

"Do you want to know a secret," Ewa had said. "You have to promise not to tell."

"I promise."

"My sister Zophia has a crush on your brother. She talks about him all the time."

"Michal likes her too. I can tell."

"If they get married, we'll be sisters," Ewa said beaming.

Michal interrupted Anna's thoughts. "You should come with us to the reading."

"I'd like that," she said, happy for the opportunity to get her mind off everything that had happened, if only for a few hours.

"Zophia's preparing for her first trip through the sewers. I'll send something for Samuel with her." He pulled what looked like a small deck of playing cards out of his pocket. "I have something for you. A miniature edition of the book *Squadron 303*," he said, handing it to her.

"Thank you," she said, opening the book. She knew all about the Polish fighter squadron that flew with the RAF and shot down the highest number of enemy aircraft in the Battle of Britain.

"It was copied onto microfilm and included in an early supply drop. We made copies, the small size makes it easier to distribute." Michal had been working nights at the *Biuletyn Informacyjny*, the Underground newspaper. "I know how much you like airplanes."

"Someday I'll fly in an airplane," she said.

"Yes, you will," he reassured her. "If you smile for me, I have another surprise for you."

She offered a weak smile. "Are you teasing me?"

"I'll be right back," he said, before leaving the room.

A few minutes later, he returned wheeling his big black bicycle with fat tires.

"It's your bike," she said.

"I want you to have it."

CHAPTER FOURTEEN

RAF Compound
Stalag IVB, Germany

The dreary days of confinement with hands bound wore on for weeks. Ulcerated sores formed on Nowak's wrists. Since the Krauts never entered the *shizen haus*, Snowshoe set up a system. There was always one man with untied hands stationed just inside the door to untie the twine on the way in and retie it on the way out, giving at least a few minutes of relief.

This morning, while Nowak waited in line to get his hands bound, word spread that Radaski, the prisoner who had escaped, had been captured and dragged back into camp. Right about now, he ought to be locked in the cooler for a few weeks in solitary. But the cooler was full. That meant he'd be standing nose to the wall.

Nowak needed to take advantage of the opportunity. He crossed his wrists and this time stretched his thumbs upwards. The guard didn't seem to notice and wrapped the rope as he always did and tied the knot.

Relaxing his thumbs gave Nowak more slack than usual within the twine. He lit a cigarette and lay his book open on the table. A new shipment was expected from the YMCA, but for now, he only had access to an algebra text. He never thought reading algebra would be entertaining, but the equations helped to occupy his mind and fend off the endless hours of boredom. He dreaded having to give up the book and pass it on to the next man on the waiting list.

Joe stomped into the hut and noticed Nowak smoking and reading a book. He narrowed his deep-set eyes and poked Nowak in the ribs with his rifle. "Ropes too loose. Wall. *Raus*."

Joe forced Nowak outside, unlocked the gate and dragged him through the Army camp to the red brick wall where a blond-haired prisoner in shabby civilian clothes stood, nose to the wall, under the watchful eyes of a guard on duty.

"Stand with toes and nose against wall," Joe ordered Nowak. Nowak moved up to the wall.

"Closer." Joe rammed the butt of his rifle into the back of his head, smashing his face against the bricks.

"Bastard," Nowak hissed, blood running down his face. He waited until Joe left and the guard on duty wasn't paying attention, before looking over at the man beside him.

"Radaski, right?" Nowak whispered, noticing Radaski's black eye.

"Who wants to know?"

"Nowak. RCAF. Where were you headed?"

"Warsaw."

"Been planning to head east myself," Nowak said.

Radaski didn't answer.

"You got contacts?"

Radaski still didn't answer. Maybe he thought Nowak was a plant. The Germans often placed their own men inside camp to pose as prisoners to get information. He waited until the guard entered the outhouse with a sign, *For Guards Only*, and tried again, saying the words symbolizing the Polish resistance movement. "*Polska walczy*. Poland fights."

Radaski glanced at him through narrowed eyes. "What do *you* know about the *Armia Krajowa*?"

"Born in Poland."

Radaski shrugged.

"Listen to me. I got shot down delivering weapons to the Polish Underground," Nowak said, anger growing inside of him. His muscles had started to cramp and his legs ached.

Radaski didn't move.

"That's the reason me and my men are locked up in this stinking camp." Nowak kicked the wall.

"Okay," Radaski said at last, without looking at him. "What do you want?"

"A way into the Army camp."

"What for?"

"To join a work party."

"Find a swap. A prisoner who wants to stay in camp. The work parties are so large, guards only take a head count on the way out."

Five hours later, Nowak heard footsteps behind him. "Thanks," he whispered just as Ukraine Joe arrived.

With a smug look, Joe led Nowak back to his compound. Little did the fucker know he'd done Nowak a favor. It was the introduction he'd been waiting for. Step one of his escape plan was in action.

On the way back to his hut, he ran smack dab into Freddie balancing a pile of *Völkischer Beobachter* newsletters on his bound wrists. According to the propaganda newsletters fed to the prisoners, Germany was winning the war and he sure as hell hoped that wasn't true. Newly captured Allied airmen provided the only reliable news on the status of the war.

Nowak followed Freddie into the *shizen haus* where he set the newsletters down for the airmen to use as toilet paper. Wind howled through the open windows.

"What happened to you?" Freddie asked. His reddish-blond hair was growing back in uneven patches. He held out his hands for the airman stationed inside to untie.

"Walked into a wall." Nowak tried to use his wrists to wipe the caked blood from his swollen nose.

"I got a letter from Izzie. The baby's due next month," Freddie said, beaming. "Have you figured a way outta here yet?"

"I'm working on it." Nowak held out his hands still bound with twine. Once they were freed, he shook his arms at his side until the feeling came back. "We're heading to Warsaw."

CHAPTER FIFTEEN

It took until early December for a shipment of metal handcuffs to arrive at camp. Medical officers had convinced the German authorities to replace the binder twine. Too many men had serious infections from open sores caused by rope burns. With the onset of winter weather, chilblains set in from exposure to the cold metal cuffs and the lack of circulation.

At least the eighteen-inch chain on the handcuffs allowed for more movement. Snowshoe set up a signal system to warn of a guard approaching, assigning two airmen as duty officers for each shift. One stood outside with a book. The other was positioned by the inside window to receive his signals. When the man outside closed his book, the lookout inside shouted out a warning. "Goon up."

Freddie had hacked off the top of the lone fir tree and set it up beside their wooden table. Nowak busied himself making Christmas decorations out of food can labels and tinsel by cutting the silver paper inside cigarette packages into strips. He thought about his family as he hung tinsel on the branches. It had been a tradition to travel out to the Rocky Mountains with his sister to search the woods for the perfect evergreen, chop it down, and bring it back to their home to decorate. The aroma of turkey in the oven would greet him when he opened the door.

The only thing he had to send home this year was a Christmas card designed by an airman in his hut. Fritz, the old guard with a belly and yellow teeth, had turned out to be friendly. He'd talked the authorities into printing copies of the card in their administration office for the airmen to send home.

A newly formed band practiced with instruments delivered by the Red Cross. The noise grated on Nowak's nerves. He checked the time on the wall clock that Freddie had made from tin cans. Lids with teeth cut into them served as gears, cans filled with sand were weights, and a can hung from the pendulum by a piece of barbed wire.

It was noon. The time of day with the fewest guards and vicious German shepherds on patrol, and the best time to walk the circuit of the RAF compound, along the inside of the locked barbed wire fence. He walked it every day at exactly 1200 hours to get himself back in shape and to wear off the angst that bubbled up inside him. Twenty circuits around the wire added up to about a mile.

He donned his greatcoat and hustled outside to start his walk. Peering through the fence, he had a clear view of the road they called International Avenue, running east and west through the center of camp, with row after row of huts full of different nationalities lining each side, all the way to the main gate. Even numbered to the north, odd to the south.

Closest to him, the French compound was filled with soldiers captured during the Battle of France back in 1940 and had little gardens beside their barracks. Australians occupied the compound next to them, South Africans on the other side.

Russians waited by the cookhouse with spoons, hoping soup would splash on the ground from cauldrons on their way out to the barracks. Next, the exercise compound and after that, a transit compound that housed transports of prisoners on a temporary basis, usually forced labor en route to other camps.

And back again.

He slowed down as he approached an area with a blind spot for the guards looking down from the towers above. Right on time, Radaski came into sight, out for his daily walk on the other side of the fence. Nowak scanned the grounds for guards nearby before he gave his friend a smile and a nod.

Radaski tossed a rock over the fence. Without missing a beat, Nowak picked up the rock and kept on walking. As he turned the corner, he unwrapped the piece of paper scrunched around it and shoved the note in his pocket.

After twenty circuits, he headed back to his hut. Freddie and Ray were inside setting up a game of Monopoly they'd rented from a British navigator by the name of Sydney Liberman for ten cigarettes. Not a bad price when they spread the cost around the three of them.

Nowak was sure Syd would've looked for a red dot on the *Free Parking* square, but he checked anyway. He'd been briefed before his first mission that a red dot meant the game had been rigged. The manufacturers of Monopoly collaborated with MI9 to make special editions of the game by hiding silk maps, German *Reichsmarks*, miniature compasses, and files inside to aid escape plans.

"Damn," Nowak said. "No red dot."

"It was worth a try." Freddie grabbed the play money and handed it out. "We might as well have a game while we have it here."

"Have you heard more about the baby?" Nowak asked.

"No. And it's got me worried."

"It's damn hard having kids at home when you're stuck in here. The little woman is madder than hell at me for signin' up," Ray said.

Nowak leaned in close and spoke quietly so the airmen playing poker at the other end of their table wouldn't hear. "I got a message from Radaski today. He's found me a swap."

"What does that do ya? We're still under lockdown." Ray spun the red-and-white spinner.

"Snowshoe thinks the lockdown will be lifted soon," Nowak said. "We gotta get our ducks in a row. Be prepared."

"Who's your swap?" Freddie asked.

"The guy that unloads the Red Cross parcels. He's gonna give me his boots."

"Bloody hell, you don't look Danish." Freddie raised his brows. "The guy's six-foot-two with blond hair and blue eyes. What if they check?"

"I've got blue eyes." Nowak sat up straight to make his five-foot-eleven frame look as tall as possible. "Besides, those guards are too stupid to know a Dane from a Pole."

"You better hope so," Freddie said. "What about me?"

"He's looking for two more swaps. For you and Ray."

"I'm stayin' put." Ray moved his wooden battleship token eight spaces. The blisters on the backs of his hands from the burns had healed, but scars remained. Even though his gold wedding ring had been cut off in the hospital, he still had a habit of touching his ring finger and twirling the imaginary band.

"What for?" Nowak spun double threes and moved his cannon token.

"If I stay, I can get an external degree from the University of London. I'm goin' study the law. Books should arrive in the

Red Cross truck any day now," Ray said. "They're setting up a camp university in Hut 108. There's a New Zealander over there by the name of Frank that's gonna give lectures on law and philosophy. My first class is on Torts."

"Tortes?" Freddie asked. "Isn't that a cake?"

Ray laughed. "It's a legal term."

"Are you sure?"

"Yeah. My ole man was a lawyer. He always wanted me to follow in his footsteps. I never liked him much, so instead of gettin' an education, I took a job on the oil rigs and married young," Ray said. "Then the kids came."

"As soon as it's warm enough to survive on the run, we're outta here." Freddie sorted his play money into stacks. "I'm gonna make an honest woman out of Izzie first chance I get. You should think about settling down one of these days too, Skipper. What do you think?"

"I'm damn hungry," Nowak said, changing the topic and grabbing the can of sardines off his shelf to share with Freddie and Ray.

A rumor circulated that each prisoner would receive a British food parcel by Christmas—the first Red Cross delivery of food since October—and even then, Nowak would have to *muck in* with Freddie and Ray, pooling and sharing one parcel equally. If a parcel was coming, they didn't have to save their last can of food any longer. Nowak snapped the key off the sardines, looked at the key, then at his cuffs. It was worth a try. He inserted the key behind the spring lock on his handcuffs and pushed down. Nothing happened. He tried again, wiggling the key back and forth inside the lock. It clicked open. He couldn't believe it.

"Bloody hell? How'd you do that?" Freddie asked.

"Well, I'll be damned," Ray said.

No sooner had Nowak removed both cuffs and rubbed his wrists, than the lookout shouted, "Goon up."

"It's Fritz," Freddie whispered.

Nowak stood up, cuffs in hand, and turned his back to the door as Fritz walked in. Sliding both his hands and the cuffs into his trouser pockets, so only the eighteen-inch heavy chain dangled in front, he turned around to face Fritz.

Fritz smiled and didn't seem to notice.

"Hey Fritz, I need to sew a button on my shirt," Nowak said. "You think you could find me a needle and some thread?"

Fritz shook his head and nervously adjusted the rifle slung over his shoulder.

"Oh, come on Fritz. I can make you a trade. I've got cigarettes. Canadian cigarettes."

Fritz shrugged and wandered off without answering.

"What was that all about?" Freddie asked.

"I'm taming him. A little at a time. You'll see soon enough," Nowak said. "We're going to need civvies on our way out of here. We'll stick out like a sore thumb crossing enemy territory in our uniforms."

As soon as Fritz left, Nowak quickly unlocked Freddie's cuffs and Ray would be next.

Nowak relished the next few hours free from the bondage of the metal cuffs. The next time the lookout shouted, "Goon up," he knew it was time for nightly inspection so he slipped his handcuffs around his wrists and snapped them shut.

Ukraine Joe and another guard stomped into the hut carrying wooden crates to collect the handcuffs for the night. Nowak sat on his bunk and waited as they made their way around. When it was his turn, he hopped off his bunk and held out his hands. Joe unlocked his cuffs and threw them onto the pile in the crate, but as soon as Joe turned his back to unlock Freddie's, Nowak reached in and snatched them back out. Freddie noticed Nowak's move and held Joe's attention while Nowak slipped his pair under his blanket. Joe didn't notice. He left, lugging the boxes of metal cuffs out of the hut until morning.

That night, Nowak drifted off to sleep thinking of the handcuffs he'd hidden behind a loose ceiling board. Right about now, the cuff count would be coming in one pair short and Ukraine Joe would face a reprimand in Commandant Müller's office.

He had outsmarted the commandant and the bastard Ukraine Joe. A small victory, but a victory, nonetheless. And very satisfying. A couple more screw-ups on Joe's part and he'd be back in the penal block where he belonged.

1943

CHAPTER SIXTEEN

On every rescue mission through the underground sewers, Samuel had been waiting inside the bunker for Anna. Until today. Not even a candle flickered in the darkness. Gun fire raged and the sound of tanks stormed down the street in the ghetto above. To settle her nerves, she paced back and forth, her fingers resting on the Vis pistol stuffed in her pocket, only daring to switch her flashlight on for brief moments at a time.

She sat in Samuel's chair for a while, then paced some more. Minutes turned to hours and now it was time to leave to get back to the Aryan side of the city before curfew. Just as she was about to go, footsteps approached the dark bunker. She pressed herself against the wall and slid the pistol out of her pocket.

Hearing what sounded like a child's cry, she switched on her flashlight. The beam fell on Samuel. He cradled a baby wrapped in a towel.

"What's going on?" she asked, relieved to see him unharmed.

"The Germans started the roundups again." He sounded out of breath.

"Oh, no!"

"People are hiding in buildings and underground bunkers. They're refusing to assemble in the holding area by the train station." He leaned forward to give the baby to her. "It's chaos up there."

She unbuttoned her coat and held out her arms.

"I don't know her name. She's an orphan," he said.

"I brought you a pistol and a couple of potatoes." She fumbled in her pocket with her free hand and offered them. He was so skinny, she always brought him something to eat: an extra turnip, a slice of bread. It wasn't much, but it was all she could spare.

He stuffed a potato in his mouth and shoved the pistol between his belt and the small of his back.

"You need to leave. It's too dangerous for you here," he said, then he took off.

She soothed the baby, then made her way through the tunnels and deep sludge, with the child tucked inside her coat. When she surfaced through the manhole, a sewer worker placed the infant in a box with air holes, covering it with a blanket for the lorry ride to the orphanage.

Her hands were still shaking when she turned the key and opened the front door of her house. The scent of pipe tobacco and two bowls of half-eaten potato soup on the table told her that Papa and Michal had rushed out.

Every time they left, she feared they wouldn't return. Just walking on the street was dangerous these days. The Nazis terrorized the citizens with mass executions and the kidnapping of children. The Underground judiciary retaliated by assassinating Nazi officials. And now the Germans had started the roundups for deportations in the ghetto again.

Feeling uneasy, she grabbed her submachine gun and curled up on the sofa with a blanket to wait for them.

*

It had been four days and Papa and Michal were still not back. Fearing they were fighting with the Jewish Underground in the ghetto, she spent her nights tossing and turning on the sofa, her gun tucked under the blanket beside her, waking with a start every few minutes, straining her ears for the sound of their return.

This time, when she started awake, she heard truck doors slam and a rustling at the front door. Running to the window, she peered outside, careful not to disturb the curtains as she looked out at a handful of men standing on her doorstep in field gray uniforms. Nazi uniforms.

The doorknob rattled.

She gripped her submachine gun. Resting the aluminum butt-plate on her shoulder, she aimed it at the dead center of the door and released the safety catch on the trigger. She wasn't sure she could take the shot. Target practice with Michal in a concrete-lined tunnel underground was one thing. Shooting a human being was another.

The door flew open.

"Put the gun down, Anna." Papa stormed into the house, dragging a man bleeding from the stomach. Michal and two others in Nazi uniforms followed.

She was relieved to see her father and Michal, but she didn't move. Her gun stayed fixed on the uniformed men.

"Don't be afraid. They're fighters from the Jewish Underground," Papa explained. "The uniforms are stolen."

She dropped the gun.

"Papa, I was so worried. Are you wounded?"

"Just tired." Her father helped the wounded man to the sofa. "We've been fighting alongside the Jewish forces in the ghetto."

"We've halted the deportations. For now," Michal said. "But they'll be back. We need military supplies to continue."

"Did you see Samuel? Did he make it out with you?" Anna asked.

"He wanted to stay," Michal replied.

"Why?"

"There's no time to talk," Papa interrupted them. "These men need medical attention. Go find Dr. Jeska."

She grabbed her coat, scarf, and hat, slipped on her winter boots, and ran out of the house. Struggling against the blowing snow, she made her way along the cobbled street to Market Square. There she entered the doorway of the burnished-yellow burgher house. Despite the unlit stairwell, she climbed the creaking stairs two at a time keeping her hand over the banister to guide her. Breathless, she opened the door to the medical office, a place she'd visited so many times before. Zophia sat behind the wooden reception desk in her nurse's uniform. The same desk where Ewa used to sit, wearing her father's stethoscope around her neck and writing prescriptions for sugar lumps and chocolate.

Zophia looked up.

"I must see your father at once," Anna said.

"He's not here," Zophia replied. "He's at the field hospital. Many wounded men were brought in this morning."

"Papa needs help."

Zophia grabbed her black medical bag. "I'll do what I can until father gets there. Where are they?"

"My house."

"Is Michal hurt?"

Anna could read the fear in Zophia's eyes. "Don't worry. He's fine," she said, giving her a quick hug before barreling back down the stairs.

The field hospital was a fair distance away, hidden in the basement of a cathedral. She rushed out of Old Town and caught a tram. Stepping inside, her eyes searched for an empty seat. There was only one. Right beside an SS officer. Not wanting to sit beside him, she reached up and gripped the grab bar.

"Why don't you take a seat, my dear?" he said.

She'd heard that voice before. Pulling her knitted hat down over her ears, she glanced at him. He smiled and flashed a gold tooth. Fear surged through her. He was the same officer that had kidnapped Ewa. She would never forget his face. His hazel eyes. Or that gold tooth.

It was too late to jump off the tram without drawing attention. She offered a smile and sat down, trying to quell the panic building inside her.

He took a candy out of his pocket and offered it to her. "*Schokolade?*"

Anna looked at his MP-40 submachine gun and accepted his candy. She held the sweet in her hand with no intention of eating it.

"*Danke*," she said.

"You're German?" he asked.

Anna nodded and smiled. She had questions of her own. Where is Ewa? What did you do to her?

The tram rumbled under the wooden footbridge that connected both sides of the ghetto at 22 Chlodna Street. Flames raged behind the brick walls topped with barbed wire that lined each side of the tracks. Thick black smoke seeped through the windows, burning the back of her throat. Her eyes watered.

"Will you go to the fair?" he asked.

"What fair?"

"We're building an amusement park."

Anna glanced out the window at Krasinski Square, opposite the ghetto wall, which was crammed with workmen and machinery alongside tanks and helmeted soldiers.

"It should be ready in time to celebrate the Easter holiday. The children will have so much fun. There will be carousels with music and swinging gondolas."

At that moment, she wanted to gouge his hazel eyes out. This man was talking about fun and holidays and amusement parks while all she could think about were the children sealed inside buildings set ablaze in the ghetto. And Samuel fighting for his life.

The tram bell rang.

"The next stop is mine," she said as she jumped out of her seat.

"Quick trip." He narrowed his eyes and looked at her suspiciously.

"I'm late."

She hustled off the tram the second it stopped. Looking up at the window, she saw him watching her. Fighting to stay calm, she put the candy in her mouth and forced a smile.

He kept staring. She waited until the tram was at a safe distance away before she spat the candy into the gutter. Then she ran to the cathedral and bolted down the stairs to the field hospital, where she found Dr. Jeska draping a sheet over a body.

"Papa needs you," she said, panting.

"Is he wounded?"

"No. We have guests."

"I'll be there as soon as I can."

This was the first time she'd seen Ewa's father since the kidnapping, and she wondered if he could see the shame she carried for not helping his daughter. She was sure it was plastered all over her like a stain. Once set, impossible to remove.

CHAPTER SEVENTEEN

Nowak held a razor blade in his hand. His uniform and unlocked cuffs were laid out on his bunk before him. He examined the rusty, dull blade. It needed sharpening to make a clean cut.

He brushed the blade back and forth against a rough piece of rock. Once sharp, he sliced the magnetized compass button off his trousers and removed the large pocket on the lower leg, designed to hold an escape kit. To ensure its safekeeping, he climbed onto the top bunk and raised the ceiling board just enough to slide the piece of material and the compass inside. After that, he sheared the raised nap off the woolen fabric of his trousers, little by little, leaving a shiny, flat material. A slow and tedious job.

If he ever made it out of this damn camp, he needed civvies. Civilian clothes to blend in with the German population.

Nowak ran his escape plan over and over in his mind. Now that the lockdown had been lifted, he could join an outgoing work party by swapping identities with the Dane in the Army compound, who wanted to stay put.

Once he and Freddie reached a work camp, they could escape when the time was right. The long winter nights without heat and with insufficient food were over. Spring had arrived, and they could survive the outdoor elements. He had walked the perimeter of the Air Force compound daily to get himself back in shape. If they made it to Warsaw, a good 600 kilometers through German occupied territory, members of the Polish Underground would provide assistance. Radaski had given him all the information he needed to make contact.

Nowak held his trousers up to show Freddie. "What do you think? Do they look like work pants?"

Freddie looked up from the book of poetry by Robert Burns that Nowak had bought for him on the black market with a tin of bully beef from a Red Cross parcel. He hated to give the food up, but Freddie hadn't been his jokester self lately and he loved poetry, and since his mother had Scottish roots, anything with a Scottish connection seemed to ease his loneliness and isolation.

"Not bad," Freddie said. "But the Air Force blue is a dead giveaway. Let's use my socks. They color my feet so they should dye your trousers darker blue."

Freddie boiled up some water in the old copper cauldron they used for just about everything: heating soup, making coffee, and washing clothes. Balancing on one foot, then the other, he took off the hand-knitted navy socks sent by his mother in a parcel from home and threw them into the water.

Nowak eyed Freddie's blue-streaked feet. "Now that's attractive. Too bad Izzie can't see those toes."

"You can talk. You're the one standing around in your boxers," Freddie said. The water turned blue after a few moments.

"Throw your trousers in. If it works, I'll do the same thing with mine."

Nowak tossed his trousers into the cauldron. Freddie plunged them up and down, and swirled them around, with the dhobi stick they used to wash clothes, a klim tin with a smaller tin fitted inside, both with holes punched into them, nailed to an old broom handle.

"I've gotta be honest, Skipper. I almost lost faith. I was beginning to think we'd never get out of here."

"*Nil Bastardo Carborundum*." Nowak unwrapped a bar of chocolate saved from an American Red Cross parcel. "Let's make some hardtack to take with us. We'll need food, and we can't be weighed down with tin cans on the run."

He broke the chocolate into pieces, dropped them into a klim sitting on the stove and sprinkled in some raisins he'd bartered for. Grabbing the kitbag he'd made by stitching two burlap sacks together, he pulled out a small can of rolled oats.

"Where'd you get those oats?" Freddie asked.

"From Ray. He's been helping out in sick bay." Nowak poured the oatmeal into the melted chocolate. "I have his escape map. And some Horlicks tablets too. They'll boost our energy when we run out of food. We've got to travel light."

"Couldn't you talk him into coming with us?" Freddie asked.

"He's determined to stay put," Nowak said. "He's studying his law books and spending time with Frank, the New Zealander that lectures at the camp university. It's just you and me."

"I'm not hanging around. Nothing's going to stop me from seeing my son."

"Maybe it's a girl," Nowak quipped.

"Maybe. It doesn't much matter to me," Freddie said. "I just want to get home. I have a wedding to attend."

"Goon up," bellowed the lookout. The shackling of prisoners had ceased but the lookout system continued to warn the prisoners of an approaching guard.

Nowak moved his eyes toward the window. "It's just Fritz. I'll take care of him." He took the klim off the stove to cool. "Quick, give me your trousers. I can't go outside in my boxers."

He'd done a damn good job of taming Fritz. It started by giving him the occasional cigarette. The one thing you could count on, the guards loved Canadian and American cigarettes received in packages from friends and relatives. He'd offered Fritz a cup of coffee, some chocolate, and a bar of soap out of his Red Cross parcels to take home to his wife. Slowly, Nowak suggested an exchange for items they needed. Innocent, harmless things at first, like a button or thread. Then larger, more significant items. Once Fritz was hooked, there was no going back. All Nowak had to do was tell the commandant what the guard had been doing and he would be reprimanded. Fritz lived in fear of being sent to the Eastern Front.

Nowak stepped out of his hut, doing up the button on Freddie's trousers, just as Fritz reached the door. "How's the *frau*?"

"She liked the coffee," Fritz said. "*Danke*."

"Did you get the pajama tops?"

"*Ja*." Fritz opened his coat and pulled them out.

"Thanks, Fritz," Nowak said. "How's that son of yours?"

"*Mein* son says *Der Führer* will solve all of Germany's problems. He—"

"You don't really believe that, do you?" Nowak should have known better than to bring up the man's son. He wasn't about to hang around and listen to Nazi propaganda.

Returning to his hut, he tossed the pajama tops on his bunk. From his shelf, he grabbed his klim and emptied a handful of broken pencil leads into his palm. He'd traded his cigarettes for indelible pencils to sketch and pass the time. In his kitbag, he'd saved one along with a couple of blank pages torn out of his *Wartime Log*, a blank journal sent to prisoners of war through the Canadian YMCA. You never knew when you'd need a pencil and a piece of paper. Besides, he didn't own much more than that these days.

He showed the leads to Freddie. "We'll grind these into powder and dye these pajamas to look like work shirts."

"Who's my swap?" Freddie asked.

"A Greek Cypriot. He doesn't speak German or English. But don't worry about it. You don't need to do any talking. Just nod your head a lot."

"When do we leave?"

"There's still a week before the next work detail."

"I hope it goes to the sugar beet factory. It's tradition for the POWs that work there to take a piss in a bag of sugar before leaving for the night. I want to give those German buggers a little something extra to take home," Freddie said.

Nowak laughed. "There's a soccer match scheduled for Saturday. Army against Air Force. The Dutch Army Band is going to play their national anthem before kick-off. That'll piss Ukraine Joe off so much he'll haul them to the cooler. That's when we'll make the switch."

CHAPTER EIGHTEEN

German units of the *Waffen-SS* restarted the final round of deportations from the ghetto on the eve of Passover, storming through the gate on Nalewki Street with machine guns, flamethrowers, and armored tanks. But this time, the Jewish insurgents were prepared to fight back with a stash of home-made grenades, Molotov cocktails, and smuggled-in weapons, finding shelter in underground bunkers and hidden passageways. Two boys climbed up onto the roof of the command center on Muranowski Square and raised two flags, flying the blue-and-white banner of the Jewish fighters alongside the red-and-white Polish flag for four days.

Papa called an emergency meeting on the fifth day of the uprising. He sat at their kitchen table with Michal, Baranek, and Dr. Jeska. Even though it was early morning, a bottle of potato vodka made the rounds. They'd been up all night.

Anna listened intently to the strained voices of the men while she prepared for her final journey through the sewers.

"Operation Action Ghetto failed. We didn't have enough weapons or explosives to blow up the wall and evacuate people. Thousands of German troops with tanks and armored vehicles surrounded us." Papa picked up his glass and gulped back a shot of vodka. He poured himself another drink. "Our sources tell us Himmler has issued orders to accelerate the liquidation. They're burning buildings. Tomorrow the *Luftwaffe* will drop bombs."

"We can expect reprisals in the coming days when Hitler hears a senior officer of his was killed," Michal said.

Anna drew in a breath. She knew what that meant: mass killings of innocent civilians.

"What happened to the air drops Churchill promised?" Baranek twisted the tip of his mustache.

"Reassigned to operations of higher priority." Michal leaned back in his chair with his arms crossed.

"What the hell is more important than stopping the liquidation?" Dr. Jeska asked.

"France and Norway," Papa said as he stuffed tobacco into his pipe.

"Polish independence is vital." Dr. Jeska drained his drink and slammed his glass on the table.

Anna checked to make sure her Vis 35 was loaded before slipping the handgun into her leather holster. She stuffed an extra box of pistol cartridges in her coat pocket and headed toward the front door.

Michal looked up. "Where are you going?"

"To meet Samuel."

Papa turned in his chair. "All rescue efforts through the sewers have been suspended," he said.

"Samuel's expecting me." She pulled on her rubber boots.

Papa stood up. "You stay here, Anna!"

"I'm bringing his family out with me. If I don't go, they'll all die."

After what seemed like a long silence, Papa said, "Promise me this will be your last trip."

"It will."

"Don't forget your pistol."

"I have it."

"Do you have candles to check the purity of the air? The Germans are pumping gas down."

"Yes, Papa. Don't worry."

"How can I help but worry?" He hugged her. "Come back to me, my dear child. May God be with you on your journey."

CHAPTER NINETEEN

Twelve Meters Underground
Warsaw, Poland

Descending into the underground sewers gave Anna purpose and some sense of control. She had grown used to the vapors and, in the areas where the passageways were narrow and the fumes suffocating, she folded her scarf into layers, pressed it against her mouth, and moved as fast as she could.

Tonight, the fumes were overpowering, with barely enough oxygen to strike a match and light her candle. She stopped at a platform to rest and gather her strength before crossing under the ghetto wall.

Gun fire from inside the ghetto raged through the grate above while music blared out of the amusement park across the street. Flashes of light siphoned down, alternating red and white splashes of color from the swinging gondola chairs on the carousel. They spun around and around, illuminating the surface of the sewage.

Noticing something floating, Anna flicked the switch on her flashlight and moved the beam back and forth. She gasped. A bloated body lay face down in the sewage.

Just then, someone shoved a lantern in her face. "Well, what do we have here?" asked a deep male voice.

A huge man in grubby overalls towered over her. She didn't answer.

"I asked you a question. Why are you down here?" He grabbed her forearm and yanked her to her feet.

"Why are *you* down here?" Anna shot back.

"I'm working."

"Oh good. You're a sewer worker."

"What do you mean *good*?" he said. "I have to hand you over to the Gestapo."

"You're supposed to help me."

"Not anymore. The Germans know we're using the sewers to move children out. They surrounded the manhole at the courthouse this afternoon and massacred a gang of smugglers when they climbed out. They'll kill me if I don't turn you over."

"They'll kill me if you do." She dug into her pant pocket for the money she carried for bribes. "I have *złotys*."

"How many?"

"Fifty."

"Not enough. I can get more if I turn you in."

"That's all I have." She handed over the coins. "Take it. Take it all."

He let go of her arm to grab the money, then held the lantern to his open palm to count it. When he looked away, Anna slid the pistol out of her holster and aimed it at him. Nothing was going to stop her from guiding Samuel and his family out of the ghetto. It was their last chance.

He must have seen her hand move. He saw the gun and stepped back. "If you fire that gun, the Germans will hear and kill us both," he said.

"I'll take my chances. Get out of here." She waved her pistol. "Or I'll bloody well shoot you."

He backed away, stirring the water, and intensifying the fumes. Her head was pounding now, but still she waded along the sewer line until she reached the next passageway and crawled through to the underground bunker.

Samuel stood waiting with his pistol sticking out from behind his belt. He appeared thinner, his beard longer. A young girl stood in the shadows behind him and he motioned her to come forward.

She ran to Anna and embraced her. It was Lieba, Samuel's seven-year-old sister.

"I'm so happy to see you," Anna said, hugging the child. Even in the dim light, Anna could tell she'd been crying. Turning back to Samuel, she asked him, "Where are your parents? All of you must come with me this time."

"Our parents are dead. Killed yesterday. Lieba is my only family now."

Anna searched for the right words. "I'm so sorry," she said.

Samuel said nothing.

"There's no reason for you to stay then. You must leave."

He shook his head. "I'll keep fighting. We've moved as many people as possible into the underground bunker under Mila Street. We're using it as a command center."

"But the Germans are sending thousands of troops. They're burning the buildings. Tomorrow will be worse. I won't leave you here." She looked at him in the scant light. He seemed so weak, yet so brave. Stepping closer, she wrapped her arms around his boney shoulders.

He didn't respond. "You must leave now, with my sister," he said, his body rigid.

"You don't have enough weapons. It's suicide," she pleaded.

Lieba reached for her brother's hand. "Please come," Lieba whimpered. "Don't leave me."

He bent down, so he was at eye level with his sister, and rested his hands on her shoulders. For a few seconds, the old Samuel was back, as his tone softened. "You must leave now, my little loved one. It's your only chance of survival. Always remember how much I love you." He kissed her on the forehead.

"Don't do this," Anna insisted, struggling to understand.

"It's a matter of honor. Take my sister and leave." He spoke without looking at her.

She wanted to break down in tears and beg him to come with her. Scream at the top of her lungs to make him listen. Anything to get through to him. But the sweet, innocent Samuel she had known and loved like a brother, was no longer there. The war had taken him from her.

Smoke from the fires above seeped into the bunker as armored tanks launched explosive shells out on the street. She had to leave.

"We have to go now," she told Lieba, taking her hand.

Lieba burst into tears.

"I'll make sure she grabs hold of the cable and follows you. Go now," he said.

"Try not to be scared. I've done this many times," Anna whispered to the sobbing child to calm her. "But remember, you must be quiet."

Anna used the series of knots to guide her on the return trip through the dark underground maze until she stopped at a junction and reached up for the rope. Then reached again. And again. But she couldn't find it.

Had the fumes gone to her head and confused her? Where was the rope? If she took the wrong turn, Lieba would die. And so would she.

Reaching for the rosary she wore around her neck, she asked for guidance. From God. From the Virgin Mary. From her mother. From anyone else who might be listening. She clutched the medallion, fingered the first bead, then the next, assigning each one a direction—right, left, right, left—as she worked her way down to the crucifix. The last bead said, right.

They turned right. Working her way forward, a faint glimmer of light filtered down through a manhole cover farther along the sewer line. Relief washed over her.

"We're almost there," she whispered to the little girl.

Lieba wiped away a tear and nodded.

When they got to the platform, Anna reached for her miniature crowbar. It wasn't there. Had someone taken it? Was she at the wrong manhole?

They were back on the Aryan side of the city and there was light above. She could scale the rungs in the shaft and push the cover up just enough to see where they were.

"Stay here," she whispered as she stepped onto the first iron rung.

One by one, she clambered up the shaft. At the top, she placed both hands under the metal cover and pushed. It didn't move. No matter how hard she pushed, it wouldn't budge. She climbed back to the bottom where Lieba sat on the platform, whimpering with her face in her hands.

Out of energy and losing hope, Anna slumped down beside her, unable to go any farther. The Germans had soldered the manhole cover shut and removed the ropes. She and a child, who depended on her for survival, were lost in the dark sewers below Warsaw.

"Take me back to my brother," Lieba pleaded and tugged on her arm. "We're going to die in here."

Anna put her arm around Lieba and listened to the sounds overhead. All she heard were the rumblings of traffic and an odd knocking echoing through the tunnels. Nothing gave her any sign of where they were.

She closed her eyes to concentrate.

Wait.

The knocking seemed in sequence. Knock, knock. Followed by a softer knock, knock. Then silence. A minute later, two loud knocks followed by two softer. Just like her secret knock with Michal. Did he sense she was in trouble?

Follow the sounds, she told herself. Let Michal guide you.

"Grab the cable, Lieba. We're almost home," she said.

CHAPTER TWENTY

Nowak and Freddie hustled along International Avenue in the Army Camp to join the outgoing work party gathered at the main gate. They wore two sets of clothes with escape rations and cigarettes sewn into the lining of their jackets.

"Hurry up, Nowak," Freddie said. "He's started the head count."

As the column of Army prisoners moved forward, each man opened his kitbag for inspection. Nearing the front, Nowak noticed Ukraine Joe marching toward the Air Force compound. To avoid being recognized, Nowak kept his head down. Just a few more steps and it was his turn for inspection.

The guard in charge adjusted his rifle strap and pushed the rolled brim of his steel helmet back on his head.

"Jesus. It's Fritz," Nowak whispered.

"Bloody hell," Freddie said.

Nowak stepped in front of Fritz.

Fritz looked stunned. He reached for his whistle. One blow and the other guards would come a-running, and Nowak would be sent to the cooler.

Nowak gave Fritz an almost imperceptible nod. His heart pounded so loudly, he was sure the others could hear. He opened his kitbag, packed for life on the run: two blank pieces of paper, his pencil, and a small packet of coffee. The escape map was hidden in his right boot.

Fritz's eyes narrowed. Nowak held his gaze.

Fritz reached into the kit and pulled out the pieces of paper, making sure no writing on them needed to be censored. He snatched the coffee, held it to his nose, and slipped it into his coat pocket.

Nowak closed his kitbag and stepped through the gate, wondering how long it would take Fritz to figure out he had brewed, dried, and reused the coffee grinds several times. Freddie was up next. He stepped forward and opened his kit.

Fritz pulled out a pack of Lucky Strike cigarettes and the dog-eared book of poetry by Robert Burns. He leafed through the pages.

Freddie shot Nowak an irritated glare.

Nowak shook his head, hoping Freddie had enough sense to keep his mouth shut, and mouthed the words, "Let him have it."

Freddie raised his arm to grab his book. But Fritz must have realized the poetry was in English because he shoved it back in Freddie's bag, pocketed the cigarettes, and called out the next name on his list. Freddie strode through the gate up to Nowak.

As soon as the inspection was over, armed guards marched the work party to the train station where they loaded them into boxcars. Nowak sat in the corner of a crowded forty-and-eight as the train chugged east. But this time, he was on his way to a limestone quarry on a rail line bordering Czechoslovakia, and not to a prison camp surrounded by barbed wire.

CHAPTER TWENTY-ONE

Limestone Quarry
Rural Germany

Nowak stood at the bottom of an open-pit quarry, dotted with kilns used to process limestone, looking up at the vast rock cliffs surrounding him. Escape would not be as easy as he'd hoped.

Nowak and Freddie worked side by side, removing limestone from the bedrock and moving the raw material to the crusher. Their supervisor was a young German guard nicknamed Squeaky because his artificial leg squeaked every time he took a step.

After about a week, Nowak said to Freddie, "Give me your watch. I want to give it to Francois." A Czech local he had befriended.

"Why should I?"

"In exchange for some decent boots." Nowak's switch from the Army camp had given him his boots but Freddie still wore wooden clogs. "You won't get far in those."

Freddie removed his watch and handed it over. "Can you trust him?"

"My gut says yes."

"Your gut?"

"He fought in World War One. His father was Czech. His mother French. And he hates the Nazis."

Nowak maneuvered his way over to where Francois was struggling to move a heavy limestone rock with a shovel. The years of labor and sorrow etched on his face left deep wrinkles around his eyes, liver spots scattered on his hands and face, and leathered skin. Their relationship had started with bartering *Zigaretten* for *Brot*. Cigarettes for bread.

"Let me get it." Nowak plied the slab of rock with a crowbar. When he bent down to lift it into the carrier, he whispered, "Did you find boots for Freddie?"

Francois nodded. "In the bushes behind the kitchen."

"Good. Squeaky never bothers to patrol over there." Nowak glanced up at the abandoned schoolhouse that housed the makeshift kitchen on the cliff above.

He checked to make sure Squeaky wasn't watching before he slid the watch and some cigarettes into Francois's jacket pocket. He knew from talking with the old war vet that he had seen many of his comrades die horrible deaths and wished he had more to give him.

At lunchtime, the workers climbed up the rock wall for a meal of watery turnip soup, while Squeaky rode up the bumpy road in a jeep. The surrounding countryside was littered with farms, the rail line, and a small village farther down the road.

After lunch, the workers assembled beside the schoolhouse to head back down the rock wall to work. A small flock of cackling geese grazed on the grass. One goose waddled off, trailing a grasshopper around the side of the building. Freddie slipped out of sight. Nowak inched closer to see what he was up to. Freddie grabbed the bird and wrung its long, thick neck. The bird squirmed and flapped its wings before falling limp. Freddie stood with his arm outstretched and the goose dangling in the air.

Freddie and Nowak locked eyes. After so much time together, they'd developed a sixth sense that enabled them to read one another's thoughts. No one else had noticed yet. Squeaky looked the other way.

Nowak took the goose and stuffed it into a huge iron pot of leftover soup sitting on the ground. Freddie picked up the carrying pole and slid it through the handles on either side of the large container. With Freddie in front and Nowak behind, they rested it on their shoulders and headed for the kitchen.

Squeaky turned around just as the two of them entered the abandoned schoolhouse. Rows of empty desks served as the only reminder that children had once filled the building with smiles and laughter.

"Jesus, now what?" Nowak lifted the dripping turnip-stained goose from the container, spilling soup on the floor. He heard the squeak approach.

Freddie snatched the bird out of Nowak's hand, shoved it under his jacket, and scurried out the back door. Seconds later, the guard hobbled in, using his rifle as a cane to speed his gait. Nowak stood in the middle of the room with a puddle of soup on the floor. He clutched his stomach and bent over as if vomiting.

The guard swung his rifle in the direction of the outhouse. Nowak wiped his mouth with the back of his hand and staggered outside. The door to the outhouse swung open and Freddie strode out, buttoning his fly.

"Bloody hell. That was close," Freddie whispered as they passed each other on the dirt path from the schoolhouse.

"Too close," Nowak muttered.

Back at work in the open-pit quarry, Nowak told Freddie, "We leave tonight."

"Not unless we come back for that bird. I'm bloody hungry."

"You've got to be kidding. You're not planning to scoop it out of the shit hole, are you?"

"I'm not that dim. I shoved it under a bush."

CHAPTER TWENTY-TWO

Limestone Quarry
Rural Germany

After a twelve-hour day in the quarry, the exhausted work party returned to their billet: a rundown barn with muddy straw scattered on the floor. As soon as Squeaky finished his final rounds and the lights in the farmhouse turned off, Nowak and Freddie changed into their civvies.

As usual, the night guard ambled into the barn to take a headcount. Nowak closed his eyes and pretended to be asleep. Afterwards, the guard headed outside to lodge himself in a chair right in front of the door, with a rifle on his lap. Most nights, he nodded off about midnight, giving them ample time to get away. With any luck, he wouldn't notice they were gone until morning.

It was a dark, moonless night. Quiet, except for the chirping and snapping sounds of crickets and grasshoppers in the wild grass. Nowak waited. Time moved slowly. It started raining and the guard moved his chair under the overhang of the roof. A good move for them because it gave Nowak and Freddie more room to sneak out.

It was well past midnight and all the workers were asleep. Nowak moved up to the door, easing it open just enough to stick his head out.

"Now's our chance," Nowak whispered to Freddie. "I'll go first. Only a few steps to get around the side of the barn and we're home free."

He grabbed his kitbag and crept outside. Grasshoppers flew out of his way as he took each step. One. Two. Three. Four. Five. Almost there. He raised his foot to take another step.

The night guard flinched, jumped out of his chair, and grabbed his rifle. Nowak froze mid-motion, sure his heart stopped beating. He glanced over, expecting to be shot. Instead, the guard was stomping his feet and mumbling to himself.

Nowak slipped around the corner. Freddie was right behind him.

"What's he doing?" Nowak whispered.

Freddie shrugged. "Must be the bloody grasshoppers that woke him up."

They slinked their way through the wet grass past the farmhouse and out of the barnyard. Reaching the road, they hustled over to the schoolhouse next to the quarry. Nowak rummaged through the bushes to find the burlap bag Francois had hidden for them. He dumped the contents onto the ground, pleased to see a pair of work boots for Freddie, a jackknife with a bone handle, a piece of cheese, and some sausage. Much more than he expected from the kind old man.

Freddie slipped the boots on, did up the laces, and raced over to the outhouse to grab the goose he'd hidden. Stuffing the bird in his kitbag, he said, "Let's follow the train track east. Best to put as many miles as possible between us before daylight."

It was safer to travel in the dark, since, with the trees in the area cleared away to discourage escape, there were few places to hide. They didn't have much time before their escape would be discovered and a *Kriegsfahndung*, a war emergency man-hunt, was ordered.

Decked out in pajama tops and sheared Air Force trousers, with their spirits high and kitbags packed, they headed off on foot toward Warsaw on a road that was nothing more than two mucky ruts running through an open field parallel to the train tracks.

As the sun rose, they cut through a sea of yellow blooming rape-seed. To Nowak, the vibrant hue of the flowers seemed brighter than usual. Taking a moment to breathe in the clean earthy scent that lingered in the air after the spring rain, it occurred to him that the smell of freedom proved very different to that of captivity.

They came upon a small village. The rhythmic sound of horses' hooves clopped in the distance. As the sound neared, they hid behind a barn and watched a man with a horse-drawn cart deliver containers of fresh milk to each house.

As soon as the horse trotted down the winding road and disappeared, Nowak said, "I can taste that milk already."

"Let's grab some," Freddie said.

"Don't take them all from one house. They might have kids."

Freddie raced toward a thatched roof cottage with purple and yellow pansies in a window box under closed wooden shutters. He snatched a bottle off the step.

Nowak crossed the street to a white house with black trim and a pink flowering cherry tree in the yard. He grabbed one of three bottles sitting in front of the gate and guzzled it on the spot.

"Let's follow the track out of town, then stop for the day. People will wake soon," Nowak said, wiping milk from his mouth with the sleeve of his jacket.

Freddie stole a second bottle farther down.

When they reached the train station, near the exit, the bruised and bloodstained body of a British airman dangled from a noose tied around a beam. His face was purple with bulging eyes. Black flies swarmed. Printed on the wall in bold red letters was the word: *TERRORFLIEGER*, the term used by the German people to refer to members of Bomber Command.

"Jesus," Nowak said. "We've got to cut the kid down."

Freddie grabbed Nowak's jacket to hold him back. "Not so fast. People are at the station. We have to leave him."

The image of the hanging airman remained fixed in Nowak's mind as they headed east out of town along the track. He stopped beside a deep ditch with tall grass and a culvert for them to hide.

"This looks like a good spot." He slid down into the gully and crawled in. Hunched forward in the cramped space, he pulled out the sausage, broke off a piece and handed the rest to Freddie.

"Bloody hell! Do you hear that?" Freddie asked.

Nowak stopped chewing. "What?"

"Shhh. They're coming this way."

Unnerving, incessant voices repeating the words to the song "*Die Fahne Hoch*"—"Raise the Flag High"—grew louder. The chant of the *Hitlerjugend*, the Hitler Youth movement.

Nowak's nerves bristled. He peeked out, shocked to see columns of teenaged girls marching in rows of three, wearing white shirts with black scarf ties and dark blue skirts. They carried backpacks and waved Hitler Youth flags: red-and-white striped with a black swastika in a white square at the center.

He hadn't noticed a row of canvas tents that were erected far down the road. "Jesus, we're in the middle of a damn girls' camp," Nowak whispered. "We've gotta get out of here."

"What if they see us?" Freddie asked.

Nowak was silent for a moment. Unsure of what to do. "We might have to stay here until dark," he said.

"I think I hear a train," Freddie said.

Nowak listened for the sounds of a steam engine. "You're right. We can jump a freight car. It won't be going fast. We're on the outskirts of town." He grabbed his kitbag. "Get ready."

"Ever done this before?" Freddie asked.

"Nope."

"Me neither."

Nowak crawled out of the culvert and stood up. The girls were marching back toward them. The chugging sounds of the train had drowned their chanting voices out. One girl pointed, the others waved their flags. The whole damn bunch of them started running toward him.

Freddie stuck his head out of the culvert.

"Ready?" Nowak asked.

"Ready, Skipper."

Nowak jumped up and ran alongside the train. Grabbing the railing on the side of the locomotive, he heaved himself inside a boxcar. Running behind, Freddie reached for the train, gripped the rail with both hands, and dangled off the side.

Nowak leaned out of the boxcar, grasped Freddie's shirt, and hauled him in.

"Well, what do we have here? Looks like boxes of ammo headed for the Eastern Front." Nowak pulled out the jackknife and jimmied open one of the wooden crates stacked inside the compartment. "Dynamite." He grabbed a stick and tapped it against his palm.

"Are you thinking what I'm thinking?" Freddie asked.

"Damn right." Nowak placed the dynamite back in the box, slipped the jackknife in his pocket, and sat on the floor. "Let's think this through." He took a package of Sweet Caps out of his pocket and held the open pack out to Freddie. "Smoke?"

Freddie reached for a cigarette and sat down.

Nowak struck a match to light his cigarette and reached over with a cupped hand to light Freddie's. "How about we throw a lit match into the crate of dynamite, jump, and run like hell." He took a drag of his cigarette.

"Do you think that'll work?"

"Should."

"What if it doesn't?"

"Got a better idea?"

"Hand me your knife."

Nowak dug the jackknife out of his pocket and handed it over.

"Watch and learn, Skipper." Freddie jumped up to grab a stick of dynamite and sat back down. "Better make yourself comfortable. This might take a while."

Nowak leaned against the wall of the boxcar and watched Freddie carve a hole in the middle of the stick of dynamite. His friend laid the explosive on the floor, careful not to spill any of the powder, then untucked his pajama top and stuck the knife blade into the cotton, cutting off a piece of material. Tearing the fabric into three narrow strips, he braided them into a short rope and inserted one end into the hole.

"Hand me your matches," Freddie said.

Nowak tossed the box of matches over to Freddie, who slid it open, took out four matchsticks, and stuck them in between the rope and the dynamite to secure the fuse in place. He examined his invention, then changed his mind and reversed two so the match heads were inside the stick.

"This oughta do the trick." Freddie leaned back against the interior of the boxcar. "Ready anytime you are."

"I'm not in any rush. We're headed in the right direction and this is a helluva lot faster than walking." Nowak closed his eyes to get some shut-eye.

Sometime later, he felt Freddie shaking his shoulder.

"Wake up, Skipper. We're slowin' down," Freddie said. "We got to get outta here before the train stops." Freddie headed over to the crate of explosives.

Nowak heard the hiss and squeal of the brakes. He poked his head outside to survey the landscape. "It looks like we're about to pass through a forest."

Freddie placed the explosive on top of the crate and positioned several more sticks on either side. He took out a match and held it close to the striker.

"Ready, Skipper?"

Nowak nodded. "Ready."

Freddie struck the match and lit the cotton braided fuse. When it started to burn, they grabbed their kits and jumped out of the moving boxcar.

Nowak hit the ground hard, ripping his shirt at the elbow. He jumped up as quickly as he could to watch the train blow up, but it continued to chug down the track.

"I thought you said you knew what you were doing," Nowak said.

Freddie stood with his hands on his hips. "Put a sock in it."

The locomotive disappeared around the bend. Disappointed, they dragged themselves into the forest. Then they heard a massive explosion, followed by another and another. Each one louder than the last. They ran back out to the side of the track. Billows of black smoke and flames rose above the towering trees. Fragments of the supply train shot into the air.

They both cheered.

"Told you it would work. That's one shipment the Home Army won't have to sabotage," Freddie said with satisfaction.

The two of them headed back into the vast forest, invigorated. After living for almost a year in the stagnant stench of the stalag, Nowak stopped to breathe in the fresh scent of the pine needles on the trees and appreciate the moment. As he stood in the tranquility, emotions surfaced that had been buried since his capture. Relief. Joy. Anticipation. Hope.

They found a place to settle in. Freddie plucked the feathers from the goose while Nowak gathered up some twigs and started a fire. They crouched around the flames, roasting the bird by taking turns rotating it on a wooden spit.

"Do you have the address memorized?" Nowak pulled Ray's map out of his kitbag.

"Twenty-four / twelve Zawalta Street."

"Żurawia Street. Z . . . u . . . r . . . a . . . w . . . i . . . a."

"That's what I said," Freddie insisted. "Apartment four."

No sense in arguing. "If anything happens to me, just remember that address. That's where you'll contact the Underground."

"I'm all turned around. Do you know where we're going?" Freddie studied the silk escape map. "Where's that navigator of ours when we need him?"

Nowak grabbed the compass button in his pocket, held the thread tied through the hole in the middle between his fingers, and let it fall. The button dangled and spun in the air. It stopped with the dot on the edge pointing north.

"Warsaw would be that-a-way." Nowak pointed in a north-easterly direction, saddened and angered by the thought that he wouldn't be able to visit his grandparents. They'd both been killed during the Siege of Warsaw when bombs with delayed-action fuses had destroyed their neighborhood.

"Let's get some rest before we head out again. I'm beat," Nowak said.

He found a tree to lean against and sat down. Freddie settled himself in a similar fashion and took off his boots. Sunlight filtered through the tight canopy of pine and beech trees. Frogs croaked in the distance. Overcome by exhaustion, they both nodded off.

A hooting eagle owl woke Nowak from a restless sleep. Memories of Polish folklore linking the sounds of an owl with bad luck and death turned him cold with dread. He remembered his mother telling him she had heard an owl the night before his father was shot.

He stood and brushed the leaves from his clothes. Damp, stiff, and eager to get moving, he waved a piece of hardtack at Freddie.

"Wake up. Have some breakfast. Let's get going."

Freddie opened one eye, stood, and stretched his arms.

Nowak edged down a steep dirt path through a white carpet of blooming anemones leading out of the forest. He stopped beside a creek and bent down to scoop the glistening clean water. After drinking his fill, he splashed his face and relished the soothing sound of the stream trickling over the rocks. He picked a reddish-brown, irregularly shaped mushroom and held the stipe and the cap close to his nostrils to smell the aroma.

He felt the cold muzzle of a gun push against the back of his head. A shiver went down his spine. The safety clicked. Turning, he saw a fat German civilian police officer in a helmet pointing a Luger in his face. The man reeked of alcohol.

Nowak dropped the mushroom and raised his hands in the air.

A young man in a black uniform stepped out of the bushes with his rifle aimed at Freddie. "*Papiere*," Papers, he demanded.

In a mix of English, Polish and the few words of German he'd picked up, Nowak tried to convince the men they were forced Polish workers. He told them Freddie was sick and needed a doctor, so they had left their work party to search for one. But when he couldn't produce any papers and neither of them had forced labor badges, yellow with a purple border and the letter P in the center, the police officer told them a war emergency manhunt had been issued for two escapees matching their description.

At gun point, they were led along a path to a small wooden shed on the side of a road. After all of this, Nowak couldn't believe he'd been stupid enough to walk right into a checkpoint.

"Kill them. Throw their bodies in the ditch," the officer ordered the teenage boy before staggering off to the shed.

With his finger on the trigger, the boy raised his rifle. Was there a momentary hesitation by the young Pole? Was he a Nazi sympathizer? Or did he hate them as much as Nowak?

"Comrade, I'm a fellow Pole," Nowak whispered in Polish.

"Bullshit."

"*Tak. Tak.* Yes. Yes. Born in Warsaw. We are fighting to save Poland from the Germans. We are your Allies."

The rifle's aim shifted ever so slightly.

Nowak felt a spark of hope. "We have contacts in the Home Army. *Polska walczy*." Poland fights.

"Herr Albert," the boy shouted to his superior. "Gestapo considers *Luftgangsters* valuable prisoners of war. You might get transferred back to your wife and family if I turn them in."

Albert appeared at the door with a bottle of Schnapps in one hand. His belly stuck out over his belt. "Goddamn *Terrorfliegers*," he slurred. His free hand went for his pistol.

The words hung in the air. The boy with his rifle cocked, the officer waving his pistol.

Not understanding a word of the animated discussion, Freddie toed the dirt, leaned over and whispered to Nowak. "At least we got to eat the goose," and then mumbled something about the best plans of mice and men going awry.

The muscles in Nowak's stomach knotted. The world moved in slow motion. One frame at a time.

The officer took his hand off his pistol. "Take them into town. Turn them over to the Gestapo." The officer motioned them off with his hand before taking a slug from the bottle.

The boy secured handcuffs around their wrists and led them to a truck. They climbed in.

Nowak leaned over to Freddie and whispered, "You silly bugger. When they're talking about whether to shoot us or not, you shouldn't be talking about mice."

After driving for about ten minutes, the young Pole pulled the vehicle off the road. He turned to Nowak and asked, "Where were you headed?"

Nowak glared at him. He wasn't saying.

The boy took a set of keys out of his pocket.

"I wasn't going to shoot you. I just let the old drunk think he's in charge. It's easier that way. Killing the pig would create major complications."

Nowak's mouth dropped open.

"Nice job on the train," the boy said as he unlocked their handcuffs. "You want a ride or not? I haven't got all day."

CHAPTER TWENTY-THREE

Anna hurried along the colonnade to the front entrance of the Franciscan convent. Her footsteps echoed off the arched ceilings of empty corridors as she made her way to the office of the mother superior. An elderly nun with soft, wrinkly skin, wearing a black-and-white habit with a large silver crucifix hanging on a black cord around her neck, opened the carved wooden door.

"Come in. I've been expecting you," Mother Superior said, sticking her head out into the hall and looking both ways to make sure no one was watching.

Anna slipped inside the office. "How is Lieba adjusting?" Anna asked, as the nun closed the door behind her.

Two days earlier, Anna and Michal had dropped Samuel's sister off at the orphanage. Anna hadn't seen her since, and now she gave the nun an envelope with Lieba's forged identification papers and a fictional biography.

"Not very well, I'm afraid. She's very scared." The nun clasped her hands in front of her, a worried look on her face. "The Gestapo raided our orphanage last night and inspected the faces of the sleeping children by flashlight. They removed several they suspected were Jewish."

Anna squeezed her eyes shut to block the image from her mind. "How about little Aaron?" she asked.

"He's safe." Mother Superior slid her fingers down the wooden beads of the rosary hooked on her belt and said, "He keeps asking when his parents are coming to get him. Some days, he stands in front of the window and waits for them. He's very confused. Do you have time to visit the children?" she asked.

"Not today. I'm heading to *Żegota* headquarters. The Germans found the Miła Street bunker with hundreds of Jews inside. They threw tear gas down. Only a few surrendered. Some fled through the sewers. But most committed suicide by cyanide." Anna's voice wavered.

The nun closed her eyes and made the sign of the cross.

"I'm hoping to hear that Samuel made it out," Anna said. Her eyes filled with tears.

The nun reached for Anna's hand and held it in hers.

"Greater love hath no man than this," the nun said, quoting from the Gospel of St. John, "that he lay down his life for a friend."

Anna hugged the nun and left, making her way back along the colonnade to the yard where she'd parked the big black bike with fat tires. She gripped the handlebars and stood as she pedaled. Zigzagging back and forth and swerving in and out on rubble-littered streets, she rode by Nazi banners, gutted churches, bombed-out buildings, and wooden crosses marking roadside graves. One had a stuffed teddy bear at the base. Another had a soldier's metal helmet resting on top. She kept pedaling.

Ahead, billows of black smoke rose behind the ghetto walls. Ash and soot from the fires settled on the outside of the buildings. She pedaled faster.

Last night, she hadn't slept. The image of the glow over the burning ghetto remained seared in her mind. In her heart, she knew she'd never see Samuel again. She should have done more to convince him to leave. Pleaded with him longer. She'd never forgive herself.

Turning onto Żurawia Street, she spotted Gestapo communication vans in the alley and cycled past the white-washed building with the *Żegota* office. At the far end of the street, she recognized Michal's friend Pawel, a Home Army plant at a check stop outside the city. He was walking with two men dressed like farm workers in gray shirts and navy trousers.

She had to warn them about the bloody Gestapo vans. There was only one way. Ramming the front tire of the bike against a pile of rubble on the road, she skidded sideways, and crashed, tumbling off the bike and scraping her arm on a mound of crumbling bricks.

The men ran toward her.

"Jesus, are you all right?" one of them asked in a mix of English and Polish.

She looked up to meet the crystal blue eyes of a good look-ing dark-haired young man. Ignoring the pain in her arm, she jumped up.

"I'm fine."

"You're bleeding."

"It's just a scratch," she said as she brushed herself off, then lowered her voice. "I crashed on purpose so I could warn you. Gestapo vans are in the alley."

Pawel tilted his head at the two men beside him. "They're Allied airmen. Escaped from a POW camp. There's a manhunt underway."

"I'm Johnnie Nowak," the man with the blue eyes said. He pointed at the other man, "And this is Freddie."

"I'll handle it from here," Anna told Pawel, ignoring Nowak. Then, grabbing her bike, she muttered, "Come with me."

They followed her past Saxon Garden and Adolf Hitler Platz to the red brick barbican entrance into Old Town Warsaw and from there along winding medieval backstreets where colorful burgher houses stood next to jagged fragments of bombed-out buildings to her house on Piwna Street.

She hurried up the steps. "Quick. Go inside," she told them, opening the door.

"Do you speak English?" Nowak asked once indoors. "My Polish is a little rusty."

"I speak English. My father insisted I learn."

"Is anyone else here?" He looked around the room.

She shook her head.

"We can't stay here. This is your home. If they find us, they'll kill you."

"It's not safe for you here in Warsaw." She bolted the door. "The Germans are everywhere. Thousands of them."

"What's with all the smoke?" he asked.

"They're burning the ghetto, block by block."

A look of shock crossed his face. "What about the people?"

"Many refused to leave. They're still inside." Her voice faltered. "They tried to fight back, but they didn't have enough weapons."

"Nazi bastards!" Freddie made a fist and shook his head in disgust.

"We don't get much information in the prison camp. We heard rumors but I had no idea it was this horrific," Nowak said.

"I'll guide you out of the city in the morning and give you directions to a safe house in the country," she said. "The owners work with us. They'll get you a *Kennkarte* to blend in."

"A what?" Freddie asked.

"Identity papers with a photo and fingerprints. You'll also need ration cards and an *Arbeitskarte*. That's a work card. Are you hungry?"

"Sure am," Nowak said.

"Starved." Freddie patted his stomach.

Anna headed to the kitchen to heat the soup she'd made from her last stash of dried mushrooms earlier in the day. The men pulled mismatched chairs up to the table and sat down.

She heated the soup and scooped it into two of the bowls Michal had painted that looked just as fancy as the top brands of Polish pottery. Carrying them to the table, she served Nowak the bowl without the chip and then Freddie.

"Aren't you eating?" Nowak asked.

"I'm not hungry," she lied. She needed to save some soup for Papa and Michal.

"What's your name?" Nowak asked.

"Hope." She hadn't used her real name since the day she'd picked up documents at the cathedral on her first assignment as a courier.

Nowak put the spoon to his mouth and sipped the broth. He closed his eyes.

"Don't you like it?" she asked him.

"It's delicious." He looked up at her. "I recognize the flavor. It reminds me of the days before I left Poland. I used to pick mushrooms for my mother. I never thought I'd be back."

"You're Polish?" she asked.

"I was born in Poland but emigrated to Canada when I was a kid. A Russian killed my father. I was very young."

She read the hurt in his kind eyes.

"The Germans murdered my mother. I miss her every day," she said. She wasn't sure why she offered that information, but she felt as if she could. Something about his eyes made her feel safe and at ease.

"I'm so sorry," he said, holding her gaze.

Freddie remained oblivious to the conversation, clearly more interested in eating than talking.

"Why were the Gestapo at the safe house on Żurawia?" Nowak asked, between mouthfuls.

"Their communication vans are trying to fix the location of our radio signals."

Nowak's eyebrows arched as if he was impressed.

"We've received reports on a German research center on the Baltic coast in a place called Peenemünde."

"What are they constructing?" Nowak asked.

"Hitler's *Vergeltungswaffe*. The V1 Flying Bomb and a V2."

"A V2?" Nowak asked. "You mean the Germans are developing another buzz bomb?"

"Not exactly. It's a long-range rocket with a bigger payload. And much faster. Faster than the speed of sound."

"How do you know all this?" he asked.

She wasn't sure he believed her.

"Sometimes I have to deliver reports from memory."

Noticing the rip in his shirt, she went upstairs to Papa's room and opened the closet. Inside were a few shirts, a pair of trousers, and various stolen German uniforms. Gone were the pristine suits and ties Papa once wore to the university.

After grabbing a blue work shirt, she checked her image in the mirror and straightened her braid. If only she had something nicer to wear than Michal's old sweater and cuffed denim trousers. It was so exciting to shelter Allied airmen at her home.

Back in the kitchen, she handed the shirt to Nowak. "You better change." When she saw the scars on his shoulder and chest, she blurted out, "What happened?"

"I was wounded when my aircraft was shot down."

"You're a pilot?"

"Yep."

A pilot. A real live Allied pilot sitting at her table. Butterflies fluttered in her stomach as she watched him put on the shirt and fasten the buttons. The blue tone in the fabric brought out the color of his eyes even more. She couldn't stop smiling.

"What kind of airplane did you fly?" she asked.

"A Wimpy," he said. "A Wellington."

"I know what a Wimpy is. I saw one once. What's it like to be inside an airplane?"

"It's a tremendous feeling of freedom." He closed his eyes as if remembering.

"It is my dream to one day be free to fly."

There were interrupted by a sudden pounding on the front door. She moved to the window, opening the burlap curtains just enough to peer out. An armored black Mercedes with running boards sat parked in front of the house.

"They must be doing bloody house checks again. Quick, you can hide in the cellar." She tore back the frayed rug covering the trapdoor and lifted the floorboards. A musty smell wafted up from below.

The men grabbed their kitbags and flew down the stairs. The pounding outside grew louder.

"I'm coming," she yelled as she replaced the boards and straightened the rug.

She ripped out her braid and messed her hair before unlatching the door. Two members of the Gestapo in black leather coats stormed inside.

"What took you so long to answer the door?" asked the one wearing a fedora while the other rushed up the stairs.

"I was sleeping."

"Stay right where you are." He pointed his walking stick at her. Looking around the room, he noticed the soup bowls on the table. "Who else is here?"

"No one." She fought the urge to glance at the rug to make sure it covered the trapdoor.

With a swing of his walking stick, he knocked her precious bowls onto the floor where they shattered.

Terrified, she backed up.

"I told you not to move." He glared at her. "Where are they?"

"I haven't had time to clean up. I'm sick."

"What's wrong with you?" He jabbed her in the stomach with his stick.

She doubled over. "Typhus," she said.

His eyes narrowed as he inched back, stopping on the carpet covering the trapdoor, right over Nowak and Freddie. She had to do something, fast.

Knowing that the early symptoms of typhus included a skin rash and itching, she scratched at the scrape on her arm until she drew blood.

"I'm so glad you're here. Please stay and help me." She reached for him with her bloody arm.

"Don't touch me, *Untermensch*."

She moved closer to him, wiped her brow and coughed. Then coughed again.

He turned away from her and called up to the second officer who was dumping the contents of drawers onto the floor upstairs. "Did you find anything?"

"*Nichts,*" came the reply.

"Let's get out of here."

After the door slammed shut and the armored car drove away, she sank into a chair. It took her a few minutes to regain her composure before she pulled back the rug and opened the trapdoor.

CHAPTER TWENTY-FOUR

Kowalski Residence
Warsaw, Poland

Nowak listened to every word from the cellar, afraid she'd get herself killed for helping them. When the trapdoor opened, he crawled out. The first thing he noticed was Anna's arm. "You're bleeding. Did the bastards hurt you?"

"I'm fine." She hurried upstairs again and returned with two worn gray blankets. "You'll have to sleep in the cellar. If they come back, use the hidden exit that leads out to the alley. I'll show you where it is."

Freddie grabbed a blanket. "Much appreciated. I'm bagged." He headed down right away.

Nowak crossed the room to peer out the window. Pulling back the burlap curtains, he noticed small numbers stamped on the hem. It looked like a partial serial number. A familiar number.

He spun around. "Where did you get this?"

"From an air drop. When the British sent us supplies."

He pulled out his jack knife, flicked the blade open, and chopped off the hem.

"What are you doing?" she shouted.

"The Gestapo might be back. If they see this serial number, they'll know you're Home Army." He tossed the strip of fabric into the fireplace. "Were you there?"

"I swung a lantern to warn the pilot of the trees. He pulled up just in time, skimming the treetops."

Nowak was at a loss for words. He just stood there looking at her.

"What's the matter?" she asked.

"That was me. The pilot assigned to the air drop with that serial number. You saved our lives."

Her eyes lit up.

"I don't know how to thank you. You've saved me twice now. You must be my guardian angel." Bubbling with appreciation, he wanted to pick her up and twirl her around like he used to do to his sister. But he hardly knew this girl. Not wanting to overreact, he said, "I'd like to give you something for helping us."

"It isn't necessary."

"All I have is this jackknife." He held it out to her.

"You better keep it. You'll need it."

She sat down on the sofa and pulled a dog-eared *Airplane Recognition Handbook* out from under one of the dark green cushions. "It's my dream to one day fly in an airplane," she said as she flipped through the pages.

"So that's how you know about Wellingtons." He sat across from her in a battered chair. "I hope that dream comes true for you," he said. And he meant it. "How old are you, anyway?"

"Eighteen."

"You're the same age as my sister." What a different life his sister Mary was living back in Canada. Graduating high school. Playing basketball. Going on dates.

She set her book down and slumped back, resting her head against a pillow.

"You look like you could use some sleep," he said, concerned about how pale she looked.

"I haven't been able to sleep for days. I have a childhood friend in the ghetto. I could have led him out but he refused to leave. I shouldn't have left without him."

Johnnie gasped. What was she talking about?

Her eyes watered. "It's the second time I've let a friend down."

"What happened?"

"The SS kidnapped a little girl I was walking to school. I was supposed to protect her. I let her down. I let everyone down."

"You can't blame yourself for the actions of those Nazi bastards." He leaned back in the chair and paused. Should he tell her that he blamed himself for the capture of his crewmembers? For Tubby's disfigurement. For Edwin's death. He hadn't admitted it to anyone, keeping his thoughts and feelings bottled up inside until they bubbled to the surface in terrifying, reoccurring nightmares.

On fire, his Wellington sped toward the water in a nosedive. Struggling with the control column, he pulled back with all his strength. He pulled and pulled, but it wouldn't budge. The aircraft crashed into the sea. Underwater, he tried to swim to the surface. Something dragged him down. The light grew dimmer. And dimmer.

For some reason, he felt safe with this girl. It might make her feel better if he told her. He cleared his throat. "I know how you feel," he said. "I blame myself too."

When she didn't answer, he realized she'd fallen asleep. Maybe she felt safe with him. Deciding to write her a note of thanks, he opened his kit and pulled out his pencil and paper. Not knowing what to say, he wrote the lines he could remember from the poem Freddie sent Izzie and slipped it under her pillow. Then covered her with the blanket she'd given him and climbed down into the darkness.

He had a fitful sleep, waking often from the cold, but finally he heard footsteps above and, giving Freddie a kick to wake him, Nowak crawled out of the cellar. In the kitchen, Hope served them each a piece of bread and a cup of tea made with dried linden leaves. He noticed that once again she didn't eat, and he realized she was giving them all the food she had. Breaking his bread in half, he placed it on the table in front of her. She looked up at him in surprise.

"Eat," he urged softly.

It looked like she was about to refuse, but then, with a nod of thanks, she stuffed the bread into her mouth.

"Are you safe here when your family is gone?" he asked, concerned about leaving her alone.

"I'm a soldier, not a child," she said.

"You're right," he said.

Once they finished, she led them through the hidden exit into the alley. Nowak and Freddie followed her back through winding streets and dark alleyways. Nowak noticed a poster on a wall next to a massive oak tree with a drawing of two hands shaking through a broken brick ghetto wall and words written in a language he didn't understand.

"What does that say?" he asked, stopping.

"*All people are equal brothers; Brown, White, Black and Yellow. To separate peoples, colors, race—is but an act of cheating!* It's Yiddish. The Jewish Fighting Organization posted them."

"I've never known a girl like you before." He rifled through his kit bag for his jackknife. Flicking open the blade, he stuck the tip into the thick trunk of the oak tree and carved the symbol of the resistance into the bark. The *Kotwica*, the letters P and W representing the words *Polska Walczy*, Poland Fights, joined together to resemble an anchor. "From now on,

I'll call it the symbol of hope," he said. "In honor of you saving us twice."

She broke out in a smile and held out her hand for the knife. He gave it to her. Bending down, she cut off the cuff on her trousers.

"For you. It's all I have." She gave the knife back to him with the piece of material.

He twisted the cuff into two loops and slipped it onto his wrist.

A block farther down, they turned onto a quiet street lined with linden trees and arching branches. Stopping under one of them, she took a miniature crowbar out of her bag and pointed at a manhole cover.

"That's the safest way out. Major sewer lines converge under the tracks at Gdanski Railway Station. Line C leads out of Old Town."

"Are you serious?" Freddie looked shocked.

"Have you done this before?" Nowak asked.

"Not this route, but I've studied the map. I used to smuggle children out of the ghetto through the sewers." Her eyes checked up and down the street for German snipers hiding in doorways. "When I signal you, come as fast as you can. Climb down the ladder inside the manhole. Wait for me at the bottom. Don't speak unless you have to. The Germans lower listening devices to check for noise."

She walked casually over to the manhole cover and dropped her bag. Bending down, she stuck the crowbar into the notch, dragged the cover off to the side, and motioned for them to come with a wave.

Nowak and Freddie ran to the hole and climbed into the entrance shaft. Anna checked the street one more time, crawled in, and slid the cover back into place. At the bottom, she slung her bag over her head and across her chest.

"Put one hand on my shoulder and follow me. Once you get the hang of it, we'll use my cable to keep us together," she whispered.

Freddie took a few steps and slipped.

Then it was Nowak's turn. "Jesus," he said.

"This will take forever," Freddie muttered.

"Shhh. It's easier if you slide your fingers along the wall to keep your balance."

Nowak sloshed forward, holding onto the cable while Anna led them through the darkness. As they approached an overhead grate, loud German voices filtered down from above. She put her finger to her lips and switched off her flashlight.

Freddie took a step backward. He slid, falling against the wall.

The men above stopped talking. Nowak didn't dare move a muscle until the men started speaking again and their voices faded into the distance. They slogged on for hours until Nowak felt a rush of cool air and the sound of running water.

"What's that noise?" he whispered.

"A stream runs through. The water level is higher than usual because of all the rain we've had," Anna told them. "The next junction might be dangerous."

"Now you tell us," Freddie said.

"I see light ahead," Nowak said.

When they reached the junction, they were stopped by rushing water.

"This is where I must leave you," she said.

"How do we cross?" Nowak asked.

"There's supposed to be a chain strung across. The Germans must have removed it."

"Bloody hell. Now what do we do?" Freddie asked.

"Use my cable," she said. "Tie one end to the rungs of the ladder under that manhole and wrap the other around your waist. If you fall, the water won't wash you away."

"I don't want to leave you here alone. Will you be all right?" Nowak asked.

She nodded.

"I hope someday I can repay you," he said as he stepped into the stream and took small, slow steps through the water. But the current was stronger than he'd expected, the water pounding incessantly at his legs. If he'd been fitter, stronger, maybe he would have made it. But he wasn't. He lost his balance and fell into the torrent.

The current swept him downstream, arms flailing as he desperately tried to stop himself from being swept away, but there was nothing to hold on to. He could see daylight ahead where the water flowed into the river and thick metal bars sealed the drain. At this speed, he'd slam into them. Inches from the bars, he braced himself for impact when the cable tightened around his waist, stopping him with a jerk.

He struggled to lift himself up, wavered, and then steadied. With water whooshing past him, he used his hands to pull himself along the length of the cable and make his way back to the junction, where he swung himself to safety on the other side. He fell against the sewer wall, coughing and panting as he bent over. Once he had recovered, he lodged his legs against the opposite wall, stringing the cable tight across the stream for Freddie to cling to.

One step at a time, Freddie held onto the cable and shuffled across. Nowak untied it from his waist and threw it back across the stream to her, taking one last look at the girl from Warsaw.

CHAPTER TWENTY-FIVE

The Cooler
Stalag IVB, Germany

A six-by-eight cell. A bare wooden bunk. A bucket for a latrine. A diet of black bread and water. Twenty minutes a day for fresh air and exercise.

With Freddie nattering in Nowak's ear and his mind focused on the girl, they had literally walked right into an ambush. Now here he was, back in prison camp, locked in solitary confinement.

He should have noticed the farmyard was too quiet. No movement whatsoever. No animals. No people. When he knocked on the front door of the safehouse, an SS officer greeted them. The bodies of the owners lay slaughtered in puddles of their own blood on the floor.

At first, Nowak welcomed the solitude. The privacy was almost a relief after close to a year in the crowded barracks. But soon the isolation and silence wore thin. To work off the tension, he did push-ups. And he paced. With every step, his hatred for the enemy grew, and the four walls of his cell seemed to move closer.

To occupy his mind, he planned his next escape. He wasn't going to let the German bastards intimidate him: he would antagonize and defy the Nazis at every opportunity. The next attempt would get him out of Germany for good. He refused to die in this miserable hole.

After a week, he craved human contact. He used to think the lack of privacy in the barracks he shared with hundreds of other men was rough going. They were in his face every minute of every day. While he slept. While he ate. While he took a shit.

Now he missed them.

He thought he knew what loss of freedom felt like. He thought he had experienced confinement at its worst. He was wrong.

Here in solitary, he was caged. He couldn't make a bloody decision for himself. The enemy decided when he could leave his cell, when to turn on the lights, when to give him food. Some days, things got so bad he felt he might suffocate. He paced. And paced. Repeating over and over to himself: *Nil Bastardo Carborundum*.

He reassured himself that a world existed beyond the four walls. He thought about the fun he used to have at The Eagle Pub back in England and the time he balanced on Freddie's shoulders to burn his initials on the ceiling with his petrol lighter. About his family. And about Hope, the girl from Warsaw.

Discovering that Hope was part of the reception party at the airdrop, was something he couldn't get out of his mind. In the darkness, she had risked her life to swing a lantern to warn him of the trees at the edge of the clearing, then appeared in his life a second time to help him. She even knew what a Wimpy was. And was a real looker too. She could see right through a guy with those blue eyes of hers.

He had all but lost count of the days when keys knocked against the bars of his cell and the door swung open. For once, the ugly pockmarked face of Ukraine Joe made him smile.

Joe escorted him out of the building. But instead of heading back to his barracks, he turned in the opposite direction.

"Where are you taking me?" Nowak asked.

Joe didn't answer.

As they neared the holding hut where men sentenced to solitary confinement waited for an empty cell, Nowak began to panic. Sometimes prisoners stayed in the holding area for weeks to serve a sentence of only a few days.

Joe opened the door and shoved him inside.

"What the hell are you doing?" Nowak asked.

Joe locked the door and left.

"Let me out. You bastard!" Nowak shouted after him.

The holding hut, a small wooden shed with no windows, had a straw mattress on the floor. He thought about kicking the door down. But there was nowhere to go. In no time flat, he'd get locked back up.

Ukraine Joe returned early the next morning and dragged Nowak back to the cooler. Joe unlocked the door to the cell.

"My sentence is over," Nowak protested. He fought with Joe not to enter. "The maximum sentence in solitary is thirty days. You're breaching the terms of the Geneva Convention."

"You were only sentenced to thirty days. The commandant released you yesterday. Today you were sentenced to another thirty days."

"For what?"

"He wants the names of your contacts."

"What contacts?" Nowak asked.

"Home Army contacts, you filthy Pole." Ukraine Joe smashed Nowak in the stomach with the butt of his rifle.

"I don't have any contacts."

Another swift blow landed across Nowak's shoulder. He fell to the ground. When he tried to get up, the metal plate on the toe of Joe's black leather jackboot struck him in the chest. He fell backwards.

Joe, towering over him, used his hobnailed boot to stomp on Nowak and uttered, "*Polnische schwein*." Polish swine.

"Fucking traitor," Nowak shouted back. His hatred for the man swelled. He crawled through the open door into the empty cell to get away from him.

Joe unbuckled his thick leather belt. He stood at the entrance, belt in hand, ready to strike. But he didn't enter the cell.

"Come out here," Joe demanded.

"Not a chance," Nowak said. Doubled over, he pressed his arms against his chest to fight the pain.

The fucker just stood there like he was afraid to enter. That must be why he always leaves the door to the guards' only outhouse open, he's scared of small spaces.

"Come in and get me, asshole," Nowak taunted him.

With a sudden motion, Joe slammed the door and locked it. Put his belt back on and left. It wasn't like Joe to give up so easily.

Nowak sat alone in the dark. In pain from the beating, he no longer paced. Too weak to do push-ups, he slept. He ate black bread to stay alive. Black bread made from tree flour. How long could a man survive on sawdust? The bread seemed heavy when he picked it up. The smell made him gag. The act of chewing and swallowing a concerted effort.

When Joe remembered to turn the lights on, they seemed to dim, then brighten. Nowak couldn't distinguish day from night. The walls moved closer and closer. Sometimes they wavered. He had trouble sleeping.

Then the voices started. Whispers. At first, he couldn't make out the words. Sitting cross-legged on the floor, staring at the walls, a voice spoke behind him.

"What? What did you say?" he asked the emptiness.

The voice didn't answer. But it came back. The next day. And the day after that. Louder, sometimes softer, then louder again. Usually from behind him. But not always. Startling. And unnerving.

When the voice spoke, he felt cold.

"Who are you?" he asked.

When the voice didn't answer, he began to sweat. One night, sitting on his mattress, staring into the darkness, he smelled the sickly-sweet stench of decaying apples—the pervasive odor of gangrene. A familiar voice spoke. Strong. And comforting.

His father's voice recited a Polish rhyme about a little star. The same rhyme his father recited to him as a small child on nights he couldn't sleep. He closed his eyes. The words flowed over his body, soothing his nerves.

When the rhyme finished, his father said, "Never lose hope."

The voice disappeared.

Left alone, he pictured the biplanes his father used to talk about, gliding in and out of the stars in the night sky, and recalled his father's dreams for their family after Poland was restored to an independent state at the end of WWI.

He thought about Hope, and touched the cuff wrapped around his wrist. A peaceful sensation settled over him. That night, he slept soundly.

In the days that followed, he could no longer distinguish between reality and his own thoughts. His emotions escalated and crashed, alternating between panic and calm. Frightening thoughts dominated his thinking. Maybe the guards had abandoned him. Maybe he would never get out.

Hopeless. And paranoid. He backed himself up against the wall. That day, he was sure he saw Hope in his cell. And his determination strengthened. He even enjoyed a soothing moment of calm. The emotional oscillation continued. He questioned whether he had ever had a life beyond the four walls.

CHAPTER TWENTY-SIX

RAF Compound
Stalag IVB, Germany

At the end of his sentence, Nowak moved back to his hut. He had to shield his eyes from the blast of sunshine. His clothes hung loose, his skin pale, legs shaky.

The noisy, crowded, smoky interior of his hut unnerved him as he walked through the door. Ray dropped the criminal law textbook he was reading and helped Nowak to his chair.

"I'll get you some grub." Ray returned with rations he'd been saving.

Nowak grabbed a cold potato off the dented tin plate and wolfed it down. "Where's Freddie?" he asked.

"Sleepin'. You look like you could stand some rest. Get your strength back."

"All I want to do is eat."

"I was hoping y'all made a home run."

Nowak didn't want to talk about his escape. Out of circulation for months, he yearned to catch up on the news.

"Any developments?" Nowak spoke slowly, the sound of his own voice oddly unfamiliar.

"The commandant got rid of the handcuffs while you were gone."

"That's bloody good news."

"I guess ya didn't hear about Operation Crossbow. The secret raid on the V-weapon factory in Peenemünde."

Nowak thought about Hope and smiled. "Sounds like they got their report to London. I guess she knew what she was talking about, after all. Maybe her father really is someone important."

"Huh?"

"Polish Home Army Intelligence."

Ray looked a little puzzled.

"Never mind. Go on." Nowak reached for another potato.

"Three waves of bombers attacked by moonlight at altitudes as low as four thousand feet."

"How did they manage that?"

"Sent a force of Mosquito decoys on ahead to perform a diversionary raid on Berlin. *Luftwaffe* followed them."

"When?"

"August seventeenth. Blew the hell out of Hitler's rocket factory," Ray reported proudly.

The news gave Nowak a rush of energy, but he was too weak to respond with more than a slight smile. "How many aircraft did we lose?"

"That's the bad news. Forty-one. And a barrack full of forced laborers killed by mistake. Mostly Poles."

"Damn." His elation slipped. He shuffled over to his bunk and flopped down. Clasping his hands behind his head, he lay there and tried to focus his thoughts. But he couldn't shake the mental fog.

Freddie lay stretched out on the bunk next door. He looked like he'd lost twenty pounds.

"Freddie?"

Freddie didn't answer.

"Freddie!" Nowak said, again. Louder.

"Yeah." He sounded despondent.

"What's the matter? Are you okay?" Nowak asked.

"Yeah."

"When did you get out?"

"A couple of hours ago."

"I need a shower and a shave." Nowak rubbed his beard. "When's the next shower brigade?"

"Five weeks. The water's turned off. We have to wait until it rains."

"Jesus." As soon as he got home, he was going to soak in the tub for hours. Maybe a whole day.

A letter and a package from home sat on the shelf beside his bunk. A strong sense of nostalgia struck him. What he wouldn't give to see his family. He opened the envelope and removed the card. Along the top were the words: *Congratulations on Your 21st Birthday*. A birthday he spent in the cooler. His fingers traced the picture of a luxurious living room with a blue-and-white-striped couch, thick carpet, and elegant curtains. A black puppy lay curled up on the sofa. Cherry blossoms and a flower garden peeked through the large picture window.

Inside the parcel, he found forty packages of Sweet Caporals—one thousand cigarettes. He kissed the box. *Thank you*. Cigarettes served as currency in camp.

The wrapped package had sat on his shelf for weeks and no one had touched it. There hadn't been any problems since Snowshoe had caught a little bastard from the neighboring hut stealing cigarettes and sentenced him to a swim in the cesspool under the *shizen haus*.

"Did you get any mail?" Nowak asked Freddie.

"No." His friend's eyes seemed to look right past him.

"Let's go for a walk," Nowak urged.

"No point in getting up."

"What are you talking about? We're finally out of the damn cooler. We've got things to do."

"I'm knackered." Freddie rolled over on his side.

"Okay, you rest."

Nowak craved fresh air and human interaction. Holding his box of cigarettes under his arm, he climbed down off his bunk and headed outside to join a group of airmen gathered around the trading table. He examined the items set out for sale on a worn army blanket: used razor blades, a can of coffee, a few German *Reichsmarks*, mismatched socks, and a couple of watches.

He picked up a wristwatch with chronographic features and a black leather strap. A watch would be useful if he needed to bribe a guard.

"How much?" he asked.

"Two hundred," said the seller.

"Sold."

He watched Ukraine Joe enter the small, for guards only, outhouse. He left the door open. Nowak inched closer, made sure no one was watching, kicked the door shut, and latched it. Not exactly the payback he'd envisioned over the last few months, but it gave him a slight sense of satisfaction. It would do, for now.

He heard Joe pounding on the door as he walked away.

"Let me out!" Joe screamed.

On his way back to his hut, he thought about how Hope navigated the underground sewers right under the noses of the Krauts. He stopped and scanned the grounds, the barracks, the machine gun towers, the barbed wire surrounding him.

An idea dawned on him. Why didn't he think of it sooner? When you can't go over, you go under.

CHAPTER TWENTY-SEVEN

Roman Catholic Cathedral
Warsaw, Poland

Angels hovered on the painted ceiling. Sunlight streamed through a stained-glass window riddled with bullet holes. The statue of the Virgin Mary lay shattered on the floor. Slashed remnants of *The Last Supper* leaned against the Gothic altar.

An SS officer carrying an MP 40 machine gun and wearing a peaked cap with a *Totenkopf*, Death's Head insignia, counted the parishioners being forced out the door. One hundred Polish civilians were being selected at random in reprisal for the killing of a senior officer during the ghetto uprising. Men, women, and children were plucked out of their house of worship to be lined up and murdered.

Anna sat on a wooden pew between Papa and Michal. Zophia was on the other side of her brother, gripping his hand. Dr. Jeska was next to her. Mrs. Jeska hadn't attended mass. Since Ewa's kidnapping, she rarely left the house.

One by one, the pews in front of them emptied.

"Eighty-two, eighty-three, eighty-four."

Just before Mass, her family delivered submachine gun components to the church cellar for assembly and testing in the concrete-lined tunnel that served as an underground shooting range. Maybe she could crawl to the back of the church and hide under a pew. Then go get a gun.

She studied the exits. All were guarded by armed members of the SS. It would be impossible to get past them.

"Eighty-five, eighty-six, eighty-seven."

She watched a family friend carry his toddler down the blood red carpet. A teacher from the Underground school dipped her fingers into a basin of holy water on the way to her death. A neighbor wiped away her granddaughter's tears with an embroidered handkerchief.

"Eighty-eight, eighty-nine, ninety."

Papa moved into the aisle as the pew in front of them emptied. Letting go of Zophia's hand, Michal stood. She grabbed the fringe on his jacket to hold him back but he pulled away and pushed ahead of Anna.

It was her turn. She didn't want to stand up. Didn't want to move into the aisle. But she couldn't imagine life without her family. Holding the crucifix of her Holy Rosary in her hand with the beads draped over her fingers, she thought of the pledge of self-sacrifice she made during her Oath of Allegiance to the Home Army and to her country.

She looked up and asked the angels to grant her strength as she edged her way out of the pew. Dr. Jeska shuffled in front of her. Zophia was right behind.

Moving up the aisle, Anna thought of Nowak and the lines from a poem about the freedom of flight he had slipped under her pillow. With her eyes focused on the floor, she silently repeated the lines and imagined soaring across the sky with him to escape the terror facing her on earth.

> *Oh! I have slipped the surly bonds of Earth*
> *And danced the skies on laughter-silvered wings;*
> *Sunward I've climbed, and joined the tumbling mirth*
> *Of sun-split clouds . . .*

A voice in the back of the church recited a Psalm:

> *The Lord is my shepherd; I shall not want.*
> *He maketh me to lie down in green pastures;*
> *He leadeth me beside the still waters.*

"Ninety-one, ninety-two, ninety-three."

The line moved forward. Papa recited the words of the Psalm. So did Michal and Dr. Jeska.

> *Yea, though I walk through the valley of the*
> *shadow of death, I will fear no evil: for thou*
> *art with me; thy rod and thy staff they comfort me.*

"Ninety-four, ninety-five, ninety-six."

The line slowed. She begged God to spare them. And the Blessed Virgin Mary, too. Her stomach churned.

More voices joined in.

> *Thou preparest a table before me in the presence*
> *of mine enemies; thou anointest my head with oil;*
> *my cup runneth over.*

"Ninety-seven, ninety-eight."

The voices of the parishioners grew louder. Anna held her breath.

> *Surely goodness and mercy shall follow me all the*
> *days of my life: and I shall dwell in the house of the*
> *Lord forever.*

"Ninety-nine, one hundred."

The line stopped. The SS officer rotated on the iron heel of his jackboot and followed the last parishioner out of the church.

Silence.

Then she heard it. Thudding machine-gun fire mixed with the screams of the dead and dying. She closed her eyes, held her fingers in her ears, and made a humming noise to block out the horrific sounds.

CHAPTER TWENTY-EIGHT

RAF Compound
Stalag IVB, Germany

One dreary morning in late October, Nowak hammered a nail in the center of a piece of wood that he'd removed from the ceiling above his bunk. Attaching a string to the nail, he tied a second sharpened nail to the other end of the string. Then he made a circle on the wood by rotating the nail around and around, each turn carving a deeper and deeper groove until he broke through.

Now he had a wheel. Once he had four wheels, he planned to build a small wagon to carry dirt along a miniature railway of wooden strips, soon to be constructed.

Freddie shuffled up. His head hung low, shoulders bent. "What are you working on?"

Nowak smiled slyly. "Nothing." It was safer for Freddie not to know about the tunnel they had started digging a few weeks back. His friend was simply not ready for another stint in solitary if they were caught.

"You're up to something."

"You're seeing things."

Freddie shrugged and settled down for a nap, which was just about the only thing he did anymore. Small talk had ceased. Living in such close proximity forced them to cherish what little silence they had.

Ray, Syd and a Lance Corporal from the British Army nicknamed Pokerface, convinced the commandant to build a six hundred seat theatre. Allowing prisoners to create costumes, writing, producing, and performing the plays would combat boredom. They didn't mention that building the Empire Theatre gave the newly formed escape committee a cover to set up shop without creating suspicion. From now on, all escape attempts had to go through the committee and Snowshoe was in charge.

Sure, they made costumes and props for the theatre, but they also made civvies and German military uniforms to prepare for their next break. The stage provided the perfect front for the hidden entrance shaft to the tunnel they were building underneath.

A secret radio receiver—started with bits and pieces scrounged on work parties, traded for cigarettes, and stolen from the administration office—was finally operational thanks to parts supplied by the Krauts to build a lighting system for the theatre. The airmen dismantled the radio and transferred it between huts daily. Each evening, one airman acted as editor and recorded the nightly BBC broadcast, then briefed runners who reported the news to the men in their huts.

Recent highlights included news that Italy had signed an Armistice Agreement with the Allies back in September. Thousands of Italian soldiers who refused to continue the war with the Germans were expected in camp any day. And the Big Three—Roosevelt, Churchill, and Stalin—planned to meet at Tehran to discuss strategies.

Nowak checked the time on the wall clock. Fritz would do his morning rounds soon, and the escape committee needed something from him.

Nowak quit working. "Hey Ray," he said. "It's time to go for that walk."

"Don't have a conniption. We've got a few minutes yet." Ray whittled a scrap of wood into a miniature sailing vessel. On the shelf beside him, he displayed his collection of boats with sails made from scraps of paper, each new creation more detailed and elaborate than the next. One for each of his children, with their names painted on the back: *Margaret's Dream* for his daughter and *Donny's Destiny* for his son.

"How did the audition go?" Nowak asked.

"Pokerface gave me a part in our first show. It's called *LET'S RAE'S A LAUGH* after the producer," Ray said.

"Who're you going to be?"

"Sugar."

Nowak burst out laughing.

"It's not that funny." Ray looked hurt. "I need you to do something for me before dress rehearsal."

"What's that?"

"Pluck my eyebrows."

Nowak tried not to laugh again.

Ray put down his knife and the piece of wood. He found a pair of tweezers in his kitbag and handed them to Nowak.

"Sit over here by the light. I'll give it a try," Nowak said.

Ray moved to the chair by the window and sat down. He tilted his head back. Nowak plucked Ray's bushy brows, randomly pulling out hairs here and there.

"I hear Snowshoe put you in charge of the tunnel." Ray squeezed his eyes shut and scrunched his nose.

"I used to work in the coal mines," Nowak said. "We need to get the entrance shaft deep enough so we can work on it over the winter. Got to be at least thirty feet. We've got another ten feet to go."

"Why so deep?"

"The bastards set up listening stations. Sunken anti-tunnelling microphones pick up the echoes underground." He handed Ray a cracked mirror.

"They're still too thick. Syd says to make finely styled arches to highlight my deep brown eyes."

"You've got to be kidding."

"Just shut up and get it over with," Ray said.

Nowak removed a few more hairs over Ray's right eye, then plucked a hair in Ray's head.

"What the hell?"

Nowak stood back and admired his work. "That'll have to do. We've got to head Fritz off." His anxiety over meeting Fritz made it hard to concentrate.

Ray held up the mirror to look.

"Now they're crooked," he said.

"Are not."

"Are too."

Nowak put on his greatcoat and hustled outside to where Fritz performed his rounds. The escape committee needed to look at his identity papers because a rumor circulated that German work passes had changed. They were more important than Ray's bloody eyebrows.

"Fritz, wait up," Nowak called. Catching up, he noticed how cold and worn out the old guard seemed. He had lost weight, his nose was red, his eyes swollen. As usual, Fritz kept his identity papers stuffed in the cuff on the sleeve of his coat. Good. That was exactly what they needed.

Ray moved in from the other direction, bumped into Fritz and slipped the identity papers out of the old guard's cuff. Apologizing, he continued on.

Nowak kept walking the circuit. The wind howled and it started to snow.

"Do you want some coffee?" Nowak rolled up his collar and blew into his hands to warm them. "I might be able to find you some. Your *frau* really likes coffee. Doesn't she?"

"*Ja,*" Fritz said.

"What's your wife's name?" Nowak asked, trying to be friendly.

"Ilse."

"You wouldn't know where I could find a camera, would you?"

"A camera? I can't bring you a camera. They'll send me to the Eastern Front if they catch me."

"Come on, Fritz. They won't find out. Besides, I might get a chocolate bar to go with that coffee. Does Ilse like chocolate?"

"*Schokolade?*"

"And some cigarettes." Nowak blew into his hands again and rubbed them together. The two of them kept walking. Hurry up, Ray. It's freezing out here. All the committee needed to do was check Fritz's papers against the ones they already had to see if any modifications were needed.

Fritz stopped. He rolled down his cuff. Patted his pockets.

"What's the matter?" Nowak asked.

"My papers."

"What about them?"

"Where are they?" Fritz looked at him suspiciously.

Nowak shrugged.

"Give me back my papers." He gripped the rifle slung over his shoulder.

Nowak raised his hands. "Honest, I don't have them."

Ray ran up. "Hey, Fritz." He waved the pass in the air and acted like he was brushing snow off it. "Look what I found. Better be more careful."

Fritz grabbed his pass and shoved it back in the cuff of his sleeve.

Nowak's shoulders relaxed. That was close. Before parting, he winked at the guard and said, "Don't forget to get some film for that camera." As he walked away, he thought he heard Fritz sigh.

He was sure Fritz knew what they were doing, and he felt a slight tinge of guilt. He had started to like the old man and didn't want any harm to come to him. Feeling unsettled, he told himself: A Kraut is a Kraut, and war is war, so it can't be helped. If the old man ended up on the Eastern Front, it wasn't his problem. He only cared about one thing—getting back to base.

CHAPTER TWENTY-NINE

Nowak stood in front of a mash of bread, raisins, jam, and water simmering in a can on top of the stove at the theatre while he tinkered with his homemade still—an old trombone and some rubber tubing that collected the steam from the fermented mixture and ran it through cold water.

"How're ya coming over there? I thought you were goin' learn to play that instrument, not make hooch." Ray looked up from the law book he was studying.

"It's working," Nowak said as he watched alcohol drip into a sauerkraut bucket. "One drink of this ought to get Freddie out of bed." He chuckled. "Cure what's ailing him. He hasn't been himself since his visit to the cooler."

"Did he get a letter from Izzie yet?" Ray asked.

"No. It's really got him worried."

"I'd be worried, too."

"I keep telling him it's just the lousy mail service."

"My mail is gettin' through. Maybe she's found someone else?"

"I sure as hell hope not," Nowak said.

"Better keep an eye on him. That barbed wire disease is pretty hard to shake once it sets in. Stayin' busy is the only way I keep my sanity. I asked him to audition for the theatre. He says he's not interested."

"He'll liven up when we get the tunnel finished, and he knows he's going home," Nowak said.

Nowak checked his watch. It was almost time for his shift in the tunnel. He scooped some hooch into a klim and hustled over to his hut, where he found Freddie sitting on his bunk, staring at the floor.

"Want a drink?" Nowak offered.

Freddie didn't answer.

"C'mon," Nowak coaxed. "Have a drink."

Freddie reached for the klim and took a sip. He coughed. "Bloody hell."

"Come to the theatre for a bit."

"Maybe later," Freddie said, his eyes still focused on the floor.

"I know it's tough, Freddie. But you've got to snap out of it. We're going to get out of here. The RAF and the Americans are bombing Berlin."

Freddie lay down and covered his eyes with his arm. "Leave me alone."

Nowak knew what Freddie was going through because he was barely holding on himself. He thought about the days back in solitary, when he didn't think he'd survive one more minute and wondered whether to tell Freddie about it, just to show he understood. But telling Freddie might make matters worse. It wouldn't do anybody any good if they both wallowed in their misery.

It was up to him now to find a way out and get Freddie back to Izzie and his baby. He couldn't let his emotions get the best of him or they'd never get back to England. He had to be strong for his friend. They'd come this far together, and they were damn well going to finish together.

Nowak rushed back to the theatre for his shift in the tunnel. He shoved a sharpened spoon in his pocket, grabbed a klim, and crawled under the stage. Squeezing through the narrow entrance shaft, he climbed thirty feet down a flimsy wooden ladder to access the twenty feet of tunnel they'd burrowed this past month.

Hunched on his knees in the dim light of a burning fat lamp, he used the spoon to loosen the dirt and his klim to scoop it up, dumping one tin at a time into a miniature wagon. Gritting his teeth, he labored on, trying to ignore the feeling of being trapped, of the walls closing in—just as they had when he was in solitary. Despite the cold and damp, he wiped sweat off his forehead. With his throat tight and his heart racing, he gripped his klim with both hands to keep them from shaking.

All he wanted to do was crawl up the ladder and scream for help—curfew and guards be damned. But the tunnel was his idea. His men depended on him. He couldn't weaken now. He hoped for a successful tunnel break, right under the noses of the bloody Krauts, by mid-summer. It was risky, with the odds stacked against him, but what was a man without hope?

Closing his eyes to focus on his breathing, he thought about Hope and the way she traveled through the underground sewers. He'd been awed by her determination and courage. She did it to help others, not herself. There was other work she could have done for the Home Army instead of crawling through human waste to rescue children. What a world they lived in.

If she could do it, so could he.

Slowly, he managed to bring his breathing under control and his heart returned to a steady rhythm. Picking up his spoon, he went back to work.

CHAPTER THIRTY

Mother Superior bolted the door to her office after Anna entered. Aaron stood waiting, dressed in a winter coat and boots. Anna bent to tuck a lock of his dark hair into the bandage wrapped around his head and pulled the woolen hat she'd knitted using multi-colored scraps of wool down over his ears.

"There you go," she said, buttoning his coat. "Don't be afraid. I'll travel with you."

"Why are you taking me away again?" Aaron asked.

"So you can live with a nice family," she reassured the child. "You'll have a mother and a father soon."

"I already have a family. I want my parents. Not someone else's. Why won't you take me home? Why don't they want me anymore?"

Anna didn't answer the barrage of questions. She didn't want to tell the boy he was the only member of his family to escape the ghetto. His parents were both dead. "What's your name?" she asked to make sure he remembered his assumed Christian identity.

"Andrzej."

"Andrzej who?"

"Andrzej Bosko."

"Very good," Anna said.

The nun slipped her hand inside the sleeve of her black habit and pulled out train tickets. She handed them to Anna.

Taking Aaron by the hand, Anna left the convent and walked through a snow-crusted backstreet between buildings with terra-cotta roofs. His tight grip told her he was scared. She saw the *Kotwica* painted in white on a wall and thought of Johnnie Nowak. Whenever she got scared or lonely, she'd recite the lines of the poem he'd written to her over and over in her head, promising herself that someday she'd learn the rest of it. Sometimes she even imagined Nowak reciting it to her. Some days she thought of little else.

They headed toward the railway station and climbed a narrow stone stairway to reach Old Town Market Square. As soon as she delivered Aaron to his new family, she had to rush home to prepare the *Wigilia* meal. To celebrate Christmas Eve, she, Papa, and Michal would sit around the table, say a prayer, and share the *opłatek* bread as a sign of love, peace, and reconciliation.

According to tradition, unless even numbers of people were seated at the table for *Wigilia,* someone would die in the New Year. Michal had planned to include his girlfriend, Zophia, and make it an even four people, but she had disappeared while out delivering copies of the *Biuletyn Informacyjny* to a butcher shop. The owner distributed the Underground newspapers to members of the Home Army by hiding copies inside packages of wrapped meat. Michal blamed himself because he had printed the copies at the Underground press.

Anna hadn't seen Michal cry since Mama died. He'd locked himself in Papa's room and wouldn't come out for days, so she'd left food for him in front of the door. To help make him feel better and to keep the numbers even, she'd invited his friend Pawel from the border patrol to join them.

Anna slowed her pace as they passed through Market Square. An SS officer and a group of German soldiers stood in front of the arched doorway of a turquoise burgher house.

"Let's play a game," she said. "If someone stops us and asks questions, let's pretend I'm your older sister."

Innocent eyes wide, Aaron nodded.

"It'll be fun. Let me do all the talking."

Veering to the left to avoid the SS, she scanned the people milling among the market stalls to find her contact, Babcia, the vegetable vendor who provided safety for children by covering them with potato sacks, hiding them under her table or inside pickle barrels.

No sign of the woman.

"Where are we going?" Aaron asked.

"To the market."

"Why? I thought we were going for a train ride. I want to go for a train ride." He tried to pull her in the other direction.

"Shhh." She tugged his hand. Her eyes darted back and forth.

He attempted to wriggle free.

She tightened her grip.

"I see my grandfather," Aaron said.

"No, you don't."

"Yes, I do," insisted the boy. He pointed to a gentleman with his back to them, using a cane to walk toward the SS officer.

"Andrzej. Be quiet. That's not your grandfather."

"*Zayde*," he shouted.

"Stop it," she said, afraid to shout and draw attention to them. Her throat felt dry. Her breathing grew rapid. Each desperate breath constricting her throat. "You'll get us killed if you don't stop."

Aaron wrenched his hand free of Anna's grasp and ran to the man shouting in Yiddish. His shrill voice cut through the cold air. "*Zayde. Zayde.*"

A flock of pigeons on the square flapped their wings and scattered. The old man turned around.

Aaron slid to a stop when he realized it wasn't his grandfather.

The SS officer pulled his Luger out of his black holster with *Totenkopf* markings and pointed the pistol at the boy. Little Aaron raised his arms in the air. The officer tore the hat and the bandages from his head, exposing his dark brown hair, then ordered his men to check for circumcision.

The aim of the Luger shifted to Anna. Cold gray eyes locked on hers. She took a step back.

"*Jude*," hollered a voice.

"Arrest her," the officer ordered.

Anna turned to run. Soldiers leveled their rifles. One stepped forward to grab her. She kicked him in the shin. A red armband with a black swastika pressed hard against her face. She pounded his arm with her fists. He dragged her to the Black Maria prisoner van, opened the door, and tossed her inside.

She landed face first on the floor. Her skirt bunched up to her thighs, cold steel chilled her legs. The inside of the vehicle smelled like urine. And sweat. And fear.

The door slammed shut. With blacked-out windows, she crawled in the darkness to the side of the van by feeling her way with her hands. The sound of a single gunshot reverberated. Lowering her face into her palms, she sobbed. She had failed another child. Dear sweet Aaron.

Visions of her family sitting at the dinner table waiting for her arrival settled in her mind. Bits of hay scattered on the table as a reminder that Christ was born in a manger. The house decorated with boughs of evergreens.

Her chair sat empty. Now there would only be three. Papa, Michal, and their friend Pawel. An odd number.

Someone in the family would die in the New Year. Concealing Jews was a crime punishable by death. If the SS figured out who she was and what she had been doing, they would murder Papa and Michal. They called it *Sippenhaft*. Family liability.

Wondering if she could endure torture, she ran her finger over the cyanide capsule sewn into the hem of her skirt. As a member of the Home Army, she would swallow the poison before betraying anyone.

1944

CHAPTER THIRTY-ONE

Railway Station
Fürstenberg, Germany

Anna peered out the window, her fingers gripping cold iron bars as brakes screeched and the train rolled to a stop. The sign at the station read: *Fürstenberg*. Anna and the other women and girls on board descended the steps to where female guards wearing warm coats and field-gray uniforms waited with leashed German shepherds at their sides.

"Ranks of five, *Untermenschen*," a guard screamed as she cracked a whip.

The group marched through the empty streets of the village. Not a soul could be seen except for a young woman peeking through the window of a small white cottage. When her eyes met Anna's, the woman looked away and closed the shutters.

They continued along a path beside a frozen lake. Dogs barked. Whips cracked. Snow crunched under Anna's feet. The air was so cold her breath billowed in front of her. A four-meter-high brick wall topped with rows of barbed wire and a high-voltage electric fence came into sight: Ravensbrück Concentration Camp for women.

Inside the gates, they were led to a humid bathhouse where they were forced to strip and shower under the watchful eyes of guards. Anna's clothes were searched and her rosary thrown on to a pile of confiscated possessions strewn on the floor: spectacles, jewelry, false teeth, money and shoes. Her body shook and her lips quivered as she sat naked on a wooden stool with her arms wrapped in front of her chest. A prisoner with deep crow's feet and tired eyes grabbed her braid, yanked her head back, and hacked off her hair. Then she shaved Anna's head and collected her blonde locks.

An attractive guard with blonde ringlets and red lipstick motioned her closer. She stood pencil straight in a tailored uniform with a jacket and skirt, and jackboots shined to perfection.

Anna approached hesitantly, stifled by the woman's pungent perfume.

"Spread your legs." The guard clutched a straight razor in her hand.

Anna closed her eyes and willed her legs to stop shaking while the woman shaved her pubic hair. A sudden sharp pain made her cry out. She opened her eyes and pressed her hand against the bleeding cut on her thigh.

The guard looked at her with a mocking smile, her teeth smudged with blood red lipstick. Turning away, she called out, "Next."

Anna moved into the adjoining room where she was issued a blue-gray striped dress, a kerchief, and wooden clogs. The red triangle on her upper left sleeve categorized her as a political prisoner, the black letter P in the center identified her as Polish.

Once dressed, she was photographed and issued a registration number. One by one, the women were told to lift their skirts above their hips and run in front of two doctors—a man and a woman—both dressed in white lab coats. The well-coiffed female with dark hair tucked behind her ears jotted down notes on a clipboard. Beside her, the man regarded them emotionlessly, his eyes magnified by his thick-lensed tortoise-shell glasses.

A middle-aged woman with a yellow triangle had trouble running because of her swollen ankles. The doctors selected her for recovery and transport to *Mittwerda*.

"What does that word mean?" Anna asked the woman standing behind her.

"SS code for gas chamber," the woman answered. "She's a Jew. She won't get farther than the Green Mina."

"The what?"

"The gas van parked out back. Their mobile gas chamber."

When it was Anna's turn, she lifted her skirt and ran across the room as fast as she could. The male doctor motioned for her to keep her skirt up. He circled, stopped, bent forward, then ran his hand up and down her leg, squeezing the muscle on her calf like he was inspecting livestock. Straightening up, he swept his hand slowly over her breasts.

Anna's stomach knotted and her cheeks burned. She smelled his putrid breath.

"Over there." He motioned to where several other women with red triangles and the letter P stood. "Report to the *Revier* tomorrow," he told the group.

A guard hollered and cracked her whip, ordering them to follow her to their assigned compound.

The *Nacht und Nebel* Block.

*

Anna soon learned that the Block of Night and Fog was a secret compound for political prisoners not slated for immediate execution, and so-called because the prisoners simply vanished into the night and fog, never to be heard from again. The barracks, built for two hundred and fifty women, housed over one thousand. Three women, and sometimes four, slept in each tier of the three-tier bunks.

Anna cowered in a corner as the prisoner who had cut off her braid and shaved her head approached her. "My name is Agata. Don't be afraid," she whispered in Polish, looking around to make sure no one was listening before extending a shaking hand to return the rosary. "Keep it hidden or they'll set the dogs on both of us."

"Oh, thank you. Thank you." Anna clutched the beads. She eyed the woman's red triangle, but she wasn't sure she could trust her.

"Did they tell you to go to the *Revier*?" Agata asked.

Anna nodded.

"You're young and pretty, so you'll be raped on the operating table to assess your suitability as a prostitute. We're the main supplier of women for the SS brothels. If you're not chosen as a prostitute, you'll be used as a *Kaninchen,* a rabbit in their medical experiments. They're looking for young Polish women in good health to test new sulfa drugs on their legs."

Anna couldn't fully grasp what she was hearing. It couldn't be. It just couldn't.

The woman leaned closer. "Chances are you won't survive. Do you understand?"

Anna nodded. Her mind swirled in fear and confusion.

"Listen to me." Agata lowered her voice even more. "As soon as morning roll call is over, we're sending a large group to the Siemens factory. I work in the administration office with access to the camp paperwork. I'm helping another young Polish woman transfer out. She's been here about a month and she's pregnant. If she stays, they'll force her to have an abortion, or worse. I'll try to put you on the list too."

"What will I do at the factory?" Anna asked.

"Build rockets."

Anna threw her shoulders back and shook her head. "I won't do that. I refuse to help the Nazi war effort," she said, remembering how hard the Home Army worked to obstruct the production of V-bombs.

"You don't have a choice."

"Why are you helping me?"

"You remind me of my daughter. She didn't listen either." Agata's eyes clouded over.

"Where is she?" Anna asked.

"*Uckermark*. A detention camp for young girls considered difficult," she said and walked away.

Sick to her stomach, Anna lay curled up on the floor without a blanket. She held her rosary to her chest. If she ever needed her mother, it was now. Mama always knew how to comfort her. She closed her eyes and imagined her mother's warm embrace and soothing voice speaking to her until she dozed off.

At four a.m., a wailing siren awakened her. The block senior yelled at her to get up. Stiff and cold from sleeping on the floor, she headed to the latrine, where hundreds of women already stood in line for toilets with no doors.

By five a.m., Anna stood shivering on the *Appelplatz* in ankle-deep snow, waiting for roll call wearing only the cotton dress issued on arrival. Women huddled in ranks of five, attempting to keep warm. A fat man with wire-rimmed glasses rode a bicycle around and around the parade square, flailing a whip, and picking out women for various work details.

A sudden hush fell over the group.

"What's going on?" Anna asked Agata, who was standing beside her.

"Shhh. Wardress Ursula Fleischer is coming. They call her the Beautiful Beast," she whispered.

The wardress marched past, wearing a warm cape and gloves, with a truncheon in one hand and a black German shepherd on a leash in the other. A cloud of heavy perfume followed her.

Anna shuddered. It was the woman who had sliced her thigh the day before.

The wardress reached the end of Parade Square and marched back. Anna's eyes dropped to the ground as she passed by. At the other end, the wardress turned and started again.

"What's she doing?" Anna asked.

"Be quiet," Agata whispered. "Don't interrupt her."

When the wardress stepped out of earshot, Agata explained. "She counts her steps. She does it four times. Always four times. It seems to calm her. She's not as vicious when she does it. If she loses count, she starts again. Don't let her looks fool you. Last week, she kicked a Jewish woman to death during roll call."

"What for?" Anna asked.

"She had a curl in her hair," Agata said. "Stay clear of her and that dog. It's trained to kill."

Anna didn't need to hear anymore. She stood in utter silence. When roll call was over, Agata motioned toward a large group of prisoners, all dressed in blue-gray striped uniforms and wooden clogs, gathered nearby. "See the women over there? They're headed for the Siemens factory. It's the safest place for you. Go quickly."

Scared to go and scared to stay, Anna thought about the hands of the horrid doctor touching her body and considered what Agata had just told her about Wardress Fleischer. It only took her a few seconds to join the group moving toward the gate. She stepped into line beside a woman with a red triangle.

"Anna, is that you?" she asked.

"Zophia?" Anna hardly recognized the woman who had stolen her brother's heart, now gaunt, with a shaven head. She threw her arms around her friend. "I'm so happy to see you. I've been so worried since you disappeared."

CHAPTER THIRTY-TWO

Empire Theatre
Stalag IVB, Germany

Nowak supervised the production of fake documents and maps for the escape committee. Fritz came through with a camera and film, an old black box Carl Zeiss Jena model with a side-winding knob that provided photographs for identity papers. A former photographer developed the film under a blanket using chemicals stolen out of the administration office.

Radaski had snitched a typewriter off a desk at a clothing factory while he was out on a work party. He hid it in a haystack and later dismantled it, then smuggled the parts into camp by distributing them between the men. After that, he slipped them to Nowak and his committee members during soccer games out in the exercise compound.

As soon as they put the typewriter back together, they could produce the Gothic script used on identity cards, travel permits, and work passes. Ray had carved a Nazi Eagle stamp out of the rubber on the heel of a flying boot to seal the documents. Now all they needed was a forger good enough to pull off the signatures of German officials.

"Where's Syd? I haven't seen him around," Nowak asked Ray.

"The commandant sent him to the concentration camp at Jacobsthal. He had to dispose of corpses by throwing them into mass graves and coverin' them with lime."

"Why?"

"He's Jewish."

"Doesn't look like a Jew."

"His father was Jewish," Ray said, not looking up from his book. "Syd should be here any minute now. I talked the commandant into bringin' him back. Syd's a Jew, but he's a prisoner of war. That means he's protected. I read up on it."

"I've got a message for him from Radaski. It has to do with his mother," Nowak said. "You're not gonna believe this. She's in Mülhberg."

"Well, I'll be damned." Ray closed his law book.

"She made contact with the work party that marches through town every morning. She blends in dressed like a man. Gives them food to smuggle back into camp. Next time we're in the Army compound, there's food there for us."

Ray's eyes widened in disbelief. "Are you making this up?"

Nowak shook his head. "And there's a big problem. She's a British woman wanted by the Gestapo, posing as a man, and living on her own in a German town. Sooner or later townspeople will get suspicious and someone will turn her in. She needs a place to hide." Nowak hesitated. "She wants into the RAF compound."

"That's impossible."

"When you think about it, what better place is there for her to hide? They'll never be looking for a woman in here."

Syd limped into the theatre carrying a costume over his arm. The Gestapo had subjected him to interrogation under torture when he was first taken in as a prisoner of war. They shoved a pair of scissors under his toenails to wedge them up and pulled them out with pliers. His feet still hadn't healed.

"My ears are burning," Syd said. "If I didn't know better, I'd think you were talking about me." He had curly, light brown, almost blond hair, green eyes, and a broad, flat nose.

"We are and wait till you hear why." Nowak told Syd all about his mother.

"What the hell is she doing in Mülhberg?" Syd looked shocked at hearing the news. "I lived with her and her second husband in Germany for a few years. He's a high-ranking *Luftwaffe* officer. I had to learn German to communicate with him. When the war started, they sent me back to Britain to live with my grandparents."

"She's married to a Kraut?" Nowak asked.

Syd nodded. "Last I heard, the Gestapo arrested her for smuggling food into an Austrian prisoner-of-war camp. If the Gestapo are after her again, her husband must have helped her flee Austria."

"We'll have to wait for an opportunity to make a switch. There's a long list of us wanting out. Not many wanting in," Nowak said.

"I don't know why she wants in. If I ever get out of this place, I'm going to spend the rest of my days making sure every last Nazi motherfucker pays for his crimes," Syd said.

"Sounds good to me," Nowak said. "How do you plan to do that?"

"Haven't figured that out yet."

"I'm thinkin' the Allies can prosecute the Nazis for war crimes. It's a matter of International Law," Ray explained. "As far as I can tell, the Hague and Geneva Conventions set out the laws and customs of war. Any violations are considered criminal. The Nazis are guilty of a whole slew of crimes. Just look at their concentration camps. And their extermination squads. They can't murder civilians like that and get away with it."

"Well, what do you know? All that studying is paying off," Nowak said. "We have our very own legal counsel right here in camp."

Syd held the dress he was making out of a bed sheet for Ray to wear in his role as Sugar in the upcoming theatre production. "I soaked blue and yellow paper in water and dabbed it onto the fabric to make the pattern. Put it on. See if it fits." A tailor by trade, Syd knew what he was doing.

"This I've got to see." Nowak poured some hooch into three klims and parked himself in a chair.

Ray changed into the dress. Syd made a few alterations around the waist and shortened the length. When he finished, Ray draped a white silk aviator scarf over his shoulders like a shawl and sashayed across the room. He sat with his legs crossed and swung his foot, clad with a boot, back and forth. At the same time, he batted his eyelids and tilted his head to rest on his hand, lifting his pinkie finger in the air.

Nowak whistled. This was going to be some show.

"By the way, I have more news," Nowak said. "We're finally rid of ugly Ukraine Joe. They shipped him out to active combat."

"Now that's a cause to celebrate." Syd knocked back his drink.

"Goon up," yelled the lookout.

Ray stared out the window. "Here comes Fritz. Better sound the warning signal."

"What's he doing here? It's his day off." Nowak jumped up and yanked a rope attached to a can of pebbles hanging from the ceiling in the tunnel, signaling to the airman below that a guard was approaching and all work had to come to a standstill. Blankets lined the underground walls to muffle the sound, but they couldn't risk letting a guard hear any noise under-neath. "Fritz isn't really such a bad guy. It's that crazy son of his who fills his head with Nazi propaganda."

"You're sayin' something nice about a German?" Ray picked up his mug.

"Don't get used to it." Nowak sat back down and took a sip of brew. "The poor bugger was a POW in World War I. He was in the bag for a year."

Fritz wandered into the building, looking downcast.

"Jesus, Fritz. What's the matter?" Nowak stood up. "Have a seat."

Fritz dragged himself over and slouched into the chair. With-out saying a word, he slipped the steel helmet off his head and dropped it on the floor.

"My son was killed." Fritz rubbed his bloodshot, glassy eyes.

"How?" Nowak filled a mug with hooch and handed it over.

Fritz reached for the klim. "He was going to Fürstenberg to visit his wife and daughter. The train was hit by enemy aircraft."

"I'm sorry, Fritz. I really am." Nowak felt bad for the poor old man. Fritz wasn't a Nazi. Never was. Never would be. He was a victim of circumstance just like the rest of them. That SS son of his was a different story. Nowak couldn't help but feel a little pleased the Nazi was dead.

Resting one hand on Fritz's shoulder, Nowak raised his mug with the other. "To your son."

Syd tapped Ray's klim, raised his mug and whispered, "I'll drink to that. Makes one less Nazi this world has to contend with."

CHAPTER THIRTY-THREE

Siemenslager
Satellite Camp
Ravensbrück Concentration Camp, Germany

Every morning, right after roll call on the *Appelplatz*, Anna and Zophia and several hundred other women marched up a steep hill to the *Siemenslager*, slipping and sliding in their wooden clogs. Fifteen noisy work halls were surrounded by an electrified fence where they made electrical components for V1 and V2 rockets. At noon, the women marched back to the main camp for a rushed lunch of watery soup and then marched up again to complete their twelve-hour shifts.

Anna stood at her station, her fingers blistered from winding copper wire around a core to make coils. To her left, a conveyor belt hummed in her ear. Zophia usually worked beside her on the other side. But today, Zophia had recognized a Home Army member in the incoming transport of women and slipped away to hear any news. Women in camp came from thirty different countries, but Polish political prisoners made up the largest national group and resistance efforts remained strong.

She'd been gone a long time and Anna was having trouble meeting their daily quota. Guards rotated through the work halls ensuring the quotas were met. Every few days, one of the aeronautical engineers, an SS officer by the name of Klaus Von

Wolff, left his private office for inspections. Tall and statuesque, his blond hair was slicked back with hair tonic and clipped short on the sides.

When Zophia returned and slid back into position, her eyes were swollen. It looked like she'd been crying. She leaned in close and whispered to Anna. "Michal has fled Warsaw. He's in hiding."

"What about Papa?"

"They have no information on him."

"No information?" Anna's lower lip trembled. "But he's alive. You know he's alive?"

Zophia hesitated. She rested her hand on Anna's forearm. "I don't know."

"Why is Michal in hiding?"

"One of our members betrayed him."

"Who?"

"Mr. Baranek from the Sanitation Department."

Anna closed her eyes and pictured her brother hunched over the grand piano with his hands in the air. Slamming his fingers down on the keys for the opening of Chopin's "Revolutionary Étude." A chord rang out like a gunshot. The rest of the piece chaotic. Dark. Tense. And passionate. Evoking a struggle and ending in ambiguity.

Holding an assembled component in her fingers, she loosened the connection and pulled out the rubber O-ring to sabotage it. She slid her hand up under her skirt to hide the piece of rubber inside her underwear.

By the time she caught a waft of the perfume, it was too late. She thought she'd left Wardress Ursula Fleischer back at the main camp, but she was wrong. To her horror, the wardress had entered the work hall with her leashed black German shepherd, Grief, and she stood watching her.

She struck Anna between the shoulder blades with her rubber truncheon. "Off to the punishment block," she ordered.

Anna stood, glancing back at Zophia with terror in her eyes, as the wardress forced her out of the Siemens compound. They marched down the half-mile path lined with budding poplar trees that led to the main camp. Dog at her side, the wardress held her head high and counted each step in a deep whisper—one, two, three, four—as her hobnailed boots scraped against the gravel.

The air thickened with the sickening smell of burned bodies as they entered the south gate and neared the crematorium where red flames and human smoke rose from stone chimneys, then marched through a narrow passageway with blood splattered walls known as the shooting alley, where executions took place by a bullet to the head. Just beyond, hundreds of Jewish women stood at attention on the *Appelplatz*.

"We'll be rid of those filthy Jews soon enough," Fleischer said. "They've been selected for S.B."

Was Anna supposed to respond or stay silent?

"Cat got your tongue?" Fleischer asked, poking her hard in the ribs with her truncheon.

"I don't know what S.B. means."

"*Sonderbehandlung*. Special treatment. They get to go to Auschwitz."

Anna broke into a cold sweat.

"Shooting them takes time, and it's so messy. Gassing is much more efficient. We're closing our Jewish block until we can build a gas chamber. There's just too many for our mobile units."

Anna's throat tightened as she pictured women gasping for air in the chambers. When they reached the *Appelplatz,* Fleischer said, "Stay here." She strode onto the square, head held high. Marching up and down the rows of Jewish women, she stopped in front of one. "I've been looking for you. Get back to work," she shouted as she yanked her out of the lineup.

Without explanation, she prodded Anna and they marched on to the stone building that housed the cell block. The sound of Fleischer's hobnails reverberated off the walls of the long corridor lined with locked doors. Anna was expecting to be thrown into a blacked-out solitary cell for Level 2 detention. It would mean up to forty-two days on bread and water, with full rations every four days, and she wasn't sure she could cope.

As they neared the end of the corridor, Fleischer stopped at Cell 75. She leaned down to pet Grief. "You be a good boy, now. Wait for Mummy out here. I won't be long." She reached into her pocket and fed the dog a piece of sausage.

Fleischer took a key out of her other pocket, unlocked the wooden door, and pushed Anna inside. She froze. A beating trestle—a low wooden table, indented in the middle with wooden sides, straps, and stirrups. Two whips hung from hooks on the wall, one plaited cellophane with metal tips and the other leather with tails.

Fleischer stepped into the cell and slammed the door shut, trapping Anna inside. "Take off your clothes."

Anna shook her head.

"I said, take off your clothes."

Anna removed her blue-gray striped dress and dropped it on the floor, careful not to expose her rosary sewn into the hem.

"Take it all off."

Anna stripped off her underwear. The rubber O-ring she'd hidden fell to the floor and rolled under the trestle.

"Tsk tsk." Fleischer shook her head in disapproval. "Pretty girls never learn."

At first, she reached for the whip with plaited cellophane but changed her mind and picked the leather one. Slipping her hand through the wrist band, she wrapped her fingers around the wooden handle.

Moving closer, she stroked Anna's cheek. Anna moved her face away in disgust. The Beast pressed the whip against Anna's chest, brushing over her skin and encircling her breasts. She ran it down Anna's body and stopped between her legs. Fleischer stuck her flushed face closer and parted her lips. Anna felt her breath. Saw smudged red lipstick on her teeth. Smelled heavy perfume.

"Do you think I'm beautiful?" Fleischer whispered.

Anna puckered her lips and gathered the saliva in her mouth. More than anything, she wanted to spit in the woman's face, but it would be the last thing she did before being beaten to death or executed. Her body would be burned in the ovens, her ashes poured into the lake.

If she wanted to survive, she needed to say something. She mustered her resolve and swallowed, forcing herself to speak. "Everyone thinks you're beautiful. They call you the Beautiful Beast." *But I think you're a Beast. An ugly Beast.*

The Beast took off her field cap with the embroidered eagle patch and ran her hand over her ringlets styled in the salon for guards only, staffed by prisoners. "I had to pull that Jew out of the lineup to Auschwitz. She's the one that does my hair."

Anna wondered how she could care so much about her hair when so many lives were at stake.

The Beast unbuttoned her tailored jacket, slipped it off, and placed it on the stool. "Get on the trestle," she ordered, rolling the sleeves of her blouse up to the elbows.

Anna promised herself she'd survive to one day get even. She lay on her stomach, her head and arms dangling over the edge as thick leather straps were secured to hold her down. Her body tensed and her fists clenched when the Beast ran her red, manicured nails down her back, gagging when a filthy rag was stuffed in her mouth.

"You're supposed to count the lashes out loud. I'll make it easier for you. I'll do the counting."

The whip cracked in the air four times. Then the flogging started.

"One. Two. Three. Four."

Excruciating pain sliced through her body with every strike. Anna tried to scream but couldn't. She struggled for air and tried to get off the table to fight back, but the straps held her down.

"You're worthless! *Untermensch*," the Beast shouted. "Five. Six. Seven. Eight."

Anna bit down hard on the rag. Sour sweat and heavy perfume smothered her. She clenched her fists tighter. Her back and buttocks burned so intensely she could no longer feel the individual lashes. But she could hear the count.

"Nine. Ten. Eleven. Twelve."

Anna forced her mind to another place by reciting the lines from the poem Nowak had written to her over and over in her mind. *Oh! I have slipped the surly bonds of Earth/And danced the skies on laughter-silvered wings . . .*

"Thirteen, Fourteen, Fifteen, Sixteen."

Sunward I've climbed, and joined the tumbling mirth/Of sun-split clouds . . .

"Seventeen, Eighteen, Nineteen, Twenty."

. . . and done a hundred things/You have not dreamed of— wheeled and soared and swung . . .

"Twenty-one. Twenty-two. Twenty-three. Twenty-four."

The flogging stopped. The Beast tore the rag out of Anna's mouth and unfastened the straps.

"Get dressed," she ordered, sweaty and breathless.

Anna tried to raise herself off the table, but darkness overwhelmed her. The last thing she remembered was the Beast's flushed face. Red lips. Smudged teeth.

CHAPTER THIRTY-FOUR

The news runner dragged a chair into the center of the hut, jumped on top, and reported: "On March twenty-fourth, seventy-six airmen escaped from Stalag Luft III near Sagan, East Germany, through a three-hundred-and-fifty-foot underground tunnel called Harry."

Instantly, cheers and whistles broke out. The runner shook his head and waved his arms for silence.

"Seventy-three out of the seventy-six officers in the mass escape were captured by the Gestapo. Fifty of those have been murdered on personal orders from Adolf Hitler. In the future, the articles of the Geneva Convention will be ignored. All prisoners caught escaping will now be shot."

After a stunned silence, expressions of shock, anger, and disbelief filled the night air.

"Now the Nazis are murdering POWs," Syd said. "I hope the bastards hang for this."

"Absolute disregard for the principles of international law," Ray said.

The escape committee called an emergency meeting after the news report. Completion of the tunnel was scheduled for mid-summer. Members held a vote to see if anyone wanted to opt out due to the threat of murder if their escape plans were discovered. No one did. As far as Nowak was concerned, hope and defiance were the only ways for him to keep his sanity. Even so, his stomach churned when he thought about it.

Early the next morning, Nowak and Ray enjoyed a game of soccer, Army against Air Force, in the sandy exercise compound. The two teams wore dyed Army vests in red and blue, and old Army boots with strips of leather nailed to the soles. Thoughts of the BBC news report from the night before still preoccupied Nowak. Ray's shouting brought his thoughts back to the soccer game. "Over yonder. He's showing off again." Ray stopped the ball with his foot and pointed at the sky.

A light blue twin-engine Junker Ju 88 had taken off from the nearby *Luftwaffe* training facility at the Lönnewitz airfield. The night fighter had 20mm cannons in the nose and machine guns in the front and rear. The pilot took a victory roll overhead. After flying the circuit, he headed back. The second time around, he dove too low, too fast.

Both teams ran for cover. A couple of airmen from Nowak's hut strolled along the perimeter of the compound, unaware the pilot had lost control of the aircraft.

"Wally, Mallory. Hit the ground!" Nowak yelled.

Too late. The nose-heavy monoplane struck a power line with one wing, hit the dirt, and barreled through the exercise compound. Wally's leg was hit by the tail and a spinning propeller slashed Mallory's head, then the Junker tore through two barbed wire fences. Moments before ploughing into the cookhouse, the pilot regained control and took off, barbed wire and a fence post dangling from the wing.

Medics rushed out of the hospital block with stretchers. Wally was still alive, his leg broken. The other airman died instantly from a crushed skull.

The next day, they placed the body in a pine box and loaded it onto the back of a farm wagon. A funeral in the camp cemetery in the neighboring village of Ncuburxdorf offered an opportunity for escape too good to pass up. The escape committee wrapped up a last-minute meeting.

"We're moving two out and two in. Both incoming switches need our protection, or they'll end up in a concentration camp. They're wanted by the Gestapo. At the graveyard, sneak away from the group. Find the chapel and go upstairs," Snowshoe said.

"Is the chapel inside the cemetery?" asked the Aussie who was one of the two up for escape.

"You can't miss it. Your switch will be waiting in the attic. Swap your clothes and your identities." Snowshoe puffed on a cigarette. "There's just one thing."

"What's that?" asked the American from Mississippi, the second airman up.

Snowshoe tapped his foot. He seemed nervous. "One of them's a woman."

"A woman? You must be joking."

"You want out of here or not?"

"I don't understand."

"You don't need to understand," Snowshoe snapped.

"Have you lost your mind?"

"The less you know, the better," Snowshoe said.

"I don't have to wear a dress, do I?"

"Are you in or not? A lot of men around here will take your place."

"I'm in," the American said.

Snowshoe turned his attention to Nowak. "You're up next on the escape list, so you're the lookout on this trip."

"Yep," Nowak said with a nod, wishing he was up for this one.

"You've been briefed on the background of the switch, codenamed Mrs. B. Any questions?"

"Nope." Nowak knew all about Syd's mother. He was more interested in the second switch. A member of the Polish Underground.

Once the meeting was over, the funeral procession headed to the graveyard. Nowak snuck away from the group when the digging of the burial site started. He waited inside the chapel until a slight figure dressed as an airman descended the stairs. A young man with dirty blond hair and a square chin followed. He wore a four-cornered officer's cap with the Polish Air Force crowned eagle insignia and a fringed brown suede jacket.

By putting his finger to his lips, Nowak motioned them closer. "Follow me and do as I do," he whispered.

Outside, airmen dug the grave while the guards chatted and smoked in the shade. They had a few minutes left before the ceremony started. No head count until they formed a column to march back.

Mrs. B's face looked a little too clean, so he reached down and picked up a handful of dirt. Smearing it on her chin, he smiled and said, "You needed some stubble."

Mrs. B nodded and pulled her cap down lower on her face. She had to be one tough lady.

Scrutinizing the area, Nowak noticed an abandoned kitten curled up in a ball outside the chapel. He bent down, shoved it in his pocket, and headed for the gravesite where the three of them joined the group.

Nowak surveyed the rows and rows of wooden crosses. He had lost count of how many POWs were buried here. Prisoners who died from malnutrition, typhus, and wounds that had never healed in the filthy conditions.

When they finished digging the grave, an eight-man German honor guard provided by the authorities because of the circumstances of the death, lined up on either side. They raised their rifles and shot into the air.

No other POWs buried there had ever received an honor guard. As if providing one made any difference.

Syd was the usual bugler, but Snowshoe ordered him to stay back at camp saying he was too close to the situation. The airman assigned as a stand-in for Syd stepped forward and played "The Last Post." Nowak stood at attention and saluted while the mournful melody echoed through the cemetery and the coffin was slowly lowered into the ground.

Many of the airmen in the funeral procession knew about a switch taking place. Only a few knew a woman was involved, and it was imperative to keep that secret. Nowak just hoped they could pull it off.

CHAPTER THIRTY-FIVE

Block 14
Ravensbrück Concentration Camp, Germany

Anna stood among the other teenaged girls from her barrack while the teacher gave a lecture on astronomy. The Resistance had organized a secret educational program that taught high school classes to the girls after their twelve-hour shifts. They had free time on Sunday afternoons, but teaching was almost impossible then because the Nazis blared music full blast through the loudspeakers.

The small group of prisoners had become her surrogate family. In a world of hunger, disease, and inhumanity, they cared for each other as best they could. Surrounded by evil, they strove for momentary pockets of normality. They called each other *Lager Schwestern*. Camp sisters.

Zophia had traded half of their meagre bread rations for bandages and some salve from a woman who worked in the hospital block for Anna while she recovered from her lashings. She had been confined to her bunk for days, waking often in a cold sweat from a reoccurring nightmare, where she waded through deep sewage in a dark tunnel and came across a body lying face down. She struggled to turn it over. Then saw the face of her father. When she screamed for help, her voice wouldn't work. She tried harder and harder to scream, but nothing came out. Her heart pounded with fear. She ran. A *Totenkopf* chased her, a skull with red lips above crossed bones. She ran faster. The skull gained on her. She felt its breath on the back of her neck. Smelled heavy perfume.

Tonight was a clear evening with the stars shining brightly overhead. Anna winced when she turned her gaze to the east, toward Poland. The coarse cotton weave of her uniform rubbed against the still raw lashes, but she barely noticed as memories flooded back to her of when she would stand outside her home on Christmas Eve, under a sky that looked just like this one, waiting for the first *gwiazda*, in remembrance of the star of Bethlehem. As soon as she saw a star, she'd run into the house to tell her family so the meal could begin.

A deep sense of sadness overtook her when she thought about her capture on the evening of the *Wigilia* meal: an empty chair at the dinner table with Papa and Michal frantic. Her determination to see them again kept her going, one day at a time.

After class, Anna found Zophia with a group that gathered to exchange recipes from memory. A woman explained how to make *uszka*—small dumplings served in soup. The hunger pains were constant and thoughts of food remained foremost in the prisoners' minds. Sharing recipes allowed for a sense of community and deep bonding, friendship being an essential ingredient for survival.

"I have to talk to you about something." Zophia moved away from the group. "I don't want anyone to hear."

"What's wrong?" Anna asked.

"I'm pregnant," Zophia whispered. So thin and wearing such a baggy uniform, she had hidden the pregnancy.

"Is the baby Michal's?" Anna asked, concerned that Zophia may have been raped by one of the officers in the camp.

Zophia nodded. "He doesn't even know." Her hand rested on her stomach. Tears ran down her cheeks.

Anna embraced her friend. "Michal loves you very much. He was heartbroken when you disappeared."

"I'm afraid for our baby. Of the *Kinderzimmer*."

Anna knew of the feared baby room. Every time a baby was born, Fleischer showed up to dispose of the child. Her usual methods involved drowning, starvation, or stomping the baby to death with her hobnailed boots. She had to find a way to protect Michal and Zophia's baby from the Beast.

"We need to get you out of this bloody camp. When is the baby due?"

"Not for a couple of months."

"We'll think of something. Maybe Agata can put your number on an outgoing work party."

"I'm worried about you, too. You can't risk another whipping."

"Why is the Beast always at the factory? I thought we'd left her behind at the main camp. We can't get away from her, she's everywhere." Even in her dreams.

"Word is she has several lovers amongst the SS officers. Her favorite is Klaus Von Wolff. The aeronautical engineer working on classified weapons development."

Anna had seen Von Wolff often enough at the factory, where he would stand and watch them to ensure they met their production quotas.

"She spends a lot of time in his private office. She's obsessed with him. He holds a lot of secrets. And to the Beast, secrets are power," Zophia said.

Anna noticed a prisoner entering the barrack with a letter. "Looks like somebody got mail today."

Several weeks earlier, she had smuggled a letter to her father out of camp with a work party. Written on paper that had cost her several days of bread rations, the first letter in each line spelled *list moczem* to inform him she had written in urine between the lines and in the margins. It was a code that several of the Polish political prisoners were using. If he held the paper over a heat source or used an iron, the invisible ink would darken, and he'd know where she was.

Her letter included details on the medical experiments performed on seventy-four Polish women. Agata had access to official camp reports and Zophia gathered information from the woman who worked in the hospital. The doctors were making incisions in the women's legs and injecting strains of bacteria to cause an infection and test the efficiency of their drugs. Once the information reached the Home Army, they could pass it on to London.

Anna waited, hoping that her father had written back. But her name wasn't called.

CHAPTER THIRTY-SIX

Mrs. B was temporarily housed under the stage in the Empire Theatre. To keep the correct head count, they rented Yuri from the Russian compound as a stand-in by giving him bits of food—the authorities never bothered to count the Russian prisoners. After a Russian died, his comrades held his corpse upright at roll call to steal his rations. When they couldn't stand the smell any longer, they left the body outside overnight for the Krauts to bury in mass graves.

Yuri Ivanenko appreciated any chance he had to get out of his compound, where he licked empty cans and ate pieces of bread that the airmen threw over the fence. His long beard camouflaged how thin he really was. It was hard to believe he was a doctor and a high-ranking officer in the NKVD, the Soviet secret police.

After the first week, Mrs. B moved into the Red Cross hut behind a false wall fashioned out of empty food parcel boxes. The guards rarely searched the storage shed. To keep her busy, they gave her bed sheets that a few airmen received in packages from home, to cut up and sew into work shirts using newspaper patterns.

Snowshoe assigned Syd, Ray, Freddie, and Nowak to protect her. He called them the Petticoat Patrol. With some twenty thousand men in camp and only one woman, keeping her existence a secret was top priority.

Nowak sprinkled a little powdered milk in a can, added water, and stirred. Carefully setting it on his mattress for the kitten, which turned out to be a popular distraction for the hut. Even Fritz dropped by on his rounds to check on her.

He'd chosen the name—*Zwiebel*—because the little white ball of fur with green eyes reminded him of an onion. When he got out of the bag, one of the first things he was going to do was have an onion sandwich. He wasn't sure why, but the craving was there. And he would never eat another turnip as long as he lived. Never. Ever.

He climbed up on his bunk to wait for the runner to appear with the nightly BBC report. To construct a wooden railway for the tunnel, he had removed the bed boards, and slept on binder twine, taken off Red Cross parcels, knotted together like a hammock. After lapping the milk, the kitten curled up and fell asleep. The soothing rhythm of her purring calmed his nerves.

To pass the time, he flipped through pages of the monthly edition of the *Flywheel*—a magazine produced by the prisoners with handwritten articles and original artwork. The school exercise book had a cardboard cover with the initials MMC for the Mühlberg Motor Club and a picture of a model motorcycle flywheel assembly.

He read an article entitled "1944 Motor Show," with pictures of sleek new cars glued to the page with fermented millet soup. Pausing, he admired a picture of a 1942 seven-passenger Cadillac on a 142-inch chassis with a V8 engine, and envisioned himself driving down the highway on a warm summer day with the Rocky Mountains in the distance.

What struck him most was the perfect handwriting. He held a page up to the light and moved it around. The lettering could pass for the typewritten word.

"Hey Freddie. Who wrote in this month's edition of the *Flywheel?*"

"Michal, something Polish. The new kid Snowshoe brought into camp. The Resistance fighter," Freddie said.

"Mighty fine lettering. Just what we've been lookin' for. I think I'll get to know him."

Nowak was pleased to see Freddie perk up a bit. Talk of the Resistance and thoughts of escape fueled his hope and usually did the trick, even though he still hadn't received a letter from Izzie. He'd be better off with a Dear John letter than he was now, left wondering every day with no word about his son. So many airmen had received Dear John letters over the years that they posted them on the bulletin board as a sign of unity and moral support for each other.

The news runner arrived, hopped up on a chair, and started his BBC report: "Land, sea, and air forces invaded the French coast . . . American, British, and Canadian infantry divisions . . . One hundred and fifty thousand Allied forces, under the command of General Eisenhower have landed on the beaches of Normandy."

Jumping off his chair, the runner made his way over to the map posted on the wall showing the battle lines as reported in the *Völkischer Beobachter* and *Allgemeine Zeitung*, the propaganda newspapers fed to the prisoners. He moved the red markers to the actual battle lines reported by the BBC.

"There's been a breakdown of the German defenses. The Allies opened a second front," he said.

Revitalized by the good news, Nowak leaped off his bunk and gathered around the map to discuss the progress of the war. The airmen studied the defensive lines and the offensive operations, asked questions, shook hands, and slapped each other on the back.

"Goon up," shouted the lookout.

The runner quickly repositioned the flags to conform to the propaganda. The airmen scattered. Nowak hopped onto his bunk.

Pick Axe walked in, an arrogant little bastard with fashionably slicked-back blond hair, belted blue overalls and ankle boots. With the second front, German forces short of manpower, and the Russian forces advancing, most of the fit guards were transferred into active combat, leaving only the old and very young at the camp.

The new guard wasn't fit for battle, but freshly graduated from the Hitler Youth and indoctrinated with Nazi ideology. His favorite slogans were *Heute Deutschland, morgen die Welt*: Today Germany, tomorrow the world, and *Ein Volk, ein Reich, ein Führer*: One people, one country, one leader. He strutted around the hut, poking and probing with an Alpine stick that had a ten-inch spike welded to the end. When he found nothing suspicious, he went outside to crawl around underneath the hut to search for tunnels. The airmen referred to him as a ferret.

That night Nowak headed to the performance in the Empire Theatre. The price of admission was three cigarettes. He nodded at Fritz. His eyes swept the rows of seated men, searching for the Polish Resistance fighter. The escape committee needed a forger and, given the work the Pole had done in the *Flywheel*, Nowak figured he was a good candidate for the job. He recognized Michal sitting beside Johnny, a West African RAF officer from the British colony of Sierra Leone, and slipped onto the wooden bench between them.

"How'd you end up in here?" Nowak asked Michal.

"We were ambushed. My father was murdered." His voice faltered and he paused before adding. "I had to flee Warsaw."

"How did it happen?"

"Betrayed by one of our members. Someone we trusted. The SS threatened to kill his family if he didn't tell them where we were hiding."

"Bet the bastards killed them anyway."

"Murdered his three young daughters and his wife by firing squad. Made him watch."

Nowak shook his head in disgust. "Do you have any other family?"

"My mother died at the start of the war. My sister Anna disappeared. So did my girlfriend."

From the look on his face, it was clear Michal found it difficult to talk about. The band played and the curtain opened. In honor of D-Day, Snowshoe descended from the ceiling, center stage. He wore a parachute and catcher's mitt, and he carried a baseball. Pulling a rope, he exposed box seats and a large sign that read: RESERVED FOR MONTGOMERY AND EISENHOWER. The crowd broke into cheers.

CHAPTER THIRTY-SEVEN

Anna stood with her camp sisters at the far end of the barrack for a lecture on Polish literature. She couldn't stop thinking about Zophia, who had been sick with dysentery for the past couple of days. A piercing scream sent her rushing past the rows of three-tier bunks to the wood-shaving stuffed mattress the two of them shared.

Zophia was in premature labor. A small crowd of women had gathered. One prisoner, with experience as a midwife, was assisting her.

"Push harder," the midwife said. "That's it. Now take a deep breath."

"I see the head. One more push should do it," a woman said.

Anna paced back and forth, watching the door, afraid the Beast would burst in at any second. She knew someone in the barracks was an informant and information came cheap. An extra cup of soup or double bread rations would be all it would take to expose the birth.

"It's a boy," announced the midwife.

While holding the baby upside down, she spanked it gently. Once. Then twice. And a third time.

The baby was silent. Skin bluish. Placing him on the mattress, the midwife tilted his head back and blew quick breaths into his mouth while using two fingers to compress his chest. Blew again. Compressed again. Blew. Compressed.

As the baby gasped for air and cried out, she wrapped him in rags and laid him across Zophia's bosom. Anna caressed the cheek of the beautiful baby. Michal's son. Her nephew.

The door flung open, and in her polished leather jackboots with the dreaded hobnails, the Beast marched straight for Zophia and ripped the naked infant out of the young mother's arms. Her dog Grief assumed attack position. Stiffened body. Head pushed forward. Lips curled. Teeth exposed.

"My baby. My baby." Zophia cried out.

Anna reached for Zophia's hand. "Shhh," she said, trying to comfort her.

With the child in her arms, the Beast turned to leave. Anna had to save Zophia and Michal's baby. She'd let Zophia down when she didn't protect Ewa and she owed it to her brother. It was up to her and only her, even though she knew she'd face another beating, or worse, death.

"Stop! Don't hurt this child," Anna screamed.

"*Untermensch*," the Beast said.

"Not Subhuman."

"*Untermensch*," she repeated.

Grief growled; eyes fixed on Anna.

"*Lebensborn*," Anna shot back, knowing SS members were encouraged to have four children, in or out of wedlock, to produce racially valuable offspring. Hitler's vision of a Master Race.

"*Lebensborn*?" The Beast narrowed her eyes and looked at her suspiciously.

"His father is SS. Good German blood," Anna said.

The Beast tilted her head to the side.

"See his blond hair? The blue eyes."

"Which SS officer?" She held the baby up to study him.

Anna hesitated, not knowing what to say.

"I asked you a question," the Beast demanded. "*Who* is the father?"

"I don't know his name. He was here with a delegation that met with the commandant. Very high-ranking."

The Beast stood stone still. After a few moments, her demeanor softened, and she cuddled the baby.

"Off to the punishment block," she ordered Anna.

They marched past poplar trees and fragrant wild chamomile along the path, the scent overpowered a few steps later by the smell of burning bodies. They stopped beside carts stacked with corpses, eyes wide open, waiting their turn in one of the three ovens.

"Stand here," the Beast said, as she stomped off, leaving Grief to stand guard.

Anna held her breath, fearing that the wardress would toss the child into the ovens. They didn't call her the Beast for nothing. She stopped to chat with a Brown Sister, the Nazi nurses who kidnapped racially desirable children. This time, Anna was glad to see one, hoping Michal's baby had a chance of survival.

She stood watching the two women. The Beast held the naked child while the Brown Sister looked in his eyes and ran her fingers through his fine hair. Grief growled and bared his teeth when Anna tried to move closer. She strained to make out their words.

"Are you going to the cinema in Fürstenberg tonight? We get free tickets," the Beast said. "After the war, I'm going to be in the movies. You'll see my name on the screen."

Anna couldn't believe her ears. The fate of Michal's baby lay in the hands of these two women who were talking about movies. Death by the enemy or life with the enemy hung in the balance. It took every ounce of strength she had left to stand there and do nothing as her hatred for the Beast flared. She heaved a sigh of relief when the Brown Sister took the child.

The Beast returned without saying a word and they continued on to the punishment block. Inside Cell 75, she picked out the plaited cellophane whip with metal tips, cracked it in the air four times to limber her wrist, which sported an ivory bracelet with painted gold swastikas.

Anna removed her clothes and crawled onto the trestle, promising herself she would survive so that one day she'd make the Beast pay for everything she'd done. Leather straps were fastened and a filthy rag stuffed in her mouth. Her tormentor traced the scars on her back with her red manicured nails.

Then, suddenly, the whip crashed down.

CHAPTER THIRTY-EIGHT

Air-raid sirens blasted. Day raids had started. American Flying Fortress long-range bombers flew overhead, in formations of fifty. White vapor condensation trails crisscrossed the sky. Smoke markers hovered on the horizon.

The Soviets had pushed the Germans out of Russia and, once again, moved their forces over the Polish border, reclaiming the eastern part of Poland. Stalin declared the Curzon Line as the boundary and proclaimed Eastern Poles as Soviet citizens. Churchill and Roosevelt didn't seem to mind.

Pick Axe marched around the RAF compound with a hammer and nails, posting notices on the huts. Nowak sauntered up to the announcement and read:

NOTICE
TO ALL PRISONERS OF WAR!
THE ESCAPE FROM PRISON CAMPS IS NO LONGER A
SPORT!
Germany is determined to safeguard her homeland, and especially her war industry and provisional centers for the fighting fronts. Therefore, it has become necessary to create strictly forbidden zones, called death zones, in

which all unauthorized trespassers will be immediately
shot on sight. Prisoners of war, entering such death zones,
will lose their lives.
URGENT WARNING IS GIVEN AGAINST MAKING
FUTURE ESCAPES
IN PLAIN ENGLISH:
Stay in the camp where you will be safe!
Breaking out of it is now a damned dangerous act.
THE CHANCES OF PRESERVING YOUR LIFE ARE
ALMOST NIL!
All police and military guards have been given the most
strict orders
to shoot on sight all suspected persons.
ESCAPING FROM PRISON CAMPS HAS CEASED TO BE
A SPORT!

Tension inside camp was at an all-time high. Now that the
Germans no longer followed the rules of warfare that protected
prisoners of war, suspicion was reason enough to be shot on
sight. Not good timing for the tunnel break that was scheduled
for that night.

Nowak hustled over to the Empire Theatre. Underneath,
the finishing touches were being made to the tunnel. Outside,
the lookouts created noise to divert attention. The band rehearsed "Land of Hope and Glory," the song played at the end
of every show.

He hummed to himself as he entered the theatre carrying a
rigged Monopoly game under his arm. Syd sewed lapels onto
a military tunic to create a suit jacket. Ray cut the stitching
around the ankle of black leather flying boots using the thin
wire saw threaded through the laces, designed to make a street
shoe by removing the tops. Snowshoe fashioned belt buck-

les and buttons out of silver paper from cigarette packages. Freddie made compasses by melting gramophone records and pouring the liquid into molds. He magnetized the needles by rubbing a metal bar to create an electrical charge through friction, embedded the needle in the plastic, and attached a thin piece of metal to the face of the compass as an indicator of magnetic north.

Michal sat at a table, forging the signatures of German officials and stamping documents with the Nazi Eagle that Ray had carved.

"Mighty fine work, Michal," Nowak said as he admired the quality of the signatures. "Will you finish in time?"

"Shouldn't take much longer," Michal said.

Nowak ripped open a package of orange crystals from a Red Cross parcel and emptied the contents into a klim, adding just enough water to dissolve the crystals. He stirred the mixture and poured it into a thin layer in a large pan. The citrus scent reminded him of how hungry he was. He fought the urge to slurp it down.

Opening the Monopoly box, he removed the game board. Then tore the paper face off the board, exposing a shallow recess with a silk escape map and a two-part miniature file. He rifled through the stack of play money. Pulling out German *Reichsmarks*, he held the wad of cash up in the air and flipped through the bills.

"How'd you know the game was rigged?" Michal asked.

"We were briefed back at base." Nowak pointed to the red dot on the *free parking* square. "Arrived inside a Red Cross parcel compliments of the Licensed Victuallers' Prisoner Relief Fund. It's a fake charity. I'm going to make a map for every man in the tunnel break."

Nowak used a blend of soot and oil to ink over the rail lines, major roads, rivers, towns, cities, and border crossings printed on the silk. Then he turned the map face down and pressed it carefully onto the orange crystal gelatin to transfer the ink. He grabbed a sheet of white paper, stolen out of the administration office, and pressed it onto the gelatin, thereby transferring a rough copy of the map onto the paper. To finish it off, he traced over the lightly transferred map by hand with a pen.

Freddie wandered over and handed Nowak a compass. "Here you go, Skipper. So you won't get lost."

"Thanks." He held it up for inspection and noticed his initials carved on the back. He slid the compass into his pocket. "I could use some help with these maps."

A few hours later, the men huddled in the corner of their hut to review their escape plans one last time.

"Everything is set. We left the shaft of the tunnel open. Once Pick Axe makes his final rounds, we'll change into our civvies. We go out one by one. Then take off in pairs. Syd's with Mrs. B," Nowak said. "Freddie's with me. Ray, you sure you're not coming?"

"Y'all go ahead. I'm staying behind," Ray said. "My final exams are comin' up."

"It's not any safer in here these days," Freddie said. "Did you hear what happened to Joe from Brighton? He spotted a strawberry on the other side of the trip wire while he was walking with Pokerface during rehearsal break. Pick Axe shot him in the back of the head when he reached under the wire to grab it."

"Jesus," Nowak said.

Freddie shifted in his chair. "But let's not talk about getting shot. Michal, which way are you headed?"

"Back to Warsaw. I'll take off on my own."

"Have you received any reports on the Uprising?" Nowak asked, thinking about Hope.

"The Home Army is mobilizing for five p.m. August first. W-hour. We plan to seize control of the capital and force the Germans out. Once we liberate Warsaw, we'll join the Allied forces advancing from the west," Michal explained.

"What about the Russians?" Nowak asked.

"They're encouraging us. They're sending radio broadcasts from Moscow in Polish calling on the Underground to rise up against their Nazi oppressors."

"And the Brits?"

"We've requested aid in the form of arms and ammunition. And we've asked Britain to return the Polish Bomber and Fighter Squadrons, and the First Polish Parachute Brigade as reinforcements."

"Do you think they'll comply?" Ray asked.

"A national uprising to win back Polish independence has always been the plan. They've pledged their support. We expect aid to arrive within four or five days."

"With any luck, I'll resume dropping supplies over Warsaw," Nowak said.

"Did you fly SOE drops?"

"Sure did," Nowak said, proudly.

Michal extended his hand. "If you ever need a favor. Anything. Just ask."

"We'll keep that in mind."

"How about some poker to pass the time?" Nowak brought out a deck of cards and moved over to the table. The group joined him. "Everybody in?" he asked while shuffling the deck and dealing each man five cards.

"You better watch out, Skipper. I'm gonna win back all the cigarettes I owe you. And then some. You can pay up in ale when we get to England," Freddie said.

Nowak could hardly sit still, anticipating this to be his last day behind barbed wire. A poker game to settle his nerves was a good idea. He couldn't help but examine each card by holding it up to the light before fanning his hand. MI9 concealed segments of an escape map between the front and back layers of some of the playing cards sent into camp.

Freddie seemed to be back to his old self, cracking jokes and telling stories. The tunnel completion and the prospect of getting home to his family had raised his spirits. Halfway through the game, he jumped up on a chair. "And now, gentlemen, for my last performance before we return to England." With one hand over his heart, he sang:

> Hitler, has only got one ball,
> Goering, has two but they are small.
> Himmler, has something sim'lar,
> But poor old Goebbels, has no balls at all.

Nowak whistled the chorus until deafening sirens blared over the loudspeakers, interrupting them.

"What the hell?" Nowak's heart hit his stomach. His hope faded. Grabbing his kitbag with the forged documents, he crawled up on a top bunk and stashed it behind a loose ceiling board.

He hopped down just as Pick Axe burst into the hut, ordering everyone onto Parade Square. One by one, the huts were emptied. The commandant shouted orders over the loudspeaker and summoned Snowshoe to his office.

"They must have found the tunnel," Nowak whispered to Freddie, giving the dirt a swift kick with the toe of his boot.

"We're snookered," Freddie said. "We're never getting out of this hole."

Standing at attention in rows of five, Nowak heard the guards tearing apart his hut. He stared straight ahead and gritted his teeth while sweat trickled down his back. If they found his kitbag with everyone's forged papers stashed inside, the entire escape committee would be lined up and shot. Even if they didn't find the bag, suspicion was reason enough to be murdered.

After what seemed like forever, Snowshoe returned from the commandant's office. He strode up and down the rows of airmen to remind them of their code of silence. If everyone kept quiet, the Germans couldn't justify shooting a thousand airmen. If anyone spoke up, Snowshoe would issue a sentence for the informant far worse than the swim in the cesspool he had sentenced that little thief to a year back.

No one said a word. The commandant finally dismissed the airmen back to their huts. The guards had seized soap, cigarettes, and chocolate. They opened Red Cross cans and dumped the precious food into the cauldrons, mixing it all together.

Nowak peered up at the ceiling boards and figured it best to leave his kit bag hidden. He looked around for Freddie and saw him back on his bunk. He was damn worried about how Freddie was going to cope with another setback.

"What the hell happened?" he asked Snowshoe.

"A worker in the potato field drove a tractor over the tunnel shaft. The bloody tire fell through the opening," Snowshoe said.

Pick Axe emptied the contents of the *shizen karts* into the tunnel. A nauseating smell permeated the barracks. As the days wore on and sunshine warmed the air, the stench thickened, lingering for weeks.

A daily reminder of a year of work fueled by sweat, hope, and determination turned to shit in a minute.

CHAPTER THIRTY-NINE

Ravensbrück Concentration Camp, Germany

Anna waited behind the thousand-volt electric fence for Zophia and Agata to return from an emergency meeting. News had been brought into camp by an influx of new arrivals captured during the Warsaw Uprising. In too much pain from the lashings to walk any distance, she stood looking out at Schwedtsee Lake through a crack in the perimeter wall. The Beast and two other female guards were enjoying the warm summer day while sitting in a rowboat on the lake. On shore, prisoners dumped ashes from the crematorium into the water.

Across the lake lay the quaint town of Fürstenberg, with its church spire poking through the horizon. Trying to picture what life was like for the German families in the village, she wondered if Ewa lived in a town like that with food on the table, a clean bed, and a German name to mask the Polish blood coursing through her veins.

Held captive inside the living nightmare of Ravensbrück, questions swirled through Anna's mind. What was wrong with those people? How could they sit in their pretty houses and pretend nothing was happening? What did they think the ashes were from? Couldn't they smell the bodies burning? Were they blind to the carts piled high with excess corpses sent to the crematorium in their town?

After spending time at Ravensbrück, she had grown numb. Death was a daily occurrence, woven into the fabric of life. You expected it, resigned yourself to it. At times, it almost seemed welcome as the only way out.

She turned when she heard footsteps behind her, catching sight of Zophia and Agata on their way back.

Agata had developed a nervous tick. Her right eye twitched as she spoke. "On August first, men, women, and children in red-and-white armbands attacked the Germans. Very few had decent weaponry. They raised Polish flags, hurled rocks, petrol bombs, and Sidolówka hand grenades. Hauled household furniture into the streets to use as barricades. Dug trenches. Captured tanks. They held their ground for days, waiting for reinforcements to arrive. Only a few aircraft came through with supplies."

"What about all the countries that pledged support for Polish independence?" Anna asked, trying to contain her rage.

"It gets worse." Zophia's voice wavered. "Nazi assault troops stormed into Warsaw on August fifth and murdered people by the thousands. Dragged families out of their homes and executed them en masse. Shot patients in hospitals, floor by floor. Slaughtered defenseless children in orphanages. Bound captured women to the front of armored tanks as human shields. Doused the wounded with gasoline and burned them on the street. Set buildings on fire."

Agata threw up her hands. "Our administration offices are in chaos with all the women and children arriving from Warsaw. We're erecting tents without access to water, lights, or latrines. We need to ship many out to forced labor camps."

Anna thought for a minute. "Can you swap two of them with Zophia and me? Put our numbers on the transit list instead?"

"You go. This is your chance to escape," Zophia said.

"I don't want to leave without you."

"I need to stay. My baby is here. Somewhere."

CHAPTER FORTY

RAF Compound
Stalag IVB, Germany

Nowak sat on his bunk with his feet dangling over the side. Another dreary morning with nothing to do and no food. Constant hunger gnawed at his gut. The only thing left to scrounge together for dinner was ground potato peel soup. Even *Zwiebel* got by on potato peels and turnip tops these days.

The close quarters and lack of privacy wore on his nerves. He'd heard the same angry stories from the men in his hut, over and over. Arguments broke out over nothing.

Some initial excitement surrounded a rumored assassination attempt against Hitler by anti-Nazi conspirators in July. Then the reality of Nazi vengeance hit when a photo in a German newspaper circulated through the camp showing the accused officers hanging naked from meat hooks and piano wire. Friends and relatives of those involved were rounded up and sent to concentration camps.

Ray and Syd spent their time strategizing over which legal principles could be used to prosecute the Nazis for their war crimes and itemized as many acts as they could think of that violated international agreements. They compiled a hit list naming men they wanted arrested, starting with Adolf Hitler and his henchmen, Hermann Göring, Heinrich Himmler, Joseph Goebbels, and Adolf Eichmann, and working their way down the ranks to Ukraine Joe and Pick Axe. Adding names as news filtered into camp on the secret radio and with the newly captured.

Freddie's mood worsened after receiving a letter from home telling him his mother was in the hospital and probably wouldn't make it. His father had died when he was just an infant, and his mother had brought him up on her own. There was nothing Freddie could do for her in her last days. She would die hundreds of miles from him, but at least she'd be buried in home soil.

Nowak received sad news, too, from a newly captured airman in his squadron, who frequented the neighborhood pub where Red worked. His friend had died when a series of V1 bombs hit while she was in London. She'd been dead for months.

Discouraged, he lay down, dozed off, and fell into another nightmare with his burning Wellington nosediving into the sea. He tried to free himself from something pulling him deeper and deeper underwater.

"Wake up. You're talking in your sleep." Michal shook his shoulder.

"What's wrong?" Nowak awoke in a cold sweat, relieved to be in his bunk and not underwater.

"The Uprising is in trouble," Michal said. "Stalin is denying the Allies access to Soviet airbases for refueling to hinder assistance and reduce the armaments brought in. Polish, British and South African squadrons are trying to drop supplies. Aircrew casualties are huge and not sustainable."

"I thought the Russians encouraged the Uprising?"

"They did, but the Red Army halted outside the city on the east bank of the Vistula. They're refusing military support. I have to find a way out of here."

"We're never getting out of here," mumbled Freddie, from the neighboring bunk.

"Don't pay any attention to him. He's in a bad mood," Nowak said, although he was inclined to agree with Freddie.

"There's got to be a way out," Michal said.

"Let me think it through. We can talk later." The words felt empty as he said them.

Nowak settled back on his bunk. If he ever got out of this godforsaken hole, he'd never take his freedom for granted. There was nothing more important.

He heard shouting outside. An airman ran into the barrack, waving his arms. "I just saw a woman."

"Jesus." Nowak jumped off his bunk. They must have found Mrs. B; she was the only woman in camp. Worried, he shook Freddie's shoulder.

"Get your arse out of bed. We've got a big problem," Nowak said.

"What's all the fuss about?" Freddie raised his head.

"Not sure, but I'm going to find out."

Men fell over each other, scrambling to get dressed, wanting to be the first out the door. Nowak headed outside, hopping on one leg and then the other as he put on his trousers.

CHAPTER FORTY-ONE

Transit Camp
Stalag IVB, Germany

Anna arrived at the transit camp, wearing a pleated navy skirt and white blouse that Agata gave her before she left Ravensbrück. A sickening stench emanated from the latrines. There wasn't much inside the building. A mud-covered floor. A couple of wooden tables and a pile of filthy straw mattresses.

She pulled one off the pile, dragged it over to Marta, a woman with a baby she'd met on the crowded train ride from Fürstenberg. Her six-month-old son, dressed only in a stained nightshirt, sucked on her nipple, then fussed and cried when he received no milk.

Anna dragged another mattress over for herself and sat down.

"Is it true Old Town fell to the Germans?" she asked Marta.

"The *Luftwaffe* dropped bombs on Old Town every fifteen minutes. They did house to house clearance and mass evictions of neighborhoods. That's when they arrested us. I don't know where my husband is," she said.

Anna thought of Papa and Michal, not knowing where they were or whether they were alive or dead. Exhausted after marching from the train station in Jacobsthal, she lay down to rest. Despite the cold emanating from the brick floor, she drifted off to sleep and another nightmare with the red lipped

Totenkopf skull chasing her through the dark tunnels, breathing down her neck. She bolted upright, heart pounding.

Looking around, she noticed women filing out the door. She heard a commotion outside. "Where is everyone going?" she asked Marta.

"Let's go see." Marta wrapped her baby in a blanket.

Anna donned her scarf and tied it under her chin. They made their way out of the building, sliding between straw-filled mattresses scattered across the muddy floor. A tall, barbed wire fence separated the transit camp from a compound where hundreds of airmen stood waving, whistling, and shouting. They threw cigarettes, food, and notes over the wire to the women.

*

Nowak, Freddie, and Ray stood amongst the crowd of airmen watching women file out of the barracks on the other side of the barbed wire. Most wore navy blue jackets, trousers, and peaked caps with red-and-white cockades.

"Where did all the women come from?" Nowak asked.

"Ravensbrück," Ray said. "Syd says it's a women's concentration camp. Mrs. B told him all about it."

Nowak elbowed Freddie. "Look. It's that girl," he said, not believing his eyes. *Could it really be her?* he asked himself, suddenly energized at the sight of Hope.

"What girl?" Freddie asked.

"The girl from Warsaw." Nowak pointed. "Standing off to the side. The one with the skirt. And the scarf around her head. She's older, but it's her." He shook his head and turned to Freddie. "I think I'm going nuts."

"Why?"

"Just when I think I can't make it a minute longer, I see that girl standing on the opposite side of the wire. Her name is Hope. Maybe I'm dead. Am I dead?" he asked, not wanting to admit to himself or to Freddie what he went through in solitary.

"Not unless we both are. You're right. It's her."

"She's my guardian angel."

"Your what?" Freddie gave him a quizzical look.

"Never mind," Nowak said.

Hope looked like skin and bones. Her shoulders slumped, her smile had disappeared, and the brightness in her eyes had dimmed.

He waved and tried to get her attention, pushing his way through the crowd of men, working his way closer to the fence.

*

A small pack of biscuits landed in no-man's land, the area between the warning wire and the barbed wire fence. Anna ran to pick it up. When she slid her arm under the wire, a gunshot rang out.

A hush settled over the crowd.

She felt pressure on her calf. Then numbness. Taking a step, she fell. The point of impact started to burn. Blood ran down her leg. She glanced up at the guard tower. The sentry stood with his finger on the trigger of a Mauser rifle aimed at her, ready to take a second shot.

Someone called out her name. It couldn't be.

Then she heard it again.

"Hope," a familiar voice shouted.

Looking over at the RAF compound, she met the calming blue eyes of Johnnie Nowak on the other side of the barbed wire.

The pilot she'd guided through the maze of sewers below Warsaw. The one who carved the *Kotwica*, the symbol of hope, on the trunk of the old oak tree.

Nowak held her gaze. He reached out his hands, palms forward, and spoke in a low, comforting voice. "Focus on me. Don't look at the guard. Do exactly as I say. Put your arms in the air. Slowly. Very slowly."

Anna raised her arms.

"That's right," he coaxed. "Stay as still as you can. I'll tell you when it's safe."

Nowak nodded at Freddie.

Freddie launched an upward swing on a really big airman, socking him in the jaw.

"Watch it," he yelled, raising his fists.

"You're the arsehole," Freddie yelled back as he tackled him to the ground.

The surrounding men moved in, shouting obscenities. Urged them on and raised a ruckus. Guards blew their whistles. The sentry in the guard tower moved the sight of his rifle off Anna and onto the men.

"Run. Don't look back," Nowak shouted.

Anna turned and limped away. With every step, the burning sensation in her leg intensified. Reaching the safety of the barrack, she staggered to her mattress and collapsed.

Marta knelt beside her to inspect her wound. Taking a jackknife out of her trouser pocket, she cut the bottom of Anna's skirt. "You're lucky. It looks like the bullet went straight through your calf muscle and missed the bone." She wrapped the material over the wound and around Anna's leg. "Give me your hand. Press down. I'll find something we can use as a tourniquet."

Anna felt the warmth of her own blood soak through the fabric. A burning sensation radiated through her entire body. She gritted her teeth and pressed harder.

Marta came back with a pencil and a shoelace. She tied the lace just under Anna's knee, inserted the pencil between it and her shin, then rotated it to stop the bleeding. Unable to get up for fear that the wound would bleed again, Anna lay confined to her mattress in excruciating pain for the rest of the day. She held her rosary and squeezed the silver crucifix so hard she pressed an image of Christ into her palm.

Hours later, Marta returned to the hut to check on her. "Look what I have." She held up a tin of powdered milk. "The airman who helped you threw it over. And he sent you a note. It looks like a poem." Marta handed Anna the paper.

Anna unfolded it and read:

> High in the sunlit silence. Hov'ring there,
> I've chased the shouting wind along, and flung
> My eager craft through footless halls of air . . .
>
> Up, up the long, delirious, burning blue
> I've topped the wind-swept heights with easy grace
> Where never lark, or even eagle flew—
> And, while with silent lifting mind I've trod
> The high untrespassed sanctity of space,
> Put out my hand, and touched the face of God.

It was the rest of the poem Nowak had written to her in his note back in Warsaw. She read it over and over and over until she fell asleep grasping the poem in her hand.

CHAPTER FORTY-TWO

RAF Compound
Stalag IVB, Germany

The next morning, Nowak rubbed the stubble on his chin. He grabbed his cigarettes and headed to the trading table, where he haggled for a used razor blade and a chocolate bar. Back at his hut, he stopped by Freddie's bunk.

"Come outside. It's time for a haircut and a shave. We both look like hell." Nowak wanted to spruce himself up before seeing Hope again. He picked up a chair. "It'll cheer you up."

He set the chair outside and Freddie sat down. Nowak draped a cloth around Freddie's shoulders and then rummaged through his kitbag for his scissors.

"Hurry," Freddie said. "The ladies are waiting."

"Sit still," Nowak said. "Hold out your hand."

Freddie obliged. Nowak snipped a lock of reddish blond hair and placed it in Freddie's palm. He inverted his hand, and the hair floated to the ground.

"Don't do that," Nowak said.

"Why not?"

"Just keep your hand out," Nowak insisted. He wanted to collect Freddie's hair so he could make paintbrushes later.

When he'd finished cutting, the two of them switched places. After a cut and a shave, they headed over to the barbed wire fence that separated him from the transit camp. Nowak carried a small package tied with a string.

"What's that?" Freddie asked.

"It's for Hope. I traded my cigarettes for a chocolate bar. I kept one Lucky Strike back for good luck." Nowak patted his shirt pocket to make sure the cigarette was still there. "I'm worried about her. She can use the chocolate to barter with. Maybe she can find someone to look at the wound in her leg." He knew the transit camp held no medical supplies.

A crowd of airmen had already gathered at the fence, communicating with the women. He stood amongst them, hoping to see Hope. A sense of relief washed over him when she limped out of her barracks.

"Hope. Over here," he yelled, and waved.

A smile broke out on her face when she saw him. He tossed the package over the fence. It landed a fair distance from no-man's-land.

He watched her hobble over and pick it up. She untied the string. Read the note. Turned around and headed back to her barrack.

"Why'd she leave?" Nowak asked. His pleasure at seeing her dissipated.

"Maybe she doesn't remember us. It was a while ago."

"How could she forget?" He remembered everything about the day they met.

A few minutes later, she came back into the yard and threw a note wrapped around a rock over the fence. It read: *Thank you. I'd hoped you'd made it to safety. Where did you get captured?*

Nowak didn't want to mention the ambush, so he scribbled: *Never made it out of Poland. How's your leg?* scrunched the note around the rock and threw it back.

Anna read the note. Answered by mouthing the word: *Better*.

Thoughts of Hope kept Nowak going for the rest of the day. He slept well that night.

The next morning, he washed, dressed, and rushed out of his hut. Making his way through the crowd to the wire, he saw her standing by herself. The way she wrapped her arms in front of her told him she was cold. It was a chilly, overcast day.

"Hope," he called.

She didn't hear him and started back to her barrack.

"Hope," he shouted as loud as he could.

This time, she turned around.

He took off his greatcoat, folded it into a bundle, and tied the sleeves together to secure it. Before heaving it over the fence, he waited until the guard in the sentry tower shifted his attention. To keep the guards from confiscating it, a group of women quickly gathered around her.

Pick Axe had marched around the corner, humming "*Die Fahne Hoch*" to himself, just in time to see what was happening. He struck Nowak across the back of the head with the butt of his rifle, knocking him to the ground.

"*Heute Deutschland, morgen die Welt!*" Today Germany, tomorrow the world, Pick Axe shouted.

The cold steel of the muzzle lodged behind his ear. He squeezed his eyes shut.

This was it. He'd run out of luck.

He heard the bolt-action of the release. The click of the trigger. Then another click.

The rifle didn't fire.

Nowak opened his eyes. The bolt action had jammed. The round wouldn't chamber.

Freddie grabbed him by the arm and jerked him to his feet. Ray stepped between him and Pick Axe. Fellow airmen moved in on both sides of Ray to form a human wall to protect Nowak.

Pick Axe scurried away.

Nowak and his two crew members gathered inside their hut, huddled between two sets of three-tier bunks.

"That was close," Ray said.

"You okay?" Freddie rested his hand on Nowak's shoulder.

"Got a headache." Nowak leaned against the wooden bunk.

"The women are being shipped out," Ray said. "Day after next."

"Bloody hell," Freddie said.

"Hope can't march to the station. She can barely walk," Nowak said as he massaged the back of his head where a bump had already formed.

"Where are they sending them?" Freddie asked.

"That depends. The Polish female soldiers are fighting for POW status. They want to be treated equivalent to men, so they'll be interned in a stalag like us. Otherwise, as civilians they'll be sent to forced labor camps or a concentration camp. The bastards send the pretty ones to brothels to service the SS and the *Wehrmacht*," Ray explained.

"Are you sure?" Freddie asked.

"You bet. They've got whorehouses in the major concentration camps. Mauthausen. Buchenwald. Sachsenhausen."

"Over my dead body. Hope's not ending up in any damn Nazi brothel. They're not getting their hands on her," Nowak said. "The poor kid's already spent time in a concentration camp."

"Keep your chin up, Skipper. We'll think of something," Freddie said.

Nowak surveyed the room to make sure nobody was listening. Nearby, New Zealand aircrew played a noisy game of poker. An airman from Ireland played the fiddle. And a couple of Brits were arguing about something or other.

"We'll have to move her over here," Nowak whispered.

"No way." Ray crossed his arms. "It's too dangerous. Besides, you're plannin' to break out. Who's goin' take care of her when you're gone?"

"I'll get her settled before I take off. Make sure she's okay."

"Y'all can't be serious," Ray said. "We've already got one woman too many with Mrs. B. Syd's been trying to find a way to move his mother out of here."

"That's it," Nowak said. "We'll switch her with Mrs. B."

"Now you're using your noggin, Skipper," Freddie said.

"Might work. Mrs. B is ready to move on. Gestapo has given up looking for her by now. How do we do the switch?" Ray asked.

"One girl wants to sell a vanity case with brushes and a manicure set for cigarettes. She passed it through the gate yesterday. We stuff it full of cigarettes. Bribe Fritz to let one of us take the case back to the girls as a going-away present." Nowak checked again to make sure no one overheard. "Mrs. B takes the case in. Hope comes back out. I'll distract Fritz. Bribe him with a cup of coffee and some hooch. Maybe a girlie magazine."

"Smashing good idea," Freddie said.

"When?" Ray asked.

"Tomorrow at dusk. Fritz can't see very well. He'll never notice the difference," Nowak said. "We can do it when the guards change shifts, so there'll be a distraction. That's about the same time the show starts in the Empire Theatre."

"You can count on me, Skipper," Freddie reassured him.

"I'll talk to Syd. I bet he'll go for it," Ray said. "I'll ask Poker-face to stand in for me in the show."

"We might need the Russian's help on this. But no one else can know. And I mean no one," Nowak insisted. "There's just one more thing. I only have one cigarette left. My last Lucky Strike." He patted his shirt pocket that held his lucky cigarette. "We'll need more than that to fill the vanity case. Maybe I can sell some of my hooch."

*

The next morning, Anna scanned the faces of the men on the other side of the barbed wire, anxious to know if Nowak was all right. His greatcoat almost dragged on the ground. The sleeves hung over her hands.

Nowak pushed through the crowd of men to the front. He motioned he had a note, checked to make sure a guard wasn't watching so he wouldn't get clobbered in the head again, and threw it over the fence.

Anna picked it up. *Gate at dusk. Wear pants.* She gave him a puzzled look.

He grinned at her. Winked. And left.

All she owned was the navy skirt she wore, the one with the missing hem they had used as a bandage.

"My trousers?" Marta said when Anna asked her friend. "You want my trousers?"

"Yes, please. Would you mind?" Anna reached into her pocket for the chocolate bar she'd been saving. As she pulled it out, the precious notes written by Nowak fell from her pock-et. She quickly shoved them back in. "I can give you this in exchange," she said, handing over the chocolate.

"But why?" Marta asked. "Why do you want my trousers?"

Anna showed Marta the note.

"Do you know what he has planned?"

Anna shook her head.

"Do you trust him?"

"Yes."

"Then you don't have a choice. You'll never keep up with us on the march."

CHAPTER FORTY-THREE

RAF Compound
Stalag IVB, Germany

Fritz unlocked the gate between the RAF compound and the transit camp. "You've got five minutes," he said.

"Just enough time for a cup of coffee." Nowak needed to distract Fritz long enough for Hope and Mrs. B to switch places.

"*Nein*. I better stay here. Who's taking the case in?"

"Ray," Nowak said.

"Where is he?"

"He's coming. Don't worry," Nowak assured Fritz. "I've got hooch. You want some?"

"Hooch?"

"And a girlie magazine you can look at." Nowak headed to his hut.

Fritz followed along.

Ray and Mrs. B strode toward the entrance of the transit camp with the vanity case stuffed full of cigarettes. They were just about to the gate when Fritz stopped abruptly and turned back around.

"Halt!" he hollered.

Mrs. B stopped in her tracks with her cap pulled low on her forehead. Ray looked at Nowak, raising his tweezed eyebrows. Mrs. B waited.

"Stay right where you are." Fritz rushed toward them.

"What's the matter, Fritz?" Ray asked.

Fritz fumbled in his pocket and pulled out a small package wrapped in a crumpled piece of newspaper. "Sausage," he said. "*Wurst fur die* girls."

Ray grabbed the sausage and gave Fritz a friendly slap on the back. "That's awful considerate of you. I always knew you were a ladies' man."

"How about that drink?" Nowak tried to nudge Fritz toward his hut.

"I'm staying right here."

Fritz wasn't moving. Time for Plan B. Always have a backup plan.

Nowak brushed his fingers through his hair to signal Syd, Freddie, and Yuri the Russian, who waited in the area that was the blind spot for the guard towers.

"Bloody Ruskki," Syd yelled as he grabbed hold of Yuri's arm.

"Let go of me," Yuri hollered back.

Freddie joined in, pointing his finger and ranting about something as Syd and Ray tussled.

"Fritz, you better see what's going on. Another guard might hear them and head over. You'll get in trouble, if they see the gate unlocked," Nowak said. "I'll look after things here."

Fritz mumbled to himself and trudged away. The second he did, Mrs. B stepped through the gate, took off her cap, and handed it to Hope. But damn it, Hope didn't move. *Come on, Hope. Take the cap. Move it.*

Nowak caught a glimpse of Fritz trying to calm things down between, Syd, Yuri, and Freddie. Looking back over at Hope, he motioned her to come. She tore off her scarf, put the cap on her head and hobbled toward the gate so slowly she'd never make it to the Red Cross hut before Fritz headed back.

Nowak gave Ray a nod.

Ray lifted Hope off the ground and carried her into the Red Cross hut.

CHAPTER FORTY-FOUR

Red Cross Hut
RAF Compound
Stalag IVB, Germany

Anna sat on a straw mattress behind a false wall constructed out of Red Cross boxes. Beside her, a rusted washbasin, a cracked mirror, and a half-used bar of soap. She wore Marta's trousers with the cuffs rolled up and Nowak's greatcoat. Her only possessions stuffed in the pockets: her black-beaded rosary, the shoelace, a pencil, and the poem written on a scrap of paper.

Her leg ached. The throbbing had worsened.

Taking off Mrs. B's cap, she looked in the mirror and ran her fingers through the wisps of hair that had grown back. The door on the other side creaked open. Footsteps entered the hut.

She put the cap back. Her tension eased when Nowak poked his head around the false wall.

"Why did you bring me here?" she asked.

Clearing his throat, he shifted his weight from one foot to the other. "You helped me. Now I want to help you. You'd never make it to the train station with that bullet wound."

He sat beside her and put his arm around her tiny frame. She leaned her head on his shoulder.

"How did you end up in Ravensbrück?" he asked. "You didn't get arrested for helping us, did you?"

"The bloody SS caught me with a Jewish child."

"You're lucky to be alive."

"Yes, I am," she said. "But the child was killed. His name was Aaron. I . . . I should have protected him." She tried to keep her voice from breaking.

"You can't blame yourself. They have no mercy killing children," he said.

Emotions she'd held back for so long, surfaced. She couldn't stop talking. She told him about the mobile gas chamber and the shooting alley. About the doctors and their experiments on the Polish women. And about working at the Siemens factory.

He listened.

She told him about the Beast. How she took pleasure in feeding her dog in front of the starving women. How she stole her brother's baby. And how she strapped women to the beating trestle and whipped them. But she didn't tell him about the lashes she endured. She didn't want him to know about the ugly scars on her back and how disfigured she was.

"Let me see your wound," he said, after she had a chance to settle down.

Anna rolled the leg of her trousers up to her knee and unwrapped the piece of material tied around her calf, now caked in dry blood. The bullet's entrance and exit points were red and swollen with a festering infection.

"I'll be back. You rest while I'm gone." He kissed her on the cheek.

She felt drained and tried to sleep, but every time she drifted off, she would awaken. With every sound, her body flinched. Closing her eyes, she touched her cheek where Nowak had kissed her.

He returned carrying two sauerkraut buckets, one with warm water and the other with hot saltwater. He set the buckets on the floor, picked up an empty box, and placed it upside down on the mattress. Then covered it with a blanket.

"Keep your leg up as much as possible." He gently lifted her leg and rested it on the box.

He removed a rag sterilized in boiling water from the first bucket. Wrung it out, rubbed it with the bar of soap, and dabbed the open wound to remove the purulent discharge.

She clenched her teeth.

After washing the wound, Nowak grabbed the cloth soaking in saltwater in the second bucket. "This is going to hurt." He wrapped the cloth around the infected area.

"Squeeze my hand." He reached his hand out to hers.

She gripped it tightly. They sat for a while in silence.

"That's enough for today." He removed the cloth and covered her with a blanket. "Try to put this leg up," he said, covering her with the blanket. "I've got to get going. It's almost curfew. Try to get some sleep."

Before leaving, he reached down to remove the cap on her head. She held it in place with both hands.

CHAPTER FORTY-FIVE

Red Cross Hut
RAF Compound
Stalag IVB, Germany

On Nowak's way out of the Red Cross hut, he saw Michal posting the latest edition of the camp newspaper on his barrack wall. Like their *Flywheel* magazine, *THE NEW TIMES* was hand-written and hand-illustrated, and it included reports on sports competitions, reviews of the theatre productions, short stories, poems, and any interesting news received in letters.

He ducked around the corner to avoid chitchat. All Michal ever wanted to talk about was either escape or his missing sister. Anna. Anna. Anna. And if it wasn't Anna, it was someone by the name of Zophia.

Nowak had his hands full with Hope and he had to keep her existence an absolute secret. He could talk to the forger later.

"How's Freddie?" Nowak asked Ray when he got back to his hut.

"He's sleeping," Ray said. "He got a letter from Izzie."

"Did he tell you what she said?"

Ray shook his head. "He's all choked up. And refusing to talk about it. This is the worst I've seen him," Ray said. "He gave me his model motorboat."

Nowak had fond memories of the day Freddie surprised them at a regatta on the dugout with a boat propelled by the spring motor from a broken gramophone. "What's her problem, anyway? What the hell does she expect him to do from here?" He looked over at his friend lying on his bunk and had no idea what to do about the situation. "We're all trying our damnedest to find him a way out of this hole."

"I checked the hospital for medicine for Hope like you asked. This is all they have." Ray handed over two round yellow pills.

"What are they?" Nowak glared down at them in the palm of his hand.

"Quinine."

"For malaria?"

Ray nodded. "They've got nuthin' that'll help a bullet wound."

Nowak thought about the kiss he gave Hope and the taste of the salt from her tears. Needing to get his mind off the girl, he gathered up his journal, the paintbrushes he'd made from Freddie's hair, and a tin can of water. He joined a crowded table of airmen painting on blank pages in their journals using watercolors that arrived in a Red Cross shipment and more colors made from foodstuffs. Dropping the quinine tablets into the water, he stirred until the mixture turned a hue of yellow.

"Found us some yellow paint," he said, placing the tin in the middle of the table to share with the others.

He opened his journal to the first page, a watercolor of the RAF badge: the Imperial Crown on top of an eagle volant with the words *Per Ardua Ad Astra* meaning *Through Adversity to the Stars*, and laughed to himself when he remembered how riled up Ray had gotten over an argument, whether the bird was an eagle or an albatross. Flipping through the pages, he stopped at a blank page and ripped it out of the book.

He had an idea.

CHAPTER FORTY-SIX

Early the next morning, Nowak stood among a group of airmen and watched the Polish women march out of the main gate on their way to the train station. Mrs. B pressed forward, clutching the vanity case. Marta carried her baby and wore Anna's torn skirt with the missing hem. When she fell behind, the guard on escort duty struck the back of her legs with his rifle.

The airmen watched in silence as their distant images vanished. Before the women arrived in camp, the men, who were emotionally and physically starved for contact with the opposite sex, survived on treasured memories from the days before barbed wire—the sound of women's voices, the touch of their skin, the warmth of their bodies. Even from the other side of the wire, the female prisoners had generated excitement and desire long ago stifled.

Now that the women had left, the bleak, tedious boredom would return. Tomorrow and each day after would be the same, one day flowing into the next with nothing to look forward to and nothing left to talk about.

But Nowak had his hands full. He pulled a chair up to the tin-bashing table cluttered with empty cans from Red Cross parcels. Powdered milk. Sardines. Dried eggs. Bully beef. Jam.

Some flattened and some not, in all shapes and sizes, and a couple of broken chair legs, too.

Each POW received one spoon. That was it. Before taking food over to the Red Cross hut for Hope, he had to make her a plate. He picked up a fat lamp: a tin of margarine with a wick made from a drawstring of a pair of pajamas. Then selected two flattened tin cans, folded over the edge of one, and slid it into the folded-over edge of the second. Using a chair leg as a mallet, he bashed the seam tight.

He rolled another piece of tin into a tube, covered one end with cloth and blew through it while holding the opposite end over the flame. With his other hand, he held the seam of a bully beef can to the flame until the solder liquefied, dripping from the can onto the seam of his invention to make a waterproof seal.

Nowak stood in line for his daily ration of soup and black bread, then headed over to the Red Cross hut with the food hidden in a bucket. Hope was sitting up on the mattress, with the blanket wrapped around her shoulders, shivering. He put the bucket down and reached out to touch her forehead.

She had a burning fever.

"Try to eat. You need your strength to fight the infection." He handed over his klim of soup.

Hope wrapped her trembling hands around the klim and slowly sipped the broth.

"Good. Now take a bite of the bread." He handed her his bread ration on the tin plate. "There's something else." Reaching into his pocket, he presented her with a paper airplane he'd made from the page he'd ripped out of his journal.

She set the klim down and took the gift in her hands. "Thank you."

It was good to see her smile. "Do you want me to contact your family? I could send a letter out for you," he offered.

"I wrote them as often as I could from Ravensbrück. They never answered."

"There could be a lot of reasons for that," he said.

"Have you heard any reports on the Uprising?"

"It's all bad," he said, not wanting to tell her how bad. He glanced at his watch. "I have to leave for a bit. I have some work to do for the escape committee. Try to get some sleep."

*

As soon as Nowak entered the Empire Theatre, Michal moved toward him. "Where have you been?"

Nowak couldn't tell his friend about Hope, so he deflected the question. "Any news on the Uprising?"

"Disaster. Warsaw is under twenty-four-hour bomb attacks by the *Luftwaffe*. Thousands of residents have been murdered," Michal said. "Have you come up with a plan?"

"Not yet."

Michal trudged away.

Nowak took a seat next to Ray and picked a navy sweater, with holes in the elbows and frayed cuffs, up off the table. To unravel the stiches and wind the wool into a ball, he grabbed a loose piece of yarn.

"Michal looks upset," Nowak said.

"He's under a lot of pressure. He's countin' on you," Ray said. "He hasn't been in camp long enough to make contacts or build up a supply of food and cigarettes to barter with."

"I want out as bad as he does. It gets tougher every day." Nowak sighed. "When did these reports surface?"

"A couple days ago."

"I haven't heard a word."

"You've been tied up with that girl."

"Can you talk to Syd about some clothes for her? And we need a travel permit. We need to be prepared."

"Prepared for what? How do we get her out of here?"

"I don't know yet. She can barely stand, let alone walk. We need a medic to look at her leg."

"Can we risk it? We can't let anyone know she's here."

"We have to. She's weaker today, and she's running a fever. I'm really worried. There's got to be someone—"

"What about Yuri the Russian? He's a doctor," Ray suggested. "He already knows something is up. He was involved with the ruckus when Fritz opened the gate."

"Damn good idea. Make something up to get him over here. Tell him it's strictly need-to-know. He has to keep this quiet."

Nowak looked around. "Where's Freddie?"

"He refused to get out of bed."

"Not again. I can't take my eyes off him for a minute. He's got me worried too." Nowak put his elbows on the table and rested his head on his hands.

It was near curfew. He had just enough time to pick up *Zwiebel* and drop by the Red Cross hut with the knitting needles he'd made out of barbed wire and the balls of navy wool. Hope needed something to get her mind off how sick she was.

"I brought someone to keep you company." He handed her the kitten."

Holding it up to her face, she brushed her cheek against its soft fur. "Awww. What's her name?"

"Zwiebel."

A smile broke out on Hope's face.

"Do you know how to knit?"

She nodded.

"Here's something to keep you busy." He placed the balls of wool and the needles on the mattress. "I'll see you in the morning."

Back at his hut, Nowak found Ray hunched over a letter.

"News from home?" Nowak asked.

"A letter welcoming me as a member of the Goldfish Club." He held up a membership card and insignia. "You'll get one too. Everyone that survives a ditching with an inflatable life preserver or a rubber dinghy is a lifetime member. Gold for the value of life. Fish for the sea," Ray explained.

Nowak stopped at Freddie's bunk. "Did you get a letter from Izzie?" he asked.

"What difference does it make?" Freddie snapped.

"Tell me what she said."

"It doesn't matter."

"Of course it matters."

"Nothing matters anymore. It's too late." Freddie rolled onto his side and turned his back to Nowak.

"Too late for what?"

Freddie didn't answer.

"I know what you're going through, Freddie. Try not to lose hope."

Freddie had livened up once the women arrived. It gave him something to think about right until the day he received the damn letter from Izzie. Freddie loved her and he loved his son. He'd do anything to get out of this hole. What the hell did she say to him?

CHAPTER FORTY-SEVEN

RAF Compound
Stalag IVB, Germany

Yuri arrived at the Red Cross hut, bone thin and scruffy, and sputtering a battery of questions. "Who is she? Where'd she come from? Are you crazy?" He confirmed Nowak's fear that the situation was critical. "We've got to do something fast. She's lost a lot of blood. She needs medication to fight the infection."

"The hospital block is out of supplies," Nowak said.

"We can try maggot debridement. They eat the poison and rotten flesh. There's no shortage of them around here," Yuri said.

"Are you sure?" Nowak felt a gagging sensation in the back of his throat.

"It's our only option."

Hope was frantic upon hearing the news. Nowak wasn't sure what upset her more. Trusting her life to a Russian or a bunch of maggots.

"Maggots? You want to put maggots on my leg?" she asked.

"Yuri says it'll work."

"You can't believe a Russian," she said. "What's he doing here?"

"He's here to help you."

"I don't want his help. He's NKVD. Soviet secret police. I see his red star badge. Keep him away from me."

"Yuri's a doctor. Your condition is serious. You don't have a choice," Nowak said.

He tried his best to reassure her, holding her hand as Yuri laid each wriggling maggot on the necrotic tissue. They stopped the procedure when Hope hyperventilated.

"Try to slow your breathing." Nowak stroked her hand. "Take slow breaths. That's right. Slow."

Once they'd placed the fly larvae on the wound and bandaged her leg, she settled down. When Yuri was ready to leave, he motioned for Nowak to follow him, stopping on the other side of the boxes. "We'll give it a couple of days for her fever to break. Monitor her carefully. And keep her hydrated," he instructed. "We don't want to amputate under these conditions. We don't have a saw sharp enough."

Nowak cringed at the thought.

"I'll come back before curfew. I can stay with her overnight. They'll never miss me in my compound," Yuri said before leaving.

Nowak knelt by Hope's side.

"How are you feeling?" He picked up a damp cloth to wipe her brow.

Before she could answer, he heard the door open and the stomping of boots.

"*Was ist los?*" came a voice.

It was Fritz. Nowak put his finger to his lips and motioned for Hope to be quiet. The footsteps stopped in front of the false wall.

"Who's here?" Fritz called out.

Nowak thought for a second. Fritz must have seen Yuri leave. He had to face him. "It's just me." He slipped out from behind the boxes.

"What are you doing?" Fritz asked.

"Looking for my cat."

"What's going on?" Fritz scrutinized the boxes and the false wall.

"Nothing."

Fritz came forward.

"Don't go back there, Fritz."

"What have you got?" He smirked. "Hooch?"

"Exactly," Nowak said, but it was the wrong answer.

Fritz wanted a drink and kept going. Stepping behind the boxes, he stopped in front of the mattress.

Hope pulled the blanket over her head.

Fritz ripped it away, knocking her cap off.

Hope recoiled in fear.

"Good God. It's a girl." Fritz stepped back in shock.

"She's sick, Fritz. Really sick," Nowak said.

"I have to report this." Fritz slung the rifle off his shoulder.

"No one needs to know."

"It's my duty to report her," Fritz said. "*Der Führer*—"

"*Der Führer,* my ass. This has nothing to do with the fucking *Führer*." Nowak grabbed the barrel of the gun. He could easily overpower the old guard. "She's sick. And I'm trying to help her. If you report her, they'll kill her. And I'll tell them you were involved."

"What are you talking about?"

"You unlocked the gate for us. Remember?"

Recognition registered in his eyes.

"They'll send you to the Eastern Front if they find out," Nowak said. "Help us. She'll lose her leg if we don't do something. All we need is a couple of days."

"And then what?" Fritz asked.

Before Nowak could answer, a German shepherd barked. The door handle rattled.

"Just a couple of days," Nowak whispered, as he stepped back behind the false wall.

The door opened.

Nowak saw Pick Axe through a narrow slit between the boxes. He held his breath and moved his finger over his mouth to motion Anna to be quiet.

"What are you doing?" Pick Axe demanded.

"My inspection," Fritz said.

"Did you find anything?"

"*Nein*."

"Let me look." Pick Axe took a step into the doorway and tried to push past Fritz.

"This is my job. Not yours." Fritz shoved him back and walked outside.

The door slammed shut.

Still holding his breath, Nowak's brain screamed for oxygen. He let out a burst of air and sucked it back in just as quick. Turning to Hope, he dropped to his knees and wiped tears from her cheeks.

"It's all good now. They're gone. Everything will be all right."

"All right? Nothing is all right. I heard you say I might lose my leg." She sobbed. "I'll never make it out of here, will I?"

"Of course you will."

"I don't think so."

"Don't talk like that. You have your whole life ahead of you. You can't give up. I'll take care of you." He brushed her cheek. "Try to sleep. You need your strength."

"I'm afraid to sleep." Hope's breathing intensified. "I might not wake up."

"I'll stay with you." He took her hand. "Take slow, deep breaths. Try to think about something else," he said. "What do you like?"

"Nothing," she sniffed.

"Come on. There must be something," he persisted.

"I used to like to dance," she said, but the thought of it only upset her more.

"What else? There must be something else."

"*Gwiazdy*," she said between hard breaths. "I like the stars."

"Do you want to see them?" He picked her up and cradled her in his arms. Carrying her to the window, he removed enough cardboard to see outside.

"There's the *Gwiazda Polarna*." She rested her head against his chest. "What's it called in English?"

"Polaris."

"Pole-Lar-Is," she pronounced slowly.

"That's right. It's also called the North Star."

They watched the night sky for some time before he said, "Close your eyes."

She closed her eyes.

Remembering when she told him in Warsaw about her dream to one day fly, he said, "Imagine us flying. Just the two of us. The sun is shining into the cockpit. I tip the wings so you can look down. Do you see the trees and the mountains in the distance?"

"I see them," she said as her breathing slowed.

"Then we climb higher and higher through the silver-rimmed clouds until we break through. Now we are gliding on top. When you look up, there's nothing but blue skies."

"Where are we going?"

"Anywhere you want. The war is over. We're free."

A searchlight scanned the grounds. The light shone through the window, onto her. She raised her hand to cover her face.

"What's the matter?" he asked.

"I must look awful. I didn't want you to see."

"I think you're beautiful."

He'd never known a girl like her. Defiant and willing to give up her life for her beliefs. So young and fragile, yet so strong. He wanted to erase her pain. Make it better. But he didn't know how.

He carried her back to the mattress and covered her with the blanket. "Try to sleep. You need to build up your strength."

"Don't leave me," she whispered before closing her eyes.

"I'm here." He lifted *Zwiebel* up to snuggle in beside her.

CHAPTER FORTY-EIGHT

Red Cross Hut
RAF Compound
Stalag IVB, Germany

Anna woke when the door squeaked open. Heavy footsteps entered. Fear shot through her like a bullet. In the dark, she couldn't make out who it was. She pulled the covers up under her chin.

"Don't be afraid," he said in a thick Russian accent.

It was Yuri.

"What are you doing here?" she asked.

"I won't hurt you," he told her.

"How can I trust you?"

"We are all prisoners here."

"You're NKVD. Russian secret police. You're responsible for the murder of four thousand Polish officers found in a mass grave in the Katyn Forest."

"I'm not proud of what my comrades have done. But the world is not the same as it was. We all do bad things now. It's a matter of survival. For all of us."

Anna didn't answer.

"You must keep yourself hydrated. Here. Have a drink." He held a tin can of water up to her mouth. "Now you must rest." He tucked the blanket in around her.

Her eyes felt heavy. Too weak to argue, she drifted off to sleep.

She awoke in a fright from another nightmare about a *Totenkopf* with blood red lips chasing her through the underground tunnels. Yuri calmed her down by humming Soviet war songs to put her back to sleep.

In the morning, she found a small doll beside her made from woven straw tied together with binder twine and barbed wire.

CHAPTER FORTY-NINE

Seated at their table, Ray and Syd reviewed the Nazi names on the hit list they wanted arrested and prosecuted. Or better yet, hanged.

"I've got more names for that list of yours," Nowak said. "You won't believe what those Nazi bastards are doing at that women's camp."

Ray pulled the pencil out from behind his ear. "Give me details."

"Ursula Fleischer. Wardress at Ravensbrück."

Ray wrote the name down.

"Sorry, Nowak, this list isn't for women," Syd said. "It's for the Nazis committing mass murder."

Nowak pulled up a chair and sat down. He filled them in on everything Hope had told him.

"Well, I'll be damned," Ray said.

"Hope calls her the Beast," Nowak told them.

"Move the Beast to the top of the list," Syd said.

"I've got more," Nowak said. "Doctors there are doing experiments on the Polish political prisoners."

"What do you mean, experiments?"

"They simulate gunshot wounds by making incisions in their legs, then add glass splinters, wood chips, and strains of bacteria."

"Bacteria?"

"Staph, strep and gangrene."

"Are you sure?" Ray asked, pencil poised to take notes. "Why?"

"To induce infections to test their sulfa drugs. Hope told me all about it. I've got the names," he pulled a piece of paper out of his pocket and read, "Dr. Karl Gebhardt, Dr. Fritz Fischer, Dr. Herta Oberhauser," he handed the list over. "Here. I've got to get going."

"We need the name of the camp commandant," Ray shouted after him.

Nowak headed over to the Red Cross hut to see Hope. Her fever remained; she drifted in and out of sleep. Yuri dropped by in the early afternoon to check on her.

"There's no change," Yuri advised. "If gangrene sets in, we'll have to amputate."

"There must be something more we can do."

"Not without medication."

"I'd get it for her if I could figure a way out of here."

"Try to get some fluids into her."

Nowak sat with Hope until curfew, waking her now and then to coax her to take a drink. Raising her head with his arm, he held the klim to her lips. "Drink. You need water."

"I can't. I'll be sick." She pushed his hand away.

"Yes, you can," he insisted.

She shook her head.

"Just a little."

She opened her mouth and took a sip.

"Good. A little more. Then I'll let you rest."

Yuri took over for the night shift. Nowak returned to his hut. He settled back on his bunk, trying to think of a way to get Hope out of camp. Memories of his father and how he had suffered with gangrene flooded his mind. He'd seen the damage untreated gunshot wounds could do in a matter of hours.

He gazed at the pictures of his mother and sister he'd received in a letter from home; thankful they were far away from the horrors he experienced. He kept their photos where he could look at them every night, stuck in the bed boards of the bunk above him. They reminded him that there was a real world outside of this hellhole and that someday he would return. But when? The uncertainty was the worst. Taking one day at a time was the only way to survive; otherwise, it was just too difficult.

In a few minutes, they'd be locked inside until morning. He stared at the bunk above him. Sometimes it seemed to move closer, almost smothering him. It was moments like this that he tried to think of the good times he and Freddie had back at the pub in England.

"Freddie," Nowak called out. "Remember that time at the Eagle pub when we burned our initials in the ceiling?"

No answer.

"Freddie?"

Nowak threw off his blanket and climbed down off his bunk.

"Where's Freddie?" He looked around.

"Saw him go outside," someone said.

"It's almost curfew." Nowak charged out the door. Freddie walked toward the barbed wire fence. Searchlights scanned the grounds, weaving back and forth across the darkness.

"Freddie," Nowak shouted. "Where are you going?"

Freddie didn't answer.

Nowak felt a surge of panic and ran after him. "Wait up," he called out.

Freddie kept walking. The beam of a searchlight caught him in its scope. A warning shot rang out. The second shot landed in front of Nowak, spraying dirt in his face.

"Jesus, Freddie," he shouted. "Stop!"

Freddie raised his leg to step over the warning wire. Nowak grabbed his shirt and jerked him back. They wrestled to the ground.

Freddie jumped up and took another step toward the wire. Nowak grabbed his ankle.

"Let me go," Freddie yelled. He tried to shake his leg free from Nowak's grip.

Nowak yanked his leg, hard. Freddie lost his balance and fell back. Nowak scrambled to his feet. Standing over Freddie, he reached down and grabbed his arm.

"Come on, Freddie. Get up. Go back to bed."

"Just let me go." Freddie pulled his arm away.

Nowak shook his head. "Everything will look better in the morning."

"Don't make the same mistakes I have." Freddie looked away.

"What are you talking about? We're going to get out of here. You'll get back to England."

"It's too late for me. I've lost everything. But it's not too late for you."

"Don't talk like that. You're not thinking straight. We can talk this through," Nowak said.

Freddie didn't answer.

"Get up. And that's an order."

Freddie stood, head hung low. Nowak put his arm around his friend and led him back to their hut. The searchlight tracked their movements.

Freddie climbed up onto his bunk and flopped down. Nowak grabbed a book, determined to watch him until Fritz came to lock the hut for the night. Freddie couldn't get out after that. He'd try to talk some sense into him in the morning.

Within minutes, Fritz entered the hut and stopped by Nowak's bunk.

"I need to talk to you," Fritz whispered.

"Not now, Fritz. I need to keep an eye on Freddie."

"Now," Fritz ordered. He looked worried.

Nowak followed Fritz outside. Fritz motioned Nowak around the corner of the hut.

"Is she gone yet?" Fritz asked.

"No."

"You've got to get her out of here."

"It's not that easy."

"What do you need?"

"A train schedule would be useful," Nowak said sarcastically.

Machine-gun fire erupted in the yard. Nowak ran back out front. Freddie stood in the beam of a searchlight only inches from the warning wire. One more step, and the guard would shoot to kill.

"Freddie . . . Don't do it!"

Freddie looked back at him.

Nowak held his hands up, palms forward, and took a tentative step. "Take it easy, Freddie," he pleaded. A spray of machine-gun fire hit the ground in front of him.

Freddie didn't answer.

"You don't want to do this."

"You don't know what I want." Freddie looked at the ground.

"Yes, I do," Nowak persisted. "Think about all the good times we've had. That's what keeps me going."

Freddie stood silent.

"Think about your son."

Freddie raised his head and looked at Nowak. He wiped a tear away from his swollen eyes. "That's all I think about."

"Please don't do this. I'm begging you," Nowak pleaded.

"It's better this way. For everyone," Freddie said.

"For Christ's sake, Freddie!" Nowak screamed.

Freddie stepped over the line and reached for the barbed wire. Slowly and deliberately, he climbed the fence. The first shot hit him in the lower back. He clung to the wire. Within seconds, machine-gun fire riddled his body with bullets. He lost his grip and slipped to the ground.

Then machine-gun fire erupted in front of Nowak. Fritz grabbed him by the scruff of the neck and pulled him back. Nowak turned toward the hut and smashed his fist into the wall, pounding it again and again until his knuckles bled.

CHAPTER FIFTY

RAF Compound
Stalag IVB, Germany

Sensing someone looking over his shoulder, Nowak slid his hand under the table to hide the cuts and bruises on his fist. Without a word, Fritz removed a train schedule from his pocket and set it in front of Nowak. Their eyes locked for a moment before the old guard walked away.

Nowak's thoughts went back to Freddie. If he hadn't spent so much time with Hope, he would have seen it coming. If he hadn't agreed to talk to Fritz, he could have stopped Freddie. After all, he'd seen it before, the way barbed wire disease ate at a man's soul. Freddie wasn't the first in the barracks to kill himself. He wouldn't be the last.

Nowak heard footsteps. He slid the train schedule inside his journal.

"Aren't you coming to the meeting?" Michal asked. "They're waiting for you."

"Give me a minute." Nowak closed his book and laid it on his shelf. By the time he arrived at the escape committee meeting, plans to smuggle a prisoner out during Freddie's funeral were underway. The mood amongst the men was glum.

"It's your turn, Nowak. You're up." Snowshoe puffed on a cigarette. "Are you ready?"

Nowak's kitbag had been packed and hidden behind the ceiling boards since the tunnel collapse. He had the forged passports for all members of the escape committee, maps, and *Reichsmarks* from the rigged Monopoly game. Syd had made civvies for him. This was his last chance.

But what about Hope? He couldn't just leave her behind. Maybe he could take her with him.

"Are we making a switch, as usual?" he asked.

"There's no one to switch with to keep the numbers. We can cover for you during the head count at the graveyard. And we'll rent a Russian as a stand-in when we get back to camp."

"Could we send someone else out instead?" He wasn't sure why he even asked that question. Hope would never make it out of Germany on her own with her bum leg. Hell, she wouldn't have a chance.

"What's with you today?" Michal said. "If you're not ready, I am."

Nowak needed time to think. A dozen men, anxious to take his place, watched. If he told them about Hope, it would jeopardize her safety. Worse yet, Snowshoe would be pissed and send him to the back of the line. And a bloody long line it was.

He had failed Freddie, but he still had a chance to save Hope. If he got out of this hellhole, he could find her some medicine and smuggle it into camp with a work party. It was risky, but so was everything else these days.

If he stayed, there was nothing more he could do. Hope's condition was critical. He couldn't just sit around and wait for gangrene to devour her.

He was out of options.

*

Anna opened her eyes and wondered how long she'd slept. She crawled out of bed and limped over to the basin to wash her face and hands. Feeling dizzy, she sat back down on her mattress. *Zwiebel* crawled onto her lap.

She had woken many times to discover Yuri at her bedside, and she wanted to do something to thank him. The only thing she had to give was the sweater she was knitting. Winter was approaching, and there was no heat in Yuri's compound. She picked up the barbed wire needles and got to work.

Her mind drifted over the events of the last few days. She couldn't remember much, but she remembered Nowak telling her: *I think you're beautiful.*

For the first time in years, she felt hopeful. Maybe someday they would be free. And when that happened, they might have a future together. Did she dare to dream?

Nowak entered the hut. She smiled at him. He didn't smile back.

"I heard gun fire last night," she said, a sense of dread washing over her. She noticed cuts on his knuckles. "What happened?"

"Freddie was killed."

"I'm so sorry. I know how close you were." She reached for him.

He pulled away.

"There's more." He sat down beside her. "I have a chance to escape during the funeral procession."

"Take me with you."

"I can't."

"Why not?"

"There's only room for one. I thought about sending you out instead, but you'd never make it on your own."

"You brought me here and now you're going to leave me here. All alone?" She turned her eyes away from his. Everything she'd hoped for came crashing down that moment.

"Yuri will come and see you later this evening. You must do what he advises. You're not out of the woods yet. The infection could spread." He touched her forehead. "I'll find you some medicine and smuggle it into camp."

"How are you going to do that?"

"I haven't figured that out yet."

"There's nothing to figure out. You'll get yourself arrested if you try." She pressed her lips together. Her chin crumpled. She held the kitten in her arms. "If you're going to leave, then leave. There's nothing left to say."

"Hope, please. Listen to me." He leaned forward.

She moved her face away and felt his lips brush against her forehead.

Then he walked out the door. Just like that.

CHAPTER FIFTY-ONE

Hut 16B
RAF Compound
Stalag IVB, Germany

Nowak felt overwhelmed with sadness at the sight of Freddie's empty bunk. A toy sailboat that Ray made sat on his shelf, carved, sanded, and painted with the words *Freddie Jr.* on the back. The book of poetry, two letters and a folded sheet of paper sat on top of the blanket on his bunk. Nowak pulled out the first letter and read:

June 5, 1944

My dearest Freddie,

It's with deep regret that I'm writing to tell you that your mother is in the hospital with pneumonia. The doctors say she is so weak she may not make it through the night.

She wanted me to tell you how very proud she has always been of you and how much she loves you. We are your only family now, so please come and visit on your return.

With love, Aunt Clara

He reached for the second letter, hesitated before opening it. He read:

August 12, 1944

Dear Frederick,

I got married yesterday to that nice man, the grocer. I know that you will understand my reasons for doing so.

Please do not contact us again. It's better for Freddie to grow up thinking that George is his father. Try to forget us.

Izzie

Nowak touched the blurred ink where Freddie's tears had stained the letter. He swallowed hard. Not stopping Freddie from climbing the wire was something he would regret for the rest of his life. What he wouldn't give to live yesterday over again.

He opened the folded piece of paper. It wasn't a letter. It was a drawing of a coffin. It took him a few minutes to understand that the coffin had a false bottom. Freddie had planned a way to give Nowak an opportunity to escape with Hope during his funeral.

Nowak hustled back to his hut to organize his gear and say his goodbyes. He had to travel light. He'd take the handcuffs, his journal, the paintbrushes made from Freddie's hair, and his last Lucky Strike cigarette. With proper documentation and decent civilian clothes, this time, he'd make it back to England.

Ray sat across from him, carving a long piece of wood.

"Anything you want me to do when I get out?" Nowak asked.

"Will you contact my wife and kids?" Ray continued to whittle.

"Yep." Nowak pulled the black-and-white photographs of his family out from between the slats of the bunk above him. His favorite was the photo of his sister wearing her gym clothes with a basketball under one arm, holding a medal from a local tournament. He slipped them between the pages of his journal and placed the book inside his kitbag.

"I'm taking her with me," he announced.

"'Bout time you came up with a plan. Fess up," Ray said.

"I found this with Freddie's things," Nowak tried to keep his voice from cracking. He handed the paper over to Ray.

"Well, I'll be damned," Ray said.

"I let Freddie down, but I can still help Hope. We build a false bottom in Freddie's coffin for her to hide in on the way to the graveyard. I go in the march. You cover for me during the head count on the way back." Nowak scratched his head. "There's just one problem. She'll have trouble walking on her own when we take off from the graveyard."

"I'm carving her a cane. I knew you'd think of somethin'." Ray held out the piece of wood he was working on. A cane with a horse's head carved on the handle. Nowak hadn't even noticed.

"What about Michal?" Ray asked.

"What about him?"

"He's your lookout. You can't pull this off without him knowing. He wants out of here as much as you do. He'll never agree."

"Let's go have a chat with him," Nowak said.

Ray hopped off his bunk, cane in hand.

Nowak developed a strategy on the way to Michal's hut. "We'll work on his sympathies. Play up how young she is. Poor little sick girl. Make him feel guilty. She's Polish. You're Polish. Stuff like that."

They found Michal making a puppet out of old socks, a two-faced villain with Hitler on one side and Stalin on the other, for the evening's theatre production organized by the Polish prisoners.

"We've got a big problem," Nowak said to his friend.

"What's wrong?" Michal asked.

"I have to smuggle someone out of camp with me. I need your help."

"No way. I've got to get to Warsaw."

"It's a girl. She's Polish."

"I thought they all left."

"Not this one. If she doesn't find a doctor, she's not going to make it," Nowak said. "Just come and meet her."

CHAPTER FIFTY-TWO

Red Cross Hut
RAF Compound
Stalag IVB, Germany

Nowak's words pounded in Anna's head, razor sharp like barbed wire and flying shrapnel. This couldn't be happening. After everything he'd said to her. After all the promises, he got up and walked out the door.

She wiped the kiss from her forehead. She'd never trust anyone again. What a fool she was. She should have known something would go wrong. She was thinking like a child. He didn't give a damn about her. Why would he? Look at her. She hadn't had a shower for weeks; she had maggots crawling on her leg. Worse yet, her back was covered in scars.

Now what was she supposed to do? Yuri was on his way over. What if he decided to amputate? With no anesthetics inside camp, the Germans would hear her scream. They'd lock her in solitary confinement. Or maybe they'd ship her back to Ravensbrück. She'd never go back there. No matter what happened.

When the door swung open, she grabbed her rosary. Was Yuri there already? *Take me now, God. Please. Take me now.*

"Hope. It's just me," Nowak whispered.

"What are you doing back here?" She picked up the paper airplane he'd made for her and threw it at him. "I trusted you. Stay away from me."

"But—"

A familiar voice spoke. "Anna."

She knew instantly who it was. Her anger vanished.

Michal rushed to his sister's side, hugging her so tightly she couldn't breathe. Turning to Nowak and Ray, he asked, "What did you do to her?"

"Nothing. I tried to help her," Nowak stammered.

"How long have you kept this from me? Why didn't you tell me?"

"I thought your sister's name was Anna. A courier who disappeared. Her name is Hope."

"Hope is her codename in the Underground. You idiot."

Anna grabbed her brother's arm. "Calm down. He's been good to me."

"Are you sure?"

"I'm sure."

"Then why are you angry with him?"

"It doesn't matter." She was so happy to see Michal. She had so much to tell him. So many questions to ask.

Michal had questions of his own. "What happened to you? Where have you been?"

"Ravensbrück. Didn't you get my letters?"

"No. We searched everywhere for you."

"I've missed you so." Anna hugged him again.

Michal noticed her bandaged leg. "What happened?" he asked. "Let me see."

She pulled back.

"Be straight with me, Nowak. How bad is it?"

"She's been really sick." Nowak crossed his arms in front of his chest. "The Russian is coming to see her this afternoon. He's worried."

"The Russian has a name," Anna interjected.

"She needs to get to a hospital. We have a plan to get her out of Germany," Ray said.

"Let's hear it," Michal said.

"We put Anna in a false bottom in the coffin. Nowak marches in the funeral procession. The three of us are pallbearers. We dig the grave at the cemetery. Take our time so the guards get bored. It's too cold for them to stand around and watch us work for long. They'll wander off, probably over by the gate where shrubs block the wind. When the coast is clear, we open the sideboard on the coffin. Nowak and Anna take off," Ray said.

"How can she take off?" Michal asked.

Ray handed him the cane he had carved for her.

Michal grabbed it by the shaft. "What if the guards hang around? What's the backup plan?"

"There isn't one," Nowak said. "We have to make this work. There should only be a few guards, so it won't be too difficult. Most of them are young and inexperienced. That should work in our favor."

"How do we cover for your absence during the head count on the march back?" Michal asked.

"That's the easy part," Ray said. "We've done it before. We'll create a commotion. Get the guards confused. Mix 'em up a bit. We can come up with a plan on the way over. Work out the exact details. When we get back, we'll rent the Russian. Use him for a couple of days as a stand-in during roll call."

"Yuri. Yuri. His name is Yuri," Anna insisted. "Yuri Ivanenko."

"What about Snowshoe?" Michal asked.

"He'll be fit to be tied," Ray said. "But he won't know about it 'til we get back. By then it'll be too late. Nowak and Hope will already be gone."

"I should be the one to take her out," Michal said.

"Nowak's up next," Ray said. "He's worked for this. It's his turn. Plain and simple."

Michal looked deep in thought. "All right. As long as Anna gets out." He turned to Nowak. "If you hurt her, you'll answer to me."

"I'd never hurt her," Nowak said.

"I won't go without you. You come too," Anna told her brother. "We must go back to Warsaw. We need to find Papa."

Michal put his hands on her shoulders. "Listen. You need medical attention. You have to go without me. It's your only chance. Do you understand?" He turned toward Ray and Nowak. "Get things ready."

*

Ray and Nowak hurried out of the Red Cross hut.

"I'll get her papers and the clothes," Ray said. "You finish packing."

Nowak thought of his family. Then he thought about Anna and Michal, reunited after such a long time. Right about now, Michal was telling her the worst news possible, that her father was dead. He wanted to go back to the Red Cross hut and hold her while she cried, but he knew it wasn't his place. Michal was family, her only living relative. They needed time alone.

Back at his bunk, Nowak pulled the photograph of his sister out of his kitbag and looked at it for a long time before sliding it back between the slats in the bunk above him. He knew what he had to do.

CHAPTER FIFTY-THREE

Anna stood beside the coffin Nowak made for Freddie out of the plywood from the Red Cross shipments. She wore Ray's dress with the blue-and-yellow pattern, altered by Syd to fit, and long enough to hide her wounded leg. A coat made of worn army blankets and a scarf wrapped around her head.

"I'm really sorry about your father," Nowak said.

She nodded and leaned her head against his chest. Not wanting to cry, she pressed her lips together and squeezed her eyes shut.

"Everything's going to work out. Trust me," he said.

"Why should I trust you?"

"What do you mean?"

"You said you were leaving me."

Nowak cupped her face. "Listen to me. I didn't mean what I said. I couldn't leave you behind. I—I—" He drew her close to him and kissed her on the lips. She burrowed closer, wishing she could stay there forever, insulated from the depravity, the starvation, and the danger. For a moment, the horror of the circumstances in which they lived ceased to exist.

The door flew open. Ray stuck his head into the woodworking shed.

"Goon up. Make it fast."

Nowak stepped back. "Right now, the only thing that matters is getting you out of Germany and to a hospital." He removed the side partition from the coffin, exposing the false bottom. "It's going to be a rough trip. You'll be in there for several hours. There isn't much room to move, and Freddie's dead body will be above you."

"I can do it," Anna said, recalling the hours spent in the dark sewers under Warsaw.

"Once the plan is in motion, there's no turning back. We'll be right beside you. Ray, Michal, Syd, and I are pallbearers. Remember, we'll signal you when it's safe. Michal will knock on the side of the coffin. He says you'll recognize the knock."

"I will."

"Here are the forged documents, a map, railway schedule, and some money. You keep them in case I get searched." He handed her a burlap pouch. "One more thing." He reached into his pocket. "Here's my lucky compass. See my initials. J.N.," he said, then shoved it in the bag. "Any questions?"

She shook her head.

"Now crawl in." He helped her slide into the narrow space. Peering in, he squeezed her hand. "Above all, don't panic. Try to control your breathing. If you get anxious, take slow, deep breaths."

He secured the wood panel back in place. Patting the side of the coffin, he whispered, "Be safe."

Nowak, Ray, Syd, and Michal carried the casket outside and loaded it onto a horse-drawn cart. Anna lay on her back, her arms to her side, with only inches between her face and the wooden partition on top of her. She felt like she was going to suffocate, so she focused on the light filtering through the air holes. Remembering what Nowak had told her, she calmed herself by taking slow, deep breaths.

Guards yelled commands. A booming voice approached the casket.

"Open it," he ordered.

The lid opened. Anna bit her lip. There was movement above her, pounding on the sideboard.

She wanted to scream. Looked for air holes again. Realized she was cold yet sweating. She could smell death and wanted to gag. Squeezing her rosary, she dug her fingernails into the palms of her hands.

The lid slammed shut. She felt movement. Heard the clattering wheels of the cart on the gravel road. Sounds of men marching. The clop of horses' hooves.

The coffin shook as the cart traveled along the rough dirt road. Closing her eyes, she felt Nowak's lips on hers. He was risking everything to smuggle her out of the camp with him. They had a chance to be free and to be together. She could do this. They'd come this far.

She tried to think about something happy. About the days before the war, when she had a home, a family, and friends. She pictured herself dancing the mazurka in the fancy folk costumes her mama used to sew, rotating around and around the floor with Papa while Michal played the piano. Revisiting her family in her mind slowed her elevated pulse.

Thoughts of her father telling her to carry the music of Polish composers in her heart brought to mind the Polish national anthem, set to a triple meter mazurka, the words defiant and hopeful. Words she had not sung out loud in years because the penalty for doing so was death. She remembered the day the Underground had tapped into the Nazi loudspeaker system and the anthem blared through the streets of Warsaw.

The footsteps of the men slowed. Then stopped. The casket moved off the cart and onto the ground.

A guard instructed the airmen to dig the grave. Shovels clanked. Dirt shifted. She readied herself for Michal's secret knock. And waited.

A guard yelled, "Bury it now!"

The digging continued.

"I said *now*," the guard repeated.

The digging stopped. Ropes slid underneath the coffin. She felt it sway.

No. No. Stop. Knock. Please knock. Oh God. Somebody do something before I'm buried alive. She stifled a scream. The Nazis would kill them all if she was discovered. If someone was going to die, it had to be her.

Her thoughts turned to Samuel. His refusal to gather on the *Umschlagplatz* to be shipped to a death camp like cattle to slaughter. A deep understanding of his last words settled over her. She would not succumb to the Nazis. Even if it was her last breath.

It was a matter of honor.

CHAPTER FIFTY-FOUR

Cemetery
Neuburxdorf, Germany

Pick Axe stood in the howling wind among the rows and rows of wooden crosses, scrutinizing every move at the gravesite. The other guards waited by the entrance gate, smoking and talking next to a clump of bushes that provided shelter from the wind. Between them, a crowd of airmen made up of Freddie's friends and members of the escape committee stood ready to act as a diversion, knowing Nowak's plan to escape. Only Nowak, Michal, Ray, and Syd knew Hope was in the coffin. Syd waited by the chapel to move in when Nowak and Hope took off.

"I told you to lower the coffin," Pick Axe bellowed.

"It's not deep enough." Nowak squeezed the handle of the shovel. Sweat trickled down his back.

"Bury it now."

Nowak ignored his commands and kept digging. Michal and Ray slid the casket closer to the grave.

"I said *now*." Pick Axe kicked the side of the coffin. "It's cold out here."

Nowak climbed out of the grave and threw his shovel on the ground. If Pick Axe kicked the coffin again, he'd kill the bloody ferret. He straightened his arm, and Nick's homemade knife slipped into his hand. He gripped the handle.

Ray fumbled with the ropes under the coffin, shaking his head to warn Nowak not to do anything stupid. If they killed one guard, they would have to kill them all. And when the funeral procession didn't show up back at camp, the Krauts would issue an emergency manhunt with instructions to shoot everyone on sight. The Gestapo would be after them within hours. With no lead-time, they didn't stand a chance.

Ray and Michal held the ropes; the casket swayed over the open grave. The color drained from Michal's face.

Now what?

Nowak stared at Pick Axe. *Walk away, you little bastard. Just walk away.*

Pick Axe didn't move. It was clear he wasn't going anywhere.

"I need a smoke," Nowak said. "Let's take a break." He raised his arm at the elbow. The knife slid back up his sleeve.

"Good idea." Ray moved the coffin onto steady ground.

"Get back to work." Pick Axe raised his rifle.

"What's your hurry?" Ray said.

"Now." Pick Axe shoved the muzzle in Ray's stomach.

Nowak pulled his last Lucky Strike out of his shirt pocket and offered it to Pick Axe.

"American cigarette?" *Take the cigarette, asshole. You know you want it.*

Pick Axe hesitated.

"Guess not." Nowak lifted his arm up as if to throw it on the ground.

Pick Axe snatched the cigarette, put it in his mouth, and patted his pockets for matches. He didn't find any. Nowak shrugged, glanced at the guards by the gate, then picked up his shovel and went back to work.

Pick Axe held the cigarette between his teeth. Ray ignored him, grabbed his shovel, and resumed digging.

"Hurry," Pick Axe mumbled as he headed off to find a match to light his cigarette.

Nowak pretended to dig while he kept one eye on him. *Keep going. Just a little farther. That's it. A few more steps.*

When Pick Axe ventured far enough away, Michal knocked on the coffin, two loud followed by two softer, opened the sideboard, and pulled Anna out. She rolled behind the mound of dirt heaped beside the graveside and curled into a fetal position to hide. Ray replaced the board.

So far, so good.

Nowak glanced at the chapel. They didn't need much time. It wasn't far. He made sure Syd waited in position, ready to make the switch to keep the count. He made a final check to make sure Pick Axe had moved far enough away to make their move.

Shit. The bastard turned around. Pick Axe headed back.

"I'll take care of him," Nowak whispered, making sure his knife was in place. "Michal, get ready to take her and *run*."

"What do you mean?" Michal looked shocked.

"Don't ask questions. There isn't time. Anna has your travel documents. Just look after her for me."

Nowak moved off in the guard's direction. He reached into his pocket and pulled out a pack of matches. "Found some. Move out of the wind so I can light it for you." He positioned himself so that Pick Axe had his back to the burial site while he kept a clear view.

Michal raised Anna up off the ground. She stumbled from the pain in her leg and dropped her rosary. Before she could pick it up, Michal scooped her into his arms and carried her inside the chapel.

CHAPTER FIFTY-FIVE

Cemetery
Neuburxdorf, Germany

Nowak bent down to pick up the rosary. The realization that he might never see Anna again, and the way she'd looked at him with her questioning eyes when Michal carried her off, hit him hard. He found himself mouthing the words, *I love you*, to her. A chance at freedom for both her and her brother was the biggest gift he could give. Her rosary and his memories were all he had now.

He could still hear the dirt falling on the coffin and the haunting notes of the bugle playing "The Last Post," as he left Freddie behind, forever buried in German soil. The emptiness of the stalag and the magnitude of what he'd given up loomed before him. Snowshoe would be furious when he found out what Nowak had done. He'd never get another chance to escape.

News on the Warsaw Uprising had filtered into camp. The runner barreled into Nowak's hut, hopped up on a chair, and announced: "The Home Army evacuated as many Polish citizens as possible out of Old Town through the underground sewer system. After sixty-three days of fighting, the Home Army surrendered. Out of food, water, and ammunition, and with up to two hundred thousand unarmed civilians dead, Warsaw is in ruins. Help from the Allies arrived too late."

Nowak dragged himself into line for his ration of soup. He grabbed his klim and flicked the boiled white maggot floating on top onto the ground. Dipping his spoon into the lukewarm turnip broth, he felt a piece of meat on the bottom. Just as he scooped it up and put the spoon to his mouth, Ray reached out and grabbed his arm.

"What's the matter?" Nowak asked.

"Look at your grub," Ray said.

It wasn't a piece of meat, as he thought. It was a goddamn horse's eye. He dropped the spoon into the mug and threw it at the stove. The contents sizzled as it hit the coal.

He felt like he was going to be sick and went outside.

"*Zwiebel*," he called. "Come here, girl." With so much going on, he had forgotten to put the kitten back in his hut before he left for the graveyard. She was probably wandering around the compound looking for him.

A group of Soviet prisoners returned from a work party with their hands shoved deep in frayed pockets. They approached the fence and pulled out handfuls of lice-infested ground grain to sell. He spotted Yuri in the group, wearing the navy sweater knitted by Hope.

"Have you seen *Zwiebel*?" Nowak asked.

"I tried to stop them," Yuri looked at the ground.

Nowak's stomach flipped. "What do you mean?"

Yuri's eyes moved to a hut in the Russian compound.

Nowak's gaze followed Yuri's. A small, white hide hung outside a Russian hut. Over the next few days, he worked on his journal. With no paints left, he resorted to pencil sketches. Quite suitable, he thought, because all color had gone out of his world.

CHAPTER FIFTY-SIX

Aboard the *Nordic Queen*
Baltic Sea

Anna and Michal had posed as German citizens after they left the Neuburxdorf Cemetery and traveled by rail to the Baltic Sea port of Danzig. The train stopped several times because of strafing by aircraft and to let cars loaded with German troops pass. Most checkpoints had light surveillance due to extensive night bombings, but they were questioned and searched at Gestapo headquarters at Görlitz, Cottbus Railway Station, and Berlin. Thanks to their Aryan features and fluency with the language, together with their forged travel permits and identity papers, they avoided suspicion.

Anna spent most of the trip sleeping, and the rest of the time thinking about Nowak. Replaying the last moments with him over and over in her mind while flooded with oscillating emotions. Heartbroken that he'd remained in camp, yet thankful that he'd sacrificed his chance to escape for her brother.

The MI9 escape map that Nowak had stuffed into the burlap pouch led them to the Baltic Sea port where Swedish ships berthed, marked the location of sentry points to avoid, and a nearby clump of bushes to hide in. During the day, the yard buzzed with activity. By nightfall, the area fell quiet. Gentle waves lapped at the sandy shore and lights from docked ships reflected on the water.

Michal crept up to the wharf where two sailors untied ropes for the *Nordic Queen*, a ship flying a blue flag with a yellow Nordic cross, heading to Stockholm. After much talk and a bribe—all the money they had left—Michal convinced them to smuggle him and Anna onboard.

He carried her onto the ship. The sailors led them to the safest place to hide: the bunker where coal was loaded onboard through a chute on the roof, forming a pyramid. German soldiers rarely crawled over it to inspect the small area in the back because they didn't want to get their uniforms covered in black dust.

Anna and Michal crouched behind the coal. The steel door slammed shut, leaving them in darkness. Engines hummed, but the ship didn't move. German voices shouted. The door to the bunker screeched open. Michal gripped her hand.

"There's nothing in there," one sailor said in a heavy Swedish accent. "Come. Have a drink of Schnapps."

"I heard something," the German said.

"Just rats."

The beam of a flashlight shone into the darkness. The soldier moved inside the bunker and edged his way over the coal. Anna pressed herself against the back of the compartment. Michal's grip grew tighter. The light inched closer. And closer. A couple more feet and the German would see Michal and then her.

Anna squeezed her eyes shut, preparing herself for capture.

Michal let go of her hand. He raised his arms.

"I surrender," he said, revealing himself.

"You're under arrest." The soldier pulled out his revolver. "Get out of there."

Michal scrambled over the coal. Anna remained motionless, frozen in fear. The door shut, leaving her alone in darkness. Voices faded into the distance.

A single gunshot rang out. She held her hand over her mouth. Her chest tightened and her heart palpitated. *Oh my God. No.* She squeezed the compass she held in her sweaty palm.

The engines roared. The ship left port. Hovering in the back of the bunker, minutes seemed like hours until the door opened.

"You can come out now," the Swede said. "We're out of German waters. It's safe."

She crawled toward the door. A muscular arm, with a navy-blue tattoo of a snake wrapped around an anchor, reached for her, and dragged her out.

As she stood on the deck of the ship, covered in black coal dust, brisk sea air washed over her face. The blue flag with the yellow cross flapped in the wind. The coastline melted into the distance as the ship sailed down the channel into the open waters of the Baltic Sea.

Turning to the sailor, she asked, "Where's my brother?"

"A German shot him. They carried him off the ship before we left port."

Her throat tightened. "Is he alive?"

"I don't know."

Every ounce of strength siphoned out of Anna's body. With nothing left to fight for, she collapsed.

CHAPTER FIFTY-SEVEN

Sjukhus
Stockholm, Sweden

Anna lay in a hospital bed in Stockholm. Her leg throbbed. She lacked the strength to get up. She didn't want to live a minute longer. She should have jumped overboard. Better yet, she should have swallowed the cyanide pill the day she was captured in Warsaw. She'd lost everyone and everything that had ever been important to her.

A doctor with a clipboard and a nurse in a white cap walked into the room. Steeped in despair, Anna rolled onto her side, turning her back to them.

"She's in rough shape. There's a bullet wound in her leg. Her back and buttocks are covered in scars," the doctor said. "Has she spoken yet?"

"No," the nurse said.

"How did she get here?"

"Stowaway. A sailor brought her in."

"Do we have a name?"

"No."

"Belongings?" he asked. "Something to identify her by?"

"Some odd clothes and a small compass."

"Maybe she doesn't remember who she is."

"She remembers. I hear her calling out in her sleep. She has terrible nightmares."

"Someone treated her wound with maggot therapy. It saved her life," he said. "She's responding well to the debridement and the medication. Once we get her medical concerns taken care of, we'll get someone to evaluate her mental state. In the meantime, get her to eat something."

They both left the room.

A few minutes later, the nurse returned with a tray of food. "You must be hungry," she said.

Anna didn't react.

The plump nurse sat on the edge of the bed. She held a bowl of yellow pea soup, spoon in hand.

"You need to build up your strength. Try to eat," she said. "My name is Sonja. If you tell me your name, I'll locate your family. The compass you're holding must be very precious. Are J.N. your initials?" she persisted.

Anna shook her head.

"Well then, it must be someone very special." The nurse lifted a spoonful of soup to Anna's lips. "If you want to see them again, you must eat. Just a little."

Anna opened her mouth.

CHAPTER FIFTY-EIGHT

DECEMBER 1944

Hut 16B
Stalag IVB, Germany

The British, Canadian, and American armies stood on the western border of Germany, positioned to cross the Rhine. Bomber Command flew past en route to their targets. Pathfinder flares lit up the night sky with green and red. Air raid sirens wailed. Bomb loads dropped.

Nowak blew on the glass and rubbed the frost with the sleeve of his greatcoat. Snowflakes glistened in the beam of the searchlights scanning the grounds. Fritz marched through the blizzard for his final inspection before going on leave. By the time he trudged through the door, snow covered his helmet and coat.

Nowak gathered the bar of soap he'd been saving. "Take this home to Ilse."

"*Danke.*"

"When will you be back?"

"Christmas Eve."

"They're not letting you stay in Dresden over Christmas?"

"*Nein.*"

Fritz returned on Christmas Eve. He placed his sack on the table and removed the can that usually contained his gas mask.

"Ilse baked for you," he said as he opened the container.

Nowak's face lit up. "A Christmas cake?"

"*Ja.*" Fritz lifted the cake, pre-cut into several pieces from the canister and arranged them on the table.

"Geez, Fritz, thanks." Nowak held his hands on his hips as he admired the cake. "Thank Ilse for me. And wish her a Merry Christmas."

"Let's decorate it," Ray said once Fritz had gone. "I have some chocolate left."

Other men in the hut pulled hoarded bits of food—biscuits, sugar, jam, and powdered milk—hidden behind ceiling boards and wall boards, under mattresses, and inside work boots, to make cakes. They held an open house and invited airmen from the other huts to see their Christmas cake display. A sheet acted as a tablecloth. Streamers and ornaments made from food can labels glued together with soap decorated the room. Tinsel, made from the silver paper in cigarette packages, hung from the ceiling.

Nowak thought about his mother and sister at home with a turkey dinner and a Christmas tree. Then he thought about Anna and told himself she was spending Christmas with Michal somewhere safe. He closed his eyes and dreamed of holding her in his arms, dancing to a slow waltz. He'd give her a gift of jewelry, something really special and expensive. Like pearls. Or maybe a diamond. He'd get down on one knee and . . .

Reality set in when thousands of American soldiers captured during the Battle of the Bulge arrived, and one hundred extra men from the 106th Infantry Division were assigned to his hut, bringing the total to well over three hundred. Having marched for miles and ridden for days in unheated and crowded cattle cars, they were exhausted, frostbitten, and suffering from

malnutrition and dysentery. Nowak and Ray pushed bunks together and removed side planks to fit three men into each
tier. Others slept on tables, or on the cold, damp brick floor. It
didn't feel much like Christmas.

1945

CHAPTER FIFTY-NINE

Air-raid sirens and darkness brought in the New Year. The airmen sang, "It's a Long Way to Tipperary" and passed hooch around. To raise their spirits, Syd and Ray entertained them by candlelight. Ray pranced around dressed like Sugar in a new costume tailored by Syd.

Syd performed his comedy routine. "I once went twelve years without sex." Syd paused for effect. Shook his head. Looked around the room. Put his hand in his pocket. "Then I turned thirteen. I had my bar mitzvah and a whole other world opened up."

The hut erupted in laughter. For a few minutes, Nowak forgot the cramped quarters, the stench, and the hunger. He felt like a human being again.

January continued into the coldest winter on record. Nowak slept in his greatcoat with his boots on. Deliveries of Red Cross parcels stopped. Raids on the coal warehouse started, well-planned operations with briefings and lookouts. When Nowak's turn came up, he crawled in darkness, hiding in shadows as searchlights scanned the grounds, returning with enough coal to survive another day. He buried the stash beneath the floor, in recesses made by chipping away the mortar and removing the bricks. The next evening, the German authorities staked out the warehouse and shot the airman assigned to the raid.

With no coal to heat the barracks, Nowak volunteered to gather firewood in the forest. He poked another hole into his leather belt with a rusty old nail; donned his boots, greatcoat, and wool gloves; rolled up his collar; and joined the group. After gathering a stack of wood under the watchful eye of armed guards, he tied the bundle together with string, threw it over his shoulder, and marched back.

The cold weather broke in early February. The BBC announced the Yalta agreement. Churchill and Roosevelt gave up Eastern Poland to Stalin and agreed to allow a provisional Soviet Communist government to control the rest of the country.

RAF Bomber Command initiated Operation Thunderclap by mobilizing eight hundred aircraft to bomb Dresden. The American Air Force flew hundreds of B-17 Flying Fortress long-range bombers overhead in tight, low-altitude formations with P-51 Mustang escorts to drop bomb loads on the communication infrastructure, industrial factories, and rail, road, and river transportation networks. The city was close enough to the stalag to see the smoke and flames.

Fritz took leave after the raid to check on his wife. Upon his return, he told Nowak the city was in such a state of devastation that German troops lit the ruins on fire to cremate the bodies trapped under the rubble. He spent days searching for his street and his apartment, but he couldn't even find his neighborhood.

"*Meine frau* is dead," Fritz reported, with bloodshot eyes.

"I'm so sorry," Nowak said. And he meant it.

Fritz lowered his tired frame into a wooden chair. He leaned forward and put his face in his hands. "It's all over for me. I have nothing left. I'm throwing my rifle in the Elbe. You'll never see me again."

"Jesus, Fritz. Where will you go?" Nowak asked.

Fritz shrugged his shoulders.

"You can't just leave." Nowak knew Fritz had nowhere to go, now that both his son and wife were dead.

Fritz looked at Nowak. "The commandant's worried about arrests. I overheard them talking. High command is shipping men out of Italy."

"Where to?" This was not good news. Even though Nowak felt sympathy for Fritz, he was also angry and knew Syd would be furious when he heard the Nazi bastards were getting away.

"I don't know. It's all very secret."

"Can you go with them?"

"They're only helping high-ranking officers. I'm just a soldier."

Nowak felt compelled to help the old man. He had no cigarettes. No money. No hooch. He rummaged around in his kitbag for the last remnant of his Red Cross parcel—a can of bully beef. He was starving and so were Ray and Syd, but he owed Fritz for helping Hope. It looked to Nowak like Fritz might cry when he handed it over. His head dropped, his shoulders slumped, and his bottom lip trembled as he walked away.

The gramophone played the only record in Nowak's hut. Vera Lynn sang about the white cliffs of Dover and a time when the world would be free.

CHAPTER SIXTY

Sjukhus
Stockholm, Sweden

After Anna's admission to the psychiatric ward, she was as-signed a new physician, Dr. Frans Eklund, who visited her every day. He couldn't speak Polish and she didn't understand Swedish, so they communicated in English. He asked her ques-tions she refused to answer, voiced theories, and used words like *catatonic*, *shell shock*, and *depression*.

Early one morning, Eklund announced his decision to treat her with electroshock therapy. After the session, she snuck down to the treatment room to investigate what he was talking about. She pushed open the door just enough to see a convuls-ing patient strapped to an examination table with paddles on his head and a cloth stuffed in his mouth.

Panic overwhelmed her. Her mind returned to the punish-ment block at Ravensbrück. She swung her arms to free herself from the straps on the beating trestle. Gagged from the taste of the filthy rag stuffed in her mouth. Smelled sour sweat and heavy perfume.

Her back burned. Her heart raced. Her breathing intensified.

She ducked into the supply room and rifled through boxes of medical supplies stacked on metal shelves, dumping the contents onto the floor. Cotton balls. Syringes. Bandages. Until she found a scalpel.

Charging back into the hallway, she checked both ways to make sure the Beast wasn't following her. With her back to the wall, she slid along the brightly lit corridor to her room where she tried to slow her breathing. She would not let anyone put electrodes on her head and pump electrical currents through her brain. No wonder patients roamed the halls disoriented, with many of their memories erased.

Anna changed into the dress and coat Syd had sewn for her. From her second-floor window, she could tell it was a warm winter day by the puddles of water from the last remnants of snow melting on the ground. She grabbed hold of the bars that secured her window and tried to pull them out of the frame. They wouldn't budge.

With the compass gripped in one hand and the scalpel in the other, she snuck out of her room. From the other end of the hall, she heard Eklund's voice.

"It's time for Anna's treatment," he said. "I'll see if she's in her room."

She ran down the hall and slipped into an empty room, where she waited until someone unlocked the stairwell door. Then crept out, catching the door before it slammed shut. When the footsteps ahead of her faded, she hurried down the stairs. Stepping out the back door of the hospital, she took one last look at the sterile environment that had been her home for months. The sooner she got away from this place, the better. There had been too many days of smelling bleach and being told what to do. She'd been probed, prodded, and analyzed.

As she rushed down the street, she saw a park ahead. Out of habit, she checked for signs forbidding her entry and reminded herself this was Sweden, a neutral country, without war.

Entering the park, she walked amongst the chestnut trees and stopped to pick up a leaf floating in a puddle of melted snow. As she twirled the stem between her fingers, she remembered with fondness how she used to walk in the park with her mother and father to collect leaves in the autumn.

Up ahead, a bench overlooked a small pond. She sat to rest her leg. The park was quiet except for the drumming of a woodpecker. It felt good to breathe fresh air after the smell of imprisonment. Her hospital ward was just another prison with locked doors and bars on the windows. Never again would she allow someone to take her freedom away.

She had finally reached a neutral country without war, but what good did that do her? Her fingers traced the initials carved on the back of the compass. Poland would be south. There was nothing to return to. Her mother and father were dead. Ewa had disappeared. Samuel had perished in the mass suicide. Warsaw was in ruins, and Russia ruled her homeland. She didn't know where her brother was or if he had survived the gunshot on the ship.

By overhearing nurses, she learned of the United Nations Tracing Bureau, an organization that kept information on missing persons and concentration camp survivors, helping them to reunite with friends and family. She needed to go there. They might have information about Ewa and Michal.

She noticed how fashionably dressed the people walking in the park were. Women wore coats with fur collars left unbuttoned showing beautiful dresses in different colors and fabrics. Red. Blue. Rose pink. Aqua. Nothing like the drab, boxy wartime fashions she remembered. Nothing like the striped blue-gray uniform she wore in Ravensbrück.

She felt self-conscious about her clothes. Were people looking at her? Her dress was made from a bed sheet. The pattern she once thought so pretty, blue and yellow blotches made from colored paper soaked in water and dabbed on a white sheet, looked ugly in the sunlight. A sheet, for God's sake, she was wearing a sheet. She tried to hide her dress by buttoning her coat, which made her feel worse because her coat was made from old blankets. This was how to dress a bed, not a woman.

If she entered the Tracing Bureau looking like this, they'd think she was crazy. Maybe she *was* crazy. Here she sat on a park bench, wearing a bed sheet.

She thought of Nowak and wondered if she'd ever see him again. He'd mouthed something to her when they were separated. Did he tell her he loved her? Did she have a future to fight for?

Her eyes darted back and forth to make sure no one was watching her. She'd left the hospital before thinking through her departure. This was not the world she was used to. She needed decent clothes and a place to live before she could make her final escape.

Better to sneak back into the hospital, start talking, and write a letter to Nowak to let him know where she was.

CHAPTER SIXTY-ONE

During the month of March, Allied air forces bombed targets in the war corridor between the advancing east and west fronts where the stalag sat. Two North American P-51Mustangs thundered overhead and strafed the camp, killing six and wounding more. To protect themselves from further attack, Nowak and Ray whitewashed large stones and arranged them on the ground to read POW, then crawled up on the roof to paint the letters there.

A burning B-17 Fortress flew over and parachutes dropped. Nowak and his fellow airmen cheered in support of the American crew when they were brought into camp. Rumor spread that Hitler had ordered the mass execution of all prisoners of war held by the Nazis as revenge for the bombings. An article in a German language newspaper circulated about Hitler's plan for *Niederlagstag*, N-Day, the Day of Defeat when the SS would execute all POWs.

Nowak lay on his bunk, considering his options. He didn't know if he could take another minute, let alone another day, of hunger, cold, and uncertainty. Fritz had left. Freddie was dead. Even *Zwiebel* was gone. And he didn't know if he would ever see Anna again.

He could get it over with if he walked out the door right now. Just like Freddie. It would only take minutes. Sitting up, he swung his legs over the side of his bunk and peered at the barbed wire outside his window. Had he come this far only to be murdered now?

He thought of Hope. And heard his father's words. "Never lose hope."

Picking up his journal, he flipped the pages, stopping at the sketch of the inside of his hut. The rows of wooden tables. Three-tiered bunks. Laundry hung on ropes. Bare light bulbs dangling from the ceiling. Men standing in line to wash their hands in cold water that dripped from a pipe.

The black-beaded rosary marked the page where he'd written lines from letters sent by his mother and sister. When things got tough and he didn't think he could hold on any longer, he read those words over and over to convince himself that he wasn't alone and someone out there gave a damn if he lived or died. And now the mail was cut off, his only lifeline to the outside world. There was nothing he could do but wait. Wait. Wait. Wait. He'd been waiting for years. He told himself there was still hope. Hope, he thought. Had she really been there? Sometimes he felt on the verge of losing his mind. Maybe he'd made the whole thing up.

He ran his fingers along the beads of the rosary and closed his eyes. The gramophone played. Vera Lynn sang about meeting again on a sunny day.

Resting the book on his chest, Nowak's mind clung to the image of Anna's face. His thoughts caressed her features, and his memory revisited the emotion that swept over him when they'd kissed. At that moment, she was there with him. The Krauts couldn't take that away.

His mind wandered on an imaginary journey, driving down the highway in a shiny red Cadillac on a warm summer day, the wind blowing in his face, the Rocky Mountains in the distance. And this time, Anna sat beside him. He took one hand off the steering wheel and wrapped his arm around her.

The bastards weren't going to get the satisfaction of wearing him down. He would see this through to the end, even if it killed him.

"Hey, Sugar? What do you make of the N-Day rumors?" he asked, catching a flea inside his shirt and cracking it between his fingernails.

"Wouldn't put it past 'em," Ray said.

"What's our plan?"

"Go down fightin'."

"Then we better get busy."

Nowak gathered up a stash of everything he could use as weapons. The metal handcuffs. Scissors. Razor blades. Dhobi stick. Homemade knife. Outnumbered and out armed by the Nazis, he planned to put up the best fight he could.

On April 13, the airmen gathered for morning *Appell*. "Roosevelt *Kaput*," Pick Axe announced. After the count, the American prisoners held a memorial service for their president in the Empire Theatre.

Pathfinder flares marked Falkenberg for attack. Trucks could no longer travel down country roads without being strafed by fighter pilots. The bread supply ceased. Electricity shut off. Nowak stood in line for hours to collect drinking water from the well beside the cesspool.

The Anglo-American and Russian forces converged on both sides of the camp. The Red Army lurked within forty kilometers of Mühlberg. District sirens sounded the first general alarm. The commandant gathered the men of confidence for each compound and asked them to assume responsibility for their men by forming an international police force. The German authorities were getting ready to abandon camp.

CHAPTER SIXTY-TWO

Eklund decided against electroshock therapy as soon as Anna started talking and apologized for leaving the hospital. He moved her sessions to his office where he wore a suit and bow tie rather than a lab coat, and sat behind a desk, taking notes and puffing on his pipe. The familiar sweet fruity scent of his tobacco brought forth memories of her father and had a calming effect on her.

She lay on a black leather chaise longue. She hated reclining and wanted to sit up, but she did her best to follow protocol, as he called it. Be nice, she told herself. Tell him what he wants to hear.

"Are you ready to talk about her yet?" Eklund asked.

"Who?"

"The guard that brutalized you."

Anna's eyes went to the bookshelf lined with psychiatric texts. She'd memorized the names on the spines and would recite them back to herself as a distraction when she got anxious. Alfred Adler, *What Life Could Mean to You*. Sigmund Freud, *The Interpretation of Dreams*. Carl Jung, *Modern Man in Search of a Soul*.

"You could start by telling me just one thing about her," he said.

"She did things in fours." Anna surprised herself by blurting that out.

"Fours?"

"That's what I said. Fours. She counted everything she did in fours or multiples of four."

"Like what?"

"Her steps. My whippings. The number of times she hit me with her truncheon."

"Isn't that interesting?" he mused, knocking his pipe on the side of the ashtray.

"Interesting? The woman was nuts. Vicious. Evil. Sadistic. Anything but interesting."

"Is that so?" he asked as he filled his pipe with fresh tobacco, pressing it down with his forefinger before lighting it. "We're just starting to understand these types of compulsions and obsessions. For some people, repetitive patterns are a way of easing fear and anxiety. A way to maintain order in a chaotic world. And a way to control unacceptable impulses."

"She didn't do a very good job of controlling her impulses," Anna said. "And it was my world that was chaotic and full of fear. Not hers." Awake or asleep, the Beast was always with Anna. Occupying her days. Infiltrating her sleep. A smell, a sound, or an inadvertent touch could take her mind back to the beating trestle.

"I would say so," Eklund agreed between puffs of smoke. "I'm very pleased with the progress you've made. I think you're ready to hear the news I have to share with you."

Anna didn't respond.

"Our government is backing the White Bus Campaign. An operation designed to rescue Scandinavian prisoners held in German concentration camps and bring them to hospitals in

Sweden. The Swedish Red Cross is in Berlin negotiating with Heinrich Himmler as we speak. He is demanding press silence."

Eklund told her the delegation feared the Nazis planned to take revenge on the prisoners as the Allies advanced. To avoid confusion with military vehicles, the campaign was using white buses with Red Cross emblems. Although they planned to target Norwegian and Danish prisoners, they would include prisoners from other European countries.

"And . . ." he took another puff of his pipe, then paused. "They hope to liberate Ravensbrück."

"When?" Anna bolted upright.

He smiled at her enthusiasm. "Right away."

"I want to help. What can I do?"

"The Red Cross needs volunteers."

"To go back to Ravensbrück?" she asked, suddenly nervous. "I can't go back there. I just can't."

"You don't have to. There's plenty for you to do here," he said. "You can start right away. They'll set you up with some clothes and a room in a boarding house. But you must return every Monday morning to talk with me."

*

The white buses departed by ferry from Malmö Harbor to Copenhagen, loaded with medical supplies and food packages. From there, the convoy made the dangerous drive under intense Allied air attack into Germany. To alert the pilots of the rescue mission, Anna had helped paint large red crosses on top of the buses the day before departure. She also slipped the delegation a piece of paper with the names of her friends in the camp.

In late April, Anna waited on the docks of Malmö, a Red Cross armband on her coat sleeve, for ferries crammed with white buses. Day after day, she searched for familiar faces as thousands of women and children arrived. Many had to be carried off on stretchers. Those who could walk, peeled off louse-ridden, blue-gray striped uniforms, and coats marked with a giant X on their backs, then showered outdoors before entering tents erected for medical care and delousing. After days of searching, she spotted Zophia standing naked under an outdoor shower.

"Zophia. Zophia." Anna grabbed a towel and ran right into the steaming spray of water asking a barrage of questions.

"Did you find your baby?" She wrapped the towel around Zophia's skeletal frame.

Zophia's eyes watered.

"Do you have any information at all?"

"They sent him to one of those *Lebensborn* homes for adoption. Agata searched the files and couldn't find any information on him. I'll never find my baby. There are hundreds of those homes."

"Come inside to warm up. I'll get you food and some clean clothes. They have dresses for all of you." Anna led her friend into the tent.

Once Zophia was dressed, Anna served her hot soup and sandwiches, then sat beside her to tell her about finding Michal.

"He's alive?" Zophia's eyes brightened.

"I don't know," Anna said. After pausing for a few moments, she told her friend how she lost her brother again. "He was so happy that I found you at Ravensbrück. I didn't tell him about the baby. It didn't seem like the right time. You should be the one to tell him." She tried to smile and

continued. "I've been in touch with your parents. They registered their new address at the Tracing Bureau."

"When can I go back to Warsaw?"

"As soon as you're medically cleared." Anna's eyes scanned
the reams of women crowded inside the tent. "Did they find
anyone else? Is Agata here?"

"She refused to come with us. She's hoping her daughter
survived Uckermark. She wouldn't leave without her."

"What about our teacher?"

"They sent her to the gas chamber. She was sick and couldn't
work."

"The Green Mina?"

"A real gas chamber. They built one after you left and gassed
thousands of women right up until the day the white buses
arrived."

"Our camp sisters?"

"Most were evacuated. Thousands were sent northward on a
death march to avoid the advancing Russians."

"Good Lord. A death march?"

"Dead women can't talk," Zophia said. "The SS tried to destroy all the evidence. Agata stole some arrival lists before they
burned all the records. I hid them inside my dress and gave
them to the Red Cross when I boarded the white bus."

"What about the Beast?" Anna asked.

"She fled with Von Wolff. That aeronautical engineer from
the rocket factory. About a week before the buses showed up."

"She won't get away with what she did," Anna said, fists
clenched. "We'll find her."

CHAPTER SIXTY-THREE

Nowak stood in line for morning roll call. The gray morning dissipated as loud cheers bellowed from the eastern end of camp. Four Russian Cossacks waving red flags with crossed gold hammer and sickle, and a gold-bordered star, galloped horses down International Avenue.

A Russian colonel gave two orders: "Russians march east toward Moscow. Other nationals stay put."

Cheers and laughter erupted.

The shaking of hands.

LIBERATION!

Nowak and the other airmen tore down the barbed wire with their bare hands, liberating themselves from the confinement they'd suffered for years. They lit the fence posts and sentry towers on fire. With freedom of movement to forage for food, they slaughtered cows, sheep, pigs, and chickens from neighboring farms.

Large caricatures of Churchill, Roosevelt, and Stalin drawn on bed sheets hung in Parade Square. Allied flags flew from the front gate. German guards hung from nooses along the main corridor.

Later that night, Nowak lay on his bunk in the dark, listening to artillery fire. Ground machine guns. Rifle shots. Demolition explosions. Tank cannons. A bomb blast lit the room with red and orange flashes. The windows rattled. It was still too dangerous to leave camp, and it would be for weeks.

Nowak held Anna's rosary. The seconds dragged on.

CHAPTER SIXTY-FOUR

Sjukhus
Stockholm, Sweden

Anna kept her promise to return weekly to visit Eklund. He sat at his desk reading a newspaper and puffing on his pipe.

"Good morning, Doctor," she said with a smile, walking over to the chaise longue.

"How very nice to see you." He put the newspaper down on his desk. "I was just reading that two of the doctors who did medical experiments on the women at Ravensbrück were arrested. They'll be tried at the Military Tribunal in Nuremberg."

"That's good news," Anna said. "My friend Zophia told me the SS made a last-minute attempt to execute those Polish women to destroy the evidence. But the other prisoners protected them so they could bear witness and testify against the doctors."

"Have any other authorities been arrested?" he asked.

"They captured the commandant at an American checkpoint. A couple of guards. And a nurse," she said. "The British have scheduled Ravensbrück war crime trials for next year."

"I thought the camp was in the Russian zone."

"It is, but the British took over the investigation and moved the pending trials to Hamburg in their occupied zone. I think it's because of the SOE women who were captured and imprisoned there. Most of them disappeared. I think they were executed."

"Do you have any information on Wardress Fleischer?"

"She fled with the aeronautical engineer from the rocket factory. They've disappeared," Anna said, her voice rising.

"I've heard people in positions of authority are moving war criminals out of Germany."

"What country would let them in?"

"It's hard to imagine. But rumors are circulating that the Allies are negotiating secret military contracts with Nazi scientists involved in atomic, biological, and chemical warfare. And aeronautical engineering," he said. "Maybe the wardress and the engineer have something to sell."

"That can't be!" The thought of the Beast getting away with everything she'd done ignited a fury inside her. "She needs to face prosecution. They all do."

"Are you still having nightmares?"

"Sometimes." She didn't want to talk about her terrifying nightmares that were so vivid she smelled stale perfume and felt hot breath on the back of her neck. Awake or asleep, the Beast was always with her.

Wanting to change the subject, she said, "I've contacted Ewa's parents. They're still living in Warsaw. They've sent me photos to post in newspaper ads. I've volunteered to join the UNRRA search team. We're opening a children's center in the American zone of Bavaria.

"We've received tens of thousands of snapshots of Eastern European children that disappeared. They were taken to *Lebensborn* reception centers for racial sorting. There's so much information streaming in, we can barely keep up."

"Racial sorting?" Eklund asked.

"Children deemed racially desirable were *Germanized*. Given German names and issued false birth certificates. Children deemed undesirable were disposed of."

"For the love of God," he said. "Are you sure you're ready to return to Germany?"

Anna hesitated. "I'll never find Ewa if I don't."

"It sounds like you still blame yourself for the kidnapping."

Anna didn't answer.

"It's normal to experience some form of guilt after such trauma. You were only a child. There was nothing you could have done under the circumstances."

He had no idea what it was like. How could she begin to explain that guilt and recrimination drove her, stole her sleep, and haunted her days? Sometimes she thought she'd never be free.

CHAPTER SIXTY-FIVE

Malmö, Sweden

Anna boarded the ferry at Malmö. Watching ships in the bustling seaport, she thought about the last time she had seen her brother, when they had huddled in the coal bunker and he surrendered to the Germans to save her life. Her chest tightened. Her heart palpitated. Coal dust filled her nose. She grabbed the cold metal railing to steady herself and tried to slow her breathing the way Nowak had taught her. Once she regained her composure, she checked the satchel strapped across her chest to make sure her scalpel and the revolver she'd bought for protection, a Russian Nagant M1895, were still there.

An American Army van picked her up in Copenhagen. On the bumpy overland journey through Germany, Anna reviewed files with photos of missing children, newspaper ads, and letters. As they neared the children's center, she put her documents away and watched rows of trees glide by as the van made its way through the Bavarian countryside. She anticipated a peaceful old convent filled with smiling children.

Instead, what she saw was barbed wire and a brick path lined on both sides by poplar trees leading to the words, *ARBEIT MACHT FREI*, WORK SETS YOU FREE, forged on the wrought-iron gate of the Dachau concentration camp. The sight made her nauseous. Her body tensed. Memories of her time behind barbed wire flashed through her mind.

Ten miles down the road, the van pulled up at her destination, the Kloster Indersdorf Children's Center, housed in a medieval building with dual steeples. The former convent was overrun with Red Cross trucks and armed forces vehicles. Soldiers, UNRRA workers, and nuns scrambled to unload cargo in an atmosphere of chaos.

"What's going on?" Anna asked an American soldier.

He placed a bundle in her arms. "There are hundreds of them," he said.

Looking down, Anna realized she was holding a baby. "Where did you find them?"

"Abandoned in Steinhöring."

"Did you find any files? Birth certificates. Records showing parentage. Any information at all?"

"All we found were children. Lots of children."

"Must have been a *Lebensborn* maternity home."

"Huh?"

Anna didn't explain. Following a throng of people, all carrying babies and toddlers, she entered the building and climbed a winding staircase. She placed the infant on a bed alongside other babies lined up. A doctor in a white coat holding a stethoscope moved down the rows, examining them one by one. Toddlers wearing only shirts, socks, and shoes sat on porcelain chamber pots on the floor. Catholic nuns clothed in habits and starched white headdresses were bathing children in metal tubs, weighing them on white scales, and feeding them with baby bottles. Cries of hunger and fear filled the air.

Surrounded by a sea of blond-haired, blue-eyed children, thoughts of Zophia ran through Anna's mind. At that very moment, she realized Zophia might never find her baby. Michal's son. Anna's nephew. Lost somewhere unknown like so many others under the Nazi regime. Eyes watering, she climbed down the creaking stairs to grab another child.

The next morning, she settled at a desk stacked with search files. A girl of about eight sat across from her in a red blouse made from confiscated Nazi flag material and a skirt out of mattress ticking. A tracing officer had located the child after a neighbor reported a suspicious adoption. She matched the age and description of several children reported missing from Poland.

"What's your name?" Anna asked in German, after reviewing her file.

"Geisla."

"Your real name, not your German name."

"That is my real name."

"You're safe here. You can tell me," Anna reassured the frightened child.

"I don't remember."

"Are you Polish?"

"I'm German."

"The file says a German family adopted you four years ago. Do you remember anything before that?"

"No."

"Do you understand Polish?" Anna asked, this time in Polish and not German.

The girl shook her head.

Anna thought for a moment, then recited a popular Polish nursery rhyme about a little star often used to lull children to sleep. Rocking herself back and forth, the girl closed her blue eyes and joined in, murmuring the words along with her.

Picking up a name board, she wrote: *Do you know who I am? Poland*, before leading the child over to a photographer, and said, "Stand here and look at the camera. Hold the board in front of your chest."

Anna spent weeks preparing name boards and listening to the stories of displaced children of more than twenty different nationalities. She showed a photo of Ewa to those old enough to remember being kidnapped, but none recognized her. Many youngsters removed from adoptive families appeared well cared for and suffered the trauma of separation from the only families they remembered. They had no memories of their birth parents. Older children yearned to be reunited with family members and gave details of their *Lebensborn* experiences. Jewish children suffered from malnutrition and disease after spending time in concentration camps.

She joined a child search team scouring farms and villages for missing children. Each team member wore a khaki uniform and carried a copy of the military order, granting them the right of entry to any German institution or home where they believed an *unaccompanied* child of the United Nations or assimilated nationality lived. They stopped at each municipality to interview residents, examine records, and disperse flyers with photos of the missing.

At every opportunity, she included a picture of Ewa and followed up on leads, but none panned out. Feeling deflated, she returned to the children's center to resume interviewing children.

Late one afternoon, a boy of about fourteen, in an issued white pullover and short pants, took a seat. Before she could ask, he spoke in Polish, "My name is Janek. Janek Bakowski. I'm from Warsaw. I want to find my parents."

"How did you end up here?" she asked, while writing notes in his file.

"I ran away."

"Start at the beginning."

"The SS kidnapped me and my younger brother. They took us to a reception center and made us undress. A doctor measured me with a caliper."

"What did they measure?"

"Everything. My nose, chin, face, cheekbones. Even my privates. When it was over, they said I was of good blood and could stay." The boy turned his head and pulled his ear forward. "Look. They branded me."

Anna was shocked to see small black markings on the nape of his neck.

"What about your brother?" she asked.

"He was rated undesirable. His ears were too big. They sent him to a concentration camp. They wouldn't tell me which one."

"I'm so sorry to hear that," she said. "Then what happened?"

"The Brown Sisters called my mother a Polish whore and my father a drunk. They changed my name and forced me to speak only German. If I spoke Polish, they beat me. They tried to turn me into a Nazi."

"Where did you go after that?"

"I don't want to talk about it."

"I understand. You don't have to," she said. "Where was the reception center?"

"Kalisz."

"A friend of mine went missing the same time you did. September 1942," Anna said, knowing Ewa was also taken to Kalisz. She showed the boy a picture. "Have you ever seen this girl?"

"I know her."

"You do?" Anna could barely contain her excitement.

"She got in trouble because she called a Brown Sister *Untermensch*. They locked her in the chapel and made her kneel on the stone floor for hours beside two locked coffins. They said her parents were dead inside."

"Her parents are alive," Anna said. "Do you know what happened to her?"

"They sent her to Austria."

"Where in Austria?"

"Vienna."

"Do you remember the German name they gave her?"

"Etta Schiller. Her father was a doctor."

"Where is she now?"

"I don't know. They moved away." He wiped a tear from his eye and looked down at the floor. "I told you. I don't want to talk about it. I just want to go home."

"You've been a lot of help. We'll try to find your parents." She wrote his real name on a board—*BAKOWSKI, Janek. Warsaw, Poland*—and led him over to the photographer.

CHAPTER SIXTY-SIX

It took Flying Officer Johnnie Nowak until early June to repatriate back to Canada. He spent time in England being debriefed, taking medical tests, filling out forms, and reconnecting with friends.

Ray moved his family back to the States for a job collecting evidence for the International Military Tribunal formed to prosecute Nazi war criminals at Nuremberg. Syd took off, determined to track down every Nazi on his hit list, minus Hitler and Goebbels who had done the job for him by committing suicide.

For Nowak, the best part about getting back to England was visiting Tubby at Ward III of the Queen Vic hospital in Sussex. It was a shock to see the skin flap fashioned into a long tube that ran from his chest up to his nose, keeping the blood vessels and nerves alive until the skin attached naturally to the nasal area. They called it a pedicle. Tubby needed a good four or five surgeries before the doctors achieved a new nose.

He was in good hands with doctors McIndoe and Tilley and their pioneering reconstructive surgery. They formed the Guinea Pig Club: as much a drinking club as a support group for their patients. Nowak joined Tubby on a visit to the local pub, tubed pedicles, and all. He even ran into a couple of pilots he trained with who were receiving treatment in the Canadian wing of the hospital. The airmen were all determined to wear their scars with pride and interacted with the community whenever they could.

Weeks later, Nowak arrived in Canada, expecting the homecoming he'd envisioned over and over in his mind. His mother and sister with outstretched arms. A dinner of roast beef and gravy.

He walked up the concrete sidewalk lined with tulips to his family home in Calgary. He carried his kitbag. His lungs carried pieces of shrapnel. Lest he forget.

The flowered curtains in the front window of the freshly painted white bungalow were pulled open, welcoming him home. He climbed the narrow wooden stairs to the front door, straightened his uniform, and ran his fingers through his thick, dark hair.

This was it.

His hand reached for the doorknob. Heart pounding, he entered. The heavy aroma of turnips cooking in the kitchen struck him like a punch in the face. He couldn't breathe. He felt nauseous. His head spun. He burst into the kitchen, charging right past his mother setting the table and his sister Mary writing the words *Welcome Home* in chocolate icing on a white frosted cake.

Before they could speak, he grabbed a butcher knife off the counter. Seizing the pot from the stove, he marched outside to the backyard. The screen door slammed shut behind him. Having hurled the contents of the pot into the dirt, he knelt down and slashed the turnips into tiny bits.

After returning to the kitchen, he placed the pot and knife on the countertop, then walked into the living room.

Rummaging through his duffle bag, he removed the handcuffs and hung them on the fieldstone fireplace and patted his pocket to make sure the rosary was still there, then settled into his big easy chair.

The cat jumped into his lap. He stroked her with his sweaty palms to calm himself. His sister peeked around the corner, looking worried.

"Sorry about that, kid," he said. "I don't know what just happened. I think it was the turnips. Never, *ever* cook them again."

Mary took a few hesitant steps into the room. When he rose, she leaped into his arms. Filled with joy, he picked her up and twirled her around just like he used to when they were kids, realizing how much time had passed by her height and weight.

His mother stood close behind, wiping her hands on her white apron, tears streaming down her face. He embraced her.

"I thought you liked turnips," she said.

"Not anymore."

"You're so thin. Didn't they feed you?" She patted him on the cheek. "I bet you're hungry. Dinner's ready."

They made their way to the kitchen and settled around the table set with their best china and silverware, along with an arrangement of scarlet peonies in a glass vase in the center. With his fork, he stabbed a slice of blood-rare roast beef off the platter. He tore into a loaf of white bread and mashed his potatoes with a large blob of butter, pouring gravy over everything.

His first bite was better than he'd ever imagined.

After dinner, he sat in the easy chair while a fire burned in the hearth. Late into the night, his mother and sister caught him up on the news from home. He didn't mention his time behind barbed wire. He couldn't find the words.

"Have you registered for nursing in the fall?"

"Not yet."

"Well, you better get on that in the morning."

"I put fresh sheets on your bed," his mother said. "Is there anything you want before I turn in?"

"I'd like to stay up for a bit. How about an onion sandwich and a hot bath?"

His mother hesitated for a moment. "An onion sandwich?"

Nowak nodded.

"We have fresh green onions in the garden." She rose from her chair.

A few minutes later, she returned to the living room with a glass of milk and a small plate with the sandwich. She kissed his forehead and went to bed. Mary hugged him and followed her mother out of the room.

Nowak examined the clean glass of cold milk. It wasn't powdered milk made with water pumped from a well next to the cesspool served in a goddamn tin can. He looked at his sandwich, made with butter, onions, and fresh white bread. Tree flour and margarine would not be missed.

Tonight, he would sleep in his own bed on a real mattress between clean sheets. Not a dirty blanket on a paillasse infested with bed bugs. He would wake up to the aroma of freshly perked coffee. Not lukewarm water with acorns and twigs floating in it.

He headed for the bathroom, where he took the rosary out of his pocket and laid it on the counter beside the sink. He took off his clothes and left them in a heap on the floor. Then he stepped into a tub full of clean, warm water. He sat down, picked up his sandwich, and took a big bite. He was home. Finally, home. Leaning back, he closed his eyes. But something was missing. Or someone. He had to find her.

CHAPTER SIXTY-SEVEN

Calgary, Canada

Nowak felt restless as he sat on his front step. He'd been naive enough to think things would be the way he'd left them, but they weren't. He thought he'd just fall back into everyday life, but he couldn't. He didn't fit in. He had nightmares. The slightest things took him back to his days behind barbed wire.

He couldn't find the words to describe what he was going through. Hell, he didn't understand it himself. He felt detached from everyone except for his fellow POWs. They shared a bond, born from the horrors they'd survived together. As strong as family. Perhaps stronger in some ways.

Anna shared that bond with him, too. If only he knew where to find her. He told himself to use his head. Anna and Michal could be in any number of places. Millions of people like them lived in Displaced Persons camps scattered throughout Europe set up in military barracks, hospitals, and hotels.

The military and civil authorities were having trouble sorting through the chaos. The Tracing Bureau of the United Nations Relief and Rehabilitation Administration received thousands of letters every day from individuals and families looking for missing persons.

He'd written to every single organization he could think of, and every afternoon he waited for the mailman, hoping for word so he could head back to Europe.

If Anna and Michal had made it to safety, they'd probably be in Sweden. Or they might have taken the south escape route into Switzerland, but that entailed a lot of walking and patrols along the German-Swiss border.

Sweden was his best bet. Then again, they might have left Sweden by now. Where would they go?

There were Polish liaison officers attached to various army units, but as former members of the Underground, Anna and Michal faced possible arrest by the communist regime in power if repatriated back to Poland. He'd read about the Trial of the Sixteen that took place after the Soviets invited high-profile members of the Polish Underground to Moscow for a conference on their entry into the provisional government. When the members got there, the NKVD arrested, interrogated, and tortured them for months, after which came bogus charges, including collaborating with the Nazis. Most of them ended up in prison. The entire process had been a complete sham to capture their leaders. She wouldn't go back to Poland.

He didn't want to think of the possibility that they hadn't made it out of Germany, but it was a very real one. Escape was risky. Their chances were slim. Anything could have happened.

Anna was a survivor. So was Michal. They were smart. They'd find a way. He couldn't lose faith.

One thing for sure, he was easier to find than she was. He'd sat on the step every day since his return, waiting for the mail. Right on time, the mailman headed up the sidewalk. Nowak gave him a nod of recognition.

The mailman dug into the bag slung over his shoulder. "There's a letter from overseas. Is this what you've been waiting for?"

Nowak ripped off the side of the envelope and found a hand-written letter.

June 28, 1945

My dearest Johnnie,

I pray you are well and made it home safely to your family in Canada.

I made it to Stockholm and spent months in hospital. After discharge, I kept busy as a volunteer with the Red Cross. Now I'm working with the Tracing Bureau.

I think of you every day and miss you deeply. Please write to me at the address below so I know you are safe.

Anna

CHAPTER SIXTY-EIGHT

Warsaw, Poland

Despite hearing reports that Warsaw stood in ruins, the extent of the devastation shocked Anna. Even though the Home Army surrendered on October 2, 1944, the German demolition squads pounded Warsaw, city block by city block, for three more months, turning eighty-five percent of its infrastructure to rubble. Soviet troops had waited until January 17, 1945, to liberate the capital from the German occupation. The prewar population dropped from 1.3 million residents to about 160,000.

Zophia waited at the train station for Anna to arrive with the UN envoy of relocated children. "I haven't found Ewa yet, but I have a lead. She was adopted by a family in Vienna with the last name of Schiller. I've informed our search teams and the Tracing Bureau. If she's alive, we'll find her," Anna told her friend. "There's a boy in our group that knew Ewa. Keep in contact with him. You might get more information from him once you gain his trust. I'll introduce you." Then she asked, "Have you received any word from Michal?"

Zophia shook her head.

"I'm only here for a few hours. I'd like to visit Papa's grave before I leave. Do you know where it is?"

"They buried him next to your mother, but German demolition teams burned and dynamited the entire area. I'm very sorry, Anna," Zophia said, hugging her.

Anna closed her eyes and tried to calm herself. There was nothing much left for her in Warsaw. The Nazis had razed the Franciscan convent to the ground so she couldn't check on Samuel's sister, Lieba. Dr. Jeska had no intelligence information on how Nazi war criminals were avoiding arrest, where they were hiding, or who was helping them. Her other contacts in the Underground were either dead, arrested, or had left the country.

Before leaving the city, she needed to do one more thing. Dig up the jar she'd buried under the linden tree in the church-yard to retrieve the cigarette papers listing the original Jewish names and the assigned Polish names of the children she'd smuggled out of the ghetto. The Tracing Bureau needed this information to reunite children with any Jewish relatives who had survived the war.

A bombing raid had destroyed the Gothic cathedral. Only a pile of red bricks and rubble remained. The fence had dis-appeared. Weeds choked the yard. But the massive linden tree stood bursting with yellow star shaped flowers and dark green foliage. The figurine of the Virgin Mary resting inside a hole cut into the trunk of the tree remained intact. She relished the familiar sweet citrus fragrance that reminded her of the tea she used to make with dried linden flowers.

Scalpel in hand, she circled the base of the trunk. Was it here? Or over here a bit? A few steps forward, then back. She moved closer to the tree, then farther away. Turning in the op-posite direction, she took three paces and knelt. She thrust the blade in the ground and burrowed a small hole before deciding she was in the wrong place. It would be closer to the trunk.

She shifted over a couple of feet and started again. The dirt seemed easier to dig in the shade. It hadn't been necessary to bury the jar deep, just enough to keep it hidden, and protect it from the elements. After all, she'd dug it out and buried it again after every trip through the sewers.

The blade struck something hard. Using it as leverage, she lifted the jar out of the ground. Cigarette papers listing the names of the children were still inside. Since the lid was rusted shut, she shattered the jar on a rock and picked the papers out of the broken glass, shaking them to get rid of the shards before shoving them into her pocket.

Standing, she brushed the dirt from her uniform. After checking her watch, she hurried out of the yard to meet back up with the UN envoy scheduled to leave Warsaw by train.

CHAPTER SIXTY-NINE

Stockholm, Sweden

It took Nowak ten days to get to Staden Mellan Broarna, the area of Old Town between the bridges in Stockholm. He'd started by taking the CPR train across Canada, three days sitting up in the coach car all night to get to Toronto, then another day crossing the border to New York. While there, he purchased a double-breasted suit and an engagement ring with the money that had accumulated during his time in prison camp. He waited a day for the RMS *Queen Mary* to depart for Southampton. Referred to as the Gray Ghost, the luxury ocean liner had been converted to a troopship at the start of the war. It took four days, eleven hours, and forty-two minutes in a cramped three-tier bunk to cross the Atlantic. From the south coast of England, he boarded a flight headed for Sweden.

Nowak charged off a crowded bus in Stortorget main square wearing his new suit. He slid his hand into his jacket pocket, his fingers stroked the red velvet box containing the single solitaire diamond with a white gold band.

After so many sleepless nights wondering where Anna was, they would be together soon. He had the letter with her address in his pocket. She was alive. That was all he cared about. He loved her and that was that.

Nowak asked a street vendor cooking sausages on a grill for directions to the address.

"No English," the vendor said, offering a sausage.

Nowak asked another man walking along the square and received the same answer. Up ahead, he noticed a flower shop and decided to buy Anna a flower. The young woman behind the counter smiled at him.

"Do you speak English?" he asked.

She nodded.

His eyes swept the inside of the shop. "I'd like to buy one of those long-stemmed red roses." He brought out the letter and pointed to the address. "Can you tell me how to find this place." He'd never been good at expressing his emotions, but he hoped the rose and the engagement ring would do the trick and she'd come back home with him.

After twenty blocks of meandering cobblestone streets and medieval architecture, he found the boarding house. A Falu red wooden structure with a sloped roof and a spindly birch tree in the yard. Anna's name and room number 3D were on a list tacked to the front door.

Nowak charged up three flights of stairs, two steps at a time, and stopped at her door. He placed his kitbag on the floor, straightened his suit jacket, ran his fingers through his hair, and knocked. Holding the single long-stemmed red rose in his hand, he waited.

No answer.

He knocked again.

Still no answer.

Movement on the stairs below made him turn, hoping to see Anna. But it was only the landlord in a bathrobe and worn brown leather slippers. He got to the landing short of breath after climbing the stairs.

"I've been knocking. Do you know where she is?" Nowak asked.

"I have to respect the privacy of my tenants," the landlord said in broken English.

"I've come all the way from Canada. Tell me where she is."

"Last I saw her, she was heading for Germany."

"Don't be ridiculous. That's the last place she'd be."

"You better leave, mister. I don't want any trouble."

Nowak picked up his kit and turned to head downstairs.

"Johnnie?" a female voice called out to him.

Anna stood on the landing below. Her blonde hair had grown back. She was even more beautiful than he remembered. She climbed the stairs and threw her arms around him. He kissed her and held her for so long, the landlord scuttled off.

"I can't begin to tell you how much I missed you." He swooped her up in his arms and carried her inside.

The room was sparse. A bed. A cardboard box jammed full of file folders and a pile of newspaper clippings scattered on a small table.

"I would've come sooner," he said as he sat beside her on the worn sofa. "But I didn't know how to find you. What took you so long to contact me?"

"I sent letters to you at the stalag. Didn't you get them?"

He shook his head. "Tell me everything that happened after the graveyard. How did you get to Sweden? Where's Michal?"

Her smile vanished. A look of grief spread across her face.

"What happened?" he asked, moving closer.

"A bloody German shot him. I don't know if he's alive."

Nowak could tell she was struggling to hold back her tears. He knelt on one knee and reached into his pocket. His fingers brushed against the red velvet box containing the ring. He'd rehearsed it over and over in his mind. This wasn't the right time. Instead, he pulled out her rosary.

"I've been holding this for you for so long," he said, slipping it back into her hand.

She clutched her mother's black beads and held them to her chest.

"I've come to take you home," he said.

"I don't have a home."

"My home. To Canada."

"I need to find out what happened to my brother. And I haven't found Ewa."

"I'll help you." He cleared his throat. "The war is over. We can—"

Her grief turned to a flash of anger. "It's not over. Not until she pays for her crimes."

"Who?"

"The Beast." Anna spat out the words like venom.

"Maybe she will. They've made a lot of arrests. The Tribunal will start prosecuting Nazis this November in Nuremberg."

"Not her. She got away." Anna pulled a piece of paper and a small photograph out of her uniform pocket and handed it over. "My friends at the Tracing Bureau gave me this."

Nowak read out loud. "Ursula Fleischer. Born Fürstenberg, February 12, 1921." He looked up. "Makes her twenty-four." He went back to reading. "Joined the SS December 26, 1941. Wardress at Ravensbrück Concentration Camp. Five-foot eight. Blonde. Wanted for war crimes. Whereabouts unknown."

He lowered the paper. "You don't have much to go on. She could be anywhere. Do you have any more information?"

"Zophia said she fled with the aeronautical engineer from the rocket factory. I think people are helping them evade prosecution. He has information to sell on weapons development."

"Do you know his name?"

She nodded. "Klaus Von Wolff."

"Syd and Ray might be able to help. We talked about this back in camp." He thought for a few moments. "I'll send Ray a telegram in the morning. I don't know how to contact Syd other than through Mrs. B back in London."

He reached for her. "You must try to forget."

"I'll never forget." Anna moved away from him. "I have to live with what she did to me every day."

"What did she do to you?"

"I don't want you to see."

"See what?"

She glared at him with those piercing eyes.

"I'm afraid you'll leave me."

"I'll never leave you."

She stood and unfastened the top button on her khaki uniform. Her hand moved to the second button. She turned her back to him and the shirt slipped off her shoulders.

He gasped. Scars lined her back like a comb. Deep, raw lines.

Reaching for her, the tips of his trembling fingers touched the scars. "No one will ever hurt you again. I'll make sure of it." His voice broke when he spoke. "We'll leave for London in the morning."

CHAPTER SEVENTY

London, England

Anna walked with Nowak up to the door of a flat on Oxford Street in the West End of London. In the stalag, she had only seen Mrs. B for a few minutes and would never have recognized her in the form-fitting navy dress, single strand of pearls, and matching earrings. The breasts she once bound were full. Dark curls cascaded down her neck, replacing her former cropped short hair.

Nowak took one look at her and whistled. "Jesus, Mrs. B, you're looking good."

Mrs. B laughed. "Aren't you a sight for sore eyes."

"Do you remember Anna? You would have known her as Hope. She was your switch in camp."

"I do. Come on in," she said.

"I'm glad to have the chance to thank you." Anna wore a belted trench coat and carried an oversized black purse she had insisted on buying for the trip.

"We did each other a favor." Mrs. B led them into the parlor.

She offered them a seat on a blue tufted velvet sofa facing a picture window and sat across from them in a flowered wingback chair, crossing her legs that were covered in silk stockings. High heels had replaced her army boots.

"What brings you to London?" Mrs. B picked up a lit cigarette from a crystal ashtray.

"I'm looking for Syd. Is he around?" Nowak asked.

"He's out of town," she said. "I get the feeling this is more than a social visit."

Nowak scanned the room before speaking. "Are you still married to that German?"

"I am. He's not here. Feel free to talk."

"I was wondering if Syd followed through on a promise he made back in the camp. That if he survived the war, he'd spend the rest of his days tracking down the Nazi war criminals on his list to face trial for their war crimes."

"Of course he kept his promise," Mrs. B said, as if she was commenting on the weather. She took a drag of her cigarette and exhaled.

"There's a Nazi we want arrested. We need Syd's help to find her," Nowak said.

"Her? You're looking for a woman?"

"Wardress Ursula Fleischer," Anna piped in.

"Can I ask why?"

"She was the wardress at Ravensbrück. She's wanted for a string of war crimes and she's disappeared." Anna's hands gripped her handbag.

"The Nazis know how to cover their tracks and stay hidden. People in high places are helping them flee Europe," Mrs. B said.

"Where to?" Nowak asked.

"South America, the Middle East and . . ." she paused, "the US."

"I thought US law prohibited Nazi officials from emigrating to the States," Nowak said. "Why the hell would they let them in?"

"Rocket designs and chemical warfare. They don't want the Soviets to get their hands on it. Even the Brits are competing."

"Jesus," Nowak said. "How do they move them out of the country?"

"Ratlines."

"Ratlines?"

"Sophisticated networks with organized smuggling."

"Where do we find these bloody ratlines?" Anna asked.

"The Vatican."

Anna was lost for words.

"Jesus," Johnnie blurted. "Are you sure?"

"It's hard to believe but it's true," she said. "Syd's in Rome now. He has a hit list."

"Fleischer is on that list. I put her there myself," Nowak said. "To be honest, I always thought it was a lot of hot air. We didn't have much to talk about other than what we were going to do if we ever got out of that hole."

"Syd's put together a team. Ray's been feeding him information from the States. As an officer in the *Luftwaffe*, my husband has handed a lot of information over. He's always hated the Nazis."

"I'll do whatever it takes to get the Beast arrested," Anna said. "She used to beat me and she stole my brother's baby, so it's personal. But I'm not just speaking for myself, I'm speaking for all of us at Ravensbrück. Those murdered, and those that survived. There has to be some justice in this world."

"How do we contact Syd?" Nowak asked.

"Make your way to Rome. Infiltrate the San Girolamo Seminary. Syd has a man on the inside. I'll get word to him you're on your way down." Mrs. B leaned forward and stamped her cigarette out in the ashtray. "Keep an eye open for a limo with diplomatic plates marked CD for *Corpo Diplomatico*. That's how they transport the Nazis from Rome to a ship in Genoa. Disguised as priests or monks. If you're looking for a woman, she'll be dressed like a nun."

CHAPTER SEVENTY-ONE

San Girolamo Seminary

Rome, Italy

The chapel inside the seminary had fresco sidewalls and arched ceilings. Nowak knelt before a stone altar. Already he felt trapped contemplating the vows of poverty, chastity, and obedience in a cloistered environment with fraternal living that sounded too much like prison camp. All too familiar, and not the future he had planned for himself.

Shuffling footsteps approached and stopped beside him. Slowly raising his head, Nowak's eyes traced the bare feet in sandals up the brown habit, the white cord cinched around a waist with a rosary and three knots, to a head hidden by a hood. A hand slid out of the cuff of the robe and motioned Nowak to follow.

Rising from his knees, he shadowed the man outside to the cloister. They stopped beside a fountain with running water, surrounded by a small garden.

"About time you got here," the monk said, face still hidden by his hood.

Nowak stepped back. Who was this man? What was he saying?

"What took you so long?" he asked Nowak as he peeled back his hood.

Nowak shook his head in amazement. "Jesus, Michal," he said. "What the hell are you doing here?"

"Hush." Michal cut him off in an urgent whisper. "Have you found her?"

"Anna's here. At a guesthouse close to St. Peter's Square."

"Thank God," Michal said. "I went to Stockholm after the war and checked every hospital. I couldn't find any record of her. I was afraid she didn't make it."

"She spent months in hospital before she told anyone who she was. What happened to you? She was devastated when you disappeared."

"Bastards shot me. I almost died."

"How'd you end up here?"

"I went back to Warsaw to look for my girlfriend. Old Town was destroyed. I couldn't find any trace of her or her family. I couldn't hang around because the Soviets were arresting all known members of the Home Army."

Michal pulled his hood back up and glanced behind him to make sure no one was listening. "I looked up Syd. He needed someone on the inside. He's Jewish. He didn't know anything about Catholicism. I offered to join the Order. With my religious background, I convinced them I did my postulancy back in Poland. They started me off as a novice."

"Huh?"

"Never mind. What about you?"

"I came to Europe to find Anna and take her back to Canada with me. She refused to leave until she found you. She's determined to find the guard at Ravensbrück who beat her. Wardress Ursula Fleischer."

"I know all about the Beast," Michal snarled. "I spent months trying to track her down before I left Germany. I found her father and sister, but they claimed they hadn't heard from her for years."

"Zophia told Anna that Fleischer fled with—"

"Zophia? Zophia's alive!" Michal's eyes brightened.

"I think so."

"Where is she?"

"No idea. All I know is this. Zophia told Anna that Fleischer fled with a scientist from the rocket factory to avoid arrest. Is there really a ratline through the Vatican?"

"There is. I'm not sure how widespread. They keep things pretty quiet. It may be just a few priests involved. I can't be seen talking to you here. Meet me in twenty minutes." Michal reached into a pocket under his robe for a matchbook cover with an address on it. "This is our meeting place," he said as he slipped away.

CHAPTER SEVENTY-TWO

Rome, Italy

Twenty minutes later, Nowak found Michal sitting at a table under a red umbrella at a sidewalk café, drinking a mug of pale lager. He wore street clothes. His brown habit was rolled into a ball stuffed under his chair.

Nowak sat down and motioned to a waiter. "How do the bloody Nazis get into Italy?" he asked Michal.

"The monastery route. Out of Austria through the Brenner Pass, dressed in Franciscan robes." Michal took a drink. "Once they arrive in Rome, they travel in Vatican cars. The bishop is the liaison for Germans living in Italy. He provides false identity documents through the Vatican Refugee Organization. Then uses his contacts in the International Red Cross for a displaced person's passport and from there a visa."

"How do you know this?"

Michal grinned. "They send students on errands. One day, I delivered false papers to the International Red Cross. They issued a passport right away."

"Without a background check?"

"Not required when the request comes from a bishop. They move them out of Italy by ship. First class."

"How are they financing it?"

"Laundered Nazi gold and counterfeit British currency through the Vatican bank."

"And I thought the Franciscans took a vow of poverty, among other things I never could understand. You're telling me they're laundering Nazi gold?"

A waiter approached, balancing a tray held high in the air. "Compliments of the man at the bar." He set a round of lager and a plastic menu on the table.

Nowak flipped the menu open to see a black-and-white photo of the Beast with ringlets wearing a cap with the embroidered eagle patch. He slammed it shut and took a drink of hoppy beer.

He wiped the foam off his lips with his knuckle and squinted so he could see across the sunny sidewalk café into the dingy restaurant. The man at the bar wore a wide-rimmed fedora that shielded his face. When he got off the stool and moved toward Nowak, the limp gave him away.

Nowak stood and extended his hand.

Syd Liberman shook hands and pulled up a chair. "Where the hell have you been? We've been trying to reach you. You put this operation in motion and then you disappear. We're almost out of time," Syd told Nowak.

"What do you mean?" Nowak asked.

"She's here. At the convent," Syd said. "There was no trace of her until you contacted Ray about Von Wolff. Ray did some digging and when he couldn't reach you, he sent the details to me."

"Does she have information to sell?" Nowak took another sip of cold beer.

"The Beast's not that bright. As the mistress of the aeronautic engineer, she's part of the deal he's making with the Feds. He won't leave without her," Syd said.

"Where are they headed?" Nowak asked.

"America. The Feds are relocating top Nazi scientists and their families to South Texas to work on missile development. Von Wolff has blueprints for the V2 rocket. Maybe even those fucking foo fighters that distracted the hell out of us while we were flying in the bombers."

"How much time do we have?"

"Less than twenty-four hours. We were afraid the whole operation would explode if you didn't make it on time. She's expecting to be picked up at six tomorrow evening to meet the Feds and the engineer at the pier in Genoa. Michal will show up dressed like a monk in a borrowed Vatican limo two hours earlier. That ought to be enough time to pull it off. The diplomatic license plates will protect him from being stopped and searched."

"What's his excuse for arriving early?"

"I'll tell her the Brits are on to her," Michal said.

"I'll drink to that," Nowak laughed and raised his glass.

"Michal will have her passport and visa. That'll make him look legit," Syd said.

Nowak arched his eyebrows. "How'd you manage that?"

"I steamed open the envelope I picked up for the bishop and forged a second set."

"It's going to be a long night," Syd said. "We've got a lot of work to do if we're gonna pull this off in time."

"I have to get word to Anna." Nowak wanted to let her know he'd made contact with Syd and Michal.

"It's best she stays out of this."

"I doubt she'll agree."

"I'm in command and I'm not taking any chances. If the Beast recognizes her, it could jeopardize the entire operation. Either you're in or you're out." Syd finished his beer and slammed the glass down on the table.

"I'm in," Nowak said. Syd was right. It was best Anna stayed out of sight.

Syd tossed him a paper napkin. "Write Anna a note. I'll make sure she gets it."

CHAPTER SEVENTY-THREE

St. Peter's Square
Vatican City, Rome

The sight of St. Peter's Square and the Basilica mesmerized Anna. She had dreamed of this moment since she was a little girl in Warsaw. How she'd feel standing on holy ground at the epicenter of the Roman Catholic Church. Where the Pope walked. Where thousands of people came daily to pray.

She'd never expected to feel anger and resentment for the people behind the very walls where she stood. It was impossible to believe what Mrs. B had told her. That the Vatican helped Nazis escape prosecution.

Thousands of Catholic clergy, monks, and nuns had been murdered, taken to concentration camps, and publicly executed at the hands of the Nazis. So many members of the clergy supported the Resistance and opposed the Nazi regime that the Germans built a separate *Priest Barracks* at Dachau Concentration Camp.

What about the Catholic churches that were confiscated and destroyed? And the Franciscans? The same religious order that had helped her shelter Jewish children back in Warsaw.

Unfathomable.

After everything she'd been through, there was one thing she knew: you could only trust a handful of people in this lifetime.

If Nowak was making contact through the Franciscan monastery, it only made sense female Nazis would hide in a convent of the same order. For hours, she'd kept an eye on the Franciscan convent, studying every nun that went in, out, or passed by. This was Rome. There were groups of nuns everywhere, roaming around in full habit. Blue. Black. Brown. White. Gray. Red. Purple.

Tired and fed up, and cold with the sun going down, she headed back to the guesthouse to meet Nowak to see if he'd found anything out at the Seminary. Upon entering the room, she noticed a note scribbled on a paper napkin that someone had slid under the door. She picked it up and read:

> *The Beast is at the convent*
> *Stay where you are*
> *Back tomorrow*

She scrunched the note and hurled it on the floor. Grabbing her handbag, she left, slamming the door behind her. She had no idea what Nowak's plan was, but nothing was going to stop her from capturing the woman. Why would he tell her to stay back? Near the convent, she found a bench, buttoned her trench, and pulled the collar up. She'd wait all night if that's what it took.

By morning, she was cold and hungry. After pacing to warm up, she returned to her seat. The sun warmed the autumn air as the hours ticked by, and now the street bustled with activity. A black limousine flying a yellow-and-white Vatican flag with an emblem of a tiara and keys drove down the street and pulled into the alley. It had a license plate marked CD for *Corpo Diplomatico,* exactly like Mrs. B had described the vehicle used to transport Nazis to the port in Genoa.

Anna crept along the narrow alleyway to the parked vehicle. Just then, she heard voices. Having nowhere to hide, she turned the lever on the trunk, crawled in, and shut the lid.

It was dark inside, and she became disoriented. To calm herself, she reached for the rosary and her fingers traced the beads on the loop. Footsteps sounded near the car.

What if someone opened the trunk and saw her?

There was no going back now. She fumbled inside her new handbag for the loaded Nagant M1895 revolver and silencer. It didn't matter that it was pitch dark in the trunk; she'd screwed a silencer onto a threaded barrel many times. With the gun gripped in one hand and the sound suppressor in the other, she turned it once, twice, three times, and readied herself.

More voices. More footsteps. Car doors opened. Then slammed shut. The engine started. The vehicle drove off.

Anna settled in for the long drive to Genoa and occupied herself by developing a plan. She had to capture the Beast in the short time between leaving the limo and reaching the pier. Once the Beast boarded the ship, she'd be under US military protection, and it would be too late. But what was she going to do with her once she caught her? This was all going too fast.

The vehicle pulled off the road and stopped. Doors opened and slammed shut. Footsteps moved away.

Anna used her scalpel to pry open the locking mechanism on the inside of the trunk. She jumped out, clenching her revolver. Crouching, she peered around the side of the limo and saw a nun in a brown habit with a briefcase, a monk in a hooded robe, and an airplane on a grass runway.

An airplane? Something was wrong. Mrs. B said they would move the Beast out by ship, not by plane. She was standing in the middle of an isolated field. Not a pier.

The monk and the nun walked fast. If she didn't do something, she'd lose her chance to capture the Beast. The Nagant revolver was a close-range weapon. The nun and the monk were a fair distance away. It didn't matter. After countless hours of target practice with Michal in the concrete-lined tunnel under the cathedral, she was a damn good shot.

She could easily take out the nun. The monk was probably the bloody aeronautic engineer dressed in disguise, and even if he wasn't, whoever he was, he was helping a Nazi escape prosecution. She could take him out, too.

The gun had seven shots. She only needed two. One for the nun. One for the monk. Problem solved. She raised the assassination weapon, cocked the hammer, placed her finger on the trigger, and took aim.

She hesitated. This was too easy.

After everything she'd been through, she couldn't bring herself to shoot the Beast in the back. It was the coward's way out. She wanted the woman to see what was coming. She wanted justice.

And what if it wasn't her?

She had to do something fast. They were only a few steps from the plane. Five, maybe six steps. The Beast would keep count in that deep whisper of hers. If she lost count, she'd turn around and start over.

That was it. Interrupt her.

Anna charged down the runway. The lowering sun casting long shadows.

"You're not going anywhere," she yelled.

The nun stopped, turned, and started back. Took four steps and stopped.

It *was* her.

Anna aimed the pistol at the Beast, right between her eyes. She stood close enough to smell the perfume.

"What do *you* want?" the Beast asked.

"Do you recognize me?" Anna shot back.

"I do." The Beast ran her tongue over her teeth. "Answer me. I asked you what you want."

"I want you to pay for your war crimes."

"I did nothing wrong. I only followed orders."

Anna's rage escalated. "You beat me with a whip. Over and over until I wished I was dead." Anger pounded at her gut. "You didn't have to steal babies. You didn't have to murder women and children."

The Beast pinched her lips together. Droplets of sweat formed on her forehead.

"You're coming with me. Head back to the limo." Anna motioned toward the vehicle with her gun.

Anna saw, for the first time, fear cross the Beast's face. Then it turned to defiance. "I'm going to America. I'm going to be a movie star."

"You're not getting on that airplane. Move it." Anna waved the gun at the monk. "You're coming too."

She raised her hand to shield her eyes from the glare of the sun behind him. The Beast took the opportunity to slip her pistol out from under her habit.

CHAPTER SEVENTY-FOUR

Airfield
Italy

Anxious to start the engines and take off, Nowak grew impatient. From the cockpit, he shouted, "What's the hold up?"

"Damned if I know," Syd said.

"Do you see the Beast?"

"I think so. There's trouble on the runway. They're just standing there."

"Maybe she's figured out this plane doesn't have long-range capabilities. It would never make it to America."

"She won't know the difference," Syd growled.

Nowak checked his watch. A delay could ruin the entire operation. It had been easy to arrange for an airplane. He was still an RAF officer, and with a little help from Snowshoe, the Brits were happy to oblige once they heard he wanted to deliver a war criminal to Hamburg for their Ravensbrück trials. They sent a civilian six-seater to make sure the RAF roundels painted on their aircraft didn't give the ruse away.

Instead of driving the Beast to the ship in Genoa, Michal had taken a major detour to the airstrip. When he didn't return, the Vatican would know something was up.

"Maybe the Vatican is making trouble," Nowak said.

"I doubt it. The Church is too afraid of negative publicity."

But the Americans were a different story. When the diplomatic vehicle didn't arrive at the pier on time, they would track them down.

"What's taking so long?" Nowak asked.

"It's Michal. He's arguing with someone on the runway."

"Who?"

"Looks like Anna." Syd hung out the exit door.

"What's she doing here?" Nowak asked as he jumped out of the pilot seat and headed for the exit. Syd stopped him.

"I hear sirens. The Feds are on to us. Start the engine."

"We can't leave without Anna and Michal."

"There's too much at stake," Syd said. "It won't do anyone any good if we all get arrested. Or shot. There's no telling what the Americans will do if they catch us." Syd straightened the military looking uniform he'd finished sewing a few hours earlier and donned an officer's visor cap. "I'll handle this."

The wail of sirens in the distance intensified.

Out of options, Nowak flung himself into the pilot seat. He had to keep his wits about him and trust Syd.

CHAPTER SEVENTY-FIVE

Airfield
Italy

Anna and the Beast stood face to face, guns aimed at each other. A man, in a military uniform, stepped off the plane and limped over to them.

The monk moved toward Anna. "Give me the gun," he said.

She recognized the voice. Her knees weak, she took a step back to steady herself. Michal ripped the gun out of her hand.

"May I be of assistance, Frau Von Wolff?" the officer asked in German.

Anna gave the man a second look. It was Syd!

"I demand to see Klaus Von Wolff." The Beast waved her pistol.

"He's waiting for you on the plane," Syd said. "A first-class seat is reserved for you."

Anna sized up the situation. Stay calm, she told herself. Play along.

"I hear sirens," the Beast said.

"The Brits are on to us. We have to hurry." Syd extended his arm. "Do you have your passport?"

She nodded.

"Visa?"

Nodded again.

"Then you're all set. Allow me the pleasure of escorting you on board." The Beast took Syd's arm and gave Anna a smug look.

"I'll take the gun," Syd said. "You won't need it where you're going."

CHAPTER SEVENTY-SIX

Airfield
Italy

Footsteps stomped up the stairs to the plane. Nowak heard a chilling scream. Jumping out of the pilot seat, he moved to the back to see Syd drag the Beast down the center aisle.

"Let go of me," she shrieked.

"Do you need any help?" Nowak asked Syd, more amused than concerned.

"I can handle her." Syd threw the Beast into a seat and secured a pair of handcuffs around her wrists.

She tried to stand up. He pushed her back down.

"The American military is supposed to protect me. I demand to speak to the person in charge," she said.

"I'm in charge. Shut your mouth or I'll shut it for you."

Nowak returned to the cockpit. They had no time to waste.

"Where's Anna and Michal?" Nowak asked.

Syd hung his head out the exit door and shouted. "Get your asses in here. The Feds are on their way."

"We've got to go now!" Michal told Anna.

Anna glared at her brother. "I'm not moving until someone tells me what's going on." She crossed her arms defiantly.

"We're not going to America." Michal locked eyes with her.

"I know that. I'm not stupid. That plane doesn't have long-range capabilities."

"We're going to Hamburg. To put the Beast on trial."

That's all Anna needed to hear. Brother and sister ran to the plane as cars with flashing lights and blaring sirens turned onto the field. The aircraft engine revved, propellers spun, and hot exhaust swept over the runway.

"Ready for take off?" Nowak shouted from the cockpit.

"Ready," Michal shouted back as he sealed the aircraft door. The plane taxied forward.

"Where are you taking me?" the Beast asked.

"Hamburg," Anna said.

"*Untermensch*," the Beast spat.

"You're the *Untermensch*." Anna made a fist and smacked her in the nose.

The Beast covered her face with her cuffed hands and whimpered. Blood seeped out of her nostrils. "I'll pay you to take me to America. You can have my briefcase."

"I've already got it," Syd snapped as he rummaged through the case stuffed with jewelry and gold teeth.

"Please take me to America," the Beast begged. She pursed her lips and wiped blood from her face with the sleeve of her habit.

"Not a hope in hell," Syd said. "You're going to stand trial for murder and brutality against prisoners."

"You'll get what you deserve," Michal said. "The death penalty."

"Anna, come up to the cockpit," Nowak called out. "And hurry up about it."

Anna maneuvered her way to the co-pilot seat as the plane sped down the bumpy runway. Nowak had both hands on the controls and his feet on the rudder pedals.

He smiled at her. "Strap yourself in. You're finally going for that airplane ride you always wanted."

Outside, vehicles screeched to a halt. Men jumped out. Engines running. Doors left open. But the Americans arrived too late to do anything other than watch the plane take off.

Nowak circled and returned. Swooping down low, he tipped the wings at the men below. Leveling the aircraft, he pulled back on the control column to begin a steep climb.

"It's just like I told you it would be. See the trees and the mountains in the distance?"

"I can see them," she said.

"Now we're rising higher and higher through the silver-rimmed clouds until we break through." He checked his pocket to make sure the engagement ring was still there. His fingers touched the velvet box. "Now we're gliding on top of the clouds. Look up. There's nothing but blue skies ahead for us."

"*Up, up the long, delirious, burning blue* . . . My favorite color."

The sun shone into the cockpit like Chopin's "Sunshine Étude" in F major. Bright. Uplifting. And free.

AFTERWORD

Metal handcuffs hang on the wall in my study; a tattered *Wartime Log* sits on the bookshelf; polished medals rest in a box. They tell a story of a time before I was born, when my father fought for my freedom. They are a testament to his courage and determination.

As a small child I knew he was a bomber pilot in the Second World War and that he had ditched his Wellington in the Zuider Zee returning from a thousand-bomber raid. I also knew he had been a prisoner of war for two years, eleven months in four different camps. But that was all I knew. Even though he wouldn't speak of his past, his experiences formed an integral part of my upbringing. His emotional scars penetrated my day-to-day existence. Shaped my very being. Framed my psyche.

We never used words to discuss it, my father and I. We didn't need to. I knew that the memories were still too raw, even after so many years. Instinctively, I faced his ghosts.

Every year, my mother and I stood beside him at the cenotaph in the bitter, prairie cold on November 11. He was stoic as wreaths were laid to honor fallen soldiers. Only his crystal blue eyes spoke to me. Those eyes told me of the terror, the regret, the suffering, and the nightmare. It was truly Remembrance Day for him.

I hoped that one day he would tell me. I imagined us sitting on the large, comfortable sofa in our living room, his precious *Wartime Log* resting on his lap. We would leaf through the pages, pausing at each black-and-white photograph, and intricate drawing, as he finally shared his memories with me.

But it never happened.

Ever since I could remember, I had struggled to understand my father. His compassion, strength, and integrity were awe-inspiring to me. At the same time, however, when I was a child he was prone to severe emotional outbursts. He was never physically abusive, but suddenly and without warning his wounds would surface and penetrate my world, turning it upside down with fear and confusion, razor-sharp like barbed wire and flying shrapnel.

I learned to walk on eggshells, unsure of my footing, never knowing when the next explosion would occur. Soon I became aware of the triggers, learning to navigate my way around them, but never cognizant of the logical connection between the past and the present. Certain things just were. Our house didn't have locks on the doors. Turnips were never served. The bread always white. The coffee black. And a lab called Skipper.

My father died of lung cancer in 1985. Those same lungs carried pieces of shrapnel back to Canada for him. Cancer and shrapnel. Lest he forget. No one will ever convince me that those two horrors were not related.

The day he died, I watched him drift in and out of consciousness. As he tossed and turned, he struggled with memories that had returned. Death, escaped many times before, was back and would not leave without him.

My daughter Andrea, his only grandchild, was less than a year old then. She is now in her thirties. When I thought about passing my father's precious piece of family history onto her, I realized that I didn't know what to say. His *Wartime Log*, handcuffs, and medals spoke of the man I never knew. The part of him that the war took from both of us.

Was I going to pass this heavy silence and the scars that it inflicts onto my daughter? Would it be her unspoken legacy? Or could I break the silence and exorcise the ghosts?

I chose to pass a proud heritage onto my daughter by embarking on a journey of exploration and understanding.

The Resistance Daughter is the culmination of my journey. By adding narrative elements, I transformed the stories I uncovered from my research into historical fiction. I pieced together the facts to the best of my ability. Yet there is much left unsaid, forever lost in the obscurity of time. Over the years memories fade. Details blur. Reports vary. Much evidence has been destroyed. Out of necessity, I consolidated camps, characters, and events, and filled in the holes with my imagination. In every instance, I tried my best to maintain the authenticity of camp conditions, the ingenuity of the prisoners, and their resiliency of spirit.

This book is a tribute to their strength, courage, and humanity.

*

I began my research by contacting members of the RAF Ex-POW Association who had spent time in one of the four prison camps with my father. Later, I served as a board member with several of these men at both the Aero Space Museum of Calgary, now known as the Hangar Flight Museum, and the Air Force Museum of Alberta.

These brave former POWs told me stories about smuggling a woman (Mrs. B) into camp and the members of the petticoat patrol who protected her. They spoke of the thousands of female members of the Polish Home Army captured during the Warsaw Uprising who were the first female combatants in history interned behind barbed wire and given prisoner-of-war status. They shared memories of times spent in handcuffs, digging tunnels, tin bashing, escape committees, starvation, and much more.

My research and network expanded to Britain with a visit to the Brooklands Museum to see one of the two surviving Wellington bombers, followed by a trip to Germany with members of the Stalag IVB Ex-POW Association, one of the largest prisoner-of-war camps in Germany located northeast of the town of Mühlberg. More than twenty thousand men and hundreds of women from the Polish Home Army served time there behind barbed wire. Each day brought memorial services in cemeteries far from home. I stood among rows and rows and rows of white crosses with tears welling in my eyes, listening to the tributes to lost lives and the recounting of horrors that I could not comprehend.

At one of the camps, a black box filled with muddy dog tags sat open on a simple white chair. Each tag represented a life. The box was a testament to the thousands of men that lay buried in the mass grave outside, strewn on top of each other, to lie together for eternity.

When I returned to Canada, I was unable to continue my research or write a word pertaining to this project for over a year.

Once I began investigating my Polish Catholic roots, I became fascinated with the Polish Underground, the Home Army, and the little-known organization of Żegota, the Council to Aid Jews. The State of Israel recognizes many members of these groups as Righteous Among the Nations for helping Jews during the Holocaust. Among them, Irena Sendler, codenamed Jolanta, a Catholic social worker who risked her life to smuggle Jewish children out of the ghetto and usher them to Roman Catholic convents and orphanages.

But my fascination turned to horror when I learned of the vast number of Christian children kidnapped under the auspices of the *Lebensborn* program and transported to Germany, to be masqueraded as German offspring whose physical attributes, such as blond hair and blue eyes, were thought to demonstrate the racial superiority of the Aryan bloodline. I have read estimates as high as 200,000 Polish children abducted as well as thousands more from other Eastern European countries. Most of whom were never returned to their birth parents.

Captivated by the history of Warsaw, I traveled back to Europe to explore the Warsaw Rising Museum with a replica of the underground sewers, the POLIN Museum of the History of Polish Jews, Old Town, and the remnants of the ghetto. Approximately six million Polish citizens, or twenty percent of the population, were killed during the Second World War—among them three million Jews. Another one million citizens perished at the hands of the Soviets.

I returned to Germany to take a heartbreaking tour of Ravensbrück Concentration Camp for women where the beating trestle in the cell block and the ovens in the crematorium were seared into my memory. It was here that Irma Grese, often referred to as the Beautiful Beast, began her career as a brutal camp guard. In 1945, she was arrested, tried, and executed by the British for war crimes. She was only twenty-two years old. Eighty percent of the inmates were political prisoners, with the largest national group being Polish. Virtually all of those subjected to medical experiments were members of the Polish Resistance. More than 120,000 women and children, from thirty different nationalities, were registered at the camp. Tens of thousands perished.

On April 23, 2023, I attended the Commemoration of the 78th Anniversary of the liberation of Stalag IVB at the Zeithein

Memorial with a small group of the Friends of Stalag IVB (Ex-POW Association). August 1, 2024, marked the 80th Anniversary of the Warsaw Uprising. The 80th Anniversary of the liberation of Stalag IVB will take place on April 23, 2025, with a Commemoration at the Zeithein Memorial.

In all, 55,573 airmen were killed serving in RAF Bomber Command, with a death rate of 44.4%. Another 9,784 were shot down and taken as prisoners of war. According to the Bomber Command Museum of Canada, one third of all Bomber Command aircrew were Canadians. The museum's best estimate for the number of Canadians killed while serving with Bomber Command is 10,250. While most airmen were held in camps administered by the German Air Force (*Luftwaffe*) called *Stammlager Lufts* or Stalag Lufts, others were detained in more brutal conditions at *Stammlagers,* Stalags administered by the Germany Army (*Wehrmacht*).

I have had the honor of attending two RAF Ex-POW reunions in my lifetime. One in Canada with my father and a second in England after his death.

Throughout my journey, one nagging question persisted in my mind—why do I know so little about this chapter of history?

In many ways, I believe that my generation, although emotionally stained by the effects of the Second World War, are at the same time still fundamentally unaware of the cruel reality that our parents and grandparents experienced. Perhaps it was too difficult for our families to talk about. Perhaps they wanted to protect us from the horrors. Perhaps they just wanted to forget.

The journey has been life-changing for me. This novel is my expression of appreciation, recognition, and understanding.

I think of my father and how much I miss him.

May he rest in peace.

—Joanne Kormylo

ACKNOWLEDGMENTS

I owe a debt of gratitude to the RAF Ex-POWs who contributed to this project. Both Wilkie Wanless (Stalag Luft 3 Sagan) and Doug Hawkes (Stalag IVB Mühlberg Elbe) spent countless hours sharing their memories with me and checking my notes for accuracy. Ray Hukee (Stalag IVB Mühlberg Elbe) and Don Hall (Stalag VIIIB Lamsdorf) recounted stories. Members of the Stalag IVB Ex-POW Association provided additional details. Sadly, all of these brave men have now passed away.

Through the years, I felt I was the guardian of their stories and I was determined to share them with readers. To do so, I had to learn to write fiction which was much more difficult than I anticipated. I took many classes and workshops through the years. The first with Donald Maass and Free Expressions. More recently, with Robert Dugoni and Steven James at the Novel Writing Intensive, Gillian Holmes at the Novelry, and Robert Rotenberg.

Special thanks to my friends and fellow board members at the Air Force Museum of Alberta, especially Colonel Gerry Morrison C.D. (Retd), and to Dave Birrell from the Bomber Command Museum of Canada. Travelling companions and providers of information from the FRIENDS OF STALAG IVB (ex-POW Association), especially Lt Col (Retd) Edward Waite-Roberts, Pauline and Tony Drewitt, Glen Fowler, and Stephen Guest. My inner circle and writing tribe for their encouragement and assistance throughout this journey: Janine di Giovanni, Sabine Modder, Wili Liberman, Dave Malone, Tara Taylor, Dr. Jane Cameron, Jacky Rom, Marjory Fallon, Valorie Scarbrough, Winnie Chow, David and Maureen Corry, Alba Arikha, Bryn Turnbull, John Liandzi, and Stan Guo, with special mention to my critique partner Teresa Hendricks and her upcoming legal thriller. And many more people I've met along the way who have contributed.

I will be forever grateful for the day the stars aligned and everything fell into place. Thanks to the talented Leigh Russell, my amazing agent Bill Goodall, and my brilliant commissioning editor Audrey Linton and her team at Hodder and Stoughton for having faith in me and making my dream of publishing this book a reality.

Most of all, I am thankful for the love and support of my precious daughter Andrea and son-in-law Robbie for never giving up on me and for the remarkable parents, John and Helen Kormylo, I was blessed with and miss every day.